Author's National Edition

THE WRITINGS OF
MARK TWAIN
VOLUME XII

This is the authorized
Uniform Edition of
my books.

Mark Twain

A CORNER IN THE CAPUCHIN CONVENT

# THE

# INNOCENTS ABROAD

OR

## THE NEW PILGRIM'S PROGRESS

BEING SOME ACCOUNT OF THE STEAMSHIP
QUAKER CITY'S PLEASURE EXCURSION
TO EUROPE AND THE HOLY LAND

BY

## MARK TWAIN

(SAMUEL L. CLEMENS)

IN TWO VOLUMES
VOL. II

ILLUSTRATED

**WILDSIDE PRESS: MMIII**

**Published by:**

**Wildside Press**
**P.O. Box 301**
**Holicong, PA 18928-0301**
**www.wildsidepress.com**

# CONTENTS

# CONTENTS

# THE
# INNOCENTS ABROAD

## CHAPTER I

FROM the sanguinary sports of the Holy Inquisition; the slaughter of the Coliseum; and the dismal tombs of the Catacombs, I naturally pass to the picturesque horrors of the Capuchin Convent. We stopped a moment in a small chapel in the church to admire a picture of St. Michael vanquishing Satan —a picture which is so beautiful that I cannot but think it belongs to the reviled "Renaissance," notwithstanding I believe they told us one of the ancient old masters painted it—and then we descended into the vast vault underneath.

Here was a spectacle for sensitive nerves! Evidently the old masters had been at work in this place. There were six divisions in the apartment, and each division was ornamented with a style of decoration peculiar to itself—and these decorations were in every instance formed of human bones! There were shapely arches, built wholly of thigh-bones; there were startling pyramids, built wholly of grinning skulls; there were quaint architectural structures of

various kinds, built of shin-bones and the bones of
the arm; on the wall were elaborate frescoes, whose
curving vines were made of knotted human verte-
bræ; whose delicate tendrils were made of sinews
and tendons; whose flowers were formed of knee-
caps and toe-nails. Every lasting portion of the
human frame was represented in these intricate designs (they were by Michael Angelo, I think), and
there was a careful finish about the work, and an
attention to details that betrayed the artist's love
of his labors as well as his schooled ability. I asked
the good-natured monk who accompanied us, who
did this? And he said, "*We* did it"—meaning
himself and his brethren up-stairs. I could see that
the old friar took a high pride in his curious show.
We made him talkative by exhibiting an interest
we never betrayed to guides.

"Who were these people?"

"We—up-stairs—Monks of the Capuchin order—
my brethren."

"How many departed monks were required to
upholster these six parlors?"

"These are the bones of four thousand."

"It took a long time to get enough?"

"Many, many centuries."

"Their different parts are well separated—skulls
in one room, legs in another, ribs in another—there
would be stirring times here for a while if the last
trump should blow. Some of the brethren might
get hold of the wrong leg, in the confusion, and the
wrong skull, and find themselves limping, and looking through eyes that were wider apart or closer

together than they were used to. You cannot tell any of these parties apart, I suppose?"

"Oh, yes, I know many of them."

He put his finger on a skull. "This was Brother Anselmo—dead three hundred years—a good man."

He touched another. "This was Brother Alexander—dead two hundred and eighty years. This was Brother Carlo—dead about as long."

Then he took a skull and held it in his hand, and looked reflectively upon it, after the manner of the grave-digger when he discourses of Yorick.

"This," he said, "was Brother Thomas. He was a young prince, the scion of a proud house that traced its lineage back to the grand old days of Rome well-nigh two thousand years ago. He loved beneath his estate. His family persecuted him; persecuted the girl, as well. They drove her from Rome; he followed; he sought her far and wide; he found no trace of her. He came back and offered his broken heart at our altar and his weary life to the service of God. But look you. Shortly his father died, and likewise his mother. The girl returned, rejoicing. She sought everywhere for him whose eyes had used to look tenderly into hers out of this poor skull, but she could not find him. At last, in this coarse garb we wear, she recognized him in the street. He knew her. It was too late. He fell where he stood. They took him up and brought him here. He never spoke afterward. Within the week he died. You can see the color of his hair—faded, somewhat—by this thin shred that clings still to the temple. This [taking up a thigh-bone] was his. The veins

3

of this leaf in the decorations over your head, were his finger-joints, a hundred and fifty years ago."

This businesslike way of illustrating a touching story of the heart by laying the several fragments of the lover before us and naming them, was as grotesque a performance, and as ghastly, as any I ever witnessed. I hardly knew whether to smile or shudder. There are nerves and muscles in our frames whose functions and whose methods of working it seems a sort of sacrilege to describe by cold physiological names and surgical technicalities, and the monk's talk suggested to me something of this kind. Fancy a surgeon, with his nippers lifting tendons, muscles, and such things into view, out of the complex machinery of a corpse, and observing, "Now this little nerve quivers—the vibration is imparted to this muscle—from here it is passed to this fibrous substance; here its ingredients are separated by the chemical action of the blood—one part goes to the heart and thrills it with what is popularly termed emotion, another part follows this nerve to the brain and communicates intelligence of a startling character—the third part glides along this passage and touches the spring connected with the fluid receptacles that lie in the rear of the eye. Thus, by this simple and beautiful process, the party is informed that his mother is dead, and he weeps." Horrible!

I asked the monk if all the brethren up-stairs expected to be put in this place when they died. He answered quietly:

"We must all lie here at last."

See what one can accustom himself to. The reflection that he must some day be taken apart like an engine or a clock, or like a house whose owner is gone, and worked up into arches and pyramids and hideous frescoes, did not distress this monk in the least. I thought he even looked as if he were thinking, with complacent vanity, that his own skull would look well on top of the heap and his own ribs add a charm to the frescoes which possibly they lacked at present.

Here and there, in ornamental alcoves stretched upon beds of bones, lay dead and dried-up monks, with lank frames dressed in the black robes one sees ordinarily upon priests. We examined one closely. The skinny hands were clasped upon the breast; two lusterless tufts of hair stuck to the skull; the skin was brown and shrunken; it stretched tightly over the cheek-bones and made them stand out sharply; the crisp dead eyes were deep in the sockets; the nostrils were painfully prominent, the end of the nose being gone; the lips had shriveled away from the yellow teeth; and brought down to us through the circling years, and petrified there, was a weird laugh a full century old!

It was the jolliest laugh, but yet the most dreadful, that one can imagine. Surely, I thought, it must have been a most extraordinary joke this veteran produced with his latest breath, that he has not got done laughing at it yet. At this moment I saw that the old instinct was strong upon the boys, and I said we had better hurry to St. Peter's. They were trying to keep from asking, "Is—is he dead?"

It makes me dizzy to think of the Vatican—of

its wilderness of statues, paintings, and curiosities of
every description and every age. The "old masters" (especially in sculpture) fairly swarm, there.
I cannot write about the Vatican. I think I shall
never remember anything I saw there distinctly but
the mummies, and the "Transfiguration," by Raphael,
and some other things it is not necessary to mention
now. I shall remember the "Transfiguration" partly
because it was placed in a room almost by itself;
partly because it is acknowledged by all to be the
first oil-painting in the world; and partly because
it was wonderfully beautiful. The colors are fresh
and rich, the "expression," I am told, is fine, the
"feeling" is lively, the "tone" is good, the "depth"
is profound, and the width is about four and a half
feet, I should judge. It is a picture that really
holds one's attention; its beauty is fascinating. It
is fine enough to be a *Renaissance*. A remark I
made a while ago suggests a thought—and a hope.
Is it not possible that the reason I find such charms
in this picture is because it is out of the crazy chaos
of the galleries? If some of the others were set
apart, might not they be beautiful? If this were
set in the midst of the tempest of pictures one finds
in the vast galleries of the Roman palaces, would I
think it so handsome? If, up to this time, I had
seen only one "old master" in each palace, instead
of acres and acres of walls and ceilings fairly papered
with them, might I not have a more civilized opinion of the old masters than I have now? I think so.
When I was a school-boy and was to have a new
knife, I could not make up my mind as to which was

the prettiest in the showcase, and I did not think any of them were particularly pretty; and so I chose with a heavy heart. But when I looked at my purchase, at home, where no glittering blades came into competition with it, I was astonished to see how handsome it was. To this day my new hats look better out of the shop than they did in it with other new hats. It begins to dawn upon me, now, that possibly, what I have been taking for uniform ugliness in the galleries may be uniform beauty after all. I honestly hope it is, to others, but certainly it is not to me. Perhaps the reason I used to enjoy going to the Academy of Fine Arts in New York was because there were but a few hundred paintings in it, and it did not surfeit me to go through the list. I suppose the Academy was bacon and beans in the Forty-Mile Desert, and a European gallery is a state dinner of thirteen courses. One leaves no sign after him of the one dish, but the thirteen frighten away his appetite and give him no satisfaction.

There is one thing I am certain of, though. With all the Michael Angelos, the Raphaels, the Guidos, and the other old masters, the sublime history of Rome remains unpainted! They painted Virgins enough, and Popes enough, and saintly scarecrows enough, to people Paradise, almost, and these things are all they did paint. "Nero fiddling o'er burning Rome," the assassination of Cæsar, the stirring spectacle of a hundred thousand people bending forward with rapt interest, in the Coliseum, to see two skilful gladiators hacking away each other's life, a tiger springing upon a kneeling martyr—these and a thousand other matters which we read of with a living interest, must be sought for only in books—not among the rubbish left by the old masters—who are no more, I have the satisfaction of informing the public.

They did paint, and they did carve in marble, one historical scene, and one only (of any great historical consequence). And what was it and why did they choose it, particularly? It was the Rape of the Sabines, and they chose it for the legs and busts.

I like to look at statues, however, and I like to look at pictures, also—even of monks looking up in sacred ecstasy, and monks looking down in meditation, and monks skirmishing for something to eat—and therefore I drop ill nature to thank the papal government for so jealously guarding and so industriously gathering up these things; and for permitting me, a stranger and not an entirely friendly one, to roam at will and unmolested among them, charging me nothing, and only requiring that I shall behave myself simply as well as I ought to behave in any other man's house. I thank the Holy Father right heartily, and I wish him long life and plenty of happiness.

The Popes have long been the patrons and preservers of art, just as our new, practical Republic is the encourager and upholder of mechanics. In their Vatican is stored up all that is curious and beautiful in art; in our Patent Office is hoarded all that is curious or useful in mechanics. When a man invents a new style of horse-collar or discovers a new and superior method of telegraphing, our govern-

THE INNOCENTS ABROAD

ment issues a patent to him that is worth a fortune;
when a man digs up an ancient statue in the Campagna, the Pope gives him a fortune in gold coin.
We can make something of a guess at a man's character by the style of nose he carries on his face.
The Vatican and the Patent Office are governmental
noses, and they bear a deal of character about them.

The guide showed us a colossal statue of Jupiter,
in the Vatican, which he said looked so damaged
and rusty—so like the God of the Vagabonds—
because it had but recently been dug up in the Campagna. He asked how much we supposed this
Jupiter was worth. I replied, with intelligent
promptness, that he was probably worth about four
dollars—maybe four and a half. "A hundred thousand dollars!" Ferguson said. Ferguson said, further, that the Pope permits no ancient work of
this kind to leave his dominions. He appoints a
commission to examine discoveries like this and report upon the value; then the Pope pays the discov-
erer one-half of that assessed value and takes the
statue. He said this Jupiter was dug from a field
which had just been bought for thirty-six thousand
dollars, so the first crop was a good one for the new
farmer. I do not know whether Ferguson always
tells the truth or not, but I suppose he does. I know
that an exorbitant export duty is exacted upon all
pictures painted by the old masters, in order to discourage the sale of those in the private collections.
I am satisfied, also, that genuine old masters hardly
exist at all, in America, because the cheapest and
most insignificant of them are valued at the price of

9

a fine farm. I proposed to buy a small trifle of a Raphael, myself, but the price of it was eighty thousand dollars, the export duty would have made it considerably over a hundred, and so I studied on it awhile and concluded not to take it.

I wish here to mention an inscription I have seen, before I forget it:

"Glory to God in the highest, peace on earth TO MEN OF GOOD WILL!" It is not good Scripture, but it is sound Catholic and human nature.

This is in letters of gold around the apsis of a mosaic group at the side of the *scala santa*, church of St. John Lateran, the Mother and Mistress of all the Catholic churches of the world. The group represents the Saviour, St. Peter, Pope Leo, St. Silvester, Constantine, and Charlemagne. Peter is giving the *pallium* to the Pope, and a standard to Charlemagne. The Saviour is giving the keys to St. Silvester, and a standard to Constantine. No prayer is offered to the Saviour, who seems to be of little importance anywhere in Rome; but an inscription below says, "*Blessed Peter, give life to Pope Leo and victory to King Charles.*" It does not say, "*Intercede for us*, through the Saviour, with the Father, for this boon," but "Blessed Peter, *give it* us."

In all seriousness—without meaning to be frivolous—without meaning to be irreverent, and more than all, without meaning to be blasphemous,—I state as my simple deduction from the things I have seen and the things I have heard, that the Holy Personages rank thus in Rome:

# THE INNOCENTS ABROAD

*First*—"The Mother of God"—otherwise the Virgin Mary.

*Second*—The Deity.

*Third*—Peter.

*Fourth*—Some twelve or fifteen canonized Popes and martyrs.

*Fifth*—Jesus Christ the Saviour—(but always as an infant in arms).

I may be wrong in this—my judgment errs often, just as is the case with other men's—but it *is* my judgment, be it good or bad.

Just here I will mention something that seems curious to me. There are no "Christ's Churches" in Rome, and no "Churches of the Holy Ghost,' that I can discover. There are some four hundred churches, but about a fourth of them seem to be named for the Madonna and St. Peter. There are so many named for Mary that they have to be distinguished by all sorts of affixes, if I understand the matter rightly. Then we have churches of St. Louis; St. Augustine; St. Agnes; St. Calixtus; St. Lorenzo in Lucina; St. Lorenzo in Damaso; St. Cecilia; St. Athanasius; St. Philip Neri; St. Catherine; St. Doménico, and a multitude of lesser saints whose names are not familiar in the world—and away down, clear out of the list of the churches, comes a couple of hospitals: one of them is named for the Saviour and the other for the Holy Ghost!

Day after day and night after night we have wandered among the crumbling wonders of Rome; day after day and night after night we have fed upon the dust and decay of five-and-twenty centuries—have brooded over them by day and dreamt of them by night till sometimes we seemed moldering away ourselves, and growing defaced and cornerless, and liable at any moment to fall a prey to some antiquary and be patched in the legs, and "restored" with an unseemly nose, and labeled wrong and dated wrong, and set up in the Vatican for poets to drivel about and vandals to scribble their names on forever and forevermore.

But the surest way to stop writing about Rome is to stop. I wished to write a real "guide-book" chapter on this fascinating city, but I could not do it, because I have felt all the time like a boy in a candy shop—there was everything to choose from, and yet no choice. I have drifted along hopelessly for a hundred pages of manuscript without knowing where to commence. I will not commence at all. Our passports have been examined. We will go to Naples.

## CHAPTER II

THE ship is lying here in the harbor of Naples—quarantined. She has been here several days and will remain several more. We that came by rail from Rome have escaped this misfortune. Of course no one is allowed to go on board the ship, or come ashore from her. She is a prison, now. The passengers probably spend the long, blazing days looking out from under the awnings at Vesuvius and the beautiful city—and in swearing. Think of ten days of this sort of pastime!—We go out every day in a boat and request them to come ashore. It soothes them. We lie ten steps from the ship and tell them how splendid the city is; and how much better the hotel fare is here than anywhere else in Europe; and how cool it is; and what frozen continents of ice-cream there are; and what a time we are having cavorting about the country and sailing to the islands in the Bay. This tranquilizes them.

### ASCENT OF VESUVIUS

I shall remember our trip to Vesuvius for many a day—partly because of its sight-seeing experiences, but chiefly on account of the fatigue of the journey. Two or three of us had been resting ourselves among the tranquil and beautiful scenery of the island of Ischia, eighteen miles out in the harbor, for two

13

days; we called it "resting," but I do not remember
now what the resting consisted of, for when we got
back to Naples we had not slept for forty-eight
hours. We were just about to go to bed early in the
evening, and catch up on some of the sleep we had
lost, when we heard of this Vesuvius expedition.
There were to be eight of us in the party, and we
were to leave Naples at midnight. We laid in some
provisions for the trip, engaged carriages to take us
to Annunciation, and then moved about the city,
to keep awake, till twelve. We got away punctually,
and in the course of an hour and a half arrived at
the town of Annunciation. Annunciation is the
very last place under the sun. In other towns in
Italy, the people lie around quietly and wait for
you to ask them a question or do some overt act
that can be charged for—but in Annunciation they
have lost even that fragment of delicacy; they seize
a lady's shawl from a chair and hand it to her and
charge a penny; they open a carriage door, and
charge for it—shut it when you get out, and charge
for it; they help you to take off a duster—two
cents; brush your clothes and make them worse
than they were before—two cents; smile upon you
—two cents; bow, with a lickspittle smirk, hat in
hand—two cents; they volunteer all information,
such as that the mules will arrive presently—two
cents—warm day, sir—two cents—take you four
hours to make the ascent—two cents. And so they
go. They crowd you—infest you—swarm about
you, and sweat and smell offensively, and look
sneaking and mean, and obsequious. There is no

office too degrading for them to perform, for money. I have had no opportunity to find out anything about the upper classes by my own observation, but from what I hear said about them I judge that what they lack in one or two of the bad traits the *canaille* have they make up in one or two others that are worse. How the people beg!—many of them very well dressed, too.

I said I knew nothing against the upper classes by personal observation. I must recall it! I had forgotten. What I saw their bravest and their fairest do last night, the lowest multitude that could be scraped up out of the purlieus of Christendom would blush to do, I think. They assembled by hundreds, and even thousands, in the great Theater of San Carlo, to do—what? Why, simply, to make fun of an old woman—to deride, to hiss, to jeer at an actress they once worshiped, but whose beauty is faded now and whose voice has lost its former richness. Everybody spoke of the rare sport there was to be. They said the theater would be crammed, because Frezzolini was going to sing. It was said she could not sing well, now, but then the people liked to see her, anyhow. And so we went. And every time the woman sang they hissed and laughed —the whole magnificent house—and as soon as she left the stage they called her on again with applause. Once or twice she was encored five and six times in succession, and received with hisses when she appeared, and discharged with hisses and laughter when she had finished—then instantly encored and insulted again! And how the high-born knaves enjoyed it! White-kidded gentlemen and ladies laughed till the tears came, and clapped their hands in very ecstasy when that unhappy old woman would come meekly out for the sixth time, with uncomplaining patience, to meet a storm of hisses! It was the cruelest exhibition—the most wanton, the most unfeeling. The singer would have conquered an audience of American rowdies by her brave, unflinching tranquillity (for she answered encore after encore, and smiled and bowed pleasantly, and sang the best she possibly could, and went bowing off, through all the jeers and hisses, without ever losing countenance or temper): and surely in any other land than Italy her sex and her helplessness must have been an ample protection to her—she could have needed no other. Think what a multitude of small souls were crowded into that theater last night. If the manager could have filled his theater with Neapolitan souls alone, without the bodies, he could not have cleared less than ninety millions of dollars. What traits of character must a man have to enable him to help three thousand miscreants to hiss, and jeer, and laugh at one friendless old woman, and shamefully humiliate her? He must have *all* the vile, mean traits there are. My observation persuades me (I do not like to venture beyond my own personal observation) that the upper classes of Naples possess those traits of character. Otherwise they may be very good people; I cannot say.

### ASCENT OF VESUVIUS—CONTINUED

In this city of Naples, they believe in and support one of the wretchedest of all the religious impostures one can find in Italy—the miraculous liquefaction of the blood of St. Januarius. Twice a year the priests assemble all the people at the Cathedral, and get out this vial of clotted blood and let them see it slowly dissolve and become liquid—and every day for eight days this dismal farce is repeated while the priests go among the crowd and collect money for the exhibition. The first day, the blood liquefies in forty-seven minutes—the church is crammed, then, and time must be allowed the collectors to get around: after that it liquefies a little quicker and a little quicker, every day, as the houses grow smaller, till on the eighth day, with only a few dozen present to see the miracle, it liquefies in four minutes.

And here, also, they used to have a grand procession, of priests, citizens, soldiers, sailors, and the high dignitaries of the City Government, once a year, to shave the head of a made-up Madonna—a stuffed and painted image, like a milliner's dummy—whose hair miraculously grew and restored itself every twelve months. They still kept up this shaving procession as late as four or five years ago. It was a source of great profit to the church that possessed the remarkable effigy, and the ceremony of the public barbering of her was always carried out with the greatest possible éclat and display—the more the better, because the more excitement there was about it the larger the crowds it drew and the heavier the revenues it produced—but at last a day came when the Pope and his servants were unpopular in Naples, and the City Government stopped the Madonna's annual show.

There we have two specimens of these Neapolitans
—two of the silliest possible frauds, which half the
population religiously and faithfully believed, and
the other half either believed also or else said nothing
about, and thus lent themselves to the support of the
imposture. I am very well satisfied to think the
whole population believed in those poor, cheap
miracles—a people who want two cents every time
they bow to you, and who abuse a woman, are
capable of it, I think.

ASCENT OF VESUVIUS—CONTINUED

These Neapolitans always ask four times as much
money as they intend to take, but if you give them
what they first demand, they feel ashamed of themselves for aiming so low, and immediately ask more.
When money is to be paid and received, there is
always some vehement jawing and gesticulating
about it. One cannot buy and pay for two cents'
worth of clams without trouble and a quarrel. One
"course," in a two-horse carriage, costs a franc—
that is law—but the hackman always demands more,
on some pretense or other, and if he gets it he makes
a new demand. It is said that a stranger took a
one-horse carriage for a course—tariff, half a franc.
He gave the man five francs, by way of experiment.
He demanded more, and received another franc.
Again he demanded more, and got a franc—demanded more, and it was refused. He grew vehement—was again refused, and became noisy. The
stranger said, "Well, give me the seven francs again,
and I will see what I can do"—and when he got

18

them, he handed the hackman half a franc, and he immediately asked for two cents to buy a drink with. It may be thought that I am prejudiced. Perhaps I am. I would be ashamed of myself if I were not.

### ASCENT OF VESUVIUS—CONTINUED

Well, as I was saying, we got our mules and horses, after an hour and a half of bargaining with the population of Annunciation, and started sleepily up the mountain, with a vagrant at each mule's tail who pretended to be driving the brute along, but was really holding on and getting himself dragged up instead. I made slow headway at first, but I began to get dissatisfied at the idea of paying my minion five francs to hold my mule back by the tail and keep him from going up the hill, and so I discharged him.

We had one magnificent picture of Naples from a high point on the mountainside. We saw nothing but the gas-lamps, of course—two-thirds of a circle, skirting the great Bay—a necklace of diamonds glinting up through the darkness from the remote distance—less brilliant than the stars overhead, but more softly, richly beautiful—and over all the great city the lights crossed and recrossed each other in many and many a sparkling line and curve. And back of the town, far around and abroad over the miles of level campagna, were scattered rows, and circles, and clusters of lights, all glowing like so many gems, and marking where a score of villages were sleeping. About this time, the fellow who was hanging on to the tail of the horse in front of me and practising all sorts of unnecessary cruelty upon the

19

animal, got kicked some fourteen rods, and this incident, together with the fairy spectacle of the lights far in the distance, made me serenely happy, and I was glad I started to Vesuvius.

### ASCENT OF MOUNT VESUVIUS—CONTINUED

This subject will be excellent matter for a chapter, and to-morrow or next day I will write it.

# CHAPTER III

## ASCENT OF VESUVIUS—CONTINUED

"SEE Naples and die." Well, I do not know that one would necessarily die after merely seeing it, but to attempt to live there might turn out a little differently. To see Naples as we saw it in the early dawn from far up on the side of Vesuvius, is to see a picture of wonderful beauty. At that distance its dingy buildings looked white—and so, rank on rank of balconies, windows, and roofs, they piled themselves up from the blue ocean till the colossal castle of St. Elmo topped the grand white pyramid and gave the picture symmetry, emphasis, and completeness And when its lilies turned to roses—when it blushed under the sun's first kiss— it was beautiful beyond all description. One might well say, then, "See Naples and die." The frame of the picture was charming, itself. In front, the smooth sea—a vast mosaic of many colors; the lofty island swimming in a dreamy haze in the distance; at our end of the city the stately double peak of Vesuvius, and its strong black ribs and seams of lava stretching down to the limitless level campagna —a green carpet that enchants the eye and leads it on and on, past clusters of trees, and isolated houses, and snowy villages, until it shreds out

21

in a fringe of mist and general vagueness far away. It is from the Hermitage, there on the side of Vesuvius, that one should "see Naples and die."

But do not go within the walls and look at it in detail. That takes away some of the romance of the thing. The people are filthy in their habits, and this makes filthy streets and breeds disagreeable sights and smells. There never was a community so prejudiced against the cholera as these Neapolitans are. But they have good reason to be. The cholera generally vanquishes a Neapolitan when it seizes him, because, you understand, before the doctor can dig through the dirt and get at the disease the man dies. The upper classes take a sea-bath every day, and are pretty decent.

The streets are generally about wide enough for one wagon, and how they do swarm with people! It is Broadway repeated in every street, in every court, in every alley! Such masses, such throngs, such multitudes of hurrying, bustling, struggling humanity! We never saw the like of it, hardly even in New York, I think. There are seldom any sidewalks, and when there are, they are not often wide enough to pass a man on without caroming on him. So everybody walks in the street—and where the street is wide enough, carriages are forever dashing along. Why a thousand people are not run over and crippled every day is a mystery that no man can solve.

But if there is an eighth wonder in the world, it must be the dwelling-houses of Naples. I honestly believe a good majority of them are a hundred feet high! And the solid brick walls are seven feet through. You go up nine flights of stairs before you get to the "first" floor. No, not nine, but there or thereabouts. There is a little bird-cage of an iron railing in front of every window clear away up, up, up, among the eternal clouds, where the roof is, and there is always somebody looking out of every window—people of ordinary size looking out from the first floor, people a shade smaller from the second, people that look a little smaller yet from the third—and from thence upward they grow smaller and smaller by a regularly graduated diminution, till the folks in the topmost windows seem more like birds in an uncommonly tall martin-box than anything else. The perspective of one of these narrow cracks of streets, with its rows of tall houses stretching away till they come together in the distance like railway-tracks; its clothes-lines crossing over at all altitudes and waving their bannered raggedness over the swarms of people below; and the white-dressed women perched in balcony railings all the way from the pavement up to the heavens— a perspective like that is really worth going into Neapolitan details to see.

### ASCENT OF VESUVIUS—CONTINUED

Naples, with its immediate suburbs, contains six hundred and twenty-five thousand inhabitants, but I am satisfied it covers no more ground than an American city of one hundred and fifty thousand. It reaches up into the air infinitely higher than three American cities, though, and there is where the secret of it lies. I will observe here, in passing, that the contrasts between opulence and poverty, and magnificence and misery, are more frequent and more striking in Naples than in Paris even. One must go to the Bois de Boulogne to see fashionable dressing, splendid equipages, and stunning liveries, and to the Faubourg St. Antoine to see vice, misery, hunger, rags, dirt—but in the thoroughfares of Naples these things are all mixed together. Naked boys of nine years and the fancy-dressed children of luxury; shreds and tatters, and brilliant uniforms; jackass carts and state carriages; beggars, princes, and bishops, jostle each other in every street. At six o'clock every evening, all Naples turns out to drive on the Riviera di Chiaja (whatever that may mean); and for two hours one may stand there and see the motliest and the worst-mixed procession go by that ever eyes beheld. Princes (there are more princes than policemen in Naples—the city is infested with them)—princes who live up seven flights of stairs and don't own any principalities, will keep a carriage and go hungry; and clerks, mechanics, milliners, and strumpets will go without their dinners and squander the money on a hack-ride in the Chiaja; the ragtag and rubbish of the city stack themselves up, to the number of twenty or thirty, on a rickety little go-cart hauled by a donkey not much bigger than a cat, and *they* drive in the Chiaja; dukes and bankers, in sumptuous carriages and with gorgeous drivers and footmen, turn out, also, and so the furious procession goes. For two hours rank and wealth, and obscurity and poverty, clatter along side by side in the wild procession, and then go home serene, happy, covered with glory!

I was looking at a magnificent marble staircase in the King's palace, the other day, which, it was said, cost five million francs, and I suppose it did cost half a million, maybe. I felt as if it must be a fine thing to live in a country where there was such comfort and such luxury as this. And then I stepped out musing, and almost walked over a vagabond who was eating his dinner on the curbstone—a piece of bread and a bunch of grapes. When I found that this mustang was clerking in a fruit establishment (he had the establishment along with him in a basket), at two cents a day, and that he had no palace at home where he lived, I lost some of my enthusiasm concerning the happiness of living in Italy.

This naturally suggests to me a thought about wages here. Lieutenants in the army get about a dollar a day, and common soldiers a couple of cents. I only know one clerk—he gets four dollars a month. Printers get six dollars and a half a month, but I have heard of a foreman who gets thirteen. To be growing suddenly and violently rich, as this man is, naturally makes him a bloated aristocrat. The airs he puts on are insufferable.

And, speaking of wages, reminds me of prices of merchandise. In Paris you pay twelve dollars a dozen for Jouvin's best kid gloves; gloves of about as good quality sell here at three or four dollars a dozen. You pay five and six dollars apiece for fine linen shirts in Paris; here and in Leghorn you pay two and a half. In Marseilles you pay forty dollars for a first-class dress-coat made by a good tailor, but in Leghorn you can get a full-dress suit for the same money. Here you get handsome business suits at from ten to twenty dollars, and in Leghorn you can get an overcoat for fifteen dollars that would cost you seventy in New York. Fine kid boots are worth eight dollars in Marseilles and four dollars here. Lyons velvets rank higher in America than those of Genoa. Yet the bulk of Lyons velvets you buy in the States are made in Genoa and imported into Lyons, where they receive the Lyons stamp and are then exported to America. You can buy enough velvet in Genoa for twenty-five dollars to make a five-hundred-dollar cloak in New York—so the ladies tell me. Of course, these things bring me back, by a natural and easy transition, to the

### ASCENT OF VESUVIUS—CONTINUED

And thus the wonderful Blue Grotto is suggested to me. It is situated on the island of Capri, twenty-two miles from Naples. We chartered a little steamer and went out there. Of course, the police boarded us and put us through a health examination, and inquired into our politics, before they would let us land. The airs these little insect governments put on are in the last degree ridiculous. They even put a policeman on board of our boat to keep an eye on us as long as we were in the Capri dominions. They thought we wanted to steal the grotto, I suppose. It was worth stealing. The entrance to the cave is four feet high and four feet wide, and is in the face of a lofty perpendicular cliff—the sea-wall. You enter in small boats—and a tight squeeze it is, too. You cannot go in at all when the tide is up. Once within, you find yourself in an arched cavern about one hundred and sixty feet long, one hundred and twenty wide, and about seventy high. How deep it is no man knows. It goes down to the bottom of the ocean. The waters of this placid subterranean lake are the brightest, loveliest blue that can be imagined. They are as transparent as plate-glass, and their coloring would shame the richest sky that ever bent over Italy. No tint could be more ravishing, no luster more superb. Throw a stone into the water, and the myriad of tiny bubbles that are created flash out a brilliant glare like blue theatrical fires. Dip an oar, and its blade turns to splendid frosted silver, tinted with blue. Let a man jump in, and instantly he is cased in an armor more gorgeous than ever kingly Crusader wore.

Then we went to Ischia, but I had already been to that island and tired myself to death "resting" a couple of days and studying human villainy, with the landlord of the Grande Sentinelle for a model. So we went to Procida, and from thence to Pozzuoli, where St. Paul landed after he sailed from Samos. I landed at precisely the same spot where St. Paul landed, and so did Dan and the others. It was a remarkable coincidence. St. Paul preached to these people seven days before he started to Rome.

Nero's Baths, the ruins of Baiæ, the Temple of Serapis; Cumæ, where the Cumæan Sibyl interpreted the oracles, the Lake Agnano, with its ancient submerged city still visible far down in its depths—these and a hundred other points of interest we examined with critical imbecility, but the Grotto of the Dog claimed our chief attention, because we had heard and read so much about it. Everybody has written about the Grotto del Cane and its poisonous vapors, from Pliny down to Smith, and every tourist has held a dog over its floor by the legs to test the capabilities of the place. The dog dies in a minute and a half—a chicken instantly. As a general thing, strangers who crawl in there to sleep do not get up until they are called. And then they don't, either. The stranger that ventures to sleep there takes a permanent contract. I longed to see this grotto. I resolved to take a dog and hold him myself; suffocate him a little, and time him; suffocate him some more, and then finish him. We reached the grotto about three in the afternoon, and proceeded at once to make the experiments. But now, an important difficulty presented itself. We had no dog.

### ASCENT OF VESUVIUS—CONTINUED

At the Hermitage we were about fifteen or eighteen hundred feet above the sea, and thus far a portion of the ascent had been pretty abrupt. For the next two miles the road was a mixture—sometimes the ascent was abrupt and sometimes it was not; but one characteristic it possessed all the time, without failure—without modification—it was all uncompromisingly and unspeakably infamous. It

was a rough, narrow trail, and led over an old lava-
flow—a black ocean which was tumbled into a
thousand fantastic shapes—a wild chaos of ruin,
desolation, and barrenness—a wilderness of billowy
upheavals, of furious whirlpools, of miniature mountains rent asunder—of gnarled and knotted, wrinkled
and twisted masses of blackness that mimicked
branching roots, great vines, trunks of trees, all
interlaced and mingled together; and all these weird
shapes, all this turbulent panorama, all this stormy,
far-stretching waste of blackness, with its thrilling
suggestiveness of life, of action, of boiling, surging,
furious motion, was petrified!—all stricken dead
and cold in the instant of its maddest rioting!—
fettered, paralyzed, and left to glower at heaven in
impotent rage forevermore!

Finally we stood in a level, narrow valley (a valley
that had been created by the terrific march of some
old-time eruption) and on either hand towered the
two steep peaks of Vesuvius. The one we had to
climb—the one that contains the active volcano—
seemed about eight hundred or one thousand feet
high, and looked almost too straight-up-and-down
for any man to climb, and certainly no mule could
climb it with a man on his back. Four of these
native pirates will carry you to the top in a sedan-
chair, if you wish it, but suppose they were to slip
and let you fall,—is it likely that you would ever
stop rolling? Not this side of eternity, perhaps.
We left the mules, sharpened our finger-nails, and
began the ascent I have been writing about so long,
at twenty minutes to six in the morning. The path

led straight up a rugged sweep of loose chunks of pumice-stone, and for about every two steps forward we took, we slid back one. It was so excessively steep that we had to stop, every fifty or sixty steps, and rest a moment. To see our comrades, we had to look very nearly straight up at those above us, and very nearly straight down at those below. We stood on the summit at last—it had taken an hour and fifteen minutes to make the trip.

What we saw there was simply a circular crater—a circular ditch, if you please—about two hundred feet deep, and four or five hundred feet wide, whose inner wall was about half a mile in circumference. In the center of the great circus-ring thus formed was a torn and ragged upheaval a hundred feet high, all snowed over with a sulphur crust of many and many a brilliant and beautiful color, and the ditch inclosed this like the moat of a castle, or surrounded it as a little river does a little island, if the simile is gaudy in the extreme—all mingled together in the richest confusion were red, blue, brown, black, yellow, white—I do not know that there was a color, or shade of a color, or combination of colors, unrepresented—and when the sun burst through the morning mists and fired this tinted magnificence, it topped imperial Vesuvius like a jeweled crown!

The crater itself—the ditch—was not so variegated in coloring, but yet, in its softness, richness, and unpretentious elegance, it was more charming, more fascinating to the eye. There was nothing "loud" about its well-bred and well-dressed look. Beautiful? One could stand and look down upon it for a week without getting tired of it. It had the semblance of a pleasant meadow, whose slender grasses and whose velvety mosses were frosted with a shining dust, and tinted with palest green that deepened gradually to the darkest hue of the orange leaf, and deepened yet again into gravest brown, then faded into orange, then into brightest gold, and culminated in the delicate pink of a new-blown rose. Where portions of the meadow had sunk, and where other portions had been broken up like an ice-floe, the cavernous openings of the one, and the ragged upturned edges exposed by the other, were hung with a lacework of soft-tinted crystals of sulphur that changed their deformities into quaint shapes and figures that were full of grace and beauty.

The walls of the ditch were brilliant with yellow banks of sulphur and with lava and pumice-stone of many colors. No fire was visible anywhere, but gusts of sulphurous steam issued silently and invisibly from a thousand little cracks and fissures in the crater, and were wafted to our noses with every breeze. But so long as we kept our nostrils buried in our handkerchiefs, there was small danger of suffocation.

Some of the boys thrust long slips of paper down into holes and set them on fire, and so achieved the glory of lighting their cigars by the flames of Vesuvius, and others cooked eggs over fissures in the rocks and were happy.

The view from the summit would have been superb but for the fact that the sun could only pierce the mists at long intervals. Thus the glimpses we had of the grand panorama below were only fitful and unsatisfactory.

### THE DESCENT

The descent of the mountain was a labor of only four minutes. Instead of stalking down the rugged path we ascended, we chose one which was bedded knee-deep in loose ashes, and plowed our way with prodigious strides that would almost have shamed the performance of him of the seven-league boots.

The Vesuvius of to-day is a very poor affair compared to the mighty volcano of Kilauea, in the Sandwich Islands, but I am glad I visited it. It was well worth it.

It is said that during one of the grand eruptions of Vesuvius it discharged massy rocks weighing many tons a thousand feet into the air, its vast jets of smoke and steam ascended thirty miles toward the firmament, and clouds of its ashes were wafted abroad and fell upon the decks of ships seven hundred and fifty miles at sea! I will take the ashes at a moderate distance, if any one will take the thirty miles of smoke, but I do not feel able to take a commanding interest in the whole story by myself.

# CHAPTER IV

THEY pronounce it Pom-*pay*-e. I always had an idea that you went down into Pompeii with torches, by the way of damp, dark stairways, just as you do in silver-mines, and traversed gloomy tunnels with lava overhead and something on either hand like dilapidated prisons gouged out of the solid earth, that faintly resembled houses. But you do nothing of the kind. Fully one-half of the buried city, perhaps, is completely exhumed and thrown open freely to the light of day; and there stand the long rows of solidly built brick houses (roofless) just as they stood eighteen hundred years ago, hot with the flaming sun; and there lie their floors, clean-swept, and not a bright fragment tarnished or wanting of the labored mosaics that pictured them with the beasts and birds and flowers which we copy in perishable carpets to-day; and there are the Venuses and Bacchuses and Adonises, making love and getting drunk in many-hued frescoes on the walls of saloon and bedchamber; and there are the narrow streets and narrower sidewalks, paved with flags of good hard lava, the one deeply rutted with the chariot-wheels, and the other with the passing feet of the Pompeiians of bygone centuries; and

33

there are the bake shops, the temples, the halls of
justice, the baths, the theaters—all clean-scraped
and neat, and suggesting nothing of the nature of a
silver-mine away down in the bowels of the earth.
The broken pillars lying about, the doorless door-
ways, and the crumbled tops of the wilderness of
walls, were wonderfully suggestive of the "burnt
district" in one of our cities, and if there had been
any charred timbers, shattered windows, heaps of
debris, and general blackness and smokiness about
the place, the resemblance would have been perfect.
But no—the sun shines as brightly down on old
Pompeii to-day as it did when Christ was born in
Bethlehem, and its streets are cleaner a hundred
times than ever Pompeiian saw them in her prime.
I know whereof I speak—for in the great, chief
thoroughfares (Merchant Street and the Street of
Fortune) have I not seen with my own eyes how for
two hundred years at least the pavements were not
repaired!—how ruts five and even ten inches deep
were worn into the thick flagstones by the chariot-
wheels of generations of swindled taxpayers? And
do I not know by these signs that street commissioners of Pompeii never attended to their business,
and that if they never mended the pavements they
never cleaned them? And, besides, is it not the
inborn nature of street commissioners to avoid their
duty whenever they get a chance? I wish I knew
the name of the last one that held office in Pompeii
so that I could give him a blast. I speak with feeling on this subject, because I caught my foot in one
of these ruts, and the sadness that came over me

when I saw the first poor skeleton, with ashes and lava sticking to it, was tempered by the reflection that maybe that party was the street commissioner.

No—Pompeii is no longer a buried city. It is a city of hundreds and hundreds of roofless houses, and a tangled maze of streets where one could easily get lost, without a guide, and have to sleep in some ghostly palace that had known no living tenant since that awful November night of eighteen centuries ago.

We passed through the gate which faces the Mediterranean (called the "Marine Gate"), and by the rusty, broken image of Minerva, still keeping tireless watch and ward over the possessions it was powerless to save, and went up a long street and stood in the broad court of the Forum of Justice. The floor was level and clean, and up and down either side was a noble colonnade of broken pillars, with their beautiful Ionic and Corinthian columns scattered about them. At the upper end were the vacant seats of the judges, and behind them we descended into a dungeon where the ashes and cinders had found two prisoners chained on that memorable November night, and tortured them to death. How they must have tugged at the pitiless fetters as the fierce fires surged around them!

Then we lounged through many and many a sumptuous private mansion which we could not have entered without a formal invitation in incomprehensible Latin, in the olden time, when the owners lived there—and we probably wouldn't have got it. These people built their houses a good deal alike.

The floors were laid in fanciful figures wrought in mosaics of many-colored marbles. At the threshold your eyes fall upon a Latin sentence of welcome, sometimes, or a picture of a dog, with the legend, "Beware of the Dog," and sometimes a picture of a bear or a faun with no inscription at all. Then you enter a sort of vestibule, where they used to keep the hat-rack, I suppose; next a room with a large marble basin in the midst and the pipes of a fountain; on either side are bedrooms; beyond the fountain is a reception-room, then a little garden dining-room, and so forth and so on. The floors were all mosaic, the walls were stuccoed, or frescoed, or ornamented with bas-reliefs, and here and there were statues, large and small, and little fish-pools, and cascades of sparkling water that sprang from secret places in the colonnade of handsome pillars that surrounded the court, and kept the flower-beds fresh and the air cool. Those Pompeiians were very luxurious in their tastes and habits. The most exquisite bronzes we have seen in Europe came from the exhumed cities of Herculaneum and Pompeii, and also the finest cameos and the most delicate engravings on precious stones; their pictures, eighteen or nineteen centuries old, are often much more pleasing than the celebrated rubbish of the old masters of three centuries ago. They were well up in art. From the creation of these works of the first, clear up to the eleventh century, art seems hardly to have existed at all—at least no remnants of it are left—and it was curious to see how far (in some things, at any rate) these old-time pagans excelled the remote generations of masters that came after them. The pride of the world in sculptures seem to be the Laocoön and the Dying Gladiator in Rome. They are as old as Pompeii, were dug from the earth like Pompeii; but their exact age or who made them can only be conjectured. But worn and cracked, without a history, and with the blemishing stains of numberless centuries upon them, they still mutely mock at all efforts to rival their perfections.

It was a quaint and curious pastime, wandering through this old silent city of the dead—lounging through utterly deserted streets where thousands and thousands of human beings once bought and sold, and walked and rode, and made the place resound with the noise and confusion of traffic and pleasure. They were not lazy. They hurried in those days. We had evidence of that. There was a temple on one corner, and it was a shorter cut to go between the columns of that temple from one street to the other than to go around—and behold, that pathway had been worn deep into the heavy flagstone floor of the building by generations of time-saving feet! They would not go around when it was quicker to go through. We do that way in our cities.

Everywhere, you see things that make you wonder how old these old houses were before the night of destruction came—things, too, which bring back those long-dead inhabitants and place them living before your eyes. For instance: The steps (two feet thick—lava blocks) that lead up out of the school, and the same kind of steps that lead up into

the dress-circle of the principal theater, are almost
worn through! For ages the boys hurried out of
that school, and for ages their parents hurried into
that theater, and the nervous feet that have been
dust and ashes for eighteen centuries have left their
record for us to read to-day. I imagined I could
see crowds of gentlemen and ladies thronging into
the theater, with tickets for secured seats in their
hands, and on the wall, I read the imaginary plac-
ard, in infamous grammar, "POSITIVELY NO FREE
LIST, EXCEPT MEMBERS OF THE PRESS!" Hanging
about the doorway (I fancied) were slouchy Pompeiian street-boys uttering slang and profanity, and
keeping a wary eye out for checks. I entered the
theater, and sat down in one of the long rows of
stone benches in the dress-circle, and looked at the
place for the orchestra, and the ruined stage, and
around at the wide sweep of empty boxes, and
thought to myself, "This house won't pay." I tried
to imagine the music in full blast, the leader of the
orchestra beating time, and the "versatile" So-and-
so (who had "just returned from a most successful
tour in the provinces to play his last and farewell
engagement of positively six nights only, in Pompeii,
previous to his departure for Herculaneum") charging around the stage and piling the agony mountains high—but I could not do it with such a "house"
as that; those empty benches tied my fancy down
to full reality. I said, these people that ought to
be here have been dead, and still, and moldering to
dust for ages and ages, and will never care for the
trifles and follies of life any more forever—"Owing

to circumstances, etc., etc., there will not be any performance to-night." Close down the curtain. Put out the lights.

And so I turned away and went through shop after shop and store after store, far down the long street of the merchants, and called for the wares of Rome and the East, but the tradesmen were gone, the marts were silent, and nothing was left but the broken jars all set in cement of cinders and ashes; the wine and the oil that once had filled them were gone with their owners.

In a bake shop was a mill for grinding the grain, and the furnaces for baking the bread; and they say that here, in the same furnaces, the exhumers of Pompeii found nice, well-baked loaves which the baker had not found time to remove from the ovens the last time he left his shop, because circumstances compelled him to leave in such a hurry.

In one house (the only building in Pompeii which no woman is now allowed to enter) were the small rooms and short beds of solid masonry, just as they were in the old times, and on the walls were pictures which looked almost as fresh as if they were painted yesterday, but which no pen could have the hardihood to describe; and here and there were Latin inscriptions—obscene scintillations of wit, scratched by hands that possibly were uplifted to Heaven for succor in the midst of a driving storm of fire before the night was done.

In one of the principal streets was a ponderous stone tank, and a water-spout that supplied it, and where the tired, heated toilers from the Campagna used to rest their right hands when they bent over to put their lips to the spout, the thick stone was worn down to a broad groove an inch or two deep. Think of the countless thousands of hands that had pressed that spot in the ages that are gone, to so reduce a stone that is as hard as iron!

They had a great public bulletin-board in Pompeii —a place where announcements for gladiatorial combats, elections, and such things, were posted— not on perishable paper, but carved in enduring stone. One lady, who, I take it, was rich and well brought up, advertised a dwelling or so to rent, with baths and all the modern improvements, and several hundred shops, stipulating that the dwellings should not be put to immoral purposes. You can find out who lived in many a house in Pompeii by the carved stone door-plates affixed to them: and in the same way you can tell who they were that occupy the tombs. Everywhere around are things that reveal to you something of the customs and history of this forgotten people. But what would a volcano leave of an American city, if it once rained its cinders on it? Hardly a sign or a symbol to tell its story.

In one of these long Pompeiian halls the skeleton of a man was found, with ten pieces of gold in one hand and a large key in the other. He had seized his money and started toward the door, but the fiery tempest caught him at the very threshold, and he sank down and died. One more minute of precious time would have saved him. I saw the skeletons of a man, a woman, and two young girls. The woman had her hands spread wide apart, as if in mortal terror, and I imagined I could still trace upon her shapeless face something of the expression of wild despair that distorted it when the heavens rained fire in these streets, so many ages ago. The girls and the man lay with their faces upon their arms, as if they had tried to shield them from the enveloping cinders. In one apartment eighteen skeletons were found, all in sitting postures, and blackened places on the walls still mark their shapes and show their attitudes, like shadows. One of them, a woman, still wore upon her skeleton throat a necklace, with her name engraved upon it—JULIE DI DIOMEDE.

But perhaps the most poetical thing Pompeii has yielded to modern research, was that grand figure of a Roman soldier, clad in complete armor; who, true to his duty, true to his proud name of a soldier of Rome, and full of the stern courage which had given to that name its glory, stood to his post by the city gate, erect and unflinching, till the hell that raged around him *burned out* the dauntless spirit it could not conquer.

We never read of Pompeii but we think of that soldier; we cannot write of Pompeii without the natural impulse to grant to him the mention he so well deserves. Let us remember that he was a soldier —not a policeman—and so, praise him. Being a soldier, he stayed—because the warrior instinct forbade him to fly. Had he been a policeman he would have stayed, also—because he would have been asleep.

There are not half a dozen flights of stairs in Pompeii, and no other evidences that the houses were more than one story high. The people did not live in the clouds, as do the Venetians, the Genoese and Neapolitans of to-day.

We came out from under the solemn mysteries of this city of the Venerable Past—this city which perished, with all its old ways and its quaint old fashions about it, remote centuries ago, when the Disciples were preaching the new religion, which is as old as the hills to us now—and went dreaming among the trees that grow over acres and acres of its still buried streets and squares, till a shrill whistle and the cry of *"All aboard—last train for Naples!"* woke me up and reminded me that I belonged in the nineteenth century, and was not a dusty mummy, caked with ashes and cinders, eighteen hundred years old. The transition was startling. The idea of a railroad-train actually running to old dead Pompeii, and whistling irreverently, and calling for passengers in the most bustling and businesslike way, was as strange a thing as one could imagine, and as unpoetical and disagreeable as it was strange.

Compare the cheerful life and the sunshine of this day with the horrors the younger Pliny saw here, the 9th of November, A.D. 79, when he was so bravely striving to remove his mother out of reach of harm, while she begged him, with all a mother's unselfishness, to leave her to perish and save himself.

By this time the murky darkness had so increased that one might have believed himself abroad in a black and moonless night, or in a chamber where all the lights had been extinguished. On every hand was heard the complaints of women, the wailing of children, and the cries of men. One called his father, another his son, and another his wife, and only by their voices could

# THE INNOCENTS ABROAD

they know each other. Many in their despair begged that death would come and end their distress.

Some implored the gods to succor them, and some believed that this night was the last, the eternal night which should engulf the universe!

Even so it seemed to me—and I consoled myself for the coming death with the reflection: BEHOLD! THE WORLD IS PASSING AWAY!

After browsing among the stately ruins of Rome, of Baiæ, of Pompeii, and after glancing down the long marble ranks of battered and nameless imperial heads that stretch down the corridors of the Vatican, one thing strikes me with a force it never had before: the unsubstantial, unlasting character of fame. Men lived long lives, in the olden time, and struggled feverishly through them, toiling like slaves, in oratory, in generalship, or in literature, and then laid them down and died, happy in the possession of an enduring history and a deathless name. Well, twenty little centuries flutter away, and what is left of these things? A crazy inscription on a block of stone, which snuffy antiquaries bother over and tangle up and make nothing out of but a bare name (which they spell wrong) —no history, no tradition, no poetry—nothing that can give it even a passing interest. What may be left of General Grant's great name forty centuries hence? This—in the Encyclopedia for A.D. 5868, possibly.

URIAH S. (or Z.) GRAUNT—popular poet of ancient times in the Aztec provinces of the United States of British America. Some authors say flourished about A.D. 742; but the learned Ah-ah Foo-foo states that he was a contemporary of Scharkspyre, the English poet, and flourished about A.D. 1328, some three centuries *after* the Trojan war instead of before it. He wrote "Rock me to Sleep, Mother."

These thoughts sadden me. I will to bed.

43

## CHAPTER V

HOME, again! For the first time, in many
weeks, the ship's entire family met and shook
hands on the quarter-deck. They had gathered
from many points of the compass and from many
lands, but not one was missing; there was no tale
of sickness or death among the flock to dampen the
pleasure of the reunion. Once more there was a
full audience on deck to listen to the sailors' chorus
as they got the anchor up, and to wave an adieu to
the land as we sped away from Naples.

The seats were full at dinner again, the domino
parties were complete, and the life and bustle on
the upper deck in the fine moonlight at night was
like old times—old times that had been gone weeks
only, but yet they were weeks so crowded with incident, adventure, and excitement, that they seemed
almost like years. There was no lack of cheerful-
ness on board the *Quaker City*. For once, her title
was a misnomer.

At seven in the evening, with the western horizon
all golden from the sunken sun, and specked with
distant ships, the full moon sailing high overhead,
the dark blue of the sea under foot, and a strange
sort of twilight affected by all these different lights
and colors around us and about us, we sighted superb
Stromboli. With what majesty the monarch held

THE INNOCENTS ABROAD

his lonely state above the level sea! Distance
clothed him in a purple gloom, and added a veil of
shimmering mist that so softened his rugged features
that we seemed to see him through a web of silver
gauze. His torch was out; his fires were smoldering;
a tall column of smoke that rose up and lost itself
in the growing moonlight was all the sign he gave
that he was a living Autocrat of the Sea and not the
specter of a dead one.

At two in the morning we swept through the
Straits of Messina, and so bright was the moonlight
that Italy on the one hand and Sicily on the other
seemed almost as distinctly visible as though we
looked at them from the middle of a street we were
traversing. The city of Messina, milk-like, and
starred and spangled all over with gaslights, was a
fairy spectacle. A great party of us were on deck
smoking and making a noise, and waiting to see
famous Scylla and Charybdis. And presently the
Oracle stepped out with his eternal spy-glass and
squared himself on the deck like another Colossus
of Rhodes. It was a surprise to see him abroad at
such an hour. Nobody supposed he cared anything
about an old fable like that of Scylla and Charybdis.
One of the boys said:

"Hello, doctor, what are you doing up here at
this time of night?—What do you want to see this
place for?"

"What do *I* want to see this place for? Young
man, little do you know me, or you wouldn't ask
such a question. I wish to see *all* the places that's
mentioned in the Bible."

# MARK TWAIN

"Stuff! This place isn't mentioned in the Bible."

"It ain't mentioned in the Bible!—*this* place ain't—well now, what place *is* this, since you know so much about it?"

"Why it's Scylla and Charybdis."

"Scylla and Cha—confound it, I thought it was Sodom and Gomorrah!"

And he closed up his glass and went below. The above is the ship story. Its plausibility is marred a little by the fact that the Oracle was not a biblical student, and did not spend much of his time instructing himself about Scriptural localities.—They say the Oracle complains, in this hot weather, lately, that the only beverage in the ship that is passable, is the butter. He did not mean butter, of course, but inasmuch as that article remains in a melted state now since we are out of ice, it is fair to give him the credit of getting one long word in the right place, anyhow, for once in his life. He said, in Rome, that the Pope was a noble-looking old man, but he never *did* think much of his Iliad.

We spent one pleasant day skirting along the Isles of Greece. They are very mountainous. Their prevailing tints are gray and brown, approaching to red. Little white villages, surrounded by trees, nestle in the valleys or roost upon the lofty perpendicular sea-walls.

We had one fine sunset—a rich carmine flush that suffused the western sky and cast a ruddy glow far over the sea. Fine sunsets seem to be rare in this part of the world—or at least, striking ones. They are soft, sensuous, lovely—they are exquisite,

46

refined, effeminate, but we have seen no sunsets here yet like the gorgeous conflagrations that flame in the track of the sinking sun in our high northern latitudes.

But what were sunsets to us, with the wild excitement upon us of approaching the most renowned of cities! What cared we for outward visions, when Agamemnon, Achilles, and a thousand other heroes of the great Past were marching in ghostly procession through our fancies? What were sunsets to us, who were about to live and breathe and walk in actual Athens; yea, and go far down into the dead centuries and bid in person for the slaves, Diogenes and Plato, in the public market-place, or gossip with the neighbors about the siege of Troy or the splendid deeds of Marathon? We scorned to consider sunsets.

We arrived, and entered the ancient harbor of the Piræus at last. We dropped anchor within half a mile of the village. Away off, across the undulating Plain of Attica, could be seen a little square-topped hill with a something on it, which our glasses soon discovered to be the ruined edifices of the citadel of the Athenians, and most prominent among them loomed the venerable Parthenon. So exquisitely clear and pure is this wonderful atmosphere that every column of the noble structure was discernible through the telescope, and even the smaller ruins about it assumed some semblance of shape. This at a distance of five or six miles. In the valley, near the Acropolis (the square-topped hill before spoken of), Athens itself could be vaguely made out with an ordinary lorgnette. Everybody was anxious to get ashore and visit these classic localities as quickly as possible. No land we had yet seen had aroused such universal interest among the passengers.

But bad news came. The commandant of the Piræus came in his boat, and said we must either depart or else get outside the harbor and remain imprisoned in our ship, under rigid quarantine, for eleven days! So we took up the anchor and moved outside, to lie a dozen hours or so, taking in supplies, and then sail for Constantinople. It was the bitterest disappointment we had yet experienced. To lie a whole day in sight of the Acropolis, and yet be obliged to go away without visiting Athens! Disappointment was hardly a strong enough word to describe the circumstances.

All hands were on deck, all the afternoon, with books and maps and glasses, trying to determine which "narrow rocky ridge" was the Areopagus, which sloping hill the Pnyx, which elevation the Museum Hill, and so on. And we got things confused. Discussion became heated, and party spirit ran high. Church-members were gazing with emotion upon a hill which they said was the one St. Paul preached from, and another faction claimed that that hill was Hymettus, and another that it was Pentelicon! After all the trouble, we could be certain of only one thing—the square-topped hill was the Acropolis, and the grand ruin that crowned it was the Parthenon, whose picture we knew in infancy in the school-books.

We inquired of everybody who came near the

ship, whether there were guards in the Piræus, whether they were strict, what the chances were of capture should any of us slip ashore, and in case any of us made the venture and were caught, what would be probably done to us? The answers were discouraging: There was a strong guard or police force; the Piræus was a small town, and any stranger seen in it would surely attract attention—capture would be certain. The commandant said the punishment would be "heavy"; when asked "How heavy?" he said it would be "very severe"—that was all we could get out of him.

At eleven o'clock at night, when most of the ship's company were abed, four of us stole softly ashore in a small boat, a clouded moon favoring the enterprise, and started two and two, and far apart, over a low hill, intending to go clear around the Piræus, out of the range of its police. Picking our way so stealthily over that rocky, nettle-grown eminence, made me feel a good deal as if I were on my way somewhere to steal something. My immediate comrade and I talked in an undertone about quarantine laws and their penalties, but we found nothing cheering in the subject. I was posted. Only a few days before, I was talking with our captain, and he mentioned the case of a man who swam ashore from a quarantined ship somewhere, and got imprisoned six months for it; and when he was in Genoa a few years ago, a captain of a quarantined ship went in his boat to a departing ship, which was already outside of the harbor, and put a letter on board to be taken to his family, and the authorities

imprisoned him three months for it, and then conducted him and his ship fairly to sea, and warned
him never to show himself in that port again while
he lived. This kind of conversation did no good,
further than to give a sort of dismal interest to our
quarantine-breaking expedition, and so we dropped
it. We made the entire circuit of the town without
seeing anybody but one man, who stared at us curiously, but said nothing, and a dozen persons asleep
on the ground before their doors, whom we walked
among and never woke—but we woke up dogs
enough, in all conscience—we always had one or
two barking at our heels, and several times we had
as many as ten and twelve at once. They made such
a preposterous din that persons aboard our ship said
they could tell how we were progressing for a long
time, and where we were, by the barking of the
dogs. The clouded moon still favored us. When
we had made the whole circuit, and were passing
among the houses on the further side of the town,
the moon came out splendidly, but we no longer
feared the light. As we approached a well, near a
house, to get a drink, the owner merely glanced at
us and went within. He left the quiet, slumbering
town at our mercy. I record it here proudly, that
we didn't do anything to it.

Seeing no road, we took a tall hill to the left of
the distant Acropolis for a mark, and steered straight
for it over all obstructions, and over a little rougher
piece of country than exists anywhere else outside
of the state of Nevada, perhaps. Part of the way it
was covered with small, loose stones—we trod on six

at a time, and they all rolled. Another part of it
was dry, loose, newly plowed ground. Still another
part of it was a long stretch of low grape vines,
which were tanglesome and troublesome, and which
we took to be brambles. The Attic Plain, barring
the grape vines, was a barren, desolate, unpoetical
waste—I wonder what it was in Greece's Age of
Glory, five hundred years before Christ?

In the neighborhood of one o'clock in the morning, when we were heated with fast walking and
parched with thirst, Denny exclaimed, "Why, these
weeds are grape vines!" and in five minutes we
had a score of bunches of large, white, delicious
grapes, and were reaching down for more when
a dark shape rose mysteriously up out of the
shadows beside us and said "Ho!" And so we
left.

In ten minutes more we struck into a beautiful
road, and unlike some others we had stumbled upon
at intervals, it led in the right direction. We followed it. It was broad and smooth and white—
handsome and in perfect repair, and shaded on both
sides for a mile or so with single ranks of trees, and
also with luxuriant vineyards. Twice we entered
and stole grapes, and the second time somebody
shouted at us from some invisible place. Whereupon we left again. We speculated in grapes no
more on that side of Athens.

Shortly we came upon an ancient stone aqueduct,
built upon arches, and from that time forth we had
ruins all about us—we were approaching our journey's end. We could not see the Acropolis now or

the high hill, either, and I wanted to follow the road
till we were abreast of them, but the others overruled
me, and we toiled laboriously up the stony hill immediately in our front—and from its summit saw
another—climbed it and saw another! It was an
hour of exhausting work. Soon we came upon a
row of open graves, cut in the solid rock—(for a
while one of them served Socrates for a prison)—
we passed around the shoulder of the hill, and the
citadel, in all its ruined magnificence, burst upon
us! We hurried across the ravine and up a winding
road, and stood on the old Acropolis, with the prodigious walls of the citadel towering above our
heads. We did not stop to inspect their massive
blocks of marble, or measure their height, or guess
at their extraordinary thickness, but passed at once
through a great arched passage like a railway-tunnel,
and went straight to the gate that leads to the
ancient temples. It was locked! So, after all, it
seemed that we were not to see the great Parthenon
face to face. We sat down and held a council of
war. Result: The gate was only a flimsy structure
of wood—we would break it down. It seemed like
desecration, but then we had traveled far, and our
necessities were urgent. We could not hunt up
guides and keepers—we must be on the ship before
daylight. So we argued. This was all very fine,
but when we came to break the gate, we could not
do it. We moved around an angle of the wall and
found a low bastion—eight feet high without—ten
or twelve within. Denny prepared to scale it, and
we got ready to follow. By dint of hard scrambling

he finally straddled the top, but some loose stones crumbled away and fell with a crash into the court within. There was instantly a banging of doors and a shout. Denny dropped from the wall in a twinkling, and we retreated in disorder to the gate. Xerxes took that mighty citadel four hundred and eighty years before Christ, when his five millions of soldiers and camp-followers followed him to Greece, and if we four Americans could have remained unmolested five minutes longer, we would have taken it too.

The garrison had turned out—four Greeks. We clamored at the gate, and they admitted us. [Bribery and corruption.]

We crossed a large court, entered a great door, and stood upon a pavement of purest white marble, deeply worn by footprints. Before us, in the flooding moonlight, rose the noblest ruins we had ever looked upon—the Propylæa; a small temple of Minerva; the Temple of Hercules, and the grand Parthenon. [We got these names from the Greek guide, who didn't seem to know more than seven men ought to know.] These edifices were all built of the whitest Pentelic marble, but have a pinkish stain upon them now. Where any part is broken, however, the fracture looks like fine loaf-sugar. Six caryatides, or marble women, clad in flowing robes, support the portico of the Temple of Hercules, but the porticoes and colonnades of the other structures are formed of massive Doric and Ionic pillars, whose flutings and capitals are still measurably perfect, notwithstanding the centuries that have gone over

53

them and the sieges they have suffered. The Parthenon, originally, was two hundred and twenty-six feet long, one hundred wide, and seventy high, and had two rows of great columns, eight in each, at either end, and single rows of seventeen each down the sides, and was one of the most graceful and beautiful edifices ever erected.

Most of the Parthenon's imposing columns are still standing, but the roof is gone. It was a perfect building two hundred and fifty years ago, when a shell dropped into the Venetian magazine stored here, and the explosion which followed wrecked and unroofed it. I remember but little about the Parthenon, and I have put in one or two facts and figures for the use of other people with short memories. Got them from the guide-book.

As we wandered thoughtfully down the marble-paved length of this stately temple, the scene about us was strangely impressive. Here and there, in lavish profusion, were gleaming white statues of men and women, propped against blocks of marble, some of them armless, some without legs, others headless —but all looking mournful in the moonlight, and startlingly human! They rose up and confronted the midnight intruder on every side—they stared at him with stony eyes from unlooked-for nooks and recesses; they peered at him over fragmentary heaps far down the desolate corridors; they barred his way in the midst of the broad forum, and solemnly pointed with handless arms the way from the sacred fane; and through the roofless temple the moon looked down, and banded the floor and darkened the scattered fragments and broken statues with the slanting shadows of the columns.

What a world of ruined sculpture was about us! Set up in rows—stacked up in piles—scattered broadcast over the wide area of the Acropolis— were hundreds of crippled statues of all sizes and of the most exquisite workmanship; and vast fragments of marble that once belonged to the entablatures, covered with bas-reliefs representing battles and sieges, ships of war with three and four tiers of oars, pageants and processions—everything one could think of. History says that the temples of the Acropolis were filled with the noblest works of Praxiteles and Phidias, and of many a great master in sculpture besides—and surely these elegant fragments attest it.

We walked out into the grass-grown, fragment-strewn court beyond the Parthenon. It startled us, every now and then, to see a stony white face stare suddenly up at us out of the grass with its dead eyes. The place seemed alive with ghosts. I half expected to see the Athenian heroes of twenty centuries ago glide out of the shadows and steal into the old temple they knew so well and regarded with such boundless pride.

The full moon was riding high in the cloudless heavens now. We sauntered carelessly and unthinkingly to the edge of the lofty battlements of the citadel, and looked down—a vision! And such a vision! Athens by moonlight! The prophet that thought the splendors of the New Jerusalem were revealed to him, surely saw this instead! It lay in

'the level plain right under our feet—all spread
abroad like a picture—and we looked down upon it
as we might have looked from a balloon. We saw
no semblance of a street, but every house, every
window, every clinging vine, every projection, was
as distinct and sharply marked as if the time were
noonday; and yet there was no glare, no glitter,
nothing harsh or repulsive—the noiseless city was
flooded with the mellowest light that ever streamed
from the moon, and seemed like some living creature
wrapped in peaceful slumber. On its further side
was a little temple, whose delicate pillars and ornate
front glowed with a rich luster that chained the eye
like a spell; and nearer by, the palace of the king
reared its creamy walls out of the midst of a great
garden of shrubbery that was flecked all over with a
random shower of amber lights—a spray of golden
sparks that lost their brightness in the glory of the
moon, and glinted softly upon the sea of dark foliage like the pallid stars of the milky way. Overhead the stately columns, majestic still in their ruin
— underfoot the dreaming city — in the distance
the silver sea—not on the broad earth is there
another picture half so beautiful!

As we turned and moved again through the
temple, I wished that the illustrious men who had
sat in it in the remote ages could visit it again and
reveal themselves to our curious eyes—Plato, Aris-
totle, Demosthenes, Socrates, Phocion, Pythagoras,
Euclid, Pindar, Xenophon, Herodotus, Praxiteles
and Phidias, Zeuxis the painter. What a constella-
tion of celebrated names! But more than all, I

wished that old Diogenes, groping so patiently with his lantern, searching so zealously for one solitary honest man in all the world, might meander along and stumble on our party. I ought not to say it, maybe, but still I suppose he would have put out his light.

We left the Parthenon to keep its watch over old Athens, as it had kept it for twenty-three hundred years, and went and stood outside the walls of the citadel. In the distance was the ancient, but still almost perfect, Temple of Theseus, and close by, looking to the West, was the Bema, from whence Demosthenes thundered his philippics and fired the wavering patriotism of his countrymen. To the right was Mars Hill, where the Areopagus sat in ancient times, and where St. Paul defined his position, and below was the market-place where he "disputed daily" with the gossip-loving Athenians. We climbed the stone steps St. Paul ascended, and stood in the square-cut place he stood in, and tried to recollect the Bible account of the matter—but for certain reasons, I could not recall the words. I have found them since:

Now while Paul waited for them at Athens, his spirit was stirred in him, when he saw the city wholly given up to idolatry.

Therefore disputed he in the synagogue with the Jews, and with the devout persons, and in the market daily with them that met with him.

. . . . . . . . .

And they took him and brought him unto Areopagus, saying, May we know what this new doctrine whereof thou speakest is?

. . . . . . . . .

Then Paul stood in the midst of Mars hill, and said, Ye men of Athens, I perceive that in all things ye are too superstitious;

# MARK TWAIN

For as I passed by and beheld your devotions, I found an altar with this inscription: To the Unknown God. Whom, therefore, ye ignorantly worship, him declare I unto you.— *Acts*, ch. xvii.

It occurred to us, after a while, that if we wanted to get home before daylight betrayed us, we had better be moving. So we hurried away. When far on our road, we had a parting view of the Parthenon, with the moonlight streaming through its open colonnades and touching its capitals with silver. As it looked then, solemn, grand, and beautiful, it will always remain in our memories.

As we marched along, we began to get over our fears, and ceased to care much about quarantine scouts or anybody else. We grew bold and reckless; and once, in a sudden burst of courage, I even threw a stone at a dog. It was a pleasant reflection, though, that I did not hit him, because his master might just possibly have been a policeman. Inspired by this happy failure, my valor became utterly uncontrollable, and at intervals I absolutely whistled, though on a moderate key. But boldness breeds boldness, and shortly I plunged into a vineyard, in the full light of the moon, and captured a gallon of superb grapes, not even minding the presence of a peasant who rode by on a mule. Denny and Birch followed my example. Now I had grapes enough for a dozen, but then Jackson was all swollen up with courage, too, and he was obliged to enter a vineyard presently. The first bunch he seized brought trouble. A frowsy, bearded brigand sprang into the road with a shout, and flourished a musket in the light of the moon! We sidled toward the Piræus—not running, you understand, but only advancing with celerity. The brigand shouted again, but still we advanced. It was getting late, and we had no time to fool away on every ass that wanted to drivel Greek platitudes to us. We would just as soon have talked with him as not if we had not been in a hurry. Presently Denny said, "Those fellows are following us!"

We turned, and, sure enough, there they were—three fantastic pirates armed with guns. We slackened our pace to let them come up, and in the mean time I got out my cargo of grapes and dropped them firmly but reluctantly into the shadows by the wayside. But I was not afraid. I only felt that it was not right to steal grapes. And all the more so when the owner was around—and not only around, but with his friends around also. The villains came up and searched a bundle Dr. Birch had in his hand, and scowled upon him when they found it had nothing in it but some holy rocks from Mars Hill, and these were not contraband. They evidently suspected him of playing some wretched fraud upon them, and seemed half inclined to scalp the party. But finally they dismissed us with a warning, couched in excellent Greek, I suppose, and dropped tranquilly in our wake. When they had gone three hundred yards they stopped, and we went on rejoiced. But behold, another armed rascal came out of the shadows and took their place, and followed us two hundred yards. Then he delivered us over to another miscreant, who emerged from some mysterious place, and he in turn to another! For a mile and a half our rear was guarded all the while by armed men. I never traveled in so much state before in all my life.

It was a good while after that before we ventured to steal any more grapes, and when we did we stirred up another troublesome brigand, and then we ceased all further speculation in that line. I suppose that fellow that rode by on the mule posted all the sentinels, from Athens to the Piræus, about us.

Every field on that long route was watched by an armed sentinel, some of whom had fallen asleep, no doubt, but were on hand, nevertheless. This shows what sort of a country modern Attica is—a community of questionable characters. These men were not there to guard their possessions against strangers, but against each other; for strangers seldom visit Athens and the Piræus, and when they do, they go in daylight, and can buy all the grapes they want for a trifle. The modern inhabitants are confiscators and falsifiers of high repute, if gossip speaks truly concerning them, and I freely believe it does.

Just as the earliest tinges of the dawn flushed the eastern sky and turned the pillared Parthenon to a broken harp hung in the pearly horizon, we closed our thirteenth mile of weary, roundabout marching, and emerged upon the seashore abreast the ships, with our usual escort of fifteen hundred Piræan dogs howling at our heels. We hailed a boat that was two or three hundred yards from shore, and discovered in a moment that it was a police-boat on the lookout for any quarantine-breakers that might chance to be abroad. So we dodged—we were used to that by this time—and when the scouts reached the spot we had so lately occupied, we were absent. They cruised along the shore, but in the wrong direction, and shortly our own boat issued from the gloom and took us aboard. They had heard our signal on the ship. We rowed noiselessly away, and before the police-boat came in sight again, we were safe at home once more.

Four more of our passengers were anxious to visit Athens, and started half an hour after we returned; but they had not been ashore five minutes till the police discovered and chased them so hotly that they barely escaped to their boat again, and that was all. They pursued the enterprise no further.

We set sail for Constantinople to-day, but some of us little care for that. We have seen all there was to see in the old city that had its birth sixteen hundred years before Christ was born, and was an old town before the foundations of Troy were laid—and saw it in its most attractive aspect. Wherefore, why should *we* worry?

Two other passengers ran the blockade successfully last night. So we learned this morning. They slipped away so quietly that they were not missed from the ship for several hours. They had the hardihood to march into the Piræus in the early dusk and hire a carriage. They ran some danger of adding two or three months' imprisonment to the other novelties of their Holy Land Pleasure Excursion. I admire "cheek."[1] But they went and came safely, and never walked a step.

[1] Quotation from the Pilgrims.

## CHAPTER VI

FROM Athens all through the islands of the Grecian Archipelago, we saw little but forbidding sea-walls and barren hills, sometimes surmounted by three or four graceful columns of some ancient temple, lonely and deserted—a fitting symbol of the desolation that has come upon all Greece in these latter ages. We saw no plowed fields, very few villages, no trees or grass or vegetation of any kind, scarcely, and hardly ever an isolated house. Greece is a bleak, unsmiling desert, without agriculture, manufactures, or commerce, apparently. What supports its poverty-stricken people or its government, is a mystery.

I suppose that ancient Greece and modern Greece compared, furnish the most extravagant contrast to be found in history. George I., an infant of eighteen, and a scraggy nest of foreign office-holders, sit in the places of Themistocles, Pericles, and the illustrious scholars and generals of the Golden Age of Greece. The fleets that were the wonder of the world when the Parthenon was new, are a beggarly handful of fishing-smacks now, and the manly people that performed such miracles of valor at Marathon are only a tribe of unconsidered slaves to-day. The classic Ilissus has gone dry, and so have all

the sources of Grecian wealth and greatness. The
nation numbers only eight hundred thousand souls,
and there is poverty and misery and mendacity
enough among them to furnish forty millions and be
liberal about it. Under King Otho the revenues of
the state were five millions of dollars—raised from
a tax of *one-tenth* of all the agricultural products of
the land (which tenth the farmer had to bring to the
royal granaries on pack-mules any distance not
exceeding six leagues) and from extravagant taxes
on trade and commerce. Out of that five millions
the small tyrant tried to keep an army of ten thousand men, pay all the hundreds of useless Grand
Equerries in Waiting, First Grooms of the Bedchamber, Lord High Chancellors of the Exploded
Exchequer, and all the other absurdities which these
puppy-kingdoms indulge in, in imitation of the great
monarchies; and in addition he set about building a
white marble palace to cost about five millions itself.
The result was, simply: Ten into five goes no times
and none over. All these things could not be done
with five millions, and Otho fell into trouble.

The Greek throne, with its unpromising adjuncts
of a ragged population of ingenious rascals who
were out of employment eight months in the year
because there was little for them to borrow and less
to confiscate, and a waste of barren hills and weed-
grown deserts, went begging for a good while. It
was offered to one of Victoria's sons, and afterward
to various other younger sons of royalty who had no
thrones and were out of business, but they all had
the charity to decline the dreary honor, and venera-

tion enough for Greece's ancient greatness to refuse
to mock her sorrowful rags and dirt with a tinsel
throne in this day of her humiliation—till they
came to this young Danish George, and he took it.
He has finished the splendid palace I saw in the radiant moonlight the other night, and is doing many
other things for the salvation of Greece, they say.

We sailed through the barren Archipelago, and
into the narrow channel they sometimes call the
Dardanelles and sometimes the Hellespont. This
part of the country is rich in historic reminiscences,
and poor as Sahara in everything else. For instance, as we approached the Dardanelles, we
coasted along the Plains of Troy and past the mouth
of the Scamander; we saw where Troy had stood
(in the distance), and where it does not stand now
—a city that perished when the world was young.
The poor Trojans are all dead now. They were
born too late to see Noah's ark, and died too soon
to see our menagerie. We saw where Agamemnon's
fleets rendezvoused, and away inland a mountain
which the map said was Mount Ida. Within the
Hellespont we saw where the original first shoddy
contract mentioned in history was carried out, and
the "parties of the second part" gently rebuked
by Xerxes. I speak of the famous bridge of boats
which Xerxes ordered to be built over the narrowest
part of the Hellespont (where it is only two or three
miles wide). A moderate gale destroyed the flimsy
structure, and the King, thinking that to publicly
rebuke the contractors might have a good effect on
the next set, called them out before the army and

had them beheaded. In the next ten minutes he let
a new contract for the bridge. It has been observed
by ancient writers that the second bridge was a very
good bridge. Xerxes crossed his host of five millions
of men on it, and if it had not been purposely
destroyed, it would probably have been there yet.
If our government would rebuke some of our shoddy
contractors occasionally, it might work much good.
In the Hellespont we saw where Leander and Lord
Byron swam across, the one to see her upon whom
his soul's affections were fixed with a devotion that
only death could impair, and the other merely for
a flyer, as Jack says. We had two noted tombs
near us, too. On one shore slept Ajax, and on the
other Hecuba.

We had water batteries and forts on both sides of
the Hellespont, flying the crimson flag of Turkey,
with its white crescent, and occasionally a village,
and sometimes a train of camels; we had all these
to look at till we entered the broad sea of Marmora,
and then the land soon fading from view, we resumed
euchre and whist once more.

We dropped anchor in the mouth of the Golden
Horn at daylight in the morning. Only three or
four of us were up to see the great Ottoman capital.
The passengers do not turn out at unseasonable
hours, as they used to, to get the earliest possible
glimpse of strange foreign cities. They are well
over that. If we were lying in sight of the Pyramids of Egypt, they would not come on deck until
after breakfast, nowadays.

The Golden Horn is a narrow arm of the sea,

which branches from the Bosporus (a sort of broad
river which connects the Marmora and Black Seas),
and, curving around, divides the city in the middle.
Galata and Pera are on one side of the Bosporus,
and the Golden Horn; Stamboul (ancient Byzan-
tium) is upon the other. On the other bank of the
Bosporus is Scutari and other suburbs of Constantinople. This great city contains a million inhabitants,
but so narrow are its streets, and so crowded together are its houses, that it does not cover much
more than half as much ground as New York City.
Seen from the anchorage or from a mile or so up
the Bosporus, it is by far the handsomest city we
have seen. Its dense array of houses swells upward
from the water's edge, and spreads over the domes
of many hills; and the gardens that peep out here
and there, the great globes of the mosques, and the
countless minarets that meet the eye everywhere,
invest the metropolis with the quaint Oriental aspect
one dreams of when he reads books of Eastern
travel. Constantinople makes a noble picture.

But its attractiveness begins and ends with its
picturesqueness. From the time one starts ashore
till he gets back again, he execrates it. The boat
he goes in is admirably miscalculated for the service
it is built for. It is handsomely and neatly fitted
up, but no man could handle it well in the turbulent
currents that sweep down the Bosporus from the
Black Sea, and few men could row it satisfactorily
even in still water. It is a long, light canoe (caique),
large at one end and tapering to a knife-blade at the
other. They make that long sharp end the bow,

and you can imagine how these boiling currents spin it about. It has two oars, and sometimes four, and no rudder. You start to go to a given point and you run in fifty different directions before you get there. First one oar is backing water, and then the other; it is seldom that both are going ahead at once. This kind of boating is calculated to drive an impatient man mad in a week. The boatmen are the awkwardest, the stupidest, and the most unscientific on earth, without question.

Ashore, it was—well, it was an eternal circus. People were thicker than bees, in those narrow streets, and the men were dressed in all the outrageous, outlandish, idolatrous, extravagant, thunder-and-lightning costumes that ever a tailor with the delirium tremens and seven devils could conceive of. There was no freak in dress too crazy to be indulged in; no absurdity too absurd to be tolerated; no frenzy in ragged diabolism too fantastic to be attempted. No two men were dressed alike. It was a wild masquerade of all imaginable costumes— every struggling throng in every street was a dissolving view of stunning contrasts. Some patriarchs wore awful turbans, but the grand mass of the infidel horde wore the fiery red skull-cap they call a fez. All the remainder of the raiment they indulged in was utterly indescribable.

The shops here are mere coops, mere boxes, bathrooms, closets—anything you please to call them— on the first floor. The Turks sit cross-legged in them, and work and trade and smoke long pipes, and smell like—like Turks. That covers the ground.

Crowding the narrow streets in front of them are beggars, who beg forever, yet never collect anything; and wonderful cripples, distorted out of all semblance of humanity, almost; vagabonds driving laden asses; porters carrying dry-goods boxes as large as cottages on their backs; peddlers of grapes, hot corn, pumpkin seeds, and a hundred other things, yelling like fiends; and sleeping happily, comfortably, serenely, among the hurrying feet, are the famed dogs of Constantinople; drifting noiselessly about are squads of Turkish women, draped from chin to feet in flowing robes, and with snowy veils bound about their heads, that disclose only the eyes and a vague, shadowy notion of their features. Seen moving about, far away in the dim, arched aisles of the Great Bazar, they look as the shrouded dead must have looked when they walked forth from their graves amid the storms and thunders and earthquakes that burst upon Calvary that awful night of the Crucifixion. A street in Constantinople is a picture which one ought to see once—not oftener.

And then there was the goose-rancher—a fellow who drove a hundred geese before him about the city, and tried to sell them. He had a pole ten feet long, with a crook in the end of it, and occasionally a goose would branch out from the flock and make a lively break around the corner, with wings half lifted and neck stretched to its utmost. Did the goose-merchant get excited? No. He took his pole and reached after that goose with unspeakable *sang froid*—took a hitch round his neck, and "yanked" him back to his place in the flock without an effort. He steered his geese with that stick as easily as another man would steer a yawl. A few hours afterward we saw him sitting on a stone at a corner, in the midst of the turmoil, sound asleep in the sun, with his geese squatting around him, or dodging out of the way of asses and men. We came by again, within the hour, and he was taking account of stock, to see whether any of his flock had strayed or been stolen. The way he did it was unique. He put the end of his stick within six or eight inches of a stone wall, and made the geese march in single file between it and the wall. He counted them as they went by. There was no dodging that arrangement.

If you want dwarfs—I mean just a few dwarfs for a curiosity—go to Genoa. If you wish to buy them by the gross, for retail, go to Milan. There are plenty of dwarfs all over Italy, but it did seem to me that in Milan the crop was luxuriant. If you would see a fair average style of assorted cripples, go to Naples, or travel through the Roman states. But if you would see the very heart and home of cripples and human monsters, both, go straight to Constantinople. A beggar in Naples who can show a foot which has all run into one horrible toe, with one shapeless nail on it, has a fortune—but such an exhibition as that would not provoke any notice in Constantinople. The man would starve. Who would pay any attention to attractions like his among the rare monsters that throng the bridges of the Golden Horn and display their deformities in the gutters of Stamboul? Oh, wretched impostor! How could he stand against the three-legged woman, and the man with his eye in his cheek? How would he blush in presence of the man with fingers on his elbow? Where would he hide himself when the dwarf with seven fingers on each hand, no upper lip, and his under-jaw gone, came down in his majesty? Bismillah! The cripples of Europe are a delusion and a fraud. The truly gifted flourish only in the byways of Pera and Stamboul.

That three-legged woman lay on the bridge, with her stock in trade so disposed as to command the most striking effect—one natural leg, and two long, slender, twisted ones with feet on them like somebody else's forearm. Then there was a man further along who had no eyes, and whose face was the color of a fly-blown beefsteak, and wrinkled and twisted like a lava-flow—and verily so tumbled and distorted were his features that no man could tell the wart that served him for a nose from his cheekbones. In Stamboul was a man with a prodigious head, an uncommonly long body, legs eight inches long, and feet like snow-shoes. He traveled on those feet and his hands, and was as sway-backed as if the Colossus of Rhodes had been riding him. Ah, a beggar has to have exceedingly good points to make a living in Constantinople. A blue-faced man, who had nothing to offer except that he had been blown up in a mine, would be regarded as a rank impostor, and a mere damaged soldier on crutches would never make a cent. It would pay him to get a piece of his head taken off, and cultivate a wen like a carpet-sack.

# THE INNOCENTS ABROAD

The Mosque of St. Sophia is the chief lion of Constantinople. You must get a firman and hurry there the first thing. We did that. We did not get a firman, but we took along four or five francs apiece, which is much the same thing.

I do not think much of the Mosque of St. Sophia. I suppose I lack appreciation. We will let it go at that. It is the rustiest old barn in heathendom. I believe all the interest that attaches to it comes from the fact that it was built for a Christian church and then turned into a mosque, without much alteration, by the Mohammedan conquerors of the land. They made me take off my boots and walk into the place in my stocking feet. I caught cold, and got myself so stuck up with a complication of gums, slime, and general corruption, that I wore out more than two thousand pair of boot-jacks getting my boots off that night, and even then some Christian hide peeled off with them. I abate not a single boot-jack.

St. Sophia is a colossal church, thirteen or fourteen hundred years old, and unsightly enough to be very, very much older. Its immense dome is said to be more wonderful than St. Peter's, but its dirt is much more wonderful than its dome, though they never mention it. The church has a hundred and seventy pillars in it, each a single piece, and all of costly marbles of various kinds, but they came from ancient temples at Baalbec, Heliopolis, Athens, and Ephesus, and are battered, ugly, and repulsive. They were a thousand years old when this church was new, and then the contrast must have been ghastly—if Justinian's architects did not trim them

71

any.  The inside of the dome is figured all over with a monstrous inscription in Turkish characters, wrought in gold mosaic, that looks as glaring as a circus bill; the pavements and the marble balustrades are all battered and dirty; the perspective is marred everywhere by a web of ropes that depend from the dizzy height of the dome, and suspend countless dingy, coarse oil-lamps, and ostrich eggs, six or seven feet above the floor.  Squatting and sitting in groups, here and there and far and near, were ragged Turks reading books, hearing sermons, or receiving lessons like children, and in fifty places were more of the same sort bowing and straightening up, bowing again and getting down to kiss the earth, muttering prayers the while, and keeping up their gymnastics till they ought to have been tired, if they were not.

Everywhere was dirt and dust and dinginess and gloom; everywhere were signs of a hoary antiquity, but with nothing touching or beautiful about it; everywhere were those groups of fantastic pagans; overhead the gaudy mosaics and the web of lamp-ropes—nowhere was there anything to win one's love or challenge his admiration.

The people who go into ecstasies over St. Sophia must surely get them out of the guide-book (where every church is spoken of as being "considered by good judges to be the most marvelous structure, in many respects, that the world has ever seen").  Or else they are those old connoisseurs from the wilds of New Jersey who laboriously learn the difference between a fresco and a fire-plug, and from that day forward feel privileged to void their critical bathos on painting, sculpture, and architecture forevermore.

We visited the Dancing Dervishes. There were twenty-one of them. They wore a long, light-colored loose robe that hung to their heels. Each in his turn went up to the priest (they were all within a large circular railing) and bowed profoundly and then went spinning away deliriously and took his appointed place in the circle, and continued to spin. When all had spun themselves to their places, they were about five or six feet apart—and so situated, the entire circle of spinning pagans spun itself three separate times around the room. It took twenty-five minutes to do it. They spun on the left foot, and kept themselves going by passing the right rapidly before it and digging it against the waxed floor. Some of them made incredible "time." Most of them spun around forty times in a minute, and one artist averaged about sixty-one times a minute, and kept it up during the whole twenty-five. His robe filled with air and stood out all around him like a balloon.

They made no noise of any kind, and most of them tilted their heads back and closed their eyes, entranced with a sort of devotional ecstasy. There was a rude kind of music, part of the time, but the musicians were not visible. None but spinners were allowed within the circle. A man had to either spin or stay outside. It was about as barbarous an exhibition as we have witnessed yet. Then sick persons came and lay down, and beside them women laid their sick children (one a babe at the breast), and the patriarch of the Dervishes walked upon their bodies. He was supposed to cure their diseases by trampling upon their breasts or backs 'or standing on the back of their necks. This is well enough for a people who think all their affairs are made or marred by viewless spirits of the air— by giants, gnomes, and genii—and who still believe, to this day, all the wild tales in the Arabian Nights. Even so an intelligent missionary tells me.

We visited the Thousand and One Columns. I do not know what it was originally intended for, but they said it was built for a reservoir. It is situated in the center of Constantinople. You go down a flight of stone steps in the middle of a barren place, and there you are. You are forty feet underground, and in the midst of a perfect wilderness of tall, slender, granite columns, of Byzantine architecture. Stand where you would, or change your position as often as you pleased, you were always a center from which radiated a dozen long archways and colonnades that lost themselves in distance and the somber twilight of the place. This old dried-up reservoir is occupied by a few ghostly silk-spinners now, and one of them showed me a cross cut high up in one of the pillars. I suppose he meant me to understand that the institution was there before the Turkish occupation, and I thought he made a remark to that effect; but he must have had an impediment in his speech, for I did not understand him.

# THE INNOCENTS ABROAD

We took off our shoes and went into the marble mausoleum of the Sultan Mahmoud, the neatest piece of architecture, inside, that I have seen lately. Mahmoud's tomb was covered with a black velvet pall, which was elaborately embroidered with silver; it stood within a fancy silver railing; at the side and corners were silver candlesticks that would weigh more than a hundred pounds, and they supported candles as large as a man's leg; on the top of the sarcophagus was a fez, with a handsome diamond ornament upon it, which an attendant said cost a hundred thousand pounds, and lied like a Turk when he said it. Mahmoud's whole family were comfortably planted around him.

We went to the Great Bazar in Stamboul, of course, and I shall not describe it further than to say it is a monstrous hive of little shops—thousands, I should say—all under one roof, and cut up into innumerable little blocks by narrow streets which are arched overhead. One street is devoted to a particular kind of merchandise, another to another, and so on. When you wish to buy a pair of shoes you have the swing of the whole street— you do not have to walk yourself down hunting stores in different localities. It is the same with silks, antiquities, shawls, etc. The place is crowded with people all the time, and as the gay-colored Eastern fabrics are lavishly displayed before every shop, the Great Bazar of Stamboul is one of the sights that are worth seeing. It is full of life, and stir, and business, dirt, beggars, asses, yelling ped- . dlers, porters, dervishes, high-born Turkish female shoppers, Greeks, and weird-looking and weirdly dressed Mohammedans from the mountains and the far provinces—and the only solitary thing one does not smell when he is in the Great Bazar, is something which smells good.

# CHAPTER VII

MOSQUES are plenty, churches are plenty, graveyards are plenty, but morals and whisky are scarce. The Koran does not permit Mohammedans to drink. Their natural instincts do not permit them to be moral. They say the Sultan has eight hundred wives. This almost amounts to bigamy. It makes our cheeks burn with shame to see such a thing permitted here in Turkey. We do not mind it so much in Salt Lake, however.

Circassian and Georgian girls are still sold in Constantinople by their parents, but not publicly. The great slave-marts we have all read so much about—where tender young girls were stripped for inspection, and criticized and discussed just as if they were horses at an agricultural fair—no longer exist. The exhibition and the sales are private now. Stocks are up, just at present, partly because of a brisk demand created by the recent return of the Sultan's suite from the courts of Europe; partly on account of an unusual abundance of breadstuffs, which leaves holders untortured by hunger and enables them to hold back for high prices; and partly because buyers are too weak to bear the market, while sellers are amply prepared to bull it. Under these circumstances, if the American metropolitan news-

77

papers were published here in Constantinople, their next commercial report would read about as follows, I suppose:

SLAVE-GIRL MARKET REPORT

Best brands Circassians, crop of 1850, £200; 1852, £250; 1854, £300. Best brands Georgian, none in market; second quality, 1851, £180. Nineteen fair to middling Wallachian girls offered at £130 @ 150, but no takers; sixteen prime A1 sold in small lots to close out—terms private.

Sales of one lot Circassians, prime to good, 1852 to 1854, at £240 @ 242½, buyer 30; one forty-niner—damaged—at £23, seller ten, no deposit. Several Georgians, fancy brands, 1852, changed hands to fill orders. The Georgians now on hand are mostly last year's crop, which was unusually poor. The new crop is a little backward, but will be coming in shortly. As regards its quantity and quality, the accounts are most encouraging. In this connection we can safely say, also, that the new crop of Circassians is looking extremely well. His Majesty the Sultan has already sent in large orders for his new harem, which will be finished within a fortnight, and this has naturally strengthened the market and given Circassian stock a strong upward tendency. Taking advantage of the inflated market, many of our shrewdest operators are selling short. There are hints of a "corner" on Wallachians.

There is nothing new in Nubians. Slow sale.

Eunuchs—none offering; however, large cargoes are expected from Egypt to-day.

I think the above would be about the style of the commercial report. Prices are pretty high now, and holders firm; but, two or three years ago, parents in a starving condition brought their young daughters down here and sold them for even twenty and thirty dollars, when they could do no better, simply to save themselves and the girls from dying of want. It is sad to think of so distressing a thing as this, and I for one am sincerely glad the prices are up again.

Commercial morals, especially, are bad. There is no gainsaying that. Greek, Turkish, and Armenian morals consist only in attending church regu‑ larly on the appointed Sabbaths, and in breaking the ten commandments all the balance of the week. It comes natural to them to lie and cheat in the first place, and then they go on and improve on nature until they arrive at perfection. In recommending his son to a merchant as a valuable salesman, a father does not say he is a nice, moral, upright boy, and goes to Sunday-school and is honest, but he says, "This boy is worth his weight in broad pieces of a hundred—for behold, he will cheat whomsoever hath dealings with him, and from the Euxine to the waters of Marmora there abideth not so gifted a liar!" How is that for a recommendation? The missionaries tell me that they hear encomiums like that passed upon people every day. They say of a person they admire, "Ah, he is a charming swindler, and a most exquisite liar!"

Everybody lies and cheats—everybody who is in business, at any rate. Even foreigners soon have to come down to the custom of the country, and they do not buy and sell long in Constantinople till they lie and cheat like a Greek. I say like a Greek, because the Greeks are called the worst transgressors in this line. Several Americans, long resident in Constantinople, contend that most Turks are pretty trustworthy, but few claim that the Greeks have any virtues that a man can discover—at least without a fire assay.

I am half willing to believe that the celebrated

dogs of Constantinople have been misrepresented—slandered. I have always been led to suppose that they were so thick in the streets that they blocked the way; that they moved about in organized companies, platoons, and regiments, and took what they wanted by determined and ferocious assault; and that at night they drowned all other sounds with their terrible howlings. The dogs I see here cannot be those I have read of.

I find them everywhere, but not in strong force. The most I have found together has been about ten or twenty. And night or day a fair proportion of them were sound asleep. Those that were not asleep always looked as if they wanted to be. I never saw such utterly wretched, starving, sad-visaged, broken-hearted looking curs in my life. It seemed a grim satire to accuse such brutes as these of taking things by force of arms. They hardly seemed to have strength enough or ambition enough to walk across the street—I do not know that I have seen one walk that far yet. They are mangy and bruised and mutilated, and often you see one with the hair singed off him in such wide and well-defined tracts that he looks like a map of the new Territories. They are the sorriest beasts that breathe—the most abject—the most pitiful. In their faces is a settled expression of melancholy, an air of hopeless despondency. The hairless patches on a scalded dog are preferred by the fleas of Constantinople to a wider range on a healthier dog; and the exposed places suit the fleas exactly. I saw a dog of this kind start to nibble at a flea—a fly attracted his attention, and he made a snatch at him; the flea called for him once more, and that forever unsettled him; he looked sadly at his flea-pasture, then sadly looked at his bald spot. Then he heaved a sigh and dropped his head resignedly upon his paws. He was not equal to the situation.

The dogs sleep in the streets, all over the city. From one end of the street to the other, I suppose they will average about eight or ten to a block. Sometimes, of course, there are fifteen or twenty to a block. They do not belong to anybody, and they seem to have no close personal friendships among each other. But they district the city themselves, and the dogs of each district, whether it be half a block in extent, or ten blocks, have to remain within its bounds. Woe to a dog if he crosses the line! His neighbors would snatch the balance of his hair off in a second. So it is said. But they don't look it.

They sleep in the streets these days. They are my compass—my guide. When I see the dogs sleep placidly on, while men, sheep, geese, and all moving things turn out and go around them, I know I am not in the great street where the hotel is, and must go further. In the Grand Rue the dogs have a sort of air of being on the lookout—an air born of being obliged to get out of the way of many carriages every day—and that expression one recognizes in a moment. It does not exist upon the face of any dog without the confines of that street. All others sleep placidly and keep no watch. They would not move, though the Sultan himself passed by.

In one narrow street (but none of them are wide) I saw three dogs lying coiled up, about a foot or two apart. End to end they lay, and so they just bridged the street neatly, from gutter to gutter. A drove of a hundred sheep came along. They stepped right over the dogs, the rear crowding the front, impatient to get on. The dogs looked lazily up, flinched a little when the impatient feet of the sheep touched their raw backs—sighed, and lay peacefully down again. No talk could be plainer than that. So some of the sheep jumped over them and others scrambled between, occasionally chipping a leg with their sharp hoofs, and when the whole flock had made the trip, the dogs sneezed a little, in the cloud of dust, but never budged their bodies an inch. I thought I was lazy, but I am a steam-engine compared to a Constantinople dog. But was not that a singular scene for a city of a million inhabitants?

These dogs are the scavengers of the city. That is their official position, and a hard one it is. However, it is their protection. But for their usefulness in partially cleansing these terrible streets, they would not be tolerated long. They eat anything and everything that comes in their way, from melon rinds and spoiled grapes up through all the grades and species of dirt and refuse to their own dead friends and relatives—and yet they are always lean, always hungry, always despondent. The people are loth to kill them—do not kill them, in fact. The Turks have an innate antipathy to taking the life of any dumb animal, it is said. But they do worse. They hang and kick and stone and scald these wretched creatures to the very verge of death, and then leave them to live and suffer.

Once a Sultan proposed to kill off all the dogs here, and did begin the work—but the populace raised such a howl of horror about it that the massacre was stayed. After a while, he proposed to remove them all to an island in the Sea of Marmora. No objection was offered, and a ship-load or so was taken away. But when it came to be known that somehow or other the dogs never got to the island, but always fell overboard in the night and perished, another howl was raised and the transportation scheme was dropped.

So the dogs remain in peaceable possession of the streets. I do not say that they do not howl at night, nor that they do not attack people who have not a red fez on their heads. I only say that it would be mean for *me* to accuse them of these unseemly things who have not seen them do them with my own eyes or heard them with my own ears.

I was a little surprised to see Turks and Greeks playing newsboy right here in the mysterious land where the giants and genii of the Arabian Nights once dwelt—where winged horses and hydra-headed dragons guarded enchanted castles—where Princes and Princesses flew through the air on carpets that obeyed a mystic talisman—where cities whose houses were made of precious stones sprang up in a night under the hand of the magician, and where busy marts were suddenly stricken with a spell and each citizen lay or sat, or stood with weapon raised or foot advanced, just as he was, speechless and motionless, till time had told a hundred years!

It was curious to see newsboys selling papers in so dreamy a land as that. And, to say truly, it is comparatively a new thing here. The selling of newspapers had its birth in Constantinople about a year ago, and was a child of the Prussian and Austrian war.

There is one paper published here in the English language—the *Levant Herald*—and there are generally a number of Greek and a few French papers rising and falling, struggling up and falling again. Newspapers are not popular with the Sultan's Government. They do not understand journalism. The proverb says, "The unknown is always great." To the court, the newspaper is a mysterious and rascally institution. They know what a pestilence is, because they have one occasionally that thins the people out at the rate of two thousand a day, and they regard a newspaper as a mild form of pestilence. When it goes astray, they suppress it—pounce upon it without warning, and throttle it. When it don't go astray for a long time, they get suspicious and throttle it anyhow, because they think it is hatching deviltry. Imagine the Grand Vizier in solemn council with the magnates of the realm, spelling his way through the hated newspaper, and finally delivering his profound decision: "This thing means mischief —it is too darkly, too suspiciously inoffensive— suppress it! Warn the publisher that we cannot have this sort of thing: put the editor in prison!"

The newspaper business has its inconveniences in

# THE INNOCENTS ABROAD

Constantinople. Two Greek papers and one French one were suppressed here within a few days of each other. No victories of the Cretans are allowed to be printed. From time to time the Grand Vizier sends a notice to the various editors that the Cretan insurrection is entirely suppressed, and although that editor knows better, he still has to print the notice. The *Levant Herald* is too fond of speaking praisefully of Americans to be popular with the Sultan, who does not relish our sympathy with the Cretans, and therefore that paper has to be particularly circumspect in order to keep out of trouble. Once the editor, forgetting the official notice in his paper that the Cretans were crushed out, printed a letter of a very different tenor, from the American Consul in Crete, and was fined two hundred and fifty dollars for it. Shortly he printed another from the same source and was imprisoned three months for his pains. I think I could get the assistant editorship of the *Levant Herald*, but I am going to try to worry along without it.

To suppress a paper here involves the ruin of the publisher, almost. But in Naples I think they speculate on misfortunes of that kind. Papers are suppressed there every day, and spring up the next day under a new name. During the ten days or a fortnight we stayed there one paper was murdered and resurrected twice. The newsboys are smart there, just as they are elsewhere. They take advantage of popular weaknesses. When they find they are not likely to sell out, they approach a citizen mysteriously, and say in a low voice—"Last copy,

85

sir: double price; paper just been suppressed!"
The man buys it, of course, and finds nothing in it.
They do say—I do not vouch for it—but they do
say that men sometimes print a vast edition of a
paper, with a ferociously seditious article in it, distribute it quickly among the newsboys, and clear out
till the Government's indignation cools. It pays
well. Confiscation don't amount to anything. The
type and presses are not worth taking care of.

There is only one English newspaper in Naples.
It has seventy subscribers. The publisher is getting
rich very deliberately—very deliberately indeed.

I shall never want another Turkish lunch. The
cooking apparatus was in a little lunch-room, near
the bazar, and it was all open to the street. The
cook was slovenly, and so was the table, and it had
no cloth on it. The fellow took a mass of sausage-
meat and coated it round a wire and laid it on a
charcoal fire to cook. When it was done, he laid it
aside and a dog walked sadly in and nipped it. He
smelt it first, and probably recognized the remains of
a friend. The cook took it away from him and
laid it before us. Jack said, "I pass"—he plays
euchre sometimes—and we all passed in turn. Then
the cook baked a broad, flat, wheaten cake, greased
it well with the sausage, and started toward us with
it. It dropped in the dirt, and he picked it up and
polished it on his breeches, and laid it before us.
Jack said, "I pass." We all passed. He put some
eggs in a frying-pan, and stood pensively prying
slabs of meat from between his teeth with a fork.
Then he used the fork to turn the eggs with—and

brought them along. Jack said "Pass again." All
followed suit. We did not know what to do, and so
we ordered a new ration of sausage. The cook got
out his wire, apportioned a proper amount of
sausage-meat, spat on his hands, and fell to work!
This time, with one accord, we all passed out. We
paid and left. That is all I learned about Turkish
lunches. A Turkish lunch is good, no doubt, but
it has its little drawbacks.

When I think how I have been swindled by books
of Oriental travel, I want a tourist for breakfast. For
years and years I have dreamed of the wonders of
the Turkish bath; for years and years I have promised myself that I would yet enjoy one. Many and
many a time, in fancy, I have lain in the marble
bath, and breathed the slumbrous fragrance of Eastern spices that filled the air; then passed through a
weird and complicated system of pulling and hauling
and drenching and scrubbing, by a gang of naked
savages who loomed vast and vaguely through the
steaming mists, like demons; then rested for a
while on a divan fit for a king; then passed through
another complex ordeal, and one more fearful than
the first; and, finally, swathed in soft fabrics, been
conveyed to a princely saloon and laid on a bed of
eiderdown, where eunuchs, gorgeous of costume,
fanned me while I drowsed and dreamed, or content-
edly gazed at the rich hangings of the apartment, the
soft carpets, the sumptuous furniture, the pictures,
and drank delicious coffee, smoked the soothing
narghili, and dropped, at the last, into tranquil
repose, lulled by sensuous odors from unseen censers,

by the gentle influence of the narghili's Persian tobacco, and by the music of fountains that counterfeited the pattering of summer rain.

That was the picture, just as I got it from incendiary books of travel. It was a poor, miserable imposture. The reality is no more like it than the Five Points are like the Garden of Eden. They received me in a great court, paved with marble slabs; around it were broad galleries, one above another, carpeted with seedy matting, railed with unpainted balustrades, and furnished with huge rickety chairs, cushioned with rusty old mattresses, indented with impressions left by the forms of nine successive generations of men who had reposed upon them. The place was vast, naked, dreary; its court a barn, its galleries stalls for human horses. The cadaverous, half-nude varlets that served in the establishment had nothing of poetry in their appearance, nothing of romance, nothing of Oriental splendor. They shed no entrancing odors—just the contrary. Their hungry eyes and their lank forms continually suggested one glaring, unsentimental fact—they wanted what they term in California "a square meal."

I went into one of the racks and undressed. An unclean starveling wrapped a gaudy table-cloth about his loins, and hung a white rag over my shoulders. If I had had a tub then, it would have come natural to me to take in washing. I was then conducted down-stairs into the wet, slippery court, and the first things that attracted my attention were my heels. My fall excited no comment. They expected it, no doubt. It belonged in the list of softening, sensuous influences peculiar to this home of Eastern luxury. It was softening enough, certainly, but its application was not happy. They now gave me a pair of wooden clogs—benches in miniature, with leather straps over them to confine my feet (which they would have done, only I do not wear No. 13's). These things dangled uncomfortably by the straps when I lifted up my feet, and came down in awkward and unexpected places when I put them on the floor again, and sometimes turned sideways and wrenched my ankles out of joint. However, it was all Oriental luxury, and I did what I could to enjoy it.

They put me in another part of the barn and laid me on a stuffy sort of pallet, which was not made of cloth of gold, or Persian shawls, but was merely the unpretending sort of thing I have seen in the negro quarters of Arkansas. There was nothing whatever in this dim marble prison but five more of these biers. It was a very solemn place. I expected that the spiced odors of Araby were going to steal over my senses, now, but they did not. A copper-colored skeleton, with a rag around him, brought me a glass decanter of water, with a lighted tobacco pipe in the top of it, and a pliant stem a yard long, with a brass mouthpiece to it.

It was the famous "narghili" of the East—the thing the Grand Turk smokes in the pictures. This began to look like luxury. I took one blast at it. and it was sufficient; the smoke went in a great volume down into my stomach, my lungs, even into the uttermost parts of my frame. I exploded one mighty cough, and it was as if Vesuvius had let go.

# MARK TWAIN

For the next five minutes I smoked at every pore, like a frame house that is on fire on the inside. Not any more narghili for me. The smoke had a vile taste, and the taste of a thousand infidel tongues that remained on that brass mouthpiece was viler still. I was getting discouraged. Whenever, hereafter, I see the cross-legged Grand Turk smoking his narghili, in pretended bliss, on the outside of a paper of Connecticut tobacco, I shall know him for the shameless humbug he is.

This prison was filled with hot air. When I had got warmed up sufficiently to prepare me for a still warmer temperature, they took me where it was—into a marble room, wet, slippery, and steamy, and laid me out on a raised platform in the center. It was very warm. Presently my man sat me down by a tank of hot water, drenched me well, gloved his hand with a coarse mitten, and began to polish me all over with it. I began to smell disagreeably. The more he polished the worse I smelt. It was alarming. I said to him:

"I perceive that I am pretty far gone. It is plain that I ought to be buried without any unnecessary delay. Perhaps you had better go after my friends at once, because the weather is warm, and I cannot 'keep' long."

He went on scrubbing, and paid no attention. I soon saw that he was reducing my size. He bore hard on his mitten, and from under it rolled little cylinders, like macaroni. It could not be dirt, for it was too white. He pared me down in this way for a long time. Finally I said:

"It is a tedious process. It will take hours to trim me to the size you want me; I will wait; go and borrow a jack-plane."

He paid no attention at all.

After a while he brought a basin, some soap, and something that seemed to be the tail of a horse. He made up a prodigious quantity of soap-suds, deluged me with them from head to foot, without warning me to shut my eyes, and then swabbed me viciously with the horse-tail. Then he left me there, a snowy statue of lather, and went away. When I got tired of waiting I went and hunted him up. He was propped against the wall, in another room, asleep. I woke him. He was not disconcerted. He took me back and flooded me with hot water, then turbaned my head, swathed me with dry table-cloths, and conducted me to a latticed chicken-coop in one of the galleries, and pointed to one of those Arkansas beds. I mounted it, and vaguely expected the odors of Araby again. They did not come.

The blank, unornamented coop had nothing about it of that oriental voluptuousness one reads of so much. It was more suggestive of the county hospital than anything else. The skinny servitor brought a narghili, and I got him to take it out again without wasting any time about it. Then he brought the world-renowned Turkish coffee that poets have sung so rapturously for many generations, and I seized upon it as the last hope that was left of my old dreams of Eastern luxury. It was another fraud. Of all the unchristian beverages that ever passed my lips, Turkish coffee is the worst. The cup is small,

# MARK TWAIN

it is smeared with grounds; the coffee is black, thick, unsavory of smell, and execrable in taste. The bottom of the cup has a muddy sediment in it half an inch deep. This goes down your throat, and portions of it lodge by the way, and produce a tickling aggravation that keeps you barking and coughing for an hour.

Here endeth my experience of the celebrated Turkish bath, and here also endeth my dream of the bliss the mortal revels in who passes through it. It is a malignant swindle. The man who enjoys it is qualified to enjoy anything that is repulsive to sight or sense, and he that can invest it with a charm of poetry is able to do the same with anything else in the world that is tedious, and wretched, and dismal, and nasty.

## CHAPTER VIII

WE left a dozen passengers in Constantinople, and sailed through the beautiful Bosporus and far up into the Black Sea. We left them in the clutches of the celebrated Turkish guide, "FAR-AWAY MOSES," who will seduce them into buying a ship-load of attar of roses, splendid Turkish vestments, and all manner of curious things they can never have any use for. Murray's invaluable guide-books have mentioned Far-away Moses' name, and he is a made man. He rejoices daily in the fact that he is a recognized celebrity. However, we cannot alter our established customs to please the whims of guides; we cannot show partialities this late in the day. Therefore, ignoring this fellow's brilliant fame, and ignoring the fanciful name he takes such pride in, we called him Ferguson, just as we had done with all other guides. It has kept him in a state of smothered exasperation all the time. Yet we meant him no harm. After he has gotten himself up regardless of expense, in showy, baggy trousers, yellow, pointed slippers, fiery fez, silken jacket of blue, voluminous waist - sash of fancy Persian stuff filled with a battery of silver-mounted horse-pistols, and has strapped on his terrible simitar, he considers it an unspeakable humiliation

93

to be called Ferguson. It cannot be helped. All guides are Ferguson to us. We cannot master their dreadful foreign names.

Sebastopol is probably the worst battered town in Russia or anywhere else. But we ought to be pleased with it, nevertheless, for we have been in no country yet where we have been so kindly received, and where we felt that to be Americans was a sufficient *visé* for our passports. The moment the anchor was down, the Governor of the town immediately despatched an officer on board to inquire if he could be of any assistance to us, and to invite us to make ourselves at home in Sebastopol! If you know Russia, you know that this was a wild stretch of hospitality. They are usually so suspicious of strangers that they worry them excessively with the delays and aggravations incident to a complicated passport system. Had we come from any other country we could not have had permission to enter Sebastopol and leave again under three days—but as it was, we were at liberty to go and come when and where we pleased. Everybody in Constantinople warned us to be very careful about our passports, see that they were strictly *en regle*, and never to mislay them for a moment: and they told us of numerous instances of Englishmen and others who were delayed days, weeks, and even months, in Sebastopol, on account of trifling informalities in their passports, and for which they were not to blame. I had lost my passport, and was traveling under my room-mate's, who stayed behind in Constantinople to await our return. To read the description of him in that passport and then look at me, any man could see that I was no more like him than I am like Hercules. So I went into the harbor of Sebastopol with fear and trembling—full of a vague, horrible apprehension that I was going to be found out and hanged. But all that time my true passport had been floating gallantly overhead—and behold it was only our flag. They never asked us for any other.

We have had a great many Russian and English gentlemen and ladies on board to-day, and the time has passed cheerfully away. They were all happy-spirited people, and I never heard our mother-tongue sound so pleasantly as it did when it fell from those English lips in this far-off land. I talked to the Russians a good deal, just to be friendly, and they talked to me from the same motive; I am sure that both enjoyed the conversation, but never a word of it either of us understood. I did most of my talking to those English people though, and I am sorry we cannot carry some of them along with us.

We have gone whithersoever we chose, to-day, and have met with nothing but the kindest attentions. Nobody inquired whether we had any passports or not.

Several of the officers of the government have suggested that we take the ship to a little watering-place thirty miles from here, and pay the Emperor of Russia a visit. He is rusticating there. These officers said they would take it upon themselves to insure us a cordial reception. They said if we would go, they would not only telegraph the Emperor, but send a special courier overland to announce our coming. Our time is so short, though, and more especially our coal is so nearly out, that we judged it best to forego the rare pleasure of holding social intercourse with an Emperor.

Ruined Pompeii is in good condition compared to Sebastopol. Here, you may look in whatsoever direction you please, and your eye encounters scarcely anything but ruin, ruin, ruin!—fragments of houses, crumbled walls, torn and ragged hills, devastation everywhere! It is as if a mighty earthquake had spent all its terrible forces upon this one little spot. For eighteen long months the storms of war beat upon the helpless town, and left it at last the saddest wreck that ever the sun has looked upon. Not one solitary house escaped unscathed— not one remained habitable, even. Such utter and complete ruin one could hardly conceive of. The houses had all been solid, dressed-stone structures; most of them were plowed through and through by cannon-balls—unroofed and sliced down from eaves to foundation—and now a row of them, half a mile long, looks merely like an endless procession of battered chimneys. No semblance of a house remains in such as these. Some of the larger buildings had corners knocked off; pillars cut in two; cornices smashed; holes driven straight through the walls. Many of these holes are as round and as cleanly cut as if they had been made with an auger. Others are half pierced through, and the clean impression is there in the rock, as smooth and as shapely as if it were done in putty. Here and there a ball still sticks in a wall, and from it iron tears trickle down and discolor the stone.

# THE INNOCENTS ABROAD

The battle-fields were pretty close together. The Malakoff tower is on a hill which is right in the edge of the town. The Redan was within rifle-shot of the Malakoff; Inkerman was a mile away; and Balaklava removed but an hour's ride. The French trenches, by which they approached and invested the Malakoff, were carried so close under its sloping sides that one might have stood by the Russian guns and tossed a stone into them. Repeatedly, during three terrible days, they swarmed up the little Malakoff hill, and were beaten back with terrible slaughter. Finally, they captured the place, and drove the Russians out, who then tried to retreat into the town, but the English had taken the Redan, and shut them off with a wall of flame; there was nothing for them to do but go back and retake the Malakoff or die under its guns. They did go back; they took the Malakoff and retook it two or three times, but their desperate valor could not avail, and they had to give up at last.

These fearful fields, where such tempests of death used to rage, are peaceful enough now; no sound is heard, hardly a living thing moves about them, they are lonely and silent—their desolation is complete.

There was nothing else to do, and so everybody went to hunting relics. They have stocked the ship with them. They brought them from the Malakoff, from the Redan, Inkerman, Balaklava—everywhere. They have brought cannon-balls, broken ramrods, fragments of shell—iron enough to freight a sloop. Some have even brought bones—brought them laboriously from great distances, and were grieved to hear the surgeon pronounce them only bones of mules and oxen. I knew Blucher would not lose an opportunity like this. He brought a sack full on board and was going for another. I prevailed upon him not to go. He has already turned his stateroom into a museum of worthless trumpery, which he has gathered up in his travels. He is labeling his trophies, now. I picked up one a while ago, and found it marked "Fragment of a Russian General." I carried it out to get a better light upon it—it was nothing but a couple of teeth and part of the jawbone of a horse. I said with some asperity:

"Fragment of a Russian General! This is absurd. Are you never going to learn any sense?"

He only said: "Go slow—the old woman won't know any different." [His aunt.]

This person gathers mementoes with a perfect recklessness, nowadays; mixes them all up together, and then serenely labels them without any regard to truth, propriety, or even plausibility. I have found him breaking a stone in two, and labeling half of it "Chunk busted from the pulpit of Demosthenes," and the other half "Dornick from the Tomb of Abelard and Heloise." I have known him to gather up a handful of pebbles by the roadside, and bring them on board ship and label them as coming from twenty celebrated localities five hundred miles apart. I remonstrate against these outrages upon reason and truth, of course, but it does no good. I get the same tranquil, unanswerable reply every time:

"It don't signify—the old woman won't know any different."

## THE INNOCENTS ABROAD

Ever since we three or four fortunate ones made the midnight trip to Athens, it has afforded him genuine satisfaction to give everybody in the ship a pebble from the Mars Hill where St. Paul preached. He got all those pebbles on the seashore, abreast the ship, but professes to have gathered them from one of our party. However, it is not of any use for me to expose the deception—it affords him pleasure, and does no harm to anybody. He says he never expects to run out of mementoes of St. Paul as long as he is in reach of a sand-bank. Well, he is no worse than others. I notice that all travelers supply deficiencies in their collections in the same way. I shall never have any confidence in such things again while I live.

# CHAPTER IX

WE have got so far East now—a hundred and fifty-five degrees of longitude from San Francisco—that my watch cannot "keep the hang" of the time any more. It has grown discouraged, and stopped. I think it did a wise thing. The difference in time between Sebastopol and the Pacific coast is enormous. When it is six o'clock in the morning here, it is somewhere about week before last in California. We are excusable for getting a little tangled as to time. These distractions and distresses about the time have worried me so much that I was afraid my mind was so much affected that I never would have any appreciation of time again; but when I noticed how handy I was yet about comprehending when it was dinner-time, a blessed tranquillity settled down upon me, and I am tortured with doubts and fears no more.

Odessa is about twenty hours' run from Sebastopol, and is the most northerly port in the Black Sea. We came here to get coal, principally. The city has a population of one hundred and thirty-three thousand, and is growing faster than any other small city out of America. It is a free port, and is the great grain mart of this particular part of the world. Its roadstead is full of ships. Engineers are at work, now, turning the open roadstead into a spacious artificial harbor. It is to be almost inclosed by massive stone piers, one of which will extend into the sea over three thousand feet in a straight line.

I have not felt so much at home for a long time as I did when I "raised the hill" and stood in Odessa for the first time. It looked just like an American city; fine, broad streets, and straight as well; low houses (two or three stories), wide, neat, and free from any quaintness of architectural ornamentation; locust trees bordering the sidewalks (they call them acacias); a stirring, business look about the streets and the stores; fast walkers; a familiar *new* look about the houses and everything; yea, and a driving and smothering cloud of dust that was so like a message from our own dear native land that we could hardly refrain from shedding a few grateful tears and execrations in the old time-honored American way. Look up the street or down the street, this way or that way, we saw only America! There was not one thing to remind us that we were in Russia. We walked for some little distance, reveling in this home vision, and then we came upon a church and a hack-driver, and presto! the illusion vanished! The church had a slender-spired dome that rounded inward at its base, and looked like a turnip turned upside down, and the hackman seemed to be dressed in a long petticoat without any hoops. These things were essentially foreign, and so were the carriages—but everybody knows about these things, and there is no occasion for my describing them.

# MARK TWAIN

We were only to stay here a day and a night and take in coal; we consulted the guide-books and were rejoiced to know that there were no sights in Odessa to see; and so we had one good, untrammeled holiday on our hands, with nothing to do but idle about the city and enjoy ourselves. We sauntered through the markets and criticized the fearful and wonderful costumes from the back country; examined the populace as far as eyes could do it; and closed the entertainment with an ice-cream debauch. We do not get ice-cream everywhere, and so, when we do, we are apt to dissipate to excess. We never cared anything about ice-cream at home, but we look upon it with a sort of idolatry now that it is so scarce in these red-hot climates of the East.

We only found two pieces of statuary, and this was another blessing. One was a bronze image of the Duc de Richelieu, grandnephew of the splendid Cardinal. It stood in a spacious, handsome promenade, overlooking the sea, and from its base a vast flight of stone steps led down to the harbor—two hundred of them, fifty feet long, and a wide landing at the bottom of every twenty. It is a noble staircase, and from a distance the people toiling up it looked like insects. I mention this statue and this stairway because they have their story. Richelieu founded Odessa—watched over it with paternal care—labored with a fertile brain and a wise understanding for its best interests—spent his fortune freely to the same end—endowed it with a sound prosperity, and one which will yet make it one of the great cities of the Old World—built this noble

stairway with money from his own private purse—
and— Well, the people for whom he had done
so much let him walk down these same steps, one
day, unattended, old, poor, without a second coat
to his back; and when, years afterward, he died in
Sebastopol in poverty and neglect, they called a
meeting, subscribed liberally, and immediately
erected this tasteful monument to his memory, and
named a great street after him. It reminds me of
what Robert Burns's mother said when they erected
a stately monument to his memory: "Ah, Robbie,
ye asked them for bread and they hae gi'en ye a
stane."

The people of Odessa have warmly recommended
us to go and call on the Emperor, as did the Sebas-
topolians. They have telegraphed his Majesty, and
he has signified his willingness to grant us an audience. So we are getting up the anchors and preparing to sail to his watering-place. What a scratch-
ing around there will be now! what a holding of
important meetings and appointing of solemn com-
mittees!—and what a furbishing up of claw-hammer
coats and white silk neckties! As this fearful ordeal
we are about to pass through pictures itself to my
fancy in all its dread sublimity, I begin to feel my
fierce desire to converse with a genuine Emperor
cooling down and passing away. What am I to do
with my hands? What am I to do with my feet?
What in the world am I to do with myself?

# CHAPTER X

WE anchored here at Yalta, Russia, two or three days ago. To me the place was a vision of the Sierras. The tall, gray mountains that back it, their sides bristling with pines—cloven with ravines—here and there a hoary rock towering into view—long, straight streaks sweeping down from the summit to the sea, marking the passage of some avalanche of former times—all these were as like what one sees in the Sierras as if the one were a portrait of the other. The little village of Yalta nestles at the foot of an amphitheater which slopes backward and upward to the wall of hills, and looks as if it might have sunk quietly down to its present position from a higher elevation. This depression is covered with the great parks and gardens of noblemen, and through the mass of green foliage the bright colors of their palaces bud out here and there like flowers. It is a beautiful spot.

We had the United States consul on board—the Odessa consul. We assembled in the cabin and commanded him to tell us what we must do to be saved, and tell us quickly. He made a speech. The first thing he said fell like a blight on every hopeful spirit; he had never seen a court reception. (Three groans for the consul.) But he said he had seen receptions at the Governor-General's in Odessa, and had often listened to people's experiences of receptions at the Russian and other courts, and believed he knew very well what sort of ordeal we were about to essay. (Hope budded again.) He said we were many; the summer-place was small—a mere mansion; doubtless we should be received in summer fashion—in the garden; we would stand in a row, all the gentlemen in swallow-tail coats, white kids, and white neckties, and the ladies in light-colored silks, or something of that kind; at the proper moment—12 meridian—the Emperor, attended by his suite arrayed in splendid uniforms, would appear and walk slowly along the line, bowing to some, and saying two or three words to others. At the moment his Majesty appeared, a universal, delighted, enthusiastic smile ought to break out like a rash among the passengers—a smile of love, of gratification, of admiration—and with one accord, the party must begin to bow—not obsequiously, but respectfully, and with dignity; at the end of fifteen minutes the Emperor would go in the house, and we could run along home again. We felt immensely relieved. It seemed, in a manner, easy. There was not a man in the party but believed that with a little practice he could stand in a row, especially if there were others along; there was not a man but believed he could bow without tripping on his coat-tail and breaking his neck; in a word, we came to believe we were equal to any item in the performance except that complicated smile. The consul also said we ought to draft a little address to the

Emperor, and present it to one of his aides-de-camp,
who would forward it to him at the proper time.
Therefore, five gentlemen were appointed to prepare
the document, and the fifty others went sadly smiling about the ship—practising. During the next
twelve hours we had the general appearance, somehow, of being at a funeral, where everybody was
sorry the death had occurred, but glad it was over—
where everybody was smiling, and yet broken-
hearted.

A committee went ashore to wait on his Excel-
lency, the Governor-General, and learn our fate.
At the end of three hours of boding suspense, they
came back and said the Emperor would receive us
at noon the next day—would send carriages for
us—would hear the address in person. The Grand
Duke Michael had sent to invite us to his palace
also. Any man could see that there was an intention here to show that Russia's friendship for
America was so genuine as to render even her
private citizens objects worthy of kindly attentions.

At the appointed hour we drove out three miles
and assembled in the handsome garden in front of
the Emperor's palace.

We formed a circle under the trees before the
door, for there was no one room in the house able to
accommodate our threescore persons comfortably,
and in a few minutes the imperial family came out
bowing and smiling, and stood in our midst. A
number of great dignitaries of the empire, in un-
dress uniforms, came with them. With every bow,
his Majesty said a word of welcome. I copy these

speeches. There is character in them—Russian character—which is politeness itself, and the genuine article. The French are polite, but it is often mere ceremonious politeness. A Russian imbues his polite things with a heartiness, both of phrase and expression, that compels belief in their sincerity. As I was saying, the Czar punctuated his speeches with bows:

"Good morning—I am glad to see you—I am gratified—I am delighted—I am happy to receive you!"

All took off their hats, and the consul inflicted the address on him. He bore it with unflinching fortitude; then took the rusty-looking document and handed it to some great officer or other, to be filed away among the archives of Russia—in the stove. He thanked us for the address, and said he was very much pleased to see us, especially as such friendly relations existed between Russia and the United States. The Empress said the Americans were favorites in Russia, and she hoped the Russians were similarly regarded in America. These were all the speeches that were made, and I recommend them to parties who present policemen with gold watches, as models of brevity and point. After this the Empress went and talked sociably (for an Empress) with various ladies around the circle; several gentlemen entered into a disjointed general conversation with the Emperor; the Dukes and Princes, Admirals and Maids of Honor dropped into free-and-easy chat with first one and then another of our party, and whoever chose stepped forward and spoke with the modest little Grand Duchess Marie, the Czar's daughter. She is fourteen years old, light-haired, blue-eyed, unassuming, and pretty. Everybody talks English.

The Emperor wore a cap, frock-coat, and pantaloons, all of some kind of plain white drilling—cotton or linen—and sported no jewelry or any insignia whatever of rank. No costume could be less ostentatious. He is very tall and spare, and a determined-looking man, though a very pleasant-looking one, nevertheless. It is easy to see that he is kind and affectionate. There is something very noble in his expression when his cap is off. There is none of that cunning in his eye that all of us noticed in Louis Napoleon's.

The Empress and the little Grand Duchess wore simple suits of foulard (or foulard silk, I don't know which is proper), with a small blue spot in it; the dresses were trimmed with blue; both ladies wore broad blue sashes about their waists; linen collars and clerical ties of muslin; low-crowned straw hats trimmed with blue velvet; parasols and flesh-colored gloves. The Grand Duchess had no heels on her shoes. I do not know this of my own knowledge, but one of our ladies told me so. I was not looking at her shoes. I was glad to observe that she wore her own hair, plaited in thick braids against the back of her head, instead of the uncomely thing they call a waterfall, which is about as much like a waterfall as a canvas-covered ham is like a cataract. Taking the kind expression that is in the Emperor's face and the gentleness that is in his young daughter's into consideration, I wondered if it would not tax the Czar's firmness to the utmost to condemn a supplicating wretch to misery in the wastes of Siberia if she pleaded for him. Every time their eyes met, I saw more and more what a tremendous power that weak, diffident school-girl could wield if she chose to do it. Many and many a time she might rule the Autocrat of Russia, whose lightest word is law to seventy millions of human beings! She was only a girl, and she looked like a thousand others I have seen, but never a girl provoked such a novel and peculiar interest in me before. A strange, new sensation is a rare thing in this humdrum life, and I had it here. There was nothing stale or worn out about the thoughts and feelings the situation and the circumstances created. It seemed strange—stranger than I can tell—to think that the central figure in the cluster of men and women, chatting here under the trees like the most ordinary individual in the land, was a man who could open his lips and ships would fly through the waves, locomotives would speed over the plains, couriers would hurry from village to village, a hundred telegraphs would flash the word to the four corners of an empire that stretches its vast proportions over a seventh part of the habitable globe, and a countless multitude of men would spring to do his bidding. I had a sort of vague desire to examine his hands and see if they were of flesh and blood, like other men's. Here was a man who could do this wonderful thing, and yet if I chose I could knock him down. The case was plain, but it seemed preposterous, nevertheless

—as preposterous as trying to knock down a mountain or wipe out a continent. If this man sprained his ankle, a million miles of telegraph would carry the news over mountains—valleys—uninhabited deserts—under the trackless sea—and ten thousand newspapers would prate of it; if he were grievously ill, all the nations would know it before the sun rose again; if he dropped lifeless where he stood, his fall might shake the thrones of half a world! If I could have stolen his coat, I would have done it. When I meet a man like that, I want something to remember him by.

As a general thing, we have been shown through palaces by some plush-legged, filigreed flunky or other, who charged a franc for it; but after talking with the company half an hour, the Emperor of Russia and his family conducted us all through their mansion themselves. They made no charge. They seemed to take a real pleasure in it.

We spent half an hour idling through the palace, admiring the cozy apartments and the rich but eminently homelike appointments of the place, and then the imperial family bade our party a kind good-by, and proceeded to count the spoons.

An invitation was extended to us to visit the palace of the eldest son, the Crown Prince of Russia, which was near at hand. The young man was absent, but the Dukes and Countesses and Princes went over the premises with us as leisurely as was the case at the Emperor's, and conversation continued as lively as ever.

It was a little after one o'clock now. We drove

to the Grand Duke Michael's, a mile away, in response to his invitation, previously given.

We arrived in twenty minutes from the Emperor's. It is a lovely place. The beautiful palace nestles among the grand old groves of the park, the park sits in the lap of the picturesque crags and hills, and both look out upon the breezy ocean. In the park are rustic seats, here and there, in secluded nooks that are dark with shade; there are rivulets of crystal water; there are lakelets, with inviting, grassy banks; there are glimpses of sparkling cascades through openings in the wilderness of foliage; there are streams of clear water gushing from mimic knots on the trunks of forest trees; there are miniature marble temples perched upon gray old crags; there are airy lookouts whence one may gaze upon a broad expanse of landscape and ocean. The palace is modeled after the choicest forms of Grecian architecture, and its wide colonnades surround a central court that is banked with rare flowers that fill the place with their fragrance, and in their midst springs a fountain that cools the summer air, and may possibly breed mosquitoes, but I do not think it does.

The Grand Duke and his Duchess came out, and the presentation ceremonies were as simple as they had been at the Emperor's. In a few minutes, conversation was under way, as before. The Empress appeared in the veranda, and the little Grand Duchess came out into the crowd. They had beaten us there. In a few minutes, the Emperor came himself on horseback. It was very pleasant. You can appreciate it if you have ever visited royalty and felt occasionally that possibly you might be wearing out your welcome—though as a general thing, I believe, royalty is not scrupulous about discharging you when it is done with you.

The Grand Duke is the third brother of the Emperor, is about thirty-seven years old, perhaps, and is the princeliest figure in Russia. He is even taller than the Czar, as straight as an Indian, and bears himself like one of those gorgeous knights we read about in romances ot the Crusades. He looks like a great-hearted fellow who would pitch an enemy into the river in a moment, and then jump in and risk his life fishing him out again. The stories they tell of him show him to be of a brave and generous nature. He must have been desirous of proving that Americans were welcome guests in the imperial palaces of Russia, because he rode all the way to Yalta and escorted our procession to the Emperor's himself, and kept his aides scurrying about, clearing the road and offering assistance wherever it could be needed. We were rather familiar with him then, because we did not know who he was. We recognized him now, and appreciated the friendly spirit that prompted him to do us a favor that any other Grand Duke in the world would have doubtless declined to do. He had plenty of servitors whom he could have sent, but he chose to attend to the matter himself.

The Grand Duke was dressed in the handsome and showy uniform of a Cossack officer. The Grand Duchess had on a white alpaca robe, with the seams and gores trimmed with black barb lace, and a little gray hat with a feather of the same color. She is young, rather pretty, modest and unpretending, and full of winning politeness.

Our party walked all through the house, and then the nobility escorted them all over the grounds, and finally brought them back to the palace about half past two o'clock to breakfast. They called it breakfast, but we would have called it luncheon. It consisted of two kinds of wine; tea, bread, cheese, and cold meats, and was served on the center-tables in the reception-room and the verandas—anywhere that was convenient; there was no ceremony. It was a sort of picnic. I had heard before that we were to breakfast there, but Blucher said he believed Baker's boy had suggested it to his Imperial Highness. I think not—though it would be like him. Baker's boy is the famine-breeder of the ship. He is always hungry. They say he goes about the staterooms when the passengers are out, and eats up all the soap. And they say he eats oakum. They say he will eat anything he can get between meals, but he prefers oakum. He does not like oakum for dinner, but he likes it for a lunch, at odd hours, or anything that way. It makes him very disagreeable, because it makes his breath bad, and keeps his teeth all stuck up with tar. Baker's boy may have suggested the breakfast, but I hope he did not. It went off well, anyhow. The illustrious host moved about from place to place, and helped to destroy the provisions and keep the conversation lively, and the Grand Duchess talked with the veranda parties and such as had satisfied their appetites and straggled out from the reception-room.

The Grand Duke's tea was delicious. They give one a lemon to squeeze into it, or iced milk, if he prefers it. The former is best. This tea is brought overland from China. It injures the article to transport it by sea.

When it was time to go, we bade our distinguished hosts good-by, and they retired happy and contented to their apartments to count *their* spoons.

We had spent the best part of half a day in the home of royalty, and had been as cheerful and comfortable all the time as we could have been in the ship. I would as soon have thought of being cheerful in Abraham's bosom as in the palace of an Emperor. I supposed that Emperors were terrible people. I thought they never did anything but wear magnificent crowns and red velvet dressing-gowns with dabs of wool sewed on them in spots, and sit on thrones and scowl at the flunkies and the people in the parquette, and order Dukes and Duchesses off to execution. I find, however, that when one is so fortunate as to get behind the scenes and see them at home and in the privacy of their firesides, they are strangely like common mortals. They are pleasanter to look upon then than they are in their theatrical aspect. It seems to come as natural to them to dress and act like other people as it is *to* put a friend's cedar pencil in your pocket when you are done using it. But I can never have any confidence in the tinsel kings of the theater after this. It will be a great loss. I used to take such a thrilling pleasure in them. But, hereafter, I will turn me sadly away and say:

"This does not answer—this isn't the style of king that *I* am acquainted with."

When they swagger around the stage in jeweled crowns and splendid robes, I shall feel bound to observe that all the Emperors that ever *I* was personally acquainted with wore the commonest sort of clothes, and did not swagger. And when they come on the stage attended by a vast body-guard of supes in helmets and tin breastplates, it will be my duty as well as my pleasure to inform the ignorant that no crowned head of my acquaintance has a soldier anywhere about his house or his person.

Possibly it may be thought that our party tarried too long, or did other improper things, but such was not the case. The company felt that they were occupying an unusually responsible position—they were representing the people of America, not the government—and therefore they were careful to do their best to perform their high mission with credit.

On the other hand, the Imperial families, no doubt, considered that in entertaining us they were more especially entertaining the people of America than they could by showering attentions on a whole platoon of ministers plenipotentiary; and therefore they gave to the event its fullest significance, as an expression of good will and friendly feeling toward the entire country. We took the kindnesses we received as attentions thus directed, of course, and not to ourselves as a party. That we felt a personal pride in being received as the representatives of a nation, we do not deny; that we felt a national pride in the warm cordiality of that reception, cannot be doubted.

Our poet has been rigidly suppressed, from the time we let go the anchor. When it was announced that we were going to visit the Emperor of Russia, the fountains of his great deep were broken up, and he rained ineffable bosh for four-and-twenty hours. Our original anxiety as to what we were going to do with ourselves, was suddenly transformed into anxiety about what we were going to do with our poet. The problem was solved at last. Two alternatives were offered him—he must either swear a dreadful oath that he would not issue a line of his poetry while he was in the Czar's dominions, or else remain under guard on board the ship until we were safe at Constantinople again. He fought the dilemma long, but yielded at last. It was a great deliverance. Perhaps the savage reader would like a specimen of his style. I do not mean this term to be offensive. I only use it because "the gentle reader" has been used so often that any change from it cannot but be refreshing:

> Save us and sanctify us, and finally, then,
> See good provisions we enjoy while we journey
>     to Jerusalem.
> For so man proposes, which it is most true,
> And time will wait for none, nor for us too.

The sea has been unusually rough all day. However, we have had a lively time of it, anyhow. We have had quite a run of visitors. The Governor-General came, and we received him with a salute of nine guns. He brought his family with him. I observed that carpets were spread from the pier-head to his carriage for him to walk on, though I have seen him walk there without any carpet when he was not on business. I thought maybe he had what the accidental insurance people might call an extra-hazardous polish ("policy"—joke, but not above mediocrity) on his boots, and wished to protect them, but I examined and could not see that they were blacked any better than usual. It may have been that he had forgotten his carpet before, but he did not have it with him, anyhow. He was an exceedingly pleasant old gentleman; we all liked him, especially Blucher. When he went away, Blucher invited him to come again and fetch his carpet along.

Prince Dolgorouki and a Grand Admiral or two, whom we had seen yesterday at the reception, came on board also. I was a little distant with these parties, at first, because when I have been visiting Emperors I do not like to be too familiar with people I only know by reputation, and whose moral characters and standing in society I cannot be thoroughly acquainted with. I judged it best to be a little offish, at first. I said to myself, Princes and Counts and Grand Admirals are very well, but they are not Emperors, and one cannot be too particular about whom he associates with.

Baron Wrangel came, also. He used to be a Russian Ambassador at Washington. I told him I had an uncle who fell down a shaft and broke himself in two, as much as a year before that. That was a falsehood, but then I was not going to let any man eclipse me on surprising adventures, merely for the want of a little invention. The Baron is a fine man, and is said to stand high in the Emperor's confidence and esteem.

Baron Ungern-Sternberg, a boisterous, whole-souled old nobleman, came with the rest. He is a man of progress and enterprise—a representative man of the age. He is the Chief Director of the railway system of Russia—a sort of railroad king. In his line he is making things move along in this country. He has traveled extensively in America. He says he has tried convict labor on his railroads, and with perfect success. He says the convicts work well, and are quiet and peaceable. He observed that he employs nearly ten thousand of them now. This appeared to be another call on my resources. I was equal to the emergency. I said we had eighty thousand convicts employed on the railways in America—all of them under sentence of death for murder in the first degree. That closed *him* out. We had General Todleben (the famous defender of Sebastopol, during the siege), and many inferior army and also navy officers, and a number of unofficial Russian ladies and gentlemen. Naturally, a champagne luncheon was in order, and was accomplished without loss of life. Toasts and jokes were discharged freely, but no speeches were made save one thanking the Emperor and the Grand Duke, through the Governor-General, for our hospitable reception, and one by the Governor-General in reply, in which he returned the Emperor's thanks for the speech, etc.

## CHAPTER XI

W E returned to Constantinople, and after a day or two spent in exhausting marches about the city and voyages up the Golden Horn in *caiques*, we steamed away again. We passed through the Sea of Marmora and the Dardanelles, and steered for a new land—a new one to us, at least—Asia. We had as yet only acquired a bowing acquaintance with it, through pleasure excursions to Scutari and the regions round about.

We passed between Lemnos and Mytilene, and saw them as we had seen Elba and the Balearic Isles —mere bulky shapes, with the softening mists of distance upon them—whales in a fog, as it were. Then we held our course southward, and began to "read up" celebrated Smyrna.

At all hours of the day and night the sailors in the forecastle amused themselves and aggravated us by burlesquing our visit to royalty. The opening paragraph of our Address to the Emperor was framed as follows:

"We are a handful of private citizens of America, traveling simply for recreation—and unostentatiously, as becomes our unofficial state—and, therefore, we have no excuse to tender for presenting ourselves before your Majesty, save the desire of offering our grateful acknowledgments to the lord of a realm which, through good and through evil report, has been the steadfast friend of the land we love so well."

The third cook, crowned with a resplendent tin basin and wrapped royally in a table-cloth mottled with grease-spots and coffee-stains, and bearing a scepter that looked strangely like a belaying pin, walked upon a dilapidated carpet and perched himself on the capstan, careless of the flying spray; his tarred and weather-beaten Chamberlains, Dukes, and Lord High Admirals surrounded him, arrayed in all the pomp that spare tarpaulins and remnants of old sails could furnish. Then the visiting "watch below," transformed into graceless ladies and uncouth pilgrims, by rude travesties upon waterfalls, hoop-skirts, white kid gloves, and swallow-tail coats, moved solemnly up the companionway, and bowing low, began a system of complicated and extraordinary smiling which few monarchs could look upon and live. Then the mock consul, a slush-plastered deck-sweep, drew out a soiled fragment of paper and proceeded to read, laboriously:

"To his Imperial Majesty, Alexander II., Emperor of Russia:

"We are a handful of private citizens of America, traveling simply for recreation—and unostentatiously, as becomes our unofficial state—and, therefore, we have no excuse to tender for presenting ourselves before your Majesty—"

*The Emperor*—"Then what the devil did you come for?"

—"Save the desire of offering our grateful acknowledgments to the lord of a realm which—"

*The Emperor*—"Oh, d—n the Address!—read it to the police. Chamberlain, take these people over to my brother, the Grand Duke's, and give them a square meal. Adieu! I am happy—I am gratified—I am delighted—I am bored. Adieu, adieu—vamose the ranch! The First Groom of the Palace will proceed to count the portable articles of value belonging to the premises."

The farce then closed, to be repeated again with every change of the watches, and embellished with new and still more extravagant inventions of pomp and conversation.

At all times of the day and night the phraseology of that tiresome address fell upon our ears. Grimy sailors came down out of the foretop placidly announcing themselves as "a handful of private citizens of America, *traveling simply for recreation* and unostentatiously," etc.; the coal-passers moved to their duties in the profound depths of the ship, explaining the blackness of their faces and their uncouthness of dress, with the reminder that *they* were "a handful of private citizens, traveling simply for recreation," etc., and when the cry rang through the vessel at midnight: "EIGHT BELLS!—LARBOARD WATCH, TURN OUT!" the larboard watch came gaping and stretching out of their den, with the everlasting formula: "Aye, aye, sir! We are a handful of private citizens of America, traveling simply for recreation, and unostentatiously, as becomes our unofficial state!"

As I was a member of the committee, and helped to frame the Address, these sarcasms came home to me. I never heard a sailor proclaiming himself as a handful of American citizens traveling for recreation, but I wished he might trip and fall overboard, and so reduce his handful by one individual, at least. I never was so tired of any one phrase as the sailors made me of the opening sentence of the Address to the Emperor of Russia.

This seaport of Smyrna, our first notable acquaintance in Asia, is a closely packed city of one hundred and thirty thousand inhabitants, and, like Constantinople, it has no outskirts. It is as closely packed at its outer edges as it is in the center, and then the habitations leave suddenly off and the plain beyond seems houseless. It is just like any other Oriental city. That is to say, its Moslem houses are heavy and dark, and as comfortless as so many tombs; its streets are crooked, rudely and roughly paved, and as narrow as an ordinary staircase; the streets uniformly carry a man to any other place than the one he wants to go to, and surprise him by landing him in the most unexpected localities; business is chiefly carried on in great covered bazars, celled like a honeycomb with innumerable shops no larger than a common closet, and the whole hive cut up into a maze of alleys about wide enough to accommodate a laden camel, and well calculated to confuse a stranger and eventually lose him; everywhere there is dirt, everywhere there are fleas, everywhere there are lean, broken-hearted dogs; every alley is thronged with people; wherever you look, your eye rests upon a wild masquerade of extravagant costumes; the workshops are all open to the streets, and the workmen visible; all manner of sounds assail the ear, and over them all rings out the muezzin's cry from some tall minaret, calling the faithful vagabonds to prayer; and superior to the call to prayer, the noises in the streets, the interest of the costumes —superior to everything, and claiming the bulk of attention first, last, and all the time—is a combination of Mohammedan stenches, to which the smell of even a Chinese quarter would be as pleasant as the roasting odors of the fatted calf to the nostrils of the returning Prodigal. Such is Oriental luxury—such is Oriental splendor! We read about it all our days, but we comprehend it not until we see it. Smyrna is a very old city. Its name occurs several times in the Bible, one or two of the disciples of Christ visited it, and here was located one of the original seven apocalyptic churches spoken of in Revelations. These churches were symbolized in the Scriptures as candlesticks, and on certain conditions there was a sort of implied promise that Smyrna should be endowed with a "crown of life." She was to "be faithful unto death"—those were the terms. She has not kept up her faith straight along, but the pilgrims that wander hither consider that she has come near enough to it to save her, and so they point to the fact that Smyrna to-day wears her crown of life, and is a great city, with a great commerce and full of energy, while the cities wherein were located the other six churches, and to which no crown of life was promised, have vanished from the earth. So

Smyrna really still possesses her crown of life, in a business point of view. Her career, for eighteen centuries, has been a chequered one, and she has been under the rule of princes of many creeds, yet there has been no season during all that time, as far as we know (and during such seasons as she was inhabited at all), that she has been without her little community of Christians "faithful unto death." Hers was the only church against which no threats were implied in the Revelation, and the only one which survived.

With Ephesus, forty miles from here, where was located another of the seven churches, the case was different. The "candlestick" has been removed from Ephesus. Her light has been put out. Pilgrims, always prone to find prophecies in the Bible, and often where none exist, speak cheerfully and complacently of poor ruined Ephesus as the victim of prophecy. And yet there is no sentence that promises, without due qualification, the destruction of the city. The words are:

Remember, therefore, from whence thou art fallen, and repent, and do the first works; or else I will come unto thee quickly, and will remove thy candlestick out of his place, except thou repent.

That is all; the other verses are singularly *complimentary* to Ephesus. The threat is qualified. There is no history to show that she did not repent. But the cruelest habit the modern prophecy-savants have is that one of coolly and arbitrarily fitting the prophetic shirt on to the wrong man. They do it without regard to rhyme or reason. Both the cases

I have just mentioned are instances in point. Those "prophecies" are distinctly leveled at the "*churches* of Ephesus, Smyrna," etc., and yet the pilgrims invariably make them refer to the *cities* instead. No crown of life is promised to the town of Smyrna and its commerce, but to the handful of Christians who formed its "church." If *they* were "faithful unto death," they have their crown now—but no amount of faithfulness and legal shrewdness combined could legitimately drag the *city* into a participation in the promises of the prophecy. The stately language of the Bible refers to a crown of life whose luster will reflect the day-beams of the endless ages of eternity, not the butterfly existence of a city built by men's hands, which must pass to dust with the builders and be forgotten even in the mere handful of centuries vouchsafed to the solid world itself between its cradle and its grave.

The fashion of delving out fulfilments of prophecy where that prophecy consists of mere "ifs," trenches upon the absurd. Suppose, a thousand years from now, a malarious swamp builds itself up in the shallow harbor of Smyrna, or something else kills the town; and suppose, also, that within that time the swamp that has filled the renowned harbor of Ephesus and rendered her ancient site deadly and uninhabitable to-day, becomes hard and healthy ground; suppose the natural consequence ensues, to wit: that Smyrna becomes a melancholy ruin, and Ephesus is rebuilt. What would the prophecy-savants say? They would coolly skip over our age of the world, and say: "Smyrna was not faithful

unto death, and so her crown of life was denied her;
Ephesus repented, and lo! her candlestick was not
removed. Behold these evidences! How wonderful is prophecy!"

Smyrna has been utterly destroyed six times. If
her crown of life had been an insurance policy, she
would have had an opportunity to collect on it the
first time she fell. But she holds it on sufferance
and by a complimentary construction of language
which does not refer to her. Six different times,
however, I suppose some infatuated prophecy-
enthusiast blundered along and said, to the infinite
disgust of Smyrna and the Smyrniotes: "In sooth,
here is astounding fulfilment of prophecy! Smyrna
hath not been faithful unto death, and behold her
crown of life is vanished from her head. Verily,
these things be astonishing!"

Such things have a bad influence. They provoke
worldly men into using light conversation concerning
sacred subjects. Thick-headed commentators upon
the Bible, and stupid preachers and teachers, work
more damage to religion than sensible, cool-brained
clergymen can fight away again, toil as they may.
It is not good judgment to fit a crown of life upon a
city which has been destroyed six times. That other
class of wiseacres who twist prophecy in such a
manner as to make it promise the destruction and
desolation of the same city, use judgment just as
bad, since the city is in a very flourishing condition
now, unhappily for them. These things put argu-
ments into the mouth of infidelity.

A portion of the city is pretty exclusively Turkish; the Jews have a quarter to themselves; the Franks another quarter; so, also, with the Armenians. The Armenians, of course, are Christians. Their houses are large, clean, airy, handsomely paved with black and white squares of marble, and in the center of many of them is a square court, which has in it a luxuriant flower-garden and a sparkling fountain; the doors of all the rooms open on this. A very wide hall leads to the street-door, and in this the women sit, the most of the day. In the cool of the evening they dress up in their best raiment and show themselves at the door. They are all comely of countenance, and exceedingly neat and cleanly; they look as if they were just out of a bandbox. Some of the young ladies—many of them, I may say—are even very beautiful; they average a shade better than American girls—which treasonable words I pray may be forgiven me. They are very sociable, and will smile back when a stranger smiles at them, bow back when he bows, and talk back if he speaks to them. No introduction is required. An hour's chat at the door with a pretty girl one never saw before, is easily obtained, and is very pleasant. I have tried it. I could not talk anything but English, and the girl knew nothing but Greek, or Armenian, or some such barbarous tongue, but we got along very well. I find that in cases like these, the fact that you cannot comprehend each other isn't much of a drawback. In that Russian town of Yalta I danced an astonishing sort of dance an hour long, and one I had not heard of before, with a very pretty girl, and we talked incessantly, and laughed exhaustingly, and neither one ever knew what the other was driving at. But it was splendid. There were twenty people in the set, and the dance was very lively and complicated. It was complicated enough without me—with me it was more so. I threw in a figure now and then that surprised those Russians. But I have never ceased to think of that girl. I have written to her, but I cannot direct the epistle because her name is one of those nine-jointed Russian affairs, and there are not letters enough in our alphabet to hold out. I am not reckless enough to try to pronounce it when I am awake, but I make a stagger at it in my dreams, and get up with the lockjaw in the morning. I am fading. I do not take my meals now, with any sort of regularity. Her dear name haunts me still in my dreams. It is awful on teeth. It never comes out of my mouth but it fetches an old snag along with it. And then the lockjaw closes down and nips off a couple of the last syllables—but they taste good.

Coming through the Dardanelles, we saw camel-trains on shore with the glasses, but we were never close to one till we got to Smyrna. These camels are very much larger than the scrawny specimens one sees in the menagerie. They stride along these streets, in single file, a dozen in a train, with heavy loads on their backs, and a fancy-looking negro in Turkish costume, or an Arab, preceding them on a little donkey and completely overshadowed and rendered insignificant by the huge beasts. To see a camel-train laden with the spices of Arabia and the rare fabrics of Persia come marching through the narrow alleys of the bazar, among porters with their burdens, money-changers, lamp-merchants, Alnaschars in the glassware business, portly cross-legged Turks smoking the famous narghili, and the crowds drifting to and fro in the fanciful costumes of the East, is a genuine revelation of the Orient. The picture lacks nothing. It casts you back at once in your forgotten boyhood, and again you dream over the wonders of the Arabian Nights; again your companions are princes, your lord is the Caliph Haroun Al Raschid, and your servants are terrific giants and genii that come with smoke and lightning and thunder, and go as a storm goes when they depart!

## CHAPTER XII

WE inquired and learned that the lions of Smyrna consisted of the ruins of the ancient citadel, whose broken and prodigious battlements frown upon the city from a lofty hill just in the edge of the town — the Mount Pagus of Scripture, they call it; the site of that one of the seven apocalyptic churches of Asia which was located here in the first century of the Christian era; and the grave and the place of martyrdom of the venerable Polycarp, who suffered in Smyrna for his religion some eighteen hundred years ago.

We took little donkeys and started. We saw Polycarp's tomb, and then hurried on.

The "Seven Churches"—thus they abbreviate it—came next on the list. We rode there—about a mile and a half in the sweltering sun—and visited a little Greek church which they said was built upon the ancient site; and we paid a small fee, and the holy attendant gave each of us a little wax candle as a remembrance of the place, and I put mine in my hat and the sun melted it and the grease all ran down the back of my neck; and so now I have not anything left but the wick, and it is a sorry and wilted-looking wick at that.

Several of us argued as well as we could that the

"church" mentioned in the Bible meant a party of
Christians, and not a building; that the Bible spoke
of them as being very poor—so poor, I thought,
and so subject to persecution (as per Polycarp's
martyrdom) that in the first place they probably
could not have afforded a church edifice, and in the
second would not have dared to build it in the open
light of day if they could; and finally, that if they
had had the privilege of building it, common judgment would have suggested that they build it somewhere near the town. But the elders of the ship's
family ruled us down and scouted our evidences.
However, retribution came to them afterward. They
found that they had been led astray and had gone to
the wrong place; they discovered that the accepted
site is in the city.

Riding through the town, we could see marks of
the six Smyrnas that have existed here and been
burned up by fire or knocked down by earthquakes.
The hills and the rocks are rent asunder in places,
excavations expose great blocks of building-stone
that have lain buried for ages, and all the mean
houses and walls of modern Smyrna along the way
are spotted white with broken pillars, capitals, and
fragments of sculptured marble that once adorned
the lordly palaces that were the glory of the city in
the olden time.

The ascent of the hill of the citadel is very steep,
and we proceeded rather slowly. But there were
matters of interest about us. In one place, five
hundred feet above the sea, the perpendicular bank
on the upper side of the road was ten or fifteen feet

high, and the cut exposed three veins of oyster-
shells, just as we have seen quartz veins exposed in
the cutting of a road in Nevada or Montana. The
veins were about eighteen inches thick and two or
three feet apart, and they slanted along downward
for a distance of thirty feet or more, and then disappeared where the cut joined the road. Heaven
only knows how far a man might trace them by
"stripping." They were clean, nice oyster-shells,
large, and just like any other oyster-shells. They
were thickly massed together, and none were scattered above or below the veins. Each one was a
well-defined lead by itself, and without a spur. My
first instinct was to set up the usual—

NOTICE

We, the undersigned, claim five claims of two hundred feet
each (and one for discovery) on this ledge or lode of oyster-
shells, with all its dips, spurs, angles, variations, and sinuosities,
and fifty feet on each side of the same, to work it, etc., etc.,
according to the mining laws of Smyrna.

They were such perfectly natural-looking leads
that I could hardly keep from "taking them up."
Among the oyster-shells were mixed many fragments
of ancient, broken crockeryware. Now how did
those masses of oyster-shells get there? I cannot
determine. Broken crockery and oyster-shells are
suggestive of restaurants—but then they could have
had no such places away up there on that mountainside in our time, because nobody has lived up there.
A restaurant would not pay in such a stony, forbidding, desolate place. And besides, there were no
champagne corks among the shells. If there ever

132

was a restaurant there, it must have been in Smyrna's palmy days, when the hills were covered with palaces. I could believe in one restaurant, on those terms; but then how about the three? Did they have restaurants there at three different periods of the world?—because there are two or three feet of solid earth between the oyster leads. Evidently, the restaurant solution will not answer.

The hill might have been the bottom of the sea, once, and been lifted up, with its oyster-beds, by an earthquake—but, then, how about the crockery? And, moreover, how about *three* oyster-beds, one above another, and thick strata of good honest earth between?

That theory will not do. It is just possible that this hill is Mount Ararat, and that Noah's Ark rested here, and he ate oysters and threw the shells overboard. But that will not do, either. There are the three layers again and the solid earth between—and, besides, there were only eight in Noah's family, and they could not have eaten all these oysters in the two or three months they stayed on top of that mountain. The beasts—however, it is simply absurd to suppose he did not know any more than to feed the beasts on oyster suppers.

It is painful—it is even humiliating—but I am reduced at last to one slender theory: that the oysters climbed up there of their own accord. But what object could they have had in view?—what did they want up there? What could any oyster want to climb a hill for? To climb a hill must necessarily be fatiguing and annoying exercise for an oyster. The most natural conclusion would be that the oysters climbed up there to look at the scenery. Yet when one comes to reflect upon the nature of an oyster, it seems plain that he does not care for scenery. An oyster has no taste for such things; he cares nothing for the beautiful. An oyster is of a retiring disposition, and not lively— not even cheerful above the average, and never enterprising. But, above all, an oyster does not take any interest in scenery—he scorns it. What have I arrived at now? Simply at the point I started from, namely, *those oyster-shells are there*, in regular layers, five hundred feet above the sea, and no man knows how they got there. I have hunted up the guide-books, and the gist of what they say is this: "They are there, but how they got there is a mystery."

Twenty-five years ago, a multitude of people in America put on their ascension robes, took a tearful leave of their friends, and made ready to fly up into heaven at the first blast of the trumpet. But the angel did not blow it. Miller's resurrection day was a failure. The Millerites were disgusted. I did not suspect that there were Millers in Asia Minor, but a gentleman tells me that they had it all set for the world to come to an end in Smyrna one day about three years ago. There was much buzzing and preparation for a long time previously, and it cul- minated in a wild excitement at the appointed time. A vast number of the populace ascended the citadel hill early in the morning, to get out of the way of the general destruction, and many of the infatuated

closed up their shops and retired from all earthly
business. But the strange part of it was that about
three in the afternoon, while this gentleman and his
friends were at dinner in the hotel, a terrific storm
of rain, accompanied by thunder and lightning,
broke forth and continued with dire fury for two or
three hours. It was a thing unprecedented in
Smyrna at that time of the year, and scared some
of the most skeptical. The streets ran rivers and
the hotel floor was flooded with water. The dinner
had to be suspended. When the storm finished and
left everybody drenched through and through, and
melancholy and half-drowned, the ascensionists came
down from the mountain as dry as so many charity-
sermons! They had been looking down upon the
fearful storm going on below, and really believed
that their proposed destruction of the world was
proving a grand success.

A railway here in Asia—in the dreamy realm of
the Orient—in the fabled land of the Arabian
Nights—is a strange thing to think of. And yet
they have one already, and are building another.
The present one is well built and well conducted, by
an English company, but is not doing an immense
amount of business. The first year it carried a good
many passengers, but its freight list only comprised
eight hundred pounds of figs!

It runs almost to the very gates of Ephesus—a
town great in all ages of the world—a city familiar
to readers of the Bible, and one which was as old as
the very hills when the disciples of Christ preached
in its streets. It dates back to the shadowy ages of

tradition, and was the birthplace of gods renowned in Grecian mythology. The idea of a locomotive tearing through such a place as this, and waking the phantoms of its old days of romance out of their dreams of dead and gone centuries, is curious enough.

We journey thither to-morrow to see the celebrated ruins.

## CHAPTER XIII

THIS has been a stirring day. The superinten-
dent of the railway put a train at our disposal,
and did us the further kindness of accompanying us
to Ephesus and giving to us his watchful care. We
brought sixty scarcely perceptible donkeys in the
freight-cars, for we had much ground to go over.
We have seen some of the most grotesque costumes,
along the line of the railroad, that can be imagined.
I am glad that no possible combination of words
could describe them, for I might then be foolish
enough to attempt it.

At ancient Ayassalook, in the midst of a forbidding desert, we came upon long lines of ruined
aqueducts, and other remnants of architectural
grandeur, that told us plainly enough we were nearing what had been a metropolis once. We left the
train and mounted the donkeys, along with our
invited guests—pleasant young gentlemen from the
officers' list of an American man-of-war.

The little donkeys had saddles upon them which
were made very high in order that the rider's feet
might not drag the ground. The preventative did
not work well in the cases of our tallest pilgrims,
however. There were no bridles—nothing but a
single rope, tied to the bit. It was purely orna-

mental, for the donkey cared nothing for it. If he
were drifting to starboard, you might put your helm
down hard the other way, if it were any satisfaction
to you to do it, but he would continue to drift to
starboard all the same. There was only one process
which could be depended on, and that was to get
down and lift his rear around until his head pointed
in the right direction, or take him under your arm
and carry him to a part of the road which he could
not get out of without climbing. The sun flamed
down as hot as a furnace, and neck-scarfs, veils, and
umbrellas seemed hardly any protection; they served
only to make the long procession look more than
ever fantastic—for be it known the ladies were all
riding astride because they could not stay on the
shapeless saddles sidewise, the men were perspiring
and out of temper, their feet were banging against
the rocks, the donkeys were capering in every direction but the right one and being belabored with
clubs for it, and every now and then a broad umbrella would suddenly go down out of the cavalcade,
announcing to all that one more pilgrim had bitten
the dust. It was a wilder picture than those solitudes had seen for many a day. No donkeys ever
existed that were as hard to navigate as these, I
think, or that had so many vile, exasperating instincts. Occasionally, we grew so tired and breathless with fighting them that we had to desist—and
immediately the donkey would come down to a deliberate walk. This, with the fatigue, and the sun,
would put a man asleep; and as soon as the man
was asleep, the donkey would lie down. My donkey

shall never see his boyhood's home again. He has lain down once too often. He must die.

We all stood in the vast theater of ancient Ephesus—the stone-benched amphitheater, I mean—and had our picture taken. We looked as proper there as we would look anywhere, I suppose. We do not embellish the general desolation of a desert much. We add what dignity we can to a stately ruin with our green umbrellas and jackasses, but it is little. However, we mean well.

I wish to say a brief word of the aspect of Ephesus.

On a high, steep hill, toward the sea, is a gray ruin of ponderous blocks of marble, wherein, tradition says, St. Paul was imprisoned eighteen centuries ago. From these old walls you have the finest view of the desolate scene where once stood Ephesus, the proudest city of ancient times, and whose Temple of Diana was so noble in design and so exquisite of workmanship, that it ranked high in the list of the Seven Wonders of the World.

Behind you is the sea; in front is a level green valley (a marsh, in fact), extending far away among the mountains; to the right of the front view is the old citadel of Ayassalook, on a high hill; the ruined mosque of the Sultan Selim stands near it in the plain (this is built over the grave of St. John, and was formerly a Christian church); further toward you is the hill of Prion, around whose front is clustered all that remains of the ruins of Ephesus that still stand; divided from it by a narrow valley is the long, rocky, rugged mountain of Coressus. The scene is a pretty one, and yet desolate—for

139

in that wide plain no man can live, and in it is no human habitation. But for the crumbling arches and monstrous piers and broken walls that rise from the foot of the hill of Prion, one could not believe that in this place once stood a city whose renown is older than tradition itself. It is incredible to reflect that things as familiar all over the world to-day as household words belong in the history and in the shadowy legends of this silent, mournful solitude. We speak of Apollo and of Diana—they were born here; of the metamorphosis of Syrinx into a reed—it was done here; of the great god Pan—he dwelt in the caves of this hill of Coressus; of the Amazons—this was their best-prized home; of Bacchus and Hercules—both fought the warlike women here; of the Cyclops—they laid the ponderous marble blocks of some of the ruins yonder; of Homer—this was one of his many birthplaces; of Cimon of Athens; of Alcibiades, Lysander, Agesilaus—they visited here; so did Alexander the Great; so did Hannibal and Antiochus, Scipio, Lucullus, and Sylla; Brutus, Cassius, Pompey, Cicero, and Augustus; Antony was a judge in this place, and left his seat in the open court, while the advocates were speaking, to run after Cleopatra, who passed the door; from this city these two sailed on pleasure excursions, in galleys with silver oars and perfumed sails, and with companies of beautiful girls to serve them, and actors and musicians to amuse them; in days that seem almost modern, so remote are they from the early history of this city, Paul the Apostle preached the new religion here.

and so did John, and here it is supposed the former was pitted against wild beasts, for in I Corinthians, xv: 32, he says:

> If after the manner of men I have fought with beasts at Ephesus [etc.]

when many men still lived who had seen the Christ; here Mary Magdalen died, and here the Virgin Mary ended her days with John, albeit Rome has since judged it best to locate her grave elsewhere; six or seven hundred years ago—almost yesterday, as it were—troops of mail-clad Crusaders thronged the streets; and to come down to trifles, we speak of meandering streams, and find a new interest in a common word when we discover that the crooked river Meander, in yonder valley, gave it to our dictionary. It makes me feel as old as these dreary hills to look down upon these moss-hung ruins, this historic desolation. One may read the Scriptures and believe, but he cannot go and stand yonder in the ruined theater and in imagination people it again with the vanished multitudes who mobbed Paul's comrades there and shouted, with one voice, "Great is Diana of the Ephesians!" The idea of a shout in such a solitude as this almost makes one shudder.

It was a wonderful city, this Ephesus. Go where you will about these broad plains, you find the most exquisitely sculptured marble fragments scattered thick among the dust and weeds; and protruding from the ground, or lying prone upon it, are beautiful fluted columns of porphyry and all precious marbles; and at every step you find elegantly carved capitals and massive bases, and polished tablets engraved with Greek inscriptions. It is a world of precious relics, a wilderness of marred and mutilated gems. And yet what are these things to the wonders that lie buried here under the ground? At Constantinople, at Pisa, in the cities of Spain, are great mosques and cathedrals, whose grandest columns came from the temples and palaces of Ephesus, and yet one has only to scratch the ground here to match them. We shall never know what magnificence is, until this imperial city is laid bare to the sun.

The finest piece of sculpture we have yet seen and the one that impressed us most (for we do not know much about art and cannot easily work up ourselves into ecstasies over it), is one that lies in this old theater of Ephesus which St. Paul's riot has made so celebrated. It is only the headless body of a man, clad in a coat of mail, with a Medusa head upon the breastplate, but we feel persuaded that such dignity and such majesty were never thrown into a form of stone before.

What builders they were, these men of antiquity! The massive arches of some of these ruins rest upon piers that are fifteen feet square and built entirely of solid blocks of marble, some of which are as large as a Saratoga trunk, and some the size of a boarding-house sofa. They are not shells or shafts of stone filled inside with rubbish, but the whole pier is a mass of solid masonry. Vast arches, that may have been the gates of the city, are built in the same way.

THE INNOCENTS ABROAD

They have braved the storms and sieges of three thousand years, and have been shaken by many an earthquake, but still they stand. When they dig alongside of them, they find ranges of ponderous masonry that are as perfect in every detail as they were the day those old Cyclopean giants finished them. An English company is going to excavate Ephesus—and then!

And now am I reminded of—

## THE LEGEND OF THE SEVEN SLEEPERS

In the Mount of Prion, yonder, is the Cave of the Seven Sleepers. Once upon a time, about fifteen hundred years ago, seven young men lived near each other in Ephesus, who belonged to the despised sect of the Christians. It came to pass that the good King Maximilianus (I am telling this story for nice little boys and girls), it came to pass, I say, that the good King Maximilianus fell to persecuting the Christians, and as time rolled on he made it very warm for them. So the seven young men said one to the other, Let us get up and travel. And they got up and traveled. They tarried not to bid their fathers and mothers good-by, or any friend they knew. They only took certain moneys which their parents had, and garments that belonged unto their friends, whereby they might remember them when far away; and they took also the dog Ketmehr, which was the property of their neighbor Malchus, because the beast did run his head into a noose which one of the young men was carrying carelessly, and

143

they had not time to release him; and they took also
certain chickens that seemed lonely in the neighboring coops, and likewise some bottles of curious
liquors that stood near the grocer's window; and
then they departed from the city. By and by they
came to a marvelous cave in the Hill of Prion and
entered into it and feasted, and presently they
hurried on again. But they forgot the bottles of
curious liquors, and left them behind. They traveled
in many lands, and had many strange adventures.
They were virtuous young men, and lost no opportunity that fell in their way to make their livelihood.
Their motto was in these words, namely, "Pro-
crastination is the thief of time." And so, whenever they did come upon a man who was alone,
they said, Behold, this person hath the where-
withal—let us go through him. And they went
through him. At the end of five years they had
waxed tired of travel and adventure, and longed to
revisit their old home again and hear the voices and
see the faces that were dear unto their youth. Therefore they went through such parties as fell in their
way where they sojourned at that time, and journeyed back toward Ephesus again. For the good
King Maximilianus was become converted unto the
new faith, and the Christians rejoiced because they
were no longer persecuted. One day as the sun went
down, they came to the cave in the Mount of Prion,
and they said, each to his fellow, Let us sleep here,
and go and feast and make merry with our friends
when the morning cometh. And each of the seven
lifted up his voice and said, It is a whiz. So they

went in, and lo, where they had put them, there lay the bottles of strange liquors, and they judged that age had not impaired their excellence. Wherein the wanderers were right, and the heads of the same were level. So each of the young men drank six bottles, and behold they felt very tired, then, and lay down and slept soundly.

When they awoke, one of them, Johannes—surnamed Smithianus—said, We are naked. And it was so. Their raiment was all gone, and the money which they had gotten from a stranger whom they had proceeded through as they approached the city, was lying upon the ground, corroded and rusted and defaced. Likewise the dog Ketmehr was gone, and nothing save the brass that was upon his collar remained. They wondered much at these things. But they took the money, and they wrapped about their bodies some leaves, and came up to the top of the hill. Then were they perplexed. The wonderful temple of Diana was gone; many grand edifices they had never seen before stood in the city; men in strange garbs moved about the streets, and every thing was changed.

Johannes said, It hardly seems like Ephesus. Yet here is the great gymnasium; here is the mighty theater, wherein I have seen seventy thousand men assembled; here is the Agora; there is the font where the sainted John the Baptist immersed the converts; yonder is the prison of the good St. Paul, where we all did use to go to touch the ancient chains that bound him and be cured of our distempers; I see the tomb of the disciple Luke, and afar off is the church wherein repose the ashes of the holy John, where the Christians of Ephesus go twice a year to gather the dust from the tomb, which is able to make bodies whole again that are corrupted by disease, and cleanse the soul from sin; but see how the wharves encroach upon the sea, and what multitudes of ships are anchored in the bay; see, also, how the city hath stretched abroad, far over the valley behind Prion, and even unto the walls of Ayassalook; and lo, all the hills are white with palaces and ribbed with colonnades of marble. How mighty is Ephesus become!

And wondering at what their eyes had seen, they went down into the city and purchased garments and clothed themselves. And when they would have passed on, the merchant bit the coins which they had given him, with his teeth, and turned them about and looked curiously upon them, and cast them upon his counter, and listened if they rang; and then he said, These be bogus. And they said, Depart thou to Hades, and went their way. When they were come to their houses, they recognized them, albeit they seemed old and mean; and they rejoiced, and were glad. They ran to the doors, and knocked, and strangers opened, and looked inquiringly upon them. And they said, with great excitement, while their hearts beat high, and the color in their faces came and went, Where is my father? Where is my mother? Where are Dionysius and Serapion, and Pericles, and Decius? And the strangers that opened said, We know not these. The Seven said, How, you know them not? How long have ye dwelt here, and whither are they gone that dwelt here before ye? And the strangers said, Ye play upon us with a jest, young men; we and our fathers have sojourned under these roofs these six generations; the names ye utter rot upon the tombs, and they that bore them have run their brief race, have laughed and sung, have borne the sorrows and the weariness that were allotted them, and are at rest; for ninescore years the summers have come and gone, and the autumn leaves have fallen, since the roses faded out of their cheeks and they laid them to sleep with the dead.

Then the seven young men turned them away from their homes, and the strangers shut the doors upon them. The wanderers marveled greatly, and looked into the faces of all they met, as hoping to find one that they knew; but all were strange, and passed them by and spake no friendly word. They were sore distressed and sad. Presently they spake unto a citizen and said, Who is King in Ephesus? And the citizen answered and said, Whence come ye that ye know not that great Laertius reigns in Ephesus? They looked one at the other, greatly perplexed, and presently asked again, Where, then, is the good King Maximilianus? The citizen moved him apart, as one who is afraid, and said, Verily these men be mad, and dream dreams, else would they know that the King whereof they speak is dead above two hundred years agone.

Then the scales fell from the eyes of the Seven, and one said, Alas, that we drank of the curious liquors. They have made us weary, and in dream-

147

less sleep these two long centuries have we lain. Our homes are desolate, our friends are dead. Behold, the jig is up—let us die. And that same day went they forth and laid them down and died. And in that selfsame day, likewise, the Seven-up did cease in Ephesus, for that the Seven that were up were down again, and departed and dead withal. And the names that be upon their tombs, even unto this time, are Johannes Smithianus, Trumps, Gift, High, and Low, Jack, and The Game. And with the sleepers lie also the bottles wherein were once the curious liquors; and upon them is writ, in ancient letters, such words as these—names of heathen gods of olden time, perchance: Rumpunch, Jinsling, Eggnog.

Such is the story of the Seven Sleepers (with slight variations), and I know it is true, because I have seen the cave myself.

Really, so firm a faith had the ancients in this legend, that as late as eight or nine hundred years ago, learned travelers held it in superstitious fear.

Two of them record that they ventured into it, but ran quickly out again, not daring to tarry lest they should fall asleep and outlive their great-grandchildren a century or so. Even at this day the ignorant denizens of the neighboring country prefer not to sleep in it.

## CHAPTER XIV

W HEN I last made a memorandum, we were
at Ephesus. We are in Syria, now, encamped
in the mountains of Lebanon. The interregnum has
been long, both as to time and distance. We
brought not a relic from Ephesus! After gathering
up fragments of sculptured marbles and breaking
ornaments from the interior work of the mosques;
and after bringing them, at a cost of infinite trouble
and fatigue, five miles on muleback to the railway
depot, a government officer compelled all who had
such things to disgorge! He had an order from
Constantinople to *look out for our party*, and see that
we carried nothing off. It was a wise, a just, and a
well-deserved rebuke, but it created a sensation. I
never resist a temptation to plunder a stranger's
premises without feeling insufferably vain about it.
This time I felt proud beyond expression. I was
serene in the midst of the scoldings that were heaped
upon the Ottoman government for its affront offered
to a pleasuring party of entirely respectable gentlemen and ladies. I said, "We that have free souls,
it touches us not." The shoe not only pinched our
party, but it pinched hard; a principal sufferer discovered that the imperial order was inclosed in an
envelope bearing the seal of the British Embassy at

Constantinople, and therefore must have been inspired by the representative of the Queen. This was bad—very bad. Coming solely from the Ottomans, it might have signified only Ottoman hatred of Christians, and a vulgar ignorance as to genteel methods of expressing it; but coming from the Christianized, educated, politic British legation, it simply intimated that we were a sort of gentlemen and ladies who would bear watching! So the party regarded it, and were incensed accordingly. The truth doubtless was, that the same precautions would have been taken against *any* travelers, because the English Company who have acquired the right to excavate Ephesus, and have paid a great sum for that right, need to be protected, and deserve to be. They cannot afford to run the risk of having their hospitality abused by travelers, especially since travelers are such notorious scorners of honest behavior.

We sailed from Smyrna, in the wildest spirit of expectancy, for the chief feature, the grand goal of the expedition, was near at hand—we were approaching the Holy Land! Such a burrowing into the hold for trunks that had lain buried for weeks, yes, for months; such a hurrying to and fro above decks and below; such a riotous system of packing and unpacking; such a littering up of the cabins with shirts and skirts, and indescribable and unclassable odds and ends; such a making up of bundles, and setting apart of umbrellas, green spectacles, and thick veils; such a critical inspection of saddles and bridles that had never yet touched horses; such a cleaning and loading of revolvers and examining of bowie-knives; such a half-soling of the seats of pantaloons with serviceable buckskin; then such a poring over ancient maps; such a reading up of Bibles and Palestine travels; such a marking out of routes; such exasperating efforts to divide up the company into little bands of congenial spirits who might make the long and arduous journey without quarreling; and morning, noon, and night, such mass-meetings in the cabins, such speech-making, such sage suggesting, such worrying and quarreling, and such a general raising of the very mischief, was never seen in the ship before!

But it is all over now. We are cut up into parties of six or eight, and by this time are scattered far and wide. Ours is the only one, however, that is venturing on what is called "the long trip"—that is, out into Syria, by Baalbec to Damascus, and thence down through the full length of Palestine. It would be a tedious, and also a too risky journey, at this hot season of the year, for any but strong, healthy men, accustomed somewhat to fatigue and rough life in the open air. The other parties will take shorter journeys.

For the last two months we have been in a worry about one portion of this Holy Land pilgrimage. I refer to transportation service. We knew very well that Palestine was a country which did not do a large passenger business, and every man we came across who knew anything about it gave us to understand that not half of our party would be able to get dragomans and animals. At Constantinople everybody fell to telegraphing the American consuls at Alexandria

and Beirout to give notice that we wanted dragomans and transportation. We were desperate—would
take horses, jackasses, camelopards, kangaroos—
anything. At Smyrna, more telegraphing was done,
to the same end. Also, fearing for the worst, we
telegraphed for a large number of seats in the diligence for Damascus, and horses for the ruins of
Baalbec.

As might have been expected, a notion got
abroad in Syria and Egypt that the whole population
of the Province of America (the Turks consider us a
trifling little province in some unvisited corner of the
world) were coming to the Holy Land—and so,
when we got to Beirout yesterday, we found the
place full of dragomans and their outfits. We had
all intended to go by diligence to Damascus, and
switch off to Baalbec as we went along—because we
expected to rejoin the ship, go to Mount Carmel,
and take to the woods from there. However, when
our own private party of eight found that it was possible, and proper enough, to make the "long trip,"
we adopted that program. We have never been
much trouble to a consul before, but we have been
a fearful nuisance to our consul at Beirout. I mention this because I cannot help admiring his patience,
his industry, and his accommodating spirit. I mention it, also, because I think some of our ship's
company did not give him as full credit for his excellent services as he deserved.

Well, out of our eight, three were selected to
attend to all business connected with the expedition.
The rest of us had nothing to do but look at the

beautiful city of Beirout, with its bright, new houses
nestled among a wilderness of green shrubbery
spread abroad over an upland that sloped gently
down to the sea; and also at the mountains of Lebanon that environ it; and likewise to bathe in the
transparent blue water that rolled its billows about
the ship (we did not know there were sharks there).
We had also to range up and down through the
town and look at the costumes.  These are picturesque and fanciful, but not so varied as at Constantinople and Smyrna; the women of Beirout add an
agony—in the two former cities the sex wear a thin
veil which one can see through (and they often expose their ankles), but at Beirout they cover their
entire faces with dark-colored or black veils, so that
they look like mummies, and then expose their
breasts to the public.  A young gentleman (I believe he was a Greek) volunteered to show us around
the city, and said it would afford him great pleasure,
because he was studying English and wanted practice
in that language.  When we had finished the rounds,
however, he called for remuneration—said he hoped
the gentlemen would give him a trifle in the way of a
few piasters (equivalent to a few five-cent pieces).
We did so.  The consul was surprised when he
heard it, and said he knew the young fellow's family
very well, and that they were an old and highly
respectable family and worth a hundred and fifty
thousand dollars!  Some people, so situated, would
have been ashamed of the berth he had with us and
his manner of crawling into it.

At the appointed time our business committee

reported, and said all things were in readiness—that
we were to start to-day, with horses, pack-animals,
and tents, and go to Baalbec, Damascus, the Sea of
Tiberias, and thence southward by the way of the
scene of Jacob's Dream and other notable Bible
localities to Jerusalem—from thence probably to the
Dead Sea, but possibly not—and then strike for the
ocean and rejoin the ship three or four weeks hence
at Joppa; terms, five dollars a day apiece, in gold,
and everything to be furnished by the dragoman.
They said we would live as well as at a hotel. I had
read something like that before, and did not shame
my judgment by believing a word of it. I said nothing, however, but packed up a blanket and a shawl
to sleep in, pipes and tobacco, two or three woolen
shirts, a portfolio, a guide-book, and a Bible. I
also took along a towel and a cake of soap, to inspire
respect in the Arabs, who would take me for a
king in disguise.

We were to select our horses at 3 P.M. At that
hour Abraham, the dragoman, marshaled them before us. With all solemnity I set it down here, that
those horses were the hardest lot I ever did come
across, and their accoutrements were in exquisite
keeping with their style. One brute had an eye out;
another had his tail sawed off close, like a rabbit, and
was proud of it; another had a bony ridge running
from his neck to his tail, like one of those ruined
aqueducts one sees about Rome, and had a neck
on him like a bowsprit; they all limped, and had
sore backs, and likewise raw places and old scales
scattered about their persons like brass nails in a hair

trunk; their gaits were marvelous to contemplate, and replete with variety—under way the procession looked like a fleet in a storm. It was fearful. Blucher shook his head and said:

"That dragon is going to get himself into trouble fetching these old crates out of the hospital the way they are, unless he has got a permit."

I said nothing. The display was exactly according to the guide-book, and were we not traveling by the guide-book? I selected a certain horse because I thought I saw him shy, and I thought that a horse that had spirit enough to shy was not to be despised.

At 6 o'clock P.M. we came to a halt here on the breezy summit of a shapely mountain overlooking the sea, and the handsome valley where dwelt some of those enterprising Phœnicians of ancient times we read so much about; all around us are what were once the dominions of Hiram, King of Tyre, who furnished timber from the cedars of these Lebanon hills to build portions of King Solomon's Temple with.

Shortly after six, our pack-train arrived. I had not seen it before, and a good right I had to be astonished. We had nineteen serving-men and twenty-six pack-mules! It was a perfect caravan. It looked like one, too, as it wound among the rocks. I wondered what in the very mischief we wanted with such a vast turnout as that, for eight men. I wondered awhile, but soon I began to long for a tin plate, and some bacon and beans. I had camped out many and many a time before, and knew just what was coming. I went off, without waiting for serving-men, and unsaddled my horse, and washed such portions of his ribs and his spine as projected through his hide, and when I came back, behold five stately circus-tents were up—tents that were brilliant, within, with blue and gold and crimson, and all manner of splendid adornment! I was speechless. Then they brought eight little iron bedsteads, and set them up in the tents; they put a soft mattress and pillows and good blankets and two snow-white sheets on each bed. Next, they rigged a table about the center-pole, and on it placed pewter pitchers, basins, soap, and the whitest of towels—one set for each man; they pointed to pockets in the tent, and said we could put our small trifles in them for convenience, and if we needed pins or such things, they were sticking everywhere. Then came the finishing touch—they spread carpets on the floor! I simply said, "If you call this camping out, all right—but it isn't the style *I* am used to; my little baggage that I brought along is at a discount."

It grew dark, and they put candles on the tables —candles set in bright, new, brazen candlesticks. And soon the bell—a genuine, simon-pure bell— rang, and we were invited to "the saloon." I had thought before that we had a tent or so too many, but now here was one, at least, provided for; it was to be used for nothing but an eating-saloon. Like the others, it was high enough for a family of giraffes to live in, and was very handsome and clean and bright-colored within. It was a gem of a place. A table for eight, and eight canvas chairs; a table-cloth and napkins whose whiteness and whose fineness laughed to scorn the things we were used to in the great excursion steamer; knives and forks, soup plates, dinner plates—everything, in the handsomest kind of style. It was wonderful! And they call *this* camping out. Those stately fellows in baggy trousers and turbaned fezes brought in a dinner which consisted of roast mutton, roast chicken, roast goose, potatoes, bread, tea, pudding, apples, and delicious grapes; the viands were better cooked than any we had eaten for weeks, and the table made a finer appearance, with its large German-silver candlesticks and other finery, than any table we had sat down to for a good while, and yet that polite dragoman, Abraham, came bowing in and apologizing for the whole affair, on account of the unavoidable confusion of getting under way for a very long trip, and promising to do a great deal better in future!

It is midnight now, and we break camp at six in the morning.

They call this camping out. At this rate it is a glorious privilege to be a pilgrim to the Holy Land.

# CHAPTER XV

WE are camped near Temnin-el-Foka—a name which the boys have simplified a good deal, for the sake of convenience in spelling. They call it Jacksonville. It sounds a little strangely, here in the Valley of Lebanon, but it has the merit of being easier to remember than the Arabic name.

COME LIKE SPIRITS, SO DEPART

The night shall be filled with music,
And the cares that infest the day
Shall fold their tents like the Arabs,
And as silently steal away.

I slept very soundly last night, yet when the dragoman's bell rang at half past five this morning and the cry went abroad of "Ten minutes to dress for breakfast!" I heard both. It surprised me, because I have not heard the breakfast gong in the ship for a month, and whenever we have had occasion to fire a salute at daylight, I have only found it out in the course of conversation afterward. However, camping out, even though it be in a gorgeous tent, makes one fresh and lively in the morning—especially if the air you are breathing is the cool, fresh air of the mountains.

I was dressed within the ten minutes, and came out. The saloon tent had been stripped of its sides, and had nothing left but its roof; so when we sat down to table we could look out over a noble panorama of mountain, sea, and hazy valley. And sitting thus, the sun rose slowly up and suffused the picture with a world of rich coloring.

Hot mutton-chops, fried chicken, omelettes, fried potatoes, and coffee—all excellent. This was the bill of fare. It was sauced with a savage appetite purchased by hard riding the day before, and refreshing sleep in a pure atmosphere. As I called for a second cup of coffee, I glanced over my shoulder, and behold, our white village was gone—the splendid tents had vanished like magic! It was wonderful how quickly those Arabs had "folded their tents"; and it was wonderful, also, how quickly they had gathered the thousand odds and ends of the camp together and disappeared with them.

By half past six we were under way, and all the Syrian world seemed to be under way also. The road was filled with mule-trains and long processions of camels. This reminds me that we have been trying for some time to think what a camel looks like, and now we have made it out. When he is down on all his knees, flat on his breast to receive his load, he looks something like a goose swimming; and when he is upright he looks like an ostrich with an extra set of legs. Camels are not beautiful, and their long under-lip gives them an exceedingly "gallus" [1] expression. They have immense flat, forked cushions of feet, that make a track in the

---

[1] Excuse the slang—no other word will describe it.

dust like a pie with a slice cut out of it.  They are not particular about their diet.  They would eat a tombstone if they could bite it.  A thistle grows about here which has needles on it that would pierce through leather, I think; if one touches you, you can find relief in nothing but profanity.  The camels eat these.  They show by their actions that they enjoy them.  I suppose it would be a real treat to a camel to have a keg of nails for supper.

While I am speaking of animals, I will mention that I have a horse now by the name of "Jericho." He is a mare.  I have seen remarkable horses before, but none so remarkable as this.  I wanted a horse that could shy, and this one fills the bill.  I had an idea that shying indicated spirit.  If I was correct, I have got the most spirited horse on earth. He shies at everything he comes across, with the utmost impartiality.  He appears to have a mortal dread of telegraph-poles, especially; and it is fortunate that these are on both sides of the road, because as it is now, I never fall off twice in succession on the same side.  If I fell on the same side always, it would get to be monotonous after a while.  This creature has scared at everything he has seen to-day, except a haystack.  He walked up to that with intrepidity and a recklessness that were astonishing.  And it would fill any one with admiration to see how he preserves his self-possession in the presence of a barley sack.  This dare devil bravery will be the death of this horse some day.

He is not particularly fast, but I think he will get me through the Holy Land.  He has only one fault

His tail has been chopped off or else he has sat down on it too hard, some time or other, and he has to fight the flies with his heels. This is all very well, but when he tries to kick a fly off the top of his head with his hind foot, it is too much variety. He is going to get himself into trouble that way some day. He reaches around and bites my legs, too. I do not care particularly about that, only I do not like to see a horse too sociable.

I think the owner of this prize had a wrong opinion about him. He had an idea that he was one of those fiery, untamed steeds, but he is not of that character. I know the Arab had this idea, because when he brought the horse out for inspection in Beirout, he kept jerking at the bridle and shouting in Arabic, "Whoa! will you? Do you want to run away, you ferocious beast, and break your neck?" when all the time the horse was not doing anything in the world, and only looked like he wanted to lean up against something and think. Whenever he is not shying at things, or reaching after a fly, he wants to do that yet. How it would surprise his owner to know this.

We have been in a historical section of country all day. At noon we camped three hours and took luncheon at Mekseh, near the junction of the Lebanon Mountains and the Jebel el Kuneiyiseh, and looked down into the immense, level, garden-like Valley of Lebanon. To-night we are camping near the same valley, and have a very wide sweep of it in view. We can see the long, whale-backed ridge of Mount Hermon projecting above the eastern hills. The "dews of Hermon" are falling upon us now, and the tents are almost soaked with them.

Over the way from us, and higher up the valley, we can discern, through the glasses, the faint outlines of the wonderful ruins of Baalbec, the supposed Baal-Gad of Scripture. Joshua and another person were the two spies who were sent into this land of Canaan by the children of Israel to report upon its character—I mean they were the spies who reported favorably. They took back with them some specimens of the grapes of this country, and in the children's picture-books they are always represented as bearing one monstrous bunch swung to a pole between them, a respectable load for a pack-train. The Sunday-school books exaggerated it a little. The grapes are most excellent to this day, but the bunches are not as large as those in the pictures. I was surprised and hurt when I saw them, because those colossal bunches of grapes were one of my most cherished juvenile traditions.

Joshua reported favorably, and the children of Israel journeyed on, with Moses at the head of the general government, and Joshua in command of the army of six hundred thousand fighting men. Of women and children and civilians there was a countless swarm. Of all that mighty host, none but the two faithful spies ever lived to set their feet in the Promised Land. They and their descendants wandered forty years in the desert, and then Moses, the gifted warrior, poet, statesman, and philosopher, went up into Pisgah and met his mysterious fate. Where he was buried no man knows—for

# THE INNOCENTS ABROAD

. . . no man dug that sepulcher,
And no man saw it e'er—
For the sons of God upturned the sod
And laid the dead man there!

Then Joshua began his terrible raid, and from Jericho clear to this Baal-Gad, he swept the land like the Genius of Destruction. He slaughtered the people, laid waste their soil, and razed their cities to the ground. He wasted thirty-one kings also. One may call it that, though really it can hardly be called wasting them, because there were always plenty of kings in those days, and to spare. At any rate, he destroyed thirty-one kings, and divided up their realms among his Israelites. He divided up this valley stretched out here before us, and so it was once Jewish territory. The Jews have long since disappeared from it, however.

Back yonder, an hour's journey from here, we passed through an Arab village of stone dry-goods boxes (they look like that), where Noah's tomb lies under lock and key. [Noah built the ark.] Over these old hills and valleys the ark that contained all that was left of a vanished world once floated.

I make no apology for detailing the above information. It will be news to some of my readers, at any rate.

Noah's tomb is built of stone, and is covered with a long stone building. Bucksheesh let us in. The building had to be long, because the grave of the honored old navigator is two hundred and ten feet long itself! It is only about four feet high, though. He must have cast a shadow like a lightning-rod.

163

The proof that this is the genuine spot where Noah was buried can only be doubted by uncommonly incredulous people. The evidence is pretty straight. Shem, the son of Noah, was present at the burial, and showed the place to his descendants, who trans‧mitted the knowledge to their descendants, and the lineal descendants of these introduced themselves to us to-day. It was pleasant to make the acquaintance of members of so respectable a family. It was a thing to be proud of. It was the next thing to being acquainted with Noah himself.

Noah's memorable voyage will always possess a living interest for me, henceforward.

If ever an oppressed race existed, it is this one we see fettered around us under the inhuman tyranny of the Ottoman empire. I wish Europe would let Russia annihilate Turkey a little—not much, but enough to make it difficult to find the place again without a divining-rod or a diving-bell. The Syrians are very poor, and yet they are ground down by a system of taxation that would drive any other nation frantic. Last year their taxes were heavy enough, in all conscience—but this year they have been increased by the addition of taxes that were forgiven them in times of famine in former years. On top of this the government has levied a tax of *one-tenth* of the whole proceeds of the land. This is only half the story. The Pasha of a Pashalic does not trouble himself with appointing tax-collectors. He figures up what all these taxes ought to amount to in a certain district. Then he farms the collection out. He calls the rich men together, the highest bidder gets the speculation, pays the Pasha on the spot, and then sells out to smaller fry, who sell in turn to a piratical horde of still smaller fry. These latter compel the peasant to bring his little trifle of grain to the village, at his own cost. It must be weighed, the various taxes set apart, and the remainder returned to the producer. But the collector delays this duty day after day, while the producer's family are perishing for bread; at last the poor wretch, who cannot but understand the game, says, "Take a quarter—take half—take two-thirds if you will, and let me go!" It is a most outrageous state of things.

These people are naturally good-hearted and intelligent, and, with education and liberty, would be a happy and contented race. They often appeal to the stranger to know if the great world will not some day come to their relief and save them. The Sultan has been lavishing money like water in England and Paris, but his subjects are suffering for it now.

This fashion of camping out bewilders me. We have bootjacks and a bathtub now, and yet all the mysteries the pack-mules carry are not revealed. What next?

## CHAPTER XVI

WE had a tedious ride of about five hours, in the sun, across the Valley of Lebanon. It proved to be not quite so much of a garden as it had seemed from the hillsides. It was a desert, weed-grown waste, littered thickly with stones the size of a man's fist. Here and there the natives had scratched the ground and reared a sickly crop of grain, but for the most part the valley was given up to a handful of shepherds, whose flocks were doing what they honestly could to get a living, but the chances were against them. We saw rude piles of stones standing near the roadside, at intervals, and recognized the custom of marking boundaries which obtained in Jacob's time. There were no walls, no fences, no hedges—nothing to secure a man's possessions but these random heaps of stones. The Israelites held them sacred in the old patriarchal times, and these other Arabs, their lineal descendants, do so likewise. An American, of ordinary intelligence, would soon widely extend his property, at an outlay of mere manual labor, performed at night, under so loose a system of fencing as this.

The plows these people use are simply a sharpened stick, such as Abraham plowed with, and they still winnow their wheat as he did—they pile it on the housetop, and then toss it by shovelfuls into the air until the wind has blown all the chaff away.

We had a fine race, of a mile, with an Arab perched on a camel. Some of the horses were fast, and made very good time, but the camel scampered by them without any very great effort. The yelling and shouting, and whipping and galloping, of all parties interested, made it an exhilarating, exciting, and particularly boisterous race.

At eleven o'clock, our eyes fell upon the walls and columns of Baalbec, a noble ruin whose history is a sealed book. It has stood there for thousands of years, the wonder and admiration of travelers; but who built it, or when it was built, are questions that may never be answered. One thing is very sure, though. Such grandeur of design, and such grace of execution, as one sees in the temples of Baalbec, have not been equaled or even approached in any work of men's hands that has been built within twenty centuries past.

The great Temple of the Sun, the Temple of Jupiter, and several smaller temples, are clustered together in the midst of one of these miserable Syrian villages, and look strangely enough in such plebeian company. These temples are built upon massive substructions that might support a world, almost; the materials used are blocks of stone as large as an omnibus—very few, if any, of them are smaller than a carpenter's tool chest—and these substructions are traversed by tunnels of masonry through which a train of cars might pass. With such foundations as these, it is little wonder that

Baalbec has lasted so long.  The Temple of the
Sun is nearly three hundred feet long and one hundred and sixty feet wide.  It had fifty-four columns
around it, but only six are standing now—the
others lie broken at its base, a confused and picturesque heap.  The six columns are perfect, as
also are their bases, Corinthian capitals and entablature—and six more shapely columns do not exist.
The columns and the entablature together are ninety
feet high—a prodigious altitude for shafts of stone
to reach, truly—and yet one only thinks of their
beauty and symmetry when looking at them; the
pillars look slender and delicate, the entablature,
with its elaborate sculpture, looks like rich stucco-
work.  But when you have gazed aloft till your eyes
are weary, you glance at the great fragments of
pillars among which you are standing, and find that
they are eight feet through; and with them lie beautiful capitals apparently as large as a small cottage;
and also single slabs of stone, superbly sculptured,
that are four or five feet thick, and would completely cover the floor of any ordinary parlor.  You
wonder where these monstrous things came from,
and it takes some little time to satisfy yourself that
the airy and graceful fabric that towers above your
head is made up of their mates.  It seems too
preposterous.

The Temple of Jupiter is a smaller ruin than the
one I have been speaking of, and yet is immense.
It is in a tolerable state of preservation.  One row
of nine columns stands almost uninjured.  They are
sixty-five feet high and support a sort of porch or

roof, which connects them with the roof of the building. This porch-roof is composed of tremendous slabs of stone, which are so finely sculptured on the under side that the work looks like a fresco from below. One or two of these slabs had fallen, and again I wondered if the gigantic masses of carved stone that lay about me were no larger than those above my head. Within the temple, the ornamentation was elaborate and colossal. What a wonder of architectural beauty and grandeur this edifice must have been when it was new! And what a noble picture it and its statelier companion, with the chaos of mighty fragments scattered about them, yet make in the moonlight!

I cannot conceive how these immense blocks of stone were ever hauled from the quarries, or how they were ever raised to the dizzy heights they occupy in the temples. And yet these sculptured blocks are trifles in size compared with the rough-hewn blocks that form the wide veranda or platform which surrounds the Great Temple. One stretch of that platform, two hundred feet long, is composed of blocks of stone as large and some of them larger, than a street-car. They surmount a wall about ten or twelve feet high. I thought those were large rocks, but they sank into insignificance compared with those which formed another section of the platform. These three in number, and I thought that each of them was about as long as three street-cars placed end to end, though, of course, they are a third wider and a third higher than a street-car. Perhaps two railway freight-cars of the largest pattern, placed end to end, might better represent their size. In combined length these three stones stretch nearly two hundred feet; they are thirteen feet square; two of them are sixty-four feet long each, and the third is sixty-nine. They are built into the massive wall some twenty feet above the ground. They are there, but how they got there is the question. I have seen the hull of a steamboat that was smaller than one of those stones. All these great walls are as exact and shapely as the flimsy things we build of bricks in these days. A race of gods or of giants must have inhabited Baalbec many a century ago. Men like the men of our day could hardly rear such temples as these.

We went to the quarry from whence the stones of Baalbec were taken. It was about a quarter of a mile off, and downhill. In a great pit lay the mate of the largest stone in the ruins. It lay there just as the giants of that old forgotten time had left it when they were called hence—just as they had left it, to remain for thousands of years, an eloquent rebuke unto such as are prone to think slightingly of the men who lived before them. This enormous block lies there, squared and ready for the builders' hands—a solid mass fourteen feet by seventeen, and but a few inches less than seventy feet long! Two buggies could be driven abreast of each other, on its surface, from one end of it to the other, and leave room enough for a man or two to walk on either side.

One might swear that all the John Smiths and

George Wilkinsons, and all the other pitiful nobodies between Kingdom Come and Baalbec would inscribe their poor little names upon the walls of Baalbec's magnificent ruins, and would add the town, the county, and the state they came from—and, swearing thus, be infallibly correct. It is a pity some great ruin does not fall in and flatten out some of these reptiles, and scare their kind out of ever giving their names to fame upon any walls or monuments again, forever.

Properly, with the sorry relics we bestrode, it was a three days' journey to Damascus. It was necessary that we should do it in less than two. It was necessary because our three pilgrims would not travel on the Sabbath day. We were all perfectly willing to keep the Sabbath day, but there are times when to keep the *letter* of a sacred law whose spirit is righteous, becomes a sin, and this was a case in point. We pleaded for the tired, ill-treated horses, and tried to show that their faithful service deserved kindness in return, and their hard lot compassion. But when did ever self-righteousness know the sentiment of pity? What were a few long hours added to the hardships of some overtaxed brutes when weighed against the peril of those human souls? It was not the most promising party to travel with and hope to gain a higher veneration for religion through the example of its devotees. We said the Saviour, who pitied dumb beasts and taught that the ox must be rescued from the mire even on the Sabbath day, would not have counseled a forced march like this. We said the "long trip" was exhausting and there-

171

fore dangerous in the blistering heats of summer, even when the ordinary days' stages were traversed, and if we persisted in this hard march, some of us might be stricken down with the fevers of the country in consequence of it. Nothing could move the pilgrims. They *must* press on. Men might die, horses might die, but they must enter upon holy soil next week, with no Sabbath-breaking stain upon them. Thus they were willing to commit a sin against the spirit of religious law, in order that they might preserve the letter of it. It was not worth while to tell them "the letter kills." I am talking now about personal friends; men whom I like; men who are good citizens; who are honorable, upright, conscientious: but whose idea of the Saviour's religion seems to me distorted. They lecture our shortcomings unsparingly, and every night they call us together and read to us chapters from the Testament that are full of gentleness, of charity, and of tender mercy; and then all the next day they stick to their saddles clear up to the summits of these rugged mountains, and clear down again. Apply the Testament's gentleness, and charity, and tender mercy to a toiling, worn, and weary horse? Nonsense—these are for God's human creatures, not His dumb ones. What the pilgrims choose to do, respect for their almost sacred character demands that I should allow to pass—but I would so like to catch any other member of the party riding his horse up one of these exhausting hills once!

We have given the pilgrims a good many examples that might benefit them, but it is virtue thrown away. They have never heard a cross word out of our lips toward each other—but *they* have quarreled once or twice. We love to hear them at it, after they have been lecturing us. The very first thing they did, coming ashore at Beirout, was to quarrel in the boat. I have said I like them, and I do like them—but every time they read me a scorcher of a lecture I mean to talk back in print.

Not content with doubling the legitimate stages, they switched off the main road and went away out of the way to visit an absurd fountain called Figia, because Balaam's ass had drank there once. So we journeyed on, through the terrible hills and deserts and the roasting sun, and then far into the night, seeking the honored pool of Balaam's ass, the patron saint of all pilgrims like us. I find no entry but this in my note-book:

Rode to-day, altogether, thirteen hours, through deserts, partly, and partly over barren, unsightly hills, and latterly through wild, rocky scenery, and camped at about eleven o'clock at night on the banks of a limpid stream, near a Syrian village. Do not know its name—do not wish to know it— want to go to bed. Two horses lame (mine and Jack's) and the others worn out. Jack and I walked three or four miles, over the hills, and led the horses. Fun—but of a mild type.

Twelve or thirteen hours in the saddle, even in a Christian land and a Christian climate, and on a good horse, is a tiresome journey; but in an oven like Syria, in a ragged spoon of a saddle that slips fore-and-aft, and "thort-ships," and every way, and on a horse that is tired and lame, and yet must be whipped and spurred with hardly a moment's cessation all day long, till the blood comes from his side, and your conscience hurts you every time you strike, if you are half a man,—it is a journey to be remembered in bitterness of spirit and execrated with emphasis for a liberal division of a man's lifetime.

## CHAPTER XVII

THE next day was an outrage upon men and horses both. It was another thirteen - hour stretch (including an hour's "nooning"). It was over the barrenest chalk-hills and through the baldest cañons that even Syria can show. The heat quivered in the air everywhere. In the cañons we almost smothered in the baking atmosphere. On high ground, the reflection from the chalk-hills was blinding. It was cruel to urge the crippled horses, but it had to be done in order to make Damascus Saturday night. We saw ancient tombs and temples of fanciful architecture carved out of the solid rock high up in the face of precipices above our heads, but we had neither time nor strength to climb up there and examine them. The terse language of my note-book will answer for the rest of this day's experiences:

Broke camp at 7 A.M., and made a ghastly trip through the Zeb Dana valley and the rough mountains—horses limping and that Arab screech-owl that does most of the singing and carries the water-skins, always a thousand miles ahead of course, and no water to drink—will he *never* die? Beautiful stream in a chasm, lined thick with pomegranate, fig, olive, and quince orchards, and nooned an hour at the celebrated Balaam's Ass Fountain of Figia, second in size in Syria, and the coldest water out of Siberia—guide-books do not say Balaam's ass ever drank

# MARK TWAIN

there — somebody been imposing on the pilgrims, maybe.
Bathed in it—Jack and I. Only a second—ice-water. It is the
principal source of the Abana River—only one-half mile down
to where it joins. Beautiful place—giant trees all around—*so*
shady and cool, if one could keep awake—vast stream gushes
straight out from under the mountain in a torrent. Over it is
a very ancient ruin, with no known history—supposed to have
been for the worship of the deity of the fountain or Balaam's
ass or somebody. Wretched nest of human vermin about the
fountain—rags, dirt, sunken cheeks, pallor of sickness, sores,
projecting bones, dull, aching misery in their eyes and ravenous
hunger speaking from every eloquent fiber and muscle from
head to foot. How they sprang upon a bone, how they crunched
the bread we gave them! Such as these to swarm about one and
watch every bite he takes with greedy looks, and swallow un-
consciously every time he swallows, as if they half fancied the
precious morsel went down their own throats—hurry up the
caravan!—I never shall enjoy a meal in this distressful country.
To think of eating three times every day under *such* circumstances for three weeks yet—it is worse punishment than riding
all day in the sun. There are sixteen starving babies from one
to six years old in the party, and their legs are no larger than
broom-handles. Left the fountain at 1 P.M. (the fountain took
us at least two hours out of our way), and reached Mohammed's
lookout perch, over Damascus, in time to get a good long look
before it was necessary to move on. Tired? Ask of the winds
that far away with fragments strewed the sea.

As the glare of day mellowed into twilight, we
looked down upon a picture which is celebrated all
over the world. I think I have read about four
hundred times that when Mohammed was a simple
camel-driver he reached this point and looked down
upon Damascus for the first time, and then made a
certain renowned remark. He said man could enter
only one paradise; he preferred to go to the one
above. So he sat down there and feasted his eyes
upon the earthly paradise of Damascus, and then

went away without entering its gates. They have erected a tower on the hill to mark the spot where he stood.

Damascus *is* beautiful from the mountain. It is beautiful even to foreigners accustomed to luxuriant vegetation, and I can easily understand how unspeakably beautiful it must be to eyes that are only used to the God-forsaken barrenness and desolation of Syria. I should think a Syrian would go wild with ecstasy when such a picture bursts upon him for the first time.

From his high perch, one sees before him and below him a wall of dreary mountains, shorn of vegetation, glaring fiercely in the sun; it fences in a level desert of yellow sand, smooth as velvet and threaded far away with fine lines that stand for roads, and dotted with creeping mites we know are camel-trains and journeying men; right in the midst of the desert is spread a billowy expanse of green foliage; and nestling in its heart sits the great white city, like an island of pearls and opals gleaming out of a sea of emeralds. This is the picture you see spread far below you, with distance to soften it, the sun to glorify it, strong contrasts to heighten the effects, and over it and about it a drowsing air of repose to spiritualize it and make it seem rather a beautiful estray from the mysterious worlds we visit in dreams than a substantial tenant of our coarse, dull globe. And when you think of the leagues of blighted, blasted, sandy, rocky, sunburnt, ugly, dreary, infamous country you have ridden over to get here, you think it is the most beautiful, beautiful picture

# MARK TWAIN

that ever human eyes rested upon in all the broad
universe! If I were to go to Damascus again, I
would camp on Mohammed's hill about a week, and
then go away. There is no need to go inside the
walls. The Prophet was wise without knowing it
when he decided not to go down into the paradise
of Damascus.

There is an honored old tradition that the immense
garden which Damascus stands in was the Garden of
Eden, and modern writers have gathered up many
chapters of evidence tending to show that it really
was the Garden of Eden, and that the rivers Pharpar and Abana are the "two rivers" that watered
Adam's Paradise. It may be so, but it is not paradise now, and one would be as happy outside of it
as he would be likely to be within. It is so crooked
and cramped and dirty that one cannot realize that
he is in the splendid city he saw from the hilltop.
The gardens are hidden by high mud-walls, and the
paradise is become a very sink of pollution and un-
comeliness. Damascus has plenty of clear, pure
water in it, though, and this is enough, of itself, to
make an Arab think it beautiful and blessed. Water
is scarce in blistered Syria. We run railways by
our large cities in America; in Syria they curve the
roads so as to make them run by the meager little
puddles they call "fountains," and which are not
found oftener on a journey than every four hours.
But the "rivers" of Pharpar and Abana of Scripture (mere creeks) run through Damascus, and so
every house and every garden have their sparkling
fountains and rivulets of water. With her forest of

178

foliage and her abundance of water, Damascus must be a wonder of wonders to the Bedouin from the deserts. Damascus is simply an oasis—that is what it is. For four thousand years its waters have not gone dry or its fertility failed. Now we can understand why the city has existed so long. It could not die. So long as its waters remain to it away out there in the midst of that howling desert, so long will Damascus live to bless the sight of the tired and thirsty wayfarer.

Though old as history itself, thou art fresh as the breath of spring, blooming as thine own rose-bud, and fragrant as thine own orange flower, O Damascus, pearl of the East!

Damascus dates back anterior to the days of Abraham, and is the oldest city in the world. It was founded by Uz, the grandson of Noah. "The early history of Damascus is shrouded in the mists of a hoary antiquity." Leave the matters written of in the first eleven chapters of the Old Testament out, and no recorded event has occurred in the world but Damascus was in existence to receive the news of it. Go back as far as you will into the vague past, there was always a Damascus. In the writings of every century for more than four thousand years, its name has been mentioned and its praises sung. To Damascus, years are only moments, decades are only flitting trifles of time. She measures time, not by days and months and years, but by the empires she has seen rise and prosper and crumble to ruin. She is a type of immortality. She saw the foundations of Baalbec, and Thebes, and Ephesus laid;

she saw these villages grow into mighty cities, and amaze the world with their grandeur—and she has lived to see them desolate, deserted, and given over to the owls and the bats. She saw the Israelitish empire exalted, and she saw it annihilated. She saw Greece rise, and flourish two thousand years, and die. In her old age she saw Rome built; she saw it overshadow the world with its power; she saw it perish. The few hundreds of years of Genoese and Venetian might and splendor were, to grave old Damascus, only a trifling scintillation hardly worth remembering. Damascus has seen all that has ever occurred on earth, and still she lives. She has looked upon the dry bones of a thousand empires, and will see the tombs of a thousand more before she dies. Though another claims the name, old Damascus is by right the Eternal City.

We reached the city gates just at sundown. They do say that one can get into any walled city of Syria, after night, for bucksheesh, except Damascus. But Damascus, with its four thousand years of respectability in the world, has many old fogy notions. There are no street-lamps there, and the law compels all who go abroad at night to carry lanterns, just as was the case in old days, when heroes and heroines of the Arabian Nights walked the streets of Damascus, or flew away toward Bagdad on enchanted carpets.

It was fairly dark a few minutes after we got within the wall, and we rode long distances through wonderfully crooked streets, eight to ten feet wide, and shut in on either side by the high mud-walls of the gardens. At last we got to where lanterns could be seen flitting about here and there, and knew we were in the midst of the curious old city. In a little narrow street, crowded with our pack-mules and with a swarm of uncouth Arabs, we alighted, and through a kind of a hole in the wall entered the hotel. We stood in a great flagged court, with flowers and citron trees about us, and a huge tank in the center that was receiving the waters of many pipes. We crossed the court and entered the rooms prepared to receive four of us. In a large marble-paved recess between the two rooms was a tank of clear, cool water, which was kept running over all the time by the streams that were pouring into it from half a dozen pipes. Nothing in this scorching, desolate land could look so refreshing as this pure water flashing in the lamplight; nothing could look so beautiful, nothing could sound so delicious as this mimic rain to ears long unaccustomed to sounds of such a nature. Our rooms were large, comfortably furnished, and even had their floors clothed with soft, cheerful-tinted carpets. It was a pleasant thing to see a carpet again, for if there is anything drearier than the tomblike, stone-paved parlors and bedrooms of Europe and Asia, I do not know what it is. They make one think of the grave all the time. A very broad, gaily capari-soned divan, some twelve or fourteen feet long, ex-tended across one side of each room, and opposite were single beds with spring mattresses. There were great looking-glasses and marble-top tables. All this luxury was as grateful to systems and senses worn out with an exhausting day's travel, as it was unexpected—for one cannot tell what to expect in a Turkish city of even a quarter of a million inhabitants.

I do not know, but I think they used that tank between the rooms to draw drinking-water from; that did not occur to me, however, until I had dipped my baking head far down into its cool depths. I thought of it then, and, superb as the bath was, I was sorry I had taken it, and was about to go and explain to the landlord. But a finely curled and scented poodle dog frisked up and nipped the calf of my leg just then, and before I had time to think I had soused him to the bottom of the tank, and when I saw a servant coming with a pitcher I went off and left the pup trying to climb out and not succeeding very well. Satisfied revenge was all I needed to make me perfectly happy, and when I walked in to supper that first night in Damascus I was in that condition. We lay on those divans a long time, after supper, smoking narghilis and long-stemmed chibouks, and talking about the dreadful ride of the day, and I knew then what I had sometimes known before—that it is worth while to get tired out, because one so enjoys resting afterward.

In the morning we sent for donkeys. It is worthy of note that we had to *send* for these things. I said Damascus was an old fossil, and she is. Anywhere else we would have been assailed by a clamorous army of donkey-drivers, guides, peddlers, and beggars—but in Damascus they so hate the very sight of a foreign Christian that they want no intercourse whatever with him; only a year or two ago, his person was not always safe in Damascus streets. It is the most fanatical Mohammedan purgatory out of Arabia. Where you see one green turban of a Hadji elsewhere (the honored sign that my lord has made the pilgrimage to Mecca), I think you will see a dozen in Damascus. The Damascenes are the ugliest, wickedest looking villains we have seen. All the veiled women we had seen yet, nearly, left their eyes exposed, but numbers of these in Damascus completely hid the face under a close-drawn black veil that made the woman look like a mummy. If ever we caught an eye exposed it was quickly hidden from our contaminating Christian vision; the beggars actually passed us by without demanding bucksheesh; the merchants in the bazars did not hold up their goods and cry out eagerly, "Hey, John!" or "Look this, Howajji!" On the contrary, they only scowled at us and said never a word.

The narrow streets swarmed like a hive with men and women in strange Oriental costumes, and our small donkeys knocked them right and left as we plowed through them, urged on by the merciless donkey-boys. These persecutors run after the animals, shouting and goading them for hours together; they keep the donkey in a gallop always, yet never get tired themselves or fall behind. The donkeys fell down and spilt us over their heads occasionally, but there was nothing for it but to mount and hurry on again. We were banged against sharp corners, loaded porters, camels, and citizens generally; and we were so taken up with looking out for collisions and casualties that we had no chance to look about us at all. We rode half through the city and through the famous "street which is called Straight" without seeing anything, hardly. Our bones were nearly knocked out of joint, we were wild with excitement, and our sides ached with the jolting we had suffered. I do not like riding in the Damascus street-cars.

We were on our way to the reputed houses of Judas and Ananias. About eighteen or nineteen hundred years ago, Saul, a native of Tarsus, was particularly bitter against the new sect called Christians, and he left Jerusalem and started across the country on a furious crusade against them. He went forth "breathing threatenings and slaughter against the disciples of the Lord."

And as he journeyed, he came near Damascus, and suddenly there shined round about him a light from heaven:

And he fell to the earth and heard a voice saying unto him, Saul, Saul, why persecutest thou me?

And when he knew that it was Jesus that spoke to him he trembled, and was astonished, and said, Lord, what wilt thou have me to do?

He was told to arise and go into the ancient city and one would tell him what to do. In the mean time his soldiers stood speechless and awe-stricken, for they heard the mysterious voice but saw no man. Saul rose up and found that that fierce supernatural light had destroyed his sight, and he was blind, so "they led him by the hand and brought him to Damascus." He was converted.

Paul lay three days blind, in the house of Judas, and during that time he neither ate nor drank.

# THE INNOCENTS ABROAD

There came a voice to a citizen of Damascus, named Ananias, saying, "Arise, and go into the street which is called Straight, and inquire at the house of Judas, for one called Saul, of Tarsus; for behold, he prayeth."

Ananias did not wish to go at first, for he had heard of Saul before, and he had his doubts about that style of a "chosen vessel" to preach the gospel of peace. However, in obedience to orders, he went into the "street called Straight" (how he ever found his way into it, and after he did, how he ever found his way out of it again, are mysteries only to be accounted for by the fact that he was acting under Divine inspiration). He found Paul and restored him, and ordained him a preacher; and from this old house we had hunted up in the street which is miscalled Straight, he had started out on that bold missionary career which he prosecuted till his death.

It was not the house of the disciple who sold the Master for thirty pieces of silver. I make this explanation in justice to Judas, who was a far different sort of man from the person just referred to. A very different style of man, and lived in a very good house. It is a pity we do not know more about him.

I have given, in the above paragraphs, some more information for people who will not read Bible history until they are defrauded into it by some such method as this. I hope that no friend of progress and education will obstruct or interfere with my peculiar mission.

The street called Straight is straighter than a corkscrew, but not as straight as a rainbow. St. Luke

is careful not to commit himself; he does not say it
is the street which *is* straight, but the "street which
is *called* Straight." It is a fine piece of irony; it
is the only facetious remark in the Bible, I believe.
We traversed the street called Straight a good way,
and then turned off and called at the reputed house
of Ananias. There is small question that a part of
the original house is there still; it is an old room
twelve or fifteen feet underground, and its masonry
is evidently ancient. If Ananias did not live there
in St. Paul's time, somebody else did, which is just
as well. I took a drink out of Ananias's well, and,
singularly enough, the water was just as fresh as if
the well had been dug yesterday.

We went out toward the north end of the city to
see the place where the disciples let Paul down over
the Damascus wall at dead of night—for he preached
Christ so fearlessly in Damascus that the people
sought to kill him, just as they would to-day for the
same offense, and he had to escape and flee to
Jerusalem.

Then we called at the tomb of Mohammed's children and at a tomb which purported to be that of St.
George who killed the dragon, and so on out to the
hollow place under a rock where Paul hid during his
flight till his pursuers gave him up; and up to the
mausoleum of the five thousand Christians who were
massacred in Damascus in 1861 by the Turks. They
say those narrow streets ran blood for several days,
and that men, women, and children were butchered
indiscriminately and left to rot by hundreds all
through the Christian quarter; they say, further,

that the stench was dreadful. All the Christians who could get away fled from the city, and the Mohammedans would not defile their hands by burying the "infidel dogs." The thirst for blood extended to the high lands of Hermon and Anti-Lebanon, and in a short time twenty-five thousand more Christians were massacred and their possessions laid waste. How they hate a Christian in Damascus!—and pretty much all over Turkeydom as well. And how they will pay for it when Russia turns her guns upon them again!

It is soothing to the heart to abuse England and France for interposing to save the Ottoman Empire from the destruction it has so richly deserved for a thousand years. It hurts my vanity to see these pagans refuse to eat of food that has been cooked for us; or to eat from a dish we have eaten from; or to drink from a goatskin which we have polluted with our Christian lips, except by filtering the water through a rag which they put over the mouth of it or through a sponge! I never disliked a Chinaman as I do these degraded Turks and Arabs, and, when Russia is ready to war with them again, I hope England and France will not find it good breeding or good judgment to interfere.

In Damascus they think there are no such rivers in all the world as their little Abana and Pharpar. The Damascenes have always thought that way. In II Kings, chapter v, Naaman boasts extravagantly about them. That was three thousand years ago. He says: "Are not Abana and Pharpar, rivers of Damascus, better than all the waters of Israel? May

I not wash in them and be clean?" But some of my readers have forgotten who Naaman was, long ago. Naaman was the commander of the Syrian armies. He was the favorite of the king and lived in great state. "He was a mighty man of valor, but he was a leper." Strangely enough, the house they point out to you now as his has been turned into a leper hospital, and the inmates expose their horrid deformities and hold up their hands and beg for bucksheesh when a stranger enters.

One cannot appreciate the horror of this disease until he looks upon it in all its ghastliness in Naaman's ancient dwelling in Damascus. Bones all twisted out of shape, great knots protruding from face and body, joints decaying and dropping away —horrible!

## CHAPTER XVIII

THE last twenty-four hours we stayed in Damascus I lay prostrate with a violent attack of cholera, or cholera morbus, and therefore had a good chance and a good excuse to lie there on that wide divan and take an honest rest. I had nothing to do but listen to the pattering of the fountains and take medicine and throw it up again. It was dangerous recreation, but it was pleasanter than traveling in Syria. I had plenty of snow from Mount Hermon, and, as it would not stay on my stomach, there was nothing to interfere with my eating it—there was always room for more. I enjoyed myself very well. Syrian travel has its interesting features, like travel in any other part of the world, and yet to break your leg or have the cholera adds a welcome variety to it.

We left Damascus at noon and rode across the plain a couple of hours, and then the party stopped awhile in the shade of some fig trees to give me a chance to rest. It was the hottest day we had seen yet—the sun-flames shot down like the shafts of fire that stream out before a blowpipe; the rays seemed to fall in a steady deluge on the head and pass downward like rain from a roof. I imagined I could distinguish between the floods of rays—I thought I

could tell when each flood struck my head, when it
reached my shoulders, and when the next one came.
It was terrible. All the desert glared so fiercely
that my eyes were swimming in tears all the time.
The boys had white umbrellas heavily lined with
dark green. They were a priceless blessing. I
thanked fortune that I had one, too, notwithstanding
it was packed up with the baggage and was ten miles
ahead. It is madness to travel in Syria without an
umbrella. They told me in Beirout (these people
who always gorge you with advice) that it was madness to travel in Syria without an umbrella. It was
on this account that I got one.

But, honestly, I think an umbrella is a nuisance
anywhere when its business is to keep the sun off.
No Arab wears a brim to his fez, or uses an umbrella,
or anything to shade his eyes or his face, and he always looks comfortable and proper in the sun. But
of all the ridiculous sights I ever have seen, our
party of eight is the most so—they do cut such an
outlandish figure. They travel single file; they all
wear the endless white rag of Constantinople wrapped
round and round their hats and dangling down their
backs; they all wear thick green spectacles, with
side-glasses to them; they all hold white umbrellas,
lined with green, over their heads; without excep-
tion their stirrups are too short—they are the very
worst gang of horsemen on earth; their animals to
a horse trot fearfully hard—and when they get
strung out one after the other, glaring straight ahead
and breathless; bouncing high and out of turn, all
along the line; knees well up and stiff, elbows flap-

OUR PARTY OF EIGHT

ping like a rooster's that is going to crow, and the long file of umbrellas popping convulsively up and down—when one sees this outrageous picture exposed to the light of day, he is amazed that the gods don't get out their thunderbolts and destroy them off the face of the earth! I do—I wonder at it. I wouldn't let any such caravan go through a country of mine.

And when the sun drops below the horizon and the boys close their umbrellas and put them under their arms, it is only a variation of the picture, not a modification of its absurdity.

But maybe you cannot see the wild extravagance of my panorama. You could if you were here. Here, you feel all the time just as if you were living about the year 1200 before Christ—or back to the patriarchs—or forward to the New Era. The scenery of the Bible is about you—the customs of the patriarchs are around you—the same people, in the same flowing robes, and in sandals, cross your path—the same long trains of stately camels go and come—the same impressive religious solemnity and silence rest upon the desert and the mountains that were upon them in the remote ages of antiquity, and behold, intruding upon a scene like this, comes this fantastic mob of green-spectacled Yanks, with their flapping elbows and bobbing umbrellas! It is Daniel in the lion's den with a green cotton umbrella under his arm, all over again.

My umbrella is with the baggage, and so are my green spectacles—and there they shall stay. I will not use them. I will show some respect for the eternal fitness of things. It will be bad enough to get sunstruck, without looking ridiculous into the bargain. If I fall, let me fall bearing about me the semblance of a Christian, at least.

Three or four hours out from Damascus we passed the spot where Saul was so abruptly converted, and from this place we looked back over the scorching desert, and had our last glimpse of beautiful Damascus, decked in its robes of shining green. After nightfall we reached our tents, just outside of the nasty Arab village of Jonesborough. Of course the real name of the place is El something or other, but the boys still refuse to recognize the Arab names or try to pronounce them. When I say that that village is of the usual style, I mean to insinuate that all Syrian villages within fifty miles of Damascus are alike—so much alike that it would require more than human intelligence to tell wherein one differed from another. A Syrian village is a hive of huts one story high (the height of a man), and as square as a dry-goods box; it is mud-plastered all over, flat roof and all, and generally whitewashed after a fashion. The same roof often extends over half the town, covering many of the *streets*, which are generally about a yard wide. When you ride through one of these villages at noonday, you first meet a melancholy dog, that looks up at you and silently begs that you won't run over him, but he does not offer to get out of the way; next you meet a young boy without any clothes on, and he holds out his hand and says "Bucksheesh!"—he don't really expect a cent, but then he learned to say that before he learned to say

mother, and now he cannot break himself of it; next
you meet a woman with a black veil drawn closely
over her face, and her bust exposed; finally, you
come to several sore-eyed children and children in
all stages of mutilation and decay; and sitting
humbly in the dust, and all fringed with filthy
rags, is a poor devil whose arms and legs are gnarled
and twisted like grape vines. These are all the people you are likely to see. The balance of the population are asleep within doors, or abroad tending
goats in the plains and on the hillsides. The village is built on some consumptive little watercourse,
and about it is a little fresh-looking vegetation. Be-
yong this charmed circle, for miles on every side,
stretches a weary desert of sand and gravel, which
produces a gray bunchy shrub like sage-brush. A
Syrian village is the sorriest sight in the world, and
its surroundings are eminently in keeping with it.

I would not have gone into this dissertation upon
Syrian villages but for the fact that Nimrod, the
Mighty Hunter of Scriptural notoriety, is buried in
Jonesborough, and I wished the public to know
about how he is located. Like Homer, he is said
to be buried in many other places, but this is the
only true and genuine place his ashes inhabit.

When the original tribes were dispersed, more than
four thousand years ago, Nimrod and a large party
traveled three or four hundred miles, and settled
where the great city of Babylon afterward stood.
Nimrod built that city. He also began to build the
famous Tower of Babel, but circumstances over
which he had no control put it out of his power to

finish it. He ran it up eight stories high, however, and two of them still stand at this day, a colossal mass of brickwork, rent down the center by earthquakes, and seared and vitrified by the lightnings of an angry God. But the vast ruin will still stand for ages, to shame the puny labors of these modern generations of men. Its huge compartments are tenanted by owls and lions, and old Nimrod lies neglected in this wretched village, far from the scene of his grand enterprise.

We left Jonesborough very early in the morning, and rode forever and forever and forever, it seemed to me, over parched deserts and rocky hills, hungry, and with no water to drink. We had drained the goatskins dry in a little while. At noon we halted before the wretched Arab town of El Yuba Dam, perched on the side of a mountain, but the dragoman said if we applied there for water we would be attacked by the whole tribe, for they did not love Christians. We had to journey on. Two hours later we reached the foot of a tall isolated mountain, which is crowned by the crumbling castle of Banias, the stateliest ruin of that kind on earth, no doubt. It is a thousand feet long and two hundred wide, all of the most symmetrical, and at the same time the most ponderous, masonry. The massive towers and bastions are more than thirty feet high, and have been sixty. From the mountain's peak its broken turrets rise above the groves of ancient oaks and olives, and look wonderfully picturesque. It is of such high antiquity that no man knows who built it or when it was built. It is utterly inaccessible except in one place, where a bridle-path winds upward among the solid rocks to the old portcullis. The horses' hoofs have bored holes in these rocks to the depth of six inches during the hundreds and hundreds of years that the castle was garrisoned. We wandered for three hours among the chambers and crypts and dungeons of the fortress, and trod where the mailed heels of many a knightly Crusader had rung, and where Phœnician heroes had walked ages before them.

We wondered how such a solid mass of masonry could be affected even by an earthquake, and could not understand what agency had made Banias a ruin; but we found the destroyer, after a while, and then our wonder was increased tenfold. Seeds had fallen in crevices in the vast walls; the seeds had sprouted; the tender, insignificant sprouts had hardened; they grew larger and larger, and by a steady, imperceptible pressure forced the great stones apart, and now are bringing sure destruction upon a giant work that has even mocked the earthquakes to scorn! Gnarled and twisted trees spring from the old walls everywhere, and beautify and overshadow the gray battlements with a wild luxuriance of foliage.

From these old towers we looked down upon a broad, far-reaching green plain, glittering with the pools and rivulets which are the sources of the sacred river Jordan. It was a grateful vision, after so much desert.

And as the evening drew near, we clambered down the mountain, through groves of the Biblical oaks of Bashan (for we were just stepping over the border and entering the long-sought Holy Land), and at its extreme foot, toward the wide valley, we entered this little execrable village of Banias and camped in a great grove of olive trees near a torrent of sparkling water whose banks are arrayed in fig trees, pomegranates, and oleanders in full leaf. Barring the proximity of the village, it is a sort of paradise.

The very first thing one feels like doing when he gets into camp, all burning up and dusty, is to hunt up a bath. We followed the stream up to where it gushes out of the mountainside, three hundred yards from the tents, and took a bath that was so icy that if I did not know this was the main source of the sacred river, I would expect harm to come of it. It was bathing at noonday in the chilly source of the Abana, "River of Damascus," that gave me the cholera, so Dr. B. said. However, it generally does give me the cholera to take a bath.

The incorrigible pilgrims have come in with their pockets full of specimens broken from the ruins. I wish this vandalism could be stopped. They broke off fragments from Noah's tomb; from the exquisite sculptures of the temples of Baalbec; from the houses of Judas and Ananias, in Damascus; from the tomb of Nimrod the Mighty Hunter in Jonesborough; from the worn Greek and Roman inscriptions set in the hoary walls of the castle of Banias; and now they have been hacking and chipping these old arches here that Jesus looked upon in the flesh. Heaven protect the Sepulcher when this tribe invades Jerusalem!

The ruins here are not very interesting. There

are the massive walls of a great square building that
was once the citadel; there are many ponderous old
arches that are so smothered with debris that they
barely project above the ground; there are heavy
walled sewers through which the crystal brook of
which Jordan is born still runs; in the hillside are
the substructions of a costly marble temple that
Herod the Great built here—patches of its handsome
mosaic floors still remain; there is a quaint old stone
bridge that was here before Herod's time, maybe;
scattered everywhere, in the paths and in the woods,
are Corinthian capitals, broken porphyry pillars, and
little fragments of sculpture; and up yonder in the
precipice where the fountain gushes out, are well-
worn Greek inscriptions over niches in the rock
where in ancient times the Greeks, and after them
the Romans, worshiped the sylvan god Pan. But
trees and bushes grow above many of these ruins
now; the miserable huts of a little crew of filthy
Arabs are perched upon the broken masonry of
antiquity, the whole place has a sleepy, stupid, rural
look about it, and one can hardly bring himself to
believe that a busy, substantially built city once
existed here, even two thousand years ago. The
place was nevertheless the scene of an event whose
effects have added page after page and volume after
volume to the world's history. For in this place
Christ stood when He said to Peter:

> Thou art Peter; and upon this rock will I build my church,
> and the gates of hell shall not prevail against it. And I will
> give unto thee the keys of the Kingdom of Heaven; and what-
> soever thou shalt bind on earth shall be bound in heaven, and
> whatsoever thou shalt loose on earth shall be loosed in heaven.

On these little sentences have been built up the mighty edifice of the Church of Rome; in them lie the authority for the imperial power of the Popes over temporal affairs, and their godlike power to curse a soul or wash it white from sin. To sustain the position of "the only true Church," which Rome claims was thus conferred upon her, she has fought and labored and struggled for many a century, and will continue to keep herself busy in the same work to the end of time. The memorable words I have quoted give to this ruined city about all the interest it possesses to people of the present day.

It seems curious enough to us to be standing on ground that was once actually pressed by the feet of the Saviour. The situation is suggestive of a reality and a tangibility that seem at variance with the vagueness and mystery and ghostliness that one naturally attaches to the character of a god. I cannot comprehend yet that I am sitting where a god has stood, and looking upon the brook and the mountains which that god looked upon, and am surrounded by dusky men and women whose ancestors saw him, and even talked with him, face to face, and carelessly, just as they would have done with any other stranger. I cannot comprehend this; the gods of my understanding have been always hidden in clouds and very far away.

This morning, during breakfast, the usual assemblage of squalid humanity sat patiently without the charmed circle of the camp and waited for such crumbs as pity might bestow upon their misery. There were old and young, brown-skinned and yellow. Some of the men were tall and stalwart (for one hardly sees anywhere such splendid-looking men as here in the East), but all the women and children looked worn and sad, and distressed with hunger. They reminded me much of Indians, did these people. They had but little clothing, but such as they had was fanciful in character and fantastic in its arrangement. Any little absurd gewgaw or gimcrack they had they disposed in such a way as to make it attract attention most readily. They sat in silence, and with tireless patience watched our every motion with that vile, uncomplaining impoliteness which is so truly Indian, and which makes a white man so nervous and uncomfortable and savage that he wants to exterminate the whole tribe.

These people about us had other peculiarities, which I have noticed in the noble red man, too: they were infested with vermin, and the dirt had caked on them till it amounted to bark.

The little children were in a pitiable condition—they all had sore eyes, and were otherwise afflicted in various ways. They say that hardly a native child in all the East is free from sore eyes, and that thousands of them go blind of one eye or both every year. I think this must be so, for I see plenty of blind people every day, and I do not remember seeing any children that hadn't sore eyes. And, would you suppose that an American mother could sit for an hour, with her child in her arms, and let a hundred flies roost upon its eyes all that time undisturbed? I see that every day. It makes my flesh creep. Yesterday we met a woman riding on a little

jackass, and she had a little child in her arms;
honestly, I thought the child had goggles on as we
approached, and I wondered how its mother could
afford so much style. But when we drew near, we
saw that the goggles were nothing but a camp-meet-
ing of flies assembled around each of the child's eyes,
and at the same time there was a detachment prospecting its nose. The flies were happy, the child
was contented, and so the mother did not interfere.

As soon as the tribe found out that we had a
doctor in our party, they began to flock in from all
quarters. Dr. B., in the charity of his nature, had
taken a child from a woman who sat near by, and
put some sort of a wash upon its diseased eyes.
That woman went off and started the whole nation,
and it was a sight to see them swarm! The lame,
the halt, the blind, the leprous—all the distempers
that are bred of indolence, dirt, and iniquity—were
represented in the congress in ten minutes, and still
they came! Every woman that had a sick baby
brought it along, and every woman that hadn't,
borrowed one. What reverent and what worshiping
looks they bent upon that dread, mysterious power,
the Doctor! They watched him take his vials out;
they watched him measure the particles of white
powder; they watched him add drops of one precious
liquid, and drops of another; they lost not the
slightest movement; their eyes were riveted upon
him with a fascination that nothing could distract.
I believe they thought he was gifted like a god.
When each individual got his portion of medicine,
his eyes were radiant with joy—notwithstanding by

nature they are a thankless and impassive race—and upon his face was written the unquestioning faith that nothing on earth could prevent the patient from getting well now.

Christ knew how to preach to these simple, superstitious, disease-tortured creatures: He healed the sick. They flocked to our poor human doctor this morning when the fame of what he had done to the sick child went abroad in the land, and they worshiped him with their eyes while they did not know as yet whether there was virtue in his simples or not. The ancestors of these—people precisely like them in color, dress, manners, customs, simplicity—flocked in vast multitudes after Christ, and when they saw Him make the afflicted whole with a word, it is no wonder they worshiped Him. No wonder His deeds were the talk of the nation. No wonder the multitude that followed Him was so great that at one time—thirty miles from here—they had to let a sick man down through the roof because no approach could be made to the door; no wonder His audiences were so great at Galilee that He had to preach from a ship removed a little distance from the shore; no wonder that even in the desert places about Bethsaida, five thousand invaded His solitude, and He had to feed them by a miracle or else see them suffer for their confiding faith and devotion; no wonder when there was a great commotion in a city in those days, one neighbor explained it to another in words to this effect: "They say that Jesus of Nazareth is come!"

Well, as I was saying, the doctor distributed

medicine as long as he had any to distribute, and his reputation is mighty in Galilee this day. Among his patients was the child of the Sheik's daughter— for even this poor, ragged handful of sores and sin has its royal Sheik—a poor old mummy that looked as if he would be more at home in a poorhouse than in the Chief Magistracy of this tribe of hopeless, shirtless, savages. The princess—I mean the Sheik's daughter—was only thirteen or fourteen years old, and had a very sweet face and a pretty one. She was the only Syrian female we have seen yet who was not so sinfully ugly that she couldn't smile after ten o'clock Saturday night without breaking the Sabbath. Her child was a hard specimen, though—there wasn't enough of it to make a pie, and the poor little thing looked so pleadingly up at all who came near it (as if it had an idea that now was its chance or never) that we were filled with compassion which was genuine and not put on.

But this last new horse I have got is trying to break his neck over the tent-ropes, and I shall have to go out and anchor him. Jericho and I have parted company. The new horse is not much to boast of, I think. One of his hind legs bends the wrong way, and the other one is as straight and stiff as a tent-pole. Most of his teeth are gone, and he is as blind as a bat. His nose has been broken at some time or other, and is arched like a culvert now. His under-lip hangs down like a camel's, and his ears are chopped off close to his head. I had some trouble at first to find a name for him, but I finally concluded to call him Baalbec, because he is such a magnificent ruin. I cannot keep from talking about my horses, because I have a very long and tedious journey before me, and they naturally occupy my thoughts about as much as matters of apparently much greater importance.

We satisfied our pilgrims by making those hard rides from Baalbec to Damascus, but Dan's horse and Jack's were so crippled we had to leave them behind and get fresh animals for them. The dragoman says Jack's horse died. I swapped horses with Mohammed, the kingly-looking Egyptian who is our Ferguson's lieutenant. By Ferguson I mean our dragoman Abraham, of course. I did not take this horse on account of his personal appearance, but because I have not seen his back. I do not wish to see it. I have seen the backs of all the other horses, and found most of them covered with dreadful saddle-boils which I know have not been washed or doctored for years. The idea of riding all day long over such ghastly inquisitions of torture is sickening. My horse must be like the others, but I have at least the consolation of not knowing it to be so.

I hope that in future I may be spared any more sentimental praises of the Arab's idolatry of his horse. In boyhood I longed to be an Arab of the desert and have a beautiful mare, and call her Selim or Benjamin or Mohammed, and feed her with my own hands, and let her come into the tent, and teach her to caress me and look fondly upon me with her great tender eyes; and I wished that a stranger might come at such a time and offer me a hundred thousand dollars for her, so that I could do like the other Arabs—hesitate, yearn for the money, but, overcome by my love for my mare, at last say, "Part with thee, my beautiful one! Never with my life! Away, tempter, I scorn thy gold!" and then bound into the saddle and speed over the desert like the wind!

But I recall those aspirations. If these Arabs be like the other Arabs, their love for their beautiful mares is a fraud. These of my acquaintance have no love for their horses, no sentiment of pity for them, and no knowledge of how to treat them or care for them. The Syrian saddle-blanket is a quilted mattress two or three inches thick. It is never removed from the horse, day or night. It gets full of dirt and hair, and becomes soaked with sweat. It is bound to breed sores. These pirates never think of washing a horse's back. They do not shelter the horses in the tents, either; they must stay out and take the weather as it comes. Look at poor cropped and dilapidated Baalbec, and weep for the sentiment that has been wasted upon the Selims of romance.

# CHAPTER XIX

ABOUT an hour's ride over a rough, rocky road, half flooded with water, and through a forest of oaks of Bashan, brought us to Dan.

From a little mound here in the plain issues a broad stream of limpid water and forms a large shallow pool, and then rushes furiously onward, augmented in volume. This puddle is an important source of the Jordan. Its banks, and those of the brook, are respectably adorned with blooming oleanders, but the unutterable beauty of the spot will not throw a well-balanced man into convulsions, as the Syrian books of travel would lead one to suppose.

From the spot I am speaking of, a cannon-ball would carry beyond the confines of Holy Land and light upon profane ground three miles away. We were only one little hour's travel within the borders of Holy Land—we had hardly begun to appreciate yet that we were standing upon any different sort of earth than that we had always been used to, and yet see how the historic names began already to cluster! Dan—Bashan—Lake Huleh—the Sources of Jordan—the Sea of Galilee. They were all in sight but the last, and it was not far away. The little township of Bashan was once the kingdom so famous in Scripture for its bulls and its oaks. Lake Huleh is the Biblical "Waters of Merom." Dan was the northern and Beersheba the southern limit of Palestine—hence the expression "from Dan to Beersheba." It is equivalent to our phrases "from Maine to Texas"—"from Baltimore to San Francisco." Our expression and that of the Israelites both mean the same—great distance. With their slow camels and asses, it was about a seven days' journey from Dan to Beersheba—say a hundred and fifty or sixty miles—it was the entire length of their country, and was not to be undertaken without great preparation and much ceremony. When the prodigal traveled to "a far country," it is not likely that he went more than eighty or ninety miles. Palestine is only from forty to sixty miles wide. The state of Missouri could be split into three Palestines, and there would then be enough material left for part of another—possibly a whole one. From Baltimore to San Francisco is several thousand miles, but it will be only a seven days' journey in the cars when I am two or three years older.[1] If I live I shall necessarily have to go across the continent every now and then in those cars, but one journey from Dan to Beersheba will be sufficient, no doubt. It must be the most trying of the two. Therefore, if we chance to discover that from Dan to Beersheba seemed a mighty stretch of country to the Israelites, let us not be airy with them, but reflect that it *was* and *is* a mighty stretch when one cannot traverse it by rail.

[1] The railroad has been completed since the above was written.

# THE INNOCENTS ABROAD

The small mound I have mentioned a while ago was once occupied by the Phœnician city of Laish. A party of filibusters from Zorah and Eshcol captured the place, and lived there in a free and easy way, worshiping gods of their own manufacture and stealing idols from their neighbors whenever they wore their own out. Jeroboam set up a golden calf here to fascinate his people and keep them from making dangerous trips to Jerusalem to worship, which might result in a return to their rightful allegiance. With all respect for those ancient Israelites, I cannot overlook the fact that they were not always virtuous enough to withstand the seductions of a golden calf. Human nature has not changed much since then.

Some forty centuries ago the city of Sodom was pillaged by the Arab princes of Mesopotamia, and among other prisoners they seized upon the patriarch Lot and brought him here on their way to their own possessions. They brought him to Dan, and father Abraham, who was pursuing them, crept softly in at dead of night, among the whispering oleanders and under the shadows of the stately oaks, and fell upon the slumbering victors and startled them from their dreams with the clash of steel. He recaptured Lot and all the other plunder.

We moved on. We were now in a green valley, five or six miles wide and fifteen long. The streams which are called the sources of the Jordan flow through it to Lake Huleh, a shallow pond three miles in diameter, and from the southern extremity of the lake the concentrated Jordan flows out. The lake is surrounded by a broad marsh, grown with reeds. Between the marsh and the mountains which wall the valley is a respectable strip of fertile land; at the end of the valley, toward Dan, as much as half the land is solid and fertile, and watered by Jordan's sources. There is enough of it to make a farm. It almost warrants the enthusiasm of the spies of that rabble of adventurers who captured Dan. They said: "We have seen the land, and behold it is very good. . . . A place where there is no want of anything that is in the earth."

Their enthusiasm was at least warranted by the fact that they had never seen a country as good as this. There was enough of it for the ample support of their six hundred men and their families, too.

When we got fairly down on the level part of the Danite farm, we came to places where we could actually run our horses. It was a notable circumstance.

We had been painfully clambering over interminable hills and rocks for days together, and when we suddenly came upon this astonishing piece of rockless plain, every man drove the spurs into his horse and sped away with a velocity he could surely enjoy to the utmost, but could never hope to comprehend in Syria.

Here were evidences of cultivation—a rare sight in this country—an acre or two of rich soil studded with last year's dead corn-stalks of the thickness of your thumb and very wide apart. But in such a land it was a thrilling spectacle. Close to it was a stream, and on its banks a great herd of curious-

looking Syrian goats and sheep were gratefully eating gravel. I do not state this as a petrified fact—
I only *suppose* they were eating gravel, because there did not appear to be anything else for them to eat.
The shepherds that tended them were the very pictures of Joseph and his brethren, I have no doubt in the world. They were tall, muscular, and very dark-skinned Bedouins, with inky black beards.
They had firm lips, unquailing eyes, and a kingly stateliness of bearing. They wore the parti-colored half bonnet, half hood, with fringed ends falling upon their shoulders, and the full, flowing robe barred with broad black stripes—the dress one sees in all pictures of the swarthy sons of the desert.
These chaps would sell their younger brothers if they had a chance, I think. They have the manners, the customs, the dress, the occupation, and the loose principles of the ancient stock. [They attacked our camp last night, and I bear them no good will.]
They had with them the pygmy jackasses one sees all over Syria and remembers in all pictures of the "Flight into Egypt," where Mary and the Young Child are riding and Joseph is walking alongside, towering high above the little donkey's shoulders.

But, really, here the man rides and carries the child, as a general thing, and the woman walks.
The customs have not changed since Joseph's time.
We would not have in our houses a picture representing Joseph riding and Mary walking; we would see profanation in it, but a Syrian Christian would not. I know that hereafter the picture I first spoke of will look odd to me.

# MARK TWAIN

We could not stop to rest two or three hours out from our camp, of course, albeit the brook was beside us. So we went on an hour longer. We saw water then, but nowhere in all the waste around was there a foot of shade, and we were scorching to death. "Like unto the shadow of a great rock in a weary land." Nothing in the Bible is more beautiful than that, and surely there is no place we have wandered to that is able to give it such touching expression as this blistering, naked, treeless land.

Here you do not stop just when you please, but when you can. We found water, but no shade. We traveled on and found a tree at last, but no water. We rested and lunched, and came on to this place, Ain Mellahah (the boys call it Baldwinsville). It was a very short day's run, but the dragoman does not want to go further, and has invented a plausible lie about the country beyond this being infested by ferocious Arabs, who would make sleeping in their midst a dangerous pastime. Well, they ought to be dangerous. They carry a rusty old weather-beaten flintlock gun, with a barrel that is longer than themselves; it has no sights on it; it will not carry farther than a brickbat, and is not half so certain. And the great sash they wear in many a fold around their waists has two or three absurd old horse-pistols in it that are rusty from eternal disuse—weapons that would hang fire just about long enough for you to walk out of range, and then burst and blow the Arab's head off. Exceedingly dangerous these sons of the desert are.

It used to make my blood run cold to read Wm.

C. Grimes's hairbreadth escapes from Bedouins, but I think I could read them now without a tremor. He never said he was attacked by Bedouins, I believe, or was ever treated uncivilly, but then in about every other chapter he discovered them approaching, anyhow, and he had a blood-curdling fashion of working up the peril; and of wondering how his relations far away would feel could they see their poor wandering boy, with his weary feet and his dim eyes, in such fearful danger; and of thinking for the last time of the old homestead, and the dear old church, and the cow, and those things; and of finally straightening his form to its utmost height in the saddle, drawing his trusty revolver, and then dashing the spurs into "Mohammed" and sweeping down upon the ferocious enemy determined to sell his life as dearly as possible. True, the Bedouins never did anything to him when he arrived, and never had any intention of doing anything to him in the first place, and wondered what in the mischief he was making all that to-do about; but still I could not divest myself of the idea, somehow, that a frightful peril had been escaped through that man's daredevil bravery, and so I never could read about Wm. C. Grimes's Bedouins and sleep comfortably afterward. But I believe the Bedouins to be a fraud, now. I have seen the monster, and I can outrun him. I shall never be afraid of his daring to stand behind his own gun and discharge it.

About fifteen hundred years before Christ, this camp-ground of ours by the Waters of Merom was the scene of one of Joshua's exterminating battles.

Jabin, King of Hazor (up yonder above Dan), called all the sheiks about him together, with their hosts, to make ready for Israel's terrible General who was approaching.

> And when all these Kings were met together, they came and pitched together by the Waters of Merom, to fight against Israel.
>
> And they went out, they and all their hosts with them, much people, even as the sand that is upon the seashore for multitude [etc.].

But Joshua fell upon them and utterly destroyed them, root and branch. That was his usual policy in war. He never left any chance for newspaper controversies about who won the battle. He made this valley, so quiet now, a reeking slaughter-pen.

Somewhere in this part of the country—I do not know exactly where—Israel fought another bloody battle a hundred years later. Deborah, the prophetess, told Barak to take ten thousand men and sally forth against another King Jabin who had been doing something. Barak came down from Mount Tabor, twenty or twenty-five miles from here, and gave battle to Jabin's forces, who were in command of Sisera. Barak won the fight, and while he was making the victory complete by the usual method of exterminating the remnant of the defeated host, Sisera fled away on foot, and when he was nearly exhausted by fatigue and thirst, one Jael, a woman he seems to have been acquainted with, invited him to come into her tent and rest himself. The weary soldier acceded readily enough, and Jael put him to bed. He said he was very thirsty, and asked his generous preserver to get him a cup of water. She

brought him some milk, and he drank of it gratefully and lay down again, to forget in pleasant
dreams his lost battle and his humbled pride.
Presently when he was asleep she came softly in
with a hammer and drove a hideous tent-pin down
through his brain!

"For he was fast asleep and weary. So he died."
Such is the touching language of the Bible. "The
Song of Deborah and Barak" praises Jael for the
memorable service she had rendered, in an exultant
strain:

> Blessed above women shall Jael the wife of Heber the Kenite
> be, blessed shall she be above women in the tent.
> He asked for water, and she gave him milk; she brought
> forth butter in a lordly dish.
> She put her hand to the nail, and her right hand to the work-
> man's hammer; and with the hammer she smote Sisera, she smote
> off his head when she had pierced and stricken through his tem-
> ples.
> At her feet he bowed, he fell, he lay down: at her feet he
> bowed, he fell; where he bowed, there he fell down dead.

Stirring scenes like these occur in this valley no
more. There is not a solitary village throughout its
whole extent—not for thirty miles in either direction. There are two or three small clusters of
Bedouin tents, but not a single permanent habitation. One may ride ten miles, hereabouts, and not
see ten human beings.

To this region one of the prophecies is applied:

> I will bring the land into desolation; and your enemies which
> dwell therein shall be astonished at it. And I will scatter you
> among the heathen, and I will draw out a sword after you; and
> your land shall be desolate and your cities waste.

# MARK TWAIN

No man can stand here by deserted Ain Mellahah and say the prophecy has not been fulfilled.

In a verse from the Bible which I have quoted above, occurs the phrase "all these kings." It attracted my attention in a moment, because it carries to my mind such a vastly different significance from what it always did at home. I can see easily enough that if I wish to profit by this tour and come to a correct understanding of the matters of interest connected with it, I must studiously and faithfully unlearn a great many things I have somehow absorbed concerning Palestine. I must begin a system of reduction. Like my grapes which the spies bore out of the Promised Land, I have got everything in Palestine on too large a scale. Some of my ideas were wild enough. The word Palestine always brought to my mind a vague suggestion of a country as large as the United States. I do not know why, but such was the case. I suppose it was because I could not conceive of a small country having so large a history. I think I was a little surprised to find that the grand Sultan of Turkey was a man of only ordinary size. I must try to reduce my ideas of Palestine to a more reasonable shape. One gets large impressions in boyhood, sometimes, which he has to fight against all his life. "All these kings." When I used to read that in Sunday-school, it suggested to me the several kings of such countries as England, France, Spain, Germany, Russia, etc., arrayed in splendid robes ablaze with jewels, marching in grave procession, with scepters of gold in their hands and flashing crowns upon their heads. But here in Ain Mellahah, after coming through Syria, and after giving serious study to the character and customs of the country, the phrase "all these kings" loses its grandeur. It suggests only a parcel of petty chiefs—ill-clad and ill-conditioned savages much like our Indians, who lived in full sight of each other and whose "kingdoms" were large when they were five miles square and contained two thousand souls. The combined monarchies of the thirty "kings" destroyed by Joshua on one of his famous campaigns, only covered an area about equal to four of our counties of ordinary size. The poor old sheik we saw at Cesarea Philippi, with his ragged band of a hundred followers, would have been called a "king" in those ancient times.

It is seven in the morning, and as we are in the country, the grass ought to be sparkling with dew, the flowers enriching the air with their fragrance, and the birds singing in the trees. But, alas! there is no dew here, nor flowers, nor birds, nor trees. There is a plain and an unshaded lake, and beyond them some barren mountains. The tents are tumbling, the Arabs are quarreling like dogs and cats, as usual, the camp-ground is strewn with packages and bundles, the labor of packing them upon the backs of the mules is progressing with great activity, the horses are saddled, the umbrellas are out, and in ten minutes we shall mount and the long procession will move again. The white city of the Mellahah, resurrected for a moment out of the dead centuries, will have disappeared again and left no sign.

# CHAPTER XX

WE traversed some miles of desolate country whose soil is rich enough, but is given over wholly to weeds—a silent, mournful expanse, wherein we saw only three persons—Arabs, with nothing on but a long coarse shirt like the "tow-linen" shirts which used to form the only summer garment of little negro boys on Southern plantations. Shepherds they were, and they charmed their flocks with the traditional shepherd's pipe—a reed instrument that made music as exquisitely infernal as these same Arabs create when they sing.

In their pipes lingered no echo of the wonderful music the shepherd forefathers heard in the Plains of Bethlehem what time the angels sang "Peace on earth, good will to men."

Part of the ground we came over was not ground at all, but rocks—cream-colored rocks, worn smooth, as if by water; with seldom an edge or a corner on them, but scooped out, honeycombed, bored out with eye-holes, and thus wrought into all manner of quaint shapes, among which the uncouth imitation of skulls was frequent. Over this part of the route were occasional remains of an old Roman road like the Appian Way, whose paving-stones still clung to their places with Roman tenacity.

Gray lizards, those heirs of ruin, of sepulchers and desolation, glided in and out among the rocks or lay still and sunned themselves. Where prosperity has reigned, and fallen; where glory has flamed, and gone out; where beauty has dwelt, and passed away; where gladness was, and sorrow is; where the pomp of life has been, and silence and death brood in its high places, there this reptile makes his home, and mocks at human vanity. His coat is the color of ashes; and ashes are the symbol of hopes that have perished, of aspirations that came to naught, of loves that are buried. If he could speak, he would say, Build temples: I will lord it in their ruins; build palaces: I will inhabit them; erect empires: I will inherit them; bury your beautiful: I will watch the worms at their work; and you, who stand here and moralize over me: I will crawl over *your* corpse at the last.

A few ants were in this desert place, but merely to spend the summer. They brought their provisions from Ain Mellahah—eleven miles.

Jack is not very well to-day, it is easy to see; but, boy as he is, he is too much of a man to speak of it. He exposed himself to the sun too much yesterday, but since it came of his earnest desire to learn, and to make this journey as useful as the opportunities will allow, no one seeks to discourage him by faultfinding. We missed him an hour from the camp, and then found him some distance away, by the edge of a brook, and with no umbrella to protect him from the fierce sun. If he had been used to going without his umbrella, it would have been well

enough, of course; but he was not. He was just in
the act of throwing a clod at a mud-turtle which was
sunning itself on a small log in the brook. We
said:

"Don't do that, Jack. What do you want to
harm him for? What has he done?"

"Well, then, I won't kill him, but I ought to,
because he is a fraud."

We asked him why, but he said it was no matter.
We asked him why, once or twice, as we walked
back to the camp, but he still said it was no matter.
But late at night, when he was sitting in a thoughtful mood on the bed, we asked him again and he
said:

"Well, it don't matter; I don't mind it now, but
I did not like it to-day, you know, because *I* don't
tell anything that isn't so, and I don't think the
Colonel ought to, either. But he did; he told us
at prayers in the Pilgrims' tent, last night, and he
seemed as if he was reading it out of the Bible, too,
about this country flowing with milk and honey, and
about the voice of the turtle being heard in the
land. I thought that was drawing it a little strong,
about the turtles, anyhow, but I asked Mr. Church
if it was so, and he said it was, and what Mr. Church
tells me, I believe. But I sat there and watched
that turtle nearly an hour to-day, and I almost
burned up in the sun; but I never heard him sing.
I believe I sweated a double handful of sweat—
I *know* I did—because it got in my eyes, and it
was running down over my nose all the time; and
you know my pants are tighter than anybody else's

# THE INNOCENTS ABROAD

—Paris foolishness—and the buckskin seat of them got wet with sweat, and then got dry again and began to draw up and pinch and tear loose—it was awful—but I never heard him sing. Finally I said, This is a fraud—that is what it is, it is a fraud—and if I had had any sense I might have known a cursed mud-turtle couldn't sing. And then I said, I don't wish to be hard on this fellow, and I will just give him ten minutes to commence; ten minutes—and then if he don't, down goes his building. But he *didn't* commence, you know. I had stayed there all that time, thinking maybe he might, pretty soon, because he kept on raising his head up and letting it down, and drawing the skin over his eyes for a minute and then opening them out again, as if he was trying to study up something to sing, but just as the ten minutes were up and I was all beat out and blistered, he laid his blamed head down on a knot and went fast asleep."

"It *was* a little hard, after you had waited so long."

"I should think so. I said, Well, if you won't sing, you sha'n't sleep, anyway; and if you fellows had let me alone I would have made him shin out of Galilee quicker than any turtle ever did yet. But it isn't any matter now—let it go. The skin is all off the back of my neck."

About ten in the morning we halted at Joseph's Pit. This is a ruined Khan of the Middle Ages, in one of whose side courts is a great walled and arched pit with water in it, and this pit, one tradition says, is the one Joseph's brethren cast him into. A

219

more authentic tradition, aided by the geography
of the country, places the pit in Dothan, some two
days' journey from here. However, since there are
many who believe in this present pit as the true one,
it has its interest.

It is hard to make a choice of the most beautiful
passage in a book which is so gemmed with beautiful
passages as the Bible; but it is certain that not
many things within its lids may take rank above the
exquisite story of Joseph. Who taught those ancient
writers their simplicity of language, their felicity of
expression, their pathos, and, above all, their faculty
of sinking themselves entirely out of sight of the
reader and making the narrative stand out alone and
seem to tell itself? Shakespeare is always present
when one reads his book; Macaulay is present when
we follow the march of his stately sentences; but
the Old Testament writers are hidden from view.

If the pit I have been speaking of is the right one,
a scene transpired there, long ages ago, which is
familiar to us all in pictures. The sons of Jacob
had been pasturing their flocks near there. Their
father grew uneasy at their long absence, and sent
Joseph, his favorite, to see if anything had gone
wrong with them. He traveled six or seven days'
journey; he was only seventeen years old, and, boy-
like, he toiled through that long stretch of the vilest,
rockiest, dustiest country in Asia, arrayed in the
pride of his heart, his beautiful claw-hammer coat
of many colors. Joseph was the favorite, and that
was one crime in the eyes of his brethren; he had
dreamed dreams, and interpreted them to fore-

shadow his elevation far above all his family in the far future, and that was another; he was dressed well and had doubtless displayed the harmless vanity of youth in keeping the fact prominently before his brothers.  These were crimes his elders fretted over among themselves and proposed to punish when the opportunity should offer.  When they saw him coming up from the Sea of Galilee, they recognized him and were glad.  They said, "Lo, here is this dreamer—let us kill him."  But Reuben pleaded for his life, and they spared it.  But they seized the boy, and stripped the hated coat from his back and pushed him into the pit.  *They* intended to let him die there, but Reuben intended to liberate him secretly.  However, while Reuben was away for a little while, the brethren sold Joseph to some Ishmaelitish merchants who were journeying toward Egypt.  Such is the history of the pit.  And the selfsame pit is there in that place, even to this day; and there it will remain until the next detachment of image-breakers and tomb-desecrators arrives from the *Quaker City* excursion, and they will infallibly dig it up and carry it away with them.  For behold in them is no reverence for the solemn monuments of the past, and whithersoever they go they destroy and spare not.

Joseph became rich, distinguished, powerful—as the Bible expresses it, "lord over all the land of Egypt."  Joseph was the real king, the strength, the brain of the monarchy, though Pharaoh held the title.  Joseph is one of the truly great men of the Old Testament.  And he was the noblest and the manliest, save Esau. Why shall we not say a good word for the princely Bedouin? The only crime that can be brought against him is that he was unfortunate. Why must everybody praise Joseph's great-hearted generosity to his cruel brethren, without stint of fervent language, and fling only a reluctant bone of praise to Esau for his still sublimer generosity to the brother who had wronged him? Jacob took advantage of Esau's consuming hunger to rob him of his birthright and the great honor and consideration that belonged to the position; by treachery and falsehood he robbed him of his father's blessing; he made of him a stranger in his home, and a wanderer. Yet after twenty years had passed away and Jacob met Esau and fell at his feet quaking with fear and begging piteously to be spared the punishment he knew he deserved, what did that magnificent savage do? He fell upon his neck and embraced him! When Jacob—who was incapable of comprehending nobility of character—still doubting, still fearing, insisted upon "finding grace with my lord" by the bribe of a present of cattle, what did the georgous son of the desert say?

"Nay, I have enough, my brother; keep that thou hast unto thyself!"

Esau found Jacob rich, beloved by wives and children, and traveling in state, with servants, herds of cattle and trains of camels—but he himself was still the uncourted outcast this brother had made him. After thirteen years of romantic mystery, the brethren who had wronged Joseph, came, strangers in a strange land, hungry and humble, to buy "a little food"; and being summoned to a palace, charged with crime, they beheld in its owner their wronged brother; they were trembling beggars— he, the lord of a mightly empire! What Joseph that ever lived would have thrown away such a chance to "show off"? Who stands first—outcast Esau forgiving Jacob in prosperity, or Joseph on a king's throne forgiving the ragged tremblers whose happy rascality placed him there?

Just before we came to Joseph's Pit, we had "raised" a hill, and there, a few miles before us, with not a tree or a shrub to interrupt the view, lay a vision which millions of worshipers in the far lands of the earth would give half their possessions to see—the sacred Sea of Galilee!

Therefore we tarried only a short time at the pit.

We rested the horses and ourselves, and felt for a few minutes the blessed shade of the ancient buildings. We were out of water, but the two or three scowling Arabs, with their long guns, who were idling about the place, said they had none and that there was none in the vicinity. They knew there was a little brackish water in the pit, but they venerated a place made sacred by their ancestor's imprisonment too much to be willing to see Christian dogs drink from it. But Ferguson tied rags and handkerchiefs together till he made a rope long enough to lower a vessel to the bottom, and we drank and then rode on; and in a short time we dismounted on those shores which the feet of the Saviour have made holy ground.

At noon we took a swim in the Sea of Galilee—a

blessed privilege in this roasting climate—and then lunched under a neglected old fig tree at the fountain they call Ain-et-Tin, a hundred yards from ruined Capernaum. Every rivulet that gurgles out of the rocks and sands of this part of the world is dubbed with the title of "fountain," and people familiar with the Hudson, the Great Lakes, and the Mississippi fall into transports of admiration over them, and exhaust their powers of composition in writing their praises. If all the poetry and nonsense that have been discharged upon the fountains and the bland scenery of this region were collected in a book, it would make a most valuable volume to burn.

During luncheon, the pilgrim enthusiasts of our party, who had been so light-hearted and happy ever since they touched holy ground that they did little but mutter incoherent rhapsodies, could scarcely eat, so anxious were they to "take shipping" and sail in very person upon the waters that had borne the vessels of the Apostles. Their anxiety grew and their excitement augmented with every fleeting moment, until my fears were aroused and I began to have misgivings that in their present condition they might break recklessly loose from all considerations of prudence and buy a whole fleet of ships to sail in instead of hiring a single one for an hour, as quiet folk are wont to do. I trembled to think of the ruined purses this day's performances might result in. I could not help reflecting bodingly upon the intemperate zeal with which middle-aged men are apt to surfeit themselves upon a seductive folly which they have tasted for the first time. And yet I did not feel that I had a right to be surprised at the state of things which was giving me so much concern. These men had been taught from infancy to revere, almost to worship, the holy places whereon their happy eyes were resting now. For many and many a year this very picture had visited their thoughts by day and floated through their dreams by night. To stand before it in the flesh—to see it as they saw it now—to sail upon the hallowed sea, and kiss the holy soil that compassed it about; these were aspirations they had cherished while a generation dragged its lagging seasons by and left its furrows in their faces and its frosts upon their hair. To look upon this picture, and sail upon this sea, they had forsaken home and its idols and journeyed thousands and thousands of miles, in weariness and tribulation. What wonder that the sordid lights of work-day prudence should pale before the glory of a hope like theirs in the full splendor of its fruition? Let them squander millions! I said—who speaks of money at a time like this?

In this frame of mind I followed, as fast as I could, the eager footsteps of the pilgrims, and stood upon the shore of the lake, and swelled, with hat and voice, the frantic hail they sent after the "ship" that was speeding by. It was a success. The toilers of the sea ran in and beached their bark. Joy sat upon every countenance.

"How much?—ask him how much, Ferguson!— how much to take us all—eight of us and you—to Bethsaida, yonder, and to the mouth of Jordan, and

to the place where the swine ran down into the
sea—quick!—and we want to coast around everywhere—everywhere!—all day long!—*I* could sail
a year in these waters!—and tell him we'll stop
at Magdala and finish at Tiberias!—ask him how
much! — anything — anything whatever! — tell him
we don't care what the expense is!" [I said to
myself, I knew how it would be.]

*Ferguson*—(interpreting)—"He says two napoleons—eight dollars."

One or two countenances fell. Then a pause.

"Too much!—we'll give him one!"

I never shall know how it was—I shudder yet
when I think how the place is given to miracles—
but in a single instant of time, as it seemed to me,
that ship was twenty paces from the shore, and
speeding away like a frightened thing! Eight crest-
fallen creatures stood upon the shore, and oh, to
think of it! this—this—after all that overmaster-
ing ecstasy! Oh, shameful, shameful ending, after
such unseemly boasting! It was to much like
"Ho! let me at him!" followed by a prudent "Two
of you hold him—one can hold me!"

Instantly there was wailing and gnashing of teeth
in the camp. The two napoleons were offered—
more if necessary—and pilgrims and dragoman
shouted themselves hoarse with pleadings to the
retreating boatmen to come back. But they sailed
serenely away and paid no further heed to pilgrims
who had dreamed all their lives of some day skim-
ming over the sacred waters of Galilee and listening
to its hallowed story in the whispering of its waves,

and had journeyed countless leagues to do it, and—
and then concluded that the fare was too high.
Impertinent Mohammedan Arabs, to think such
things of gentlemen of another faith.

Well, there was nothing to do but just submit and
forego the privilege of voyaging on Gennesaret, after
coming half around the globe to taste that pleasure.
There was a time, when the Saviour taught here,
that boats were plenty among the fishermen of the
coasts—but boats and fishermen both are gone
now; and old Josephus had a fleet of men-of-war in
these waters eighteen centuries ago—a hundred and
thirty bold canoes—but they, also, have passed
away and left no sign. They battle here no more
by sea, and the commercial marine of Galilee numbers only two small ships, just of a pattern with the
little skiffs the disciples knew. One was lost to us
for good—the other was miles away and far out of
hail. So we mounted the horses and rode grimly
on toward Magdala, cantering along in the edge of
the water for want of the means of passing over it.

How the pilgrims abused each other! Each said
it was the other's fault, and each in turn denied it.
No word was spoken by the sinners—even the
mildest sarcasm might have been dangerous at such
a time. Sinners that have been kept down and had
examples held up to them, and suffered frequent
lectures, and been so put upon in a moral way and
in the matter of going slow and being serious and
bottling up slang, and so crowded in regard to the
matter of being proper and always and forever
behaving, that their lives have become a burden to

them, would not lag behind pilgrims at such a time as this, and wink furtively, and be joyful, and commit other such crimes—because it would not occur to them to do it. Otherwise they would. But they did do it, though—and it did them a world of good to hear the pilgrims abuse each other, too. We took an unworthy satisfaction in seeing them fall out, now and then, because it showed that they were only poor human people like us, after all.

So we all rode down to Magdala, while the gnashing of teeth waxed and waned by turns, and harsh words troubled the holy calm of Galilee.

Lest any man think I mean to be ill-natured when I talk about our pilgrims as I have been talking, I wish to say in all sincerity that I do not. I would not listen to lectures from men I did not like and could not respect; and none of these can say I ever took their lectures unkindly, or was restive under the infliction, or failed to try to profit by what they said to me. They are better men than I am; I can say that honestly; they are good friends of mine, too—and besides, if they did not wish to be stirred up occasionally in print, why in the mischief did they travel with me? They knew me. They knew my liberal way—that I like to give and take— when it is for me to give and other people to take. When one of them threatened to leave me in Damascus when I had the cholera, he had no real idea of doing it—I know his passionate nature and the good impulses that underlie it. And did I not overhear Church, another pilgrim, say he did not care who went or who stayed, *he* would stand by me till I walked out of Damascus on my own feet or was carried out in a coffin, if it was a year? And do I not include Church every time I abuse the pilgrims —and would I be likely to speak ill-naturedly of him? I wish to stir them up and make them healthy; that is all.

We had left Capernaum behind us. It was only a shapeless ruin. It bore no semblance to a town, and had nothing about it to suggest that it had ever been a town. But all desolate and unpeopled as it was, it was illustrious ground. From it sprang that tree of Christianity whose broad arms overshadow so many distant lands to-day. After Christ was tempted of the devil in the desert, he came here and began his teachings; and during the three or four years he lived afterward, this place was his home almost altogether. He began to heal the sick, and his fame soon spread so widely that sufferers came from Syria and beyond Jordan, and even from Jerusalem, several days' journey away, to be cured of their diseases. Here he healed the centurion's servant and Peter's mother-in-law, and multitudes of the lame and the blind and persons possessed of devils; and here, also, he raised Jairus's daughter from the dead. He went into a ship with his disciples, and when they roused him from sleep in the midst of a storm, he quieted the winds and lulled the troubled sea to rest with his voice. He passed over to the other side, a few miles away, and relieved two men of devils, which passed into some swine. After his return he called Matthew from the receipt of customs, performed some cures, and created scandal

by eating with publicans and sinners. Then he went
healing and teaching through Galilee, and even
journeyed to Tyre and Sidon. He chose the twelve
disciples, and sent them abroad to preach the new
gospel. He worked miracles in Bethsaida and
Chorazin—villages two or three miles from Capernaum. It was near one of them that the miraculous
draft of fishes is supposed to have been taken, and
it was in the desert places near the other that he fed
the thousands by the miracles of the loaves and
fishes. He cursed them both, and Capernaum also,
for not repenting, after all the great works he had
done in their midst, and prophesied against them.
They are all in ruins now—which is gratifying to
the pilgrims, for, as usual, they fit the eternal words
of gods to the evanescent things of this earth;
Christ, it is more probable, referred to the *people*,
not their shabby villages of wigwams; he said it
would be sad for them at "the Day of Judgment"—
and what business have mud-hovels at the Day of
Judgment? it would not affect the prophecy in the
least—it would neither prove it nor disprove it—if
these towns were splendid cities now instead of the
almost vanished ruins they are. Christ visited Magdala, which is near by Capernaum, and he also
visited Cesarea Philippi. He went up to his old
home at Nazareth, and saw his brothers Joses, and
Judas, and James, and Simon—those persons who,
being own brothers to Jesus Christ, one would expect to hear mentioned sometimes, yet who ever saw
their names in a newspaper or heard them from a
pulpit? Who ever inquires what manner of youths

they were; and whether they slept with Jesus, played with him and romped about him; quarreled with him concerning toys and trifles; struck him in anger, not suspecting what he was? Who ever wonders what they thought when they saw him come back to Nazareth a celebrity, and looked long at his unfamiliar face to make sure, and then said, "It *is* Jesus"? Who wonders what passed in their minds when they saw this brother (who was *only* a brother to them, however much he might be to others a mysterious stranger who was a god and had stood face to face with God above the clouds) doing strange miracles with crowds of astonished people for witnesses? Who wonders if the brothers of Jesus asked him to come home with them, and said his mother and his sisters were grieved at his long absence, and would be wild with delight to see his face again? Who ever gives a thought to the sisters of Jesus at all?—yet he had sisters; and memories of them must have stolen into his mind often when he was ill treated among strangers; when he was homeless and said he had not where to lay his head; when all deserted him, even Peter, and he stood alone among his enemies.

Christ did few miracles in Nazareth, and stayed but a little while. The people said, "*This* the Son of God! Why, his father is nothing but a carpenter. We know the family. We see them every day. Are not his brothers named so and so, and his sisters so and so, and is not his mother the person they call Mary? This is absurd." He did not curse his home, but he shook its dust from his feet and went away.

Capernaum lies close to the edge of the little sea, in a small plain some five miles long and a mile or two wide, which is mildly adorned with oleanders which look all the better contrasted with the bald hills and the howling deserts which surround them, but they are not as deliriously beautiful as the books paint them. If one be calm and resolute he can look upon their comeliness and live.

One of the most astonishing things that have yet fallen under our observation is the exceedingly small portion of the earth from which sprang the now flourishing plant of Christianity. The longest journey our Saviour ever performed was from here to Jerusalem—about one hundred to one hundred and twenty miles. The next longest was from here to Sidon—say about sixty or seventy miles. Instead of being wide apart—as American appreciation of distances would naturally suggest—the places made most particularly celebrated by the presence of Christ are nearly all right here in full view, and within cannon-shot of Capernaum. Leaving out two or three short journeys of the Saviour, he spent his life, preached his gospel, and performed his miracles within a compass no larger than an ordinary county in the United States. It is as much as I can do to comprehend this stupefying fact. How it wears a man out to have to read up a hundred pages of history every two or three miles—for verily the celebrated localities of Palestine occur that close together. How wearily, how bewilderingly they swarm about your path!

In due time we reached the ancient village of Magdala.

# CHAPTER XXI

MAGDALA is not a beautiful place. It is thoroughly Syrian, and that is to say that it is thoroughly ugly, and cramped, squalid, uncomfortable, and filthy—just the style of cities that have adorned the country since Adam's time, as all writers have labored hard to prove, and have succeeded. The streets of Magdala are anywhere from three to six feet wide, and reeking with uncleanliness. The houses are from five to seven feet high, and all built upon one arbitrary plan—the ungraceful form of a dry-goods box. The sides are daubed with a smooth white plaster, and tastefully frescoed aloft and alow with disks of camel-dung placed there to dry. This gives the edifice the romantic appearance of having been riddled with cannon-balls, and imparts to it a very warlike aspect. When the artist has arranged his materials with an eye to just proportion—the small and the large flakes in alternate rows, and separated by carefully considered intervals—I know of nothing more cheerful to look upon than a spirited Syrian fresco. The flat, plastered roof is garnished by picturesque stacks of fresco materials, which, having become thoroughly dried and cured, are placed there where it will be convenient. It is used for fuel. There is no timber of any consequence in Palestine—none at all to waste upon fires—and neither are there any mines of coal. If my description has been intelligible, you will perceive, now, that a square, flat-roofed hovel, neatly frescoed, with its wall-tops gallantly bastioned and turreted with dried camel-refuse, gives to a landscape a feature that is exceedingly festive and picturesque, especially if one is careful to remember to stick in a cat wherever, about the premises, there is room for a cat to sit. There are no windows to a Syrian hut, and no chimneys. When I used to read that they let a bedridden man down through the roof of a house in Capernaum to get him into the presence of the Saviour, I generally had a three-story brick in my mind, and marveled that they did not break his neck with the strange experiment. I perceive now, however, that they might have taken him by the heels and thrown him clear over the house without discommoding him very much. Palestine is not changed any since those days, in manners, customs, architecture, or people.

As we rode into Magdala not a soul was visible. But the rings of the horses' hoofs roused the stupid population, and they all came trooping out—old men and old women, boys and girls, the blind, the crazy, and the crippled, all in ragged, soiled, and scanty raiment, and all abject beggars by nature, instinct, and education. How the vermin-tortured vagabonds did swarm! How they showed their scars and sores, and piteously pointed to their maimed and crooked limbs, and begged with their

THE INNOCENTS ABROAD

pleading eyes for charity! We had invoked a spirit
we could not lay. They hung to the horses' tails,
clung to their manes and the stirrups, closed in on
every side in scorn of dangerous hoofs—and out of
their infidel throats, with one accord, burst an
agonizing and most infernal chorus: "Howajji,
bucksheesh! howajji, bucksheesh! howajji, bucksheesh! bucksheesh! bucksheesh!" I never was
in a storm like that before.

As we paid the bucksheesh out to sore-eyed
children and brown, buxom girls with repulsively
tattooed lips and chins, we filed through the town
and by many an exquisite fresco, till we came to a
bramble-infested inclosure and a Roman-looking ruin
which had been the veritable dwelling of St. Mary
Magdalene, the friend and follower of Jesus. The
guide believed it, and so did I. I could not well do
otherwise, with the house right there before my eyes
as plain as day. The pilgrims took down portions
of the front walls for specimens, as is their honored
custom, and then we departed.

We are camped in this place, now, just within the
city walls of Tiberias. We went into the town before nightfall and looked at its people—we cared
nothing about its houses. Its people are best examined at a distance. They are particularly uncomely Jews, Arabs, and negroes. Squalor and
poverty are the pride of Tiberias. The young
women wear their dower strung upon a strong wire
that curves downward from the top of the head to
the jaw—Turkish silver coins which they have raked
together or inherited. Most of these maidens were

not wealthy, but some few had been very kindly dealt with by fortune. I saw heiresses there worth, in their own right—worth, well, I suppose I might venture to say, as much as nine dollars and a half. But such cases are rare. When you come across one of these, she naturally puts on airs. She will not ask for bucksheesh. She will not even permit of undue familiarity. She assumes a crushing dignity and goes on serenely practising with her fine-tooth comb and quoting poetry just the same as if you were not present at all. Some people cannot stand prosperity.

They say that the long-nosed, lanky, dyspeptic-looking body-snatchers, with the indescribable hats on, and a long curl dangling down in front of each ear, are the old, familiar, self-righteous Pharisees we read of in the Scriptures. Verily, they look it. Judging merely by their general style, and without other evidence, one might easily suspect that self-righteousness was their specialty.

From various authorities I have culled information concerning Tiberias. It was built by Herod Antipas, the murderer of John the Baptist, and named after the Emperor Tiberius. It is believed that it stands upon the site of what must have been, ages ago, a city of considerable architectural pretensions, judging by the fine porphyry pillars that are scattered through Tiberias and down the lake-shore southward. These were fluted once, and yet, although the stone is about as hard as iron, the flutings are almost worn away. These pillars are small, and doubtless the edifices they adorned were distin-

guished more for elegance than grandeur. This
modern town—Tiberias—is only mentioned in the
New Testament; never in the Old.

The Sanhedrim met here last, and for three hundred years Tiberias was the metropolis of the Jews
in Palestine. It is one of the four holy cities of the
Israelites, and is to them what Mecca is to the
Mohammedan and Jerusalem to the Christian. It
has been the abiding-place of many learned and
famous Jewish rabbins. They lie buried here, and
near them lie also twenty-five thousand of their
faith who traveled far to be near them while they
lived and lie with them when they died. The great
Rabbi Ben Israel spent three years here in the early
part of the third century. He is dead, now.

The celebrated Sea of Galilee is not so large a sea
as Lake Tahoe [1] by a good deal—it is just about
two-thirds as large. And when we come to speak
of beauty, this sea is no more to be compared to
Tahoe than a meridian of longitude is to a rainbow.
The dim waters of this pool cannot suggest the limpid
brilliancy of Tahoe; these low, shaven, yellow hil-
locks of rocks and sand, so devoid of perspective,
cannot suggest the grand peaks that compass Tahoe
like a wall, and whose ribbed and chasmed fronts
are clad with stately pines that seem to grow small
and smaller as they climb, till one might fancy them
reduced to weeds and shrubs far upward, where they

[1] I measure all lakes by Tahoe, partly because I am far more
familiar with it than with any other, and partly because I have
such a high admiration for it and such a world of pleasant recollections of it, that it is very nearly impossible for me to speak of
lakes and not mention it.

join the everlasting snows. Silence and solitude
brood over Tahoe; and silence and solitude brood
also over this lake of Gennesaret. But the solitude
of the one is as cheerful and fascinating as the solitude of the other is dismal and repellent.

In the early morning one watches the silent battle
of dawn and darkness upon the waters of Tahoe
with a placid interest; but when the shadows sulk
away and one by one the hidden beauties of the
shore unfold themselves in the full splendor of
noon; when the still surface is belted like a rainbow
with broad bars of blue and green and white, half
the distance from circumference to center; when, in
the lazy summer afternoon, he lies in a boat, far out
to where the dead blue of the deep water begins,
and smokes the pipe of peace and idly winks at the
distant crags and patches of snow from under his
cap-brim; when the boat drifts shoreward to the
white water, and he lolls over the gunwale and gazes
by the hour down through the crystal depths and
notes the colors of the pebbles and reviews the finny
armies gliding in procession a hundred feet below;
when at night he sees moon and stars, mountain
ridges feathered with pines, jutting white capes, bold
promontories, grand sweeps of rugged scenery
topped with bald, glimmering peaks, all magnifi-
cently pictured in the polished mirror of the lake,
in richest, softest detail, the tranquil interest that
was born with the morning deepens and deepens, by
sure degrees, till it culminates at last in resistless
fascination!

It is solitude, for birds and squirrels on the shore

and fishes in the water are all the creatures that are near to make it otherwise, but it is not the sort of solitude to make one dreary. Come to Galilee for that. If these unpeopled deserts, these rusty mounds of barrenness, that never, never, never do shake the glare from their harsh outlines, and fade and faint into vague perspective; that melancholy ruin of Capernaum; this stupid village of Tiberias, slumbering under its six funereal plumes of palms; yonder desolate declivity where the swine of the miracle ran down into the sea, and doubtless thought it was better to swallow a devil or two and get drowned into the bargain than have to live longer in such a place; this cloudless, blistering sky; this solemn, sailless, tintless lake, reposing within its rim of yellow hills and low, steep banks, and looking just as expressionless and unpoetical (when we leave its sublime history out of the question) as any metropolitan reservoir in Christendom—if these things are not food for rock me to sleep, mother, none exist, I think.

But I should not offer the evidence for the prosecution and leave the defense unheard. Wm. C. Grimes deposes as follows:

We had taken ship to go over to the other side. The sea was not more than six miles wide. Of the beauty of the scene, however, I cannot say enough, nor can I imagine where those travelers carried their eyes who have described the scenery of the lake as tame or uninteresting. The first great characteristic of it is the deep basin in which it lies. This is from three to four hundred feet deep on all sides except at the lower end, and the sharp slope of the banks, which are all of the richest green, is broken and diversified by the wâdys and watercourses which work their way down through the sides of the basin, forming

dark chasms or light sunny valleys. Near Tiberias these banks
are rocky, and ancient sepulchers open in them, with their
doors toward the water. They selected grand spots, as did
the Egyptians of old, for burial places, as if they designed that
when the voice of God should reach the sleepers they should
walk forth and open their eyes on scenes of glorious beauty.
On the east, the wild and desolate mountains contrast finely
with the deep-blue lake; and toward the north, sublime and
majestic, Hermon looks down on the sea, lifting his white crown
to heaven with the pride of a hill that has seen the departing
footsteps of a hundred generations. On the northeast shore
of the sea was a single tree, and this is the only tree of any
size visible from the water of the lake, except a few lonely palms
in the city of Tiberias, and by its solitary position attracts
more attention than would a forest. The whole appearance of
the scene is precisely what we would expect and desire the
scenery of Gennesaret to be, grand beauty, but quiet calm. The
very mountains are calm.

It is an ingeniously written description, and well
calculated to deceive. But if the paint and the rib-
bons and the flowers be stripped from it, a skeleton
will be found beneath.

So stripped, there remains a lake six miles wide
and neutral in color; with steep green banks, unre-
lieved by shrubbery; at one end bare, unsightly
rocks, with (almost invisible) holes in them of no
consequence to the picture; eastward, "wild and
desolate mountains" (low, desolate hills, he should
have said); in the north, a mountain called Hermon,
with snow on it; peculiarity of the picture, "calm-
ness"; its prominent feature, one tree.

No ingenuity could make such a picture beautiful
—to one's actual vision.

I claim the right to correct misstatements, and
have so corrected the color of the water in the above

recapitulation. The waters of Gennesaret are of an exceedingly mild blue, even from a high elevation and a distance of five miles. Close at hand (the witness was sailing on the lake), it is hardly proper to call them blue at all, much less "deep" blue. I wish to state, also, not as a correction, but as a matter of opinion, that Mount Hermon is not a striking or picturesque mountain, by any means, being too near the height of its immediate neighbors to be so. That is all. I do not object to the witness dragging a mountain forty-five miles to help the scenery under consideration, because it is entirely proper to do it, and, besides, the picture needs it.

"C. W. E." (of *Life in the Holy Land*) deposes as follows:

A beautiful sea lies unbosomed among the Galilean hills, in the midst of that land once possessed by Zebulon and Naphtali, Asher and Dan. The azure of the sky penetrates the depths of the lake, and the waters are sweet and cool. On the west, stretch broad fertile plains; on the north the rocky shores rise step by step until in the far distance tower the snowy heights of Hermon; on the east through a misty veil are seen the high plains of Perea, which stretch away in rugged mountains leading the mind by varied paths toward Jerusalem the Holy. Flowers bloom in this terrestrial paradise, once beautiful and verdant with waving trees; singing birds enchant the ear; the turtle-dove soothes with its soft note; the crested lark sends up its song toward heaven, and the grave and stately stork inspires the mind with thought, and leads it on to meditation and repose. Life here was once idyllic, charming; here were once no rich, no poor, no high, no low. It was a world of ease, simplicity, and beauty; now it is a scene of desolation and misery.

This is not an ingenious picture. It is the worst I ever saw. It describes in elaborate detail what it terms a "terrestrial paradise," and closes with the startling information that this paradise is "a scene of *desolation and misery*."

I have given two fair, average specimens of the character of the testimony offered by the majority of the writers who visit this region. One says, "Of the beauty of the scene I cannot say enough," and then proceeds to cover up with a woof of glittering sentences a thing which, when stripped for inspection, proves to be only an unobtrusive basin of water, some mountainous desolation, and one tree. The other, after a conscientious effort to build a terrestrial paradise out of the same materials, with the addition of a "grave and stately stork," spoils it all by blundering upon the ghastly truth at the last.

Nearly every book concerning Galilee and its lake describes the scenery as beautiful. No—not always so straightforward as that. Sometimes the *impression* intentionally conveyed is that it is beautiful, at the same time that the author is careful not to *say* that it is, in plain Saxon. But a careful analysis of these descriptions will show that the materials of which they are formed are not individually beautiful and cannot be wrought into combinations that are beautiful. The veneration and the affection which some of these men felt for the scenes they were speaking of heated their fancies and biased their judgment; but the pleasant falsities they wrote were full of honest sincerity, at any rate. Others wrote as they did, because they feared it would be unpopular to write otherwise. Others were hypocrites and deliberately meant to deceive. Any of them would

say in a moment, if asked, that it was *always* right
and always *best* to tell the truth.  They would say
that, at any rate, if they did not perceive the drift
of the question.

But why should not the truth be spoken of this
region?  Is the truth harmful?  Has it ever needed
to hide its face?  God made the Sea of Galilee and
its surroundings as they are.  Is it the province of
Mr. Grimes to improve upon the work?

I am sure, from the tenor of books I have read,
that many who have visited this land in years gone
by, were Presbyterians, and came seeking evidences
in support of their particular creed; they found a
Presbyterian Palestine, and they had already made
up their minds to find no other, though possibly
they did not know it, being blinded by their zeal.
Others were Baptists, seeking Baptist evidences and
a Baptist Palestine.  Others were Catholics, Metho-
dists, Episcopalians, seeking evidences indorsing their
several creeds, and a Catholic, a Methodist, an
Episcopalian Palestine.  Honest as these men's in-
tentions may have been, they were full of partialities
and prejudices, they entered the country with their
verdicts already prepared, and they could no more
write dispassionately and impartially about it than
they could about their own wives and children.
Our pilgrims have brought *their* verdicts with them.
They have shown it in their conversation ever since
we left Beirout.  I can almost tell, in set phrase,
what they will say when they see Tabor, Nazareth,
Jericho, and Jerusalem—*because I have the books
they will "smouch" their ideas from.*  These authors

write pictures and frame rhapsodies, and lesser men follow and see with the author's eyes instead of their own, and speak with his tongue. What the pilgrims said at Cesarea Philippi surprised me with its wisdom. I found it afterward in Robinson. What they said when Gennesaret burst upon their vision charmed me with its grace. I find it in Mr. Thompson's *Land and the Book*. They have spoken often, in happily worded language which never varied, of how they mean to lay their weary heads upon a stone at Bethel, as Jacob did, and close their dim eyes, and dream, perchance, of angels descending out of heaven on a ladder. It was very pretty. But I have recognized the weary head and the dim eyes, finally. They borrowed the idea—and the words —and the construction—and the punctuation—from Grimes. The pilgrims will tell of Palestine, when they get home, not as it appeared to *them*, but as it appeared to Thompson and Robinson and Grimes— with the tints varied to suit each pilgrim's creed.

Pilgrims, sinners, and Arabs are all abed, now, and the camp is still. Labor in loneliness is irksome. Since I made my last few notes, I have been sitting outside the tent for half an hour. Night is the time to see Galilee. Gennesaret under these lustrous stars has nothing repulsive about it. Gennesaret with the glittering reflections of the constellations flecking its surface, almost makes me regret that I ever saw the rude glare of the day upon it. Its history and its associations are its chiefest charm, in any eyes, and the spells they weave are feeble in the searching light of the sun. *Then*, we scarcely feel the fetters. Our

thoughts wander constantly to the practical concerns
of life, and refuse to dwell upon things that seem
vague and unreal. But when the day is done, even
the most unimpressible must yield to the dreamy influences of this tranquil starlight. The old traditions
of the place steal upon his memory and haunt his
reveries, and then his fancy clothes all sights and
sounds with the supernatural. In the lapping of the
waves upon the beach, he hears the dip of ghostly
oars; in the secret noises of the night he hears spirit
voices; in the soft sweep of the breeze, the rush of
invisible wings. Phantom ships are on the sea, the
dead of twenty centuries come forth from the tombs,
and in the dirges of the night wind the songs of old
forgotten ages find utterance again.

In the starlight, Galilee has no boundaries but the
broad compass of the heavens, and is a theater meet
for great events; meet for the birth of a religion able
to save a world; and meet for the stately Figure
appointed to stand upon its stage and proclaim its
high decrees. But in the sunlight, one says: Is it
for the deeds which were done and the words which
were spoken in this little acre of rocks and sand
eighteen centuries gone, that the bells are ringing
to-day in the remote islands of the sea and far and
wide over continents that clasp the circumference of
the huge globe?

One can comprehend it only when night has hidden
all incongruities and created a theater proper for so
grand a drama.

# CHAPTER XXII

WE took another swim in the Sea of Galilee at twilight yesterday, and another at sunrise this morning. We have not sailed, but three swims are equal to a sail, are they not? There were plenty of fish visible in the water, but we have no outside aids in this pilgrimage but *Tent Life in the Holy Land*, *The Land and the Book*, and other literature of like description—no fishing-tackle. There were no fish to be had in the village of Tiberias. True, we saw two or three vagabonds mending their nets, but never trying to catch anything with them.

We did not go to the ancient warm baths two miles below Tiberias. I had no desire in the world to go there. This seemed a little strange, and prompted me to try to discover what the cause of this unreasonable indifference was. It turned out to be simply because Pliny mentions them. I have conceived a sort of unwarrantable unfriendliness toward Pliny and St. Paul, because it seems as if I can never ferret out a place that I can have to myself. It always and eternally transpires that St. Paul has been to that place, and Pliny has "mentioned" it.

In the early morning we mounted and started. And then a weird apparition marched forth at the head of the procession—a pirate, I thought, if ever a pirate dwelt upon land. It was a tall Arab, as swarthy as an Indian, young—say thirty years of age. On his head he had closely bound a gorgeous yellow and red striped silk scarf, whose ends, lavishly fringed with tassels, hung down between his shoulders and dallied with the wind. From his neck to his knees, in ample folds, a robe swept down that was a very star-spangled banner of curved and sinuous bars of black and white. Out of his back, somewhere, apparently, the long stem of a chibouk projected, and reached far above his right shoulder. Athwart his back, diagonally, and extending high above his left shoulder, was an Arab gun of Saladin's time, that was splendid with silver plating from stock clear up to the end of its measureless stretch of barrel. About his waist was bound many and many a yard of elaborately figured but sadly tarnished stuff that came from sumptuous Persia, and among the baggy folds in front the sunbeams glinted from a formidable battery of old brass-mounted horse-pistols and the gilded hilts of bloodthirsty knives. There were holsters for more pistols appended to the wonderful stack of long-haired goatskins and Persian carpets, which the man had been taught to regard in the light of a saddle; and down among the pendulous rank of vast tassels that swung from that saddle, and clanging against the iron shovel of a stirrup that propped the warrior's knees up toward his chin, was a crooked, silver-clad simitar of such awful dimensions and such implacable expression that no man might hope to look upon it and not shudder. The fringed and bedizened prince whose privilege it

is to ride the pony and lead the elephant into a
country village is poor and naked compared to this
chaos of paraphernalia, and the happy vanity of the
one is the very poverty of satisfaction compared to
the majestic serenity, the overwhelming complacency
of the other.

"*Who* is this? *What* is this?" That was the
trembling inquiry all down the line.

"Our guard! From Galilee to the birthplace of
the Saviour, the country is infested with fierce
Bedouins, whose sole happiness it is, in this life, to
cut and stab and mangle and murder unoffending
Christians. Allah be with us!"

"Then hire a regiment! Would you send us out
among these desperate hordes, with no salvation in
our utmost need but this old turret?"

The dragoman laughed—not at the facetiousness of
the simile, for verily, that guide or that courier or
that dragoman never yet lived upon earth who had
in him the faintest appreciation of a joke, even
though that joke were so broad and so ponderous
that if it fell on him it would flatten him out like a
postage-stamp—the dragoman laughed, and then,
emboldened by some thought that was in his brain,
no doubt, proceeded to extremities and winked.

In straits like these, when a man laughs, it is encouraging; when he winks, it is positively reassuring.
He finally intimated that one guard would be sufficient to protect us, but that that one was an absolute
necessity. It was because of the moral weight his
awful panoply would have with the Bedouins. Then
I said we didn't want any guard at all. If one fan-

tastic vagabond could protect eight armed Christians and a pack of Arab servants from all harm, surely that detachment could protect themselves. He shook his head doubtfully. Then I said, just think of how it looks—think of how it would read, to self-reliant Americans, that we went sneaking through this deserted wilderness under the protection of this masquerading Arab, who would break his neck getting out of the country if a man that *was* a man ever started after him. It was a mean, low, degrading position. Why were we ever told to bring navy revolvers with us if we had to be protected at last by this infamous star-spangled scum of the desert? These appeals were vain—the dragoman only smiled and shook his head.

I rode to the front and struck up an acquaintance with King Solomon-in-all-his-glory, and got him to show me his lingering eternity of a gun. It had a rusty flintlock; it was ringed and barred and plated with silver from end to end, but it was as desperately out of the perpendicular as are the billiard cues of '49 that one finds yet in service in the ancient mining-camps of California. The muzzle was eaten by the rust of centuries into a ragged filigree-work, like the end of a burnt-out stove-pipe. I shut one eye and peered within—it was flaked with iron rust like an old steamboat-boiler. I borrowed the ponderous pistols and snapped them. They were rusty inside, too—had not been loaded for a generation. I went back, full of encouragement, and reported to the guide, and asked him to discharge this dismantled fortress. It came out, then. This fellow was a

retainer of the Sheik of Tiberias. He was a source
of Government revenue. He was to the Empire of
Tiberias what the customs are to America. The
Sheik imposed guards upon travelers and charged
them for it. It is a lucrative source of emolument,
and sometimes brings into the national treasury as
much as thirty-five or forty dollars a year.

I knew the warrior's secret now; I knew the hollow vanity of his rusty trumpery, and despised his
asinine complacency. I told on him, and with reckless daring the cavalcade rode straight ahead into
the perilous solitudes of the desert, and scorned his
frantic warnings of the mutilation and death that
hovered about them on every side.

Arrived at an elevation of twelve hundred feet
above the lake (I ought to mention that the lake lies
six hundred feet below the level of the Mediterranean—no traveler ever neglects to flourish that
fragment of news in his letters), as bald and un-
thrilling a panorama as any land can afford, perhaps,
was spread out before us. Yet it was so crowded
with historical interest, that if all the pages that have
been written about it were spread upon its surface,
they would flag it from horizon to horizon like a
pavement. Among the localities comprised in this
view, were Mount Hermon; the hills that border
Cesarea Philippi, Dan, the Sources of the Jordan
and the Waters of Merom; Tiberias; the Sea of
Galilee; Joseph's Pit; Capernaum; Bethsaida; the
supposed scenes of the Sermon on the Mount, the
feeding of the multitudes and the miraculous draft
of fishes; the declivity down which the swine ran to

# THE INNOCENTS ABROAD

the sea; the entrance and the exit of the Jordan;
Safed, "the city set upon a hill," one of the four
holy cities of the Jews, and the place where they
believe the real Messiah will appear when he comes
to redeem the world; part of the battle-field of
Hattin, where the knightly Crusaders fought their
last fight, and in a blaze of glory passed from the
stage and ended their splendid career forever;
Mount Tabor, the traditional scene of the Lord's
Transfiguration. And down toward the southeast
lay a landscape that suggested to my mind a quotation (imperfectly remembered, no doubt):

The Ephraimites, not being called upon to share in the rich
spoils of the Ammonitish war, assembled a mighty host to fight
against Jeptha, Judge of Israel; who being apprised of their
approach, gathered together the men of Israel and gave them
battle and put them to flight. To make his victory the more
secure, he stationed guards at the different fords and passages
of the Jordan, with instructions to let none pass who could not
say Shibboleth. The Ephraimites, being of a different tribe,
could not frame to pronounce the word aright, but called it
Sibboleth, which proved them enemies and cost them their
lives; wherefore forty and two thousand fell at the different
fords and passages of the Jordan that day.

We jogged along peacefully over the great caravan
route from Damascus to Jerusalem and Egypt, past
Lubia and other Syrian hamlets, perched in the
unvarying style, upon the summit of steep mounds
and hills, and fenced round about with giant cactuses
(the sign of worthless land), with prickly pears upon
them like hams, and came at last to the battle-field of
Hattin.

It is a grand, irregular plateau, and looks as if it

might have been created for a battle-field. Here
the peerless Saladin met the Christian host some
seven hundred years ago, and broke their power in
Palestine for all time to come. There had long
been a truce between the opposing forces, but according to the Guide-Book, Raynauld of Chatillon,
Lord of Kerak, broke it by plundering a Damascus
caravan, and refusing to give up either the merchants
or their goods when Saladin demanded them. This
conduct of an insolent petty chieftain stung the
Sultan to the quick, and he swore that he would
slaughter Raynauld with his own hand, no matter
how, or when, or where he found him. Both
armies prepared for war. Under the weak King of
Jerusalem was the very flower of the Christian
chivalry. He foolishly compelled them to undergo
a long, exhausting march, in the scorching sun, and
then, without water or other refreshment, ordered
them to encamp in this open plain. The splendidly
mounted masses of Moslem soldiers swept round the
north end of Gennesaret, burning and destroying as
they came, and pitched their camp in front of the
opposing lines. At dawn the terrific fight began.
Surrounded on all sides by the Sultan's swarming
battalions, the Christian Knights fought on without
a hope for their lives. They fought with desperate
valor, but to no purpose; the odds of heat and
numbers and consuming thirst were too great against
them. Toward the middle of the day the bravest
of their band cut their way through the Moslem
ranks and gained the summit of a little hill, and
there, hour after hour, they closed around the banner

of the Cross, and beat back the charging squadrons of the enemy.

But the doom of the Christian power was sealed. Sunset found Saladin Lord of Palestine, the Christian chivalry strewn in heaps upon the field, and the King of Jerusalem, the Grand Master of the Templars, and Raynauld of Chatillon, captives in the Sultan's tent. Saladin treated two of the prisoners with princely courtesy, and ordered refreshments to be set before them. When the King handed an iced sherbet to Chatillon, the Sultan said, "It is thou that givest it to him, not I." He remembered his oath, and slaughtered the hapless Knight of Chatillon with his own hand.

It was hard to realize that this silent plain had once resounded with martial music and trembled to the tramp of armed men. It was hard to people this solitude with rushing columns of cavalry, and stir its torpid pulses with the shouts of victors, the shrieks of the wounded, and the flash of banner and steel above the surging billows of war. A desolation is here that not even imagination can grace with the pomp of life and action.

We reached Tabor safely, and considerably in advance of that old iron-clad swindle of a guard. We never saw a human being on the whole route, much less lawless hordes of Bedouins. Tabor stands solitary and alone, a giant sentinel above the Plain of Esdraelon. It rises some fourteen hundred feet above the surrounding level, a green, wooded cone, symmetrical and full of grace—a prominent landmark, and one that is exceedingly pleasant to eyes

surfeited with the repulsive monotony of desert
Syria. We climbed the steep path to its summit,
through breezy glades of thorn and oak. The view
presented from its highest peak was almost beautiful.
Below, was the broad, level plain of Esdraelon,
checkered with fields like a chess-board, and full as
smooth and level, seemingly; dotted about its
borders with white, compact villages, and faintly
penciled, far and near, with the curving lines of
roads and trails. When it is robed in the fresh
verdure of spring, it must form a charming picture,
even by itself. Skirting its southern border rises
"Little Hermon," over whose summit a glimpse of
Gilboa is caught. Nain, famous for the raising of
the widow's son, and Endor, as famous for the
performances of her witch, are in view. To the
eastward lies the Valley of the Jordan and beyond
it the mountains of Gilead. Westward is Mount
Carmel. Hermon in the north—the table lands of
Bashan—Safed, the holy city, gleaming white upon
a tall spur of the mountains of Lebanon—a steel-blue
corner of the Sea of Galilee—saddle-peaked Hattin,
traditional "Mount of Beatitudes" and mute witness
of the last brave fight of the Crusading host for Holy
Cross—these fill up the picture.

To glance at the salient features of this landscape
through the picturesque framework of a ragged and
ruined stone window-arch of the time of Christ, thus
hiding from sight all that is unattractive, is to secure
to yourself a pleasure worth climbing the mountain
to enjoy. One must stand on his head to get the
best effect in a fine sunset, and set a landscape in a

bold, strong framework that is very close at hand, to bring out all its beauty.  One learns this latter truth never more to forget it, in that mimic land of enchantment, the wonderful garden of my lord the Count Pallavicini, near Genoa.  You go wandering for hours among hills and wooded glens, artfully contrived to leave the impression that Nature shaped them and not man; following winding paths and coming suddenly upon leaping cascades and rustic bridges; finding sylvan lakes where you expected them not; loitering through battered medieval castles in miniature that seem hoary with age and yet were built a dozen years ago; meditating over ancient crumbling tombs, whose marble columns were marred and broken purposely by the modern artist that made them; stumbling unawares upon toy palaces, wrought of rare and costly materials, and again upon a peasant's hut, whose dilapidated furniture would never suggest that it was made so to order; sweeping round and round in the midst of a forest on an enchanted wooden horse that is moved by some invisible agency; traversing Roman roads and passing under majestic triumphal arches; resting in quaint bowers where unseen spirits discharge jets of water on you from every possible direction, and where even the flowers you touch assail you with a shower; boating on a subterranean lake among caverns and arches royally draped with clustering stalactites, and passing out into open day upon another lake, which is bordered with sloping banks of grass and gay with patrician barges that swim at anchor in the shadow of a miniature marble temple that rises out of the clear water and glasses its white statues, its rich capitals and fluted columns in the tranquil depths.  So, from marvel to marvel you have drifted on, thinking all the time that the one last seen must be the chiefest.  And, verily, the chiefest wonder *is* reserved until the last, but you do not see it until you step ashore, and passing through a wilderness of rare flowers, collected from every corner of the earth, you stand at the door of one more mimic temple.  Right in this place the artist taxed his genius to the utmost, and fairly opened the gates of fairy-land.  You look through an unpretending pane of glass, stained yellow; the first thing you see is a mass of quivering foliage, ten short steps before you, in the midst of which is a ragged opening like a gateway—a thing that is common enough in nature, and not apt to excite suspicions of a deep human design—and above the bottom of the gateway, project, in the most careless way, a few broad tropic leaves and brilliant flowers. All of a sudden, through this bright, bold gateway, you catch a glimpse of the faintest, softest, richest picture that ever graced the dream of a dying Saint, since John saw the New Jerusalem glimmering above the clouds of Heaven.  A broad sweep of sea, flecked with careening sails; a sharp, jutting cape, and a lofty lighthouse on it; a sloping lawn behind it; beyond, a portion of the old "city of palaces," with its parks and hills and stately mansions; beyond these, a prodigious mountain, with its strong out- lines sharply cut against ocean and sky; and, over all, vagrant shreds and flakes of cloud, floating in a sea of gold. The ocean is gold, the city is gold, the meadow, the mountain, the sky—everything is golden—rich, and mellow, and dreamy as a vision of Paradise. No artist could put upon canvas its entrancing beauty, and yet, without the yellow glass, and the carefully contrived accident of a framework that cast it into enchanted distance and shut out from it all unattractive features, it was not a picture to fall into ecstasies over. Such is life, and the trail of the serpent is over us all.

There is nothing for it now but to come back to old Tabor, though the subject is tiresome enough, and I cannot stick to it for wandering off to scenes that are pleasanter to remember. I think I will skip, anyhow. There is nothing about Tabor (except we concede that it was the scene of the Transfiguration), but some gray old ruins, stacked up there in all ages of the world from the days of stout Gideon and parties that flourished thirty centuries ago to the fresh yesterday of Crusading times. It has its Greek Convent, and the coffee there is good, but never a splinter of the true cross or bone of a hallowed saint to arrest the idle thoughts of worldlings and turn them into graver channels. A Catholic church is nothing to me that has no relics.

The plain of Esdraelon—"the battle-field of the nations"—only sets one to dreaming of Joshua, and Benhadad, and Saul, and Gideon; Tamerlane, Tancred, Cœur de Lion, and Saladin; the warrior Kings of Persia, Egypt's heroes, and Napoleon—for they all fought here. If the magic of the moonlight could summon from the graves of forgotten

centuries and many lands the countless myriads that
have battled on this wide, far-reaching floor, and
array them in the thousand strange costumes of their
hundred nationalities, and send the vast host sweeping down the plain, splendid with plumes and ban-
ners and glittering lances, I could stay here an age
to see the phantom pageant. But the magic of the
moonlight is a vanity and a fraud; and whoso
putteth his trust in it shall suffer sorrow and disappointment.

Down at the foot of Tabor, and just at the edge
of the storied Plain of Esdraelon, is the insignificant
village of Deburieh, where Deborah, prophetess of
Israel, lived. It is just like Magdala.

## CHAPTER XXIII

WE descended from Mount Tabor, crossed a deep ravine, and followed a hilly, rocky road to Nazareth—distant two hours. All distances in the East are measured by hours, not miles. A good horse will walk three miles an hour over nearly any kind of a road; therefore, an hour here always stands for three miles. This method of computation is bothersome and annoying; and until one gets thoroughly accustomed to it, it carries no intelligence to his mind until he has stopped and translated the pagan hours into Christian miles, just as people do with the spoken words of a foreign language they are acquainted with, but not familiarly enough to catch the meaning in a moment. Distances traveled by human feet are also estimated by hours and minutes, though I do not know what the base of the calculation is. In Constantinople you ask, "How far is it to the Consulate?" and they answer, "About ten minutes." "How far is it to the Lloyds' Agency?" "Quarter of an hour." "How far is it to the lower bridge?" "Four minutes." I cannot be positive about it, but I think that there, when a man orders a pair of pantaloons, he says he wants them a quarter of a minute in the legs and nine seconds around the waist.

MARK TWAIN

Two hours from Tabor to Nazareth—and as it was an uncommonly narrow, crooked trail, we necessarily met all the camel-trains and jackass-caravans between Jericho and Jacksonville in that particular place and nowhere else. The donkeys do not matter so much, because they are so small that you can jump your horse over them if he is an animal of spirit, but a camel is not jumpable. A camel is as tall as any ordinary dwelling-house in Syria—which is to say a camel is from one to two, and sometimes nearly three feet taller than a good-sized man. In this part of the country his load is oftenest in the shape of colossal sacks—one on each side. He and his cargo take up as much room as a carriage. Think of meeting this style of obstruction in a narrow trail. The camel would not turn out for a king. He stalks serenely along, bringing his cushioned stilts forward with the long, regular swing of a pendulum, and whatever is in the way must get out of the way peaceably, or be wiped out forcibly by the bulky sacks. It was a tiresome ride to us, and perfectly exhausting to the horses. We were compelled to jump over upward of eighteen hundred donkeys, and only one person in the party was unseated less than sixty times by the camels. This seems like a powerful statement, but the poet has said, "Things are not what they seem." I cannot think of anything now more certain to make one shudder, than to have a soft-footed camel sneak up behind him and touch him on the ear with its cold, flabby under-lip. A camel did this for one of the boys, who was drooping over his saddle in a brown-

study. He glanced up and saw the majestic apparition hovering above him, and made frantic efforts to
get out of the way, but the camel reached out and
bit him on the shoulder before he accomplished it.
This was the only pleasant incident of the journey.

At Nazareth we camped in an olive grove near
the Virgin Mary's fountain, and that wonderful
Arab "guard" came to collect some bucksheesh
for his "services" in following us from Tiberias
and warding off invisible dangers with the terrors of
his armament. The dragoman had paid his master,
but that counted as nothing—if you hire a man to
sneeze for you here, and another man chooses to
help him, you have got to pay both. They do
nothing whatever without pay. How it must have
surprised these people to hear the way of salvation
offered to them *"without money and without price."*
If the manners, the people, or the customs of this
country have changed since the Saviour's time, the
figures and metaphors of the Bible are not the
evidences to prove it by.

We entered the great Latin Convent which is
built over the traditional dwelling-place of the Holy
Family. We went down a flight of fifteen steps
below the ground-level, and stood in a small chapel
tricked out with tapestry hangings, silver lamps, and
oil-paintings. A spot marked by a cross, in the
marble floor, under the altar, was exhibited as the
place made forever holy by the feet of the Virgin
when she stood up to receive the message of the
angel. So simple, so unpretending a locality, to be
the scene of so mighty an event! The very scene

of the Annunciation—an event which has been commemorated by splendid shrines and august temples all over the civilized world, and one which the princes of art have made it their loftiest ambition to picture worthily on their canvas; a spot whose history is familiar to the very children of every house, and city, and obscure hamlet of the furthest lands of Christendom; a spot which myriads of men would toil across the breadth of a world to see, would consider it a priceless privilege to look upon. It was easy to think these thoughts. But it was not easy to bring myself up to the magnitude of the situation. I could sit off several thousand miles and imagine the angel appearing, with shadowy wings and lustrous countenance, and note the glory that streamed downward upon the Virgin's head while the message from the Throne of God fell upon her ears—any one can do that, beyond the ocean, but few can do it here. I saw the little recess from which the angel stepped, but could not fill its void. The angels that I know are creatures of unstable fancy—they will not fit in niches of substantial stone. Imagination labors best in distant fields. I doubt if any man can stand in the Grotto of the Annunciation and people with the phantom images of his mind its too tangible walls of stone.

They showed us a broken granite pillar, depending from the roof, which they said was hacked in two by the Moslem conquerors of Nazareth, in the vain hope of pulling down the sanctuary. But the pillar remained miraculously suspended in the air, and, unsupported itself, supported then and still supports the roof. By dividing this statement up among eight, it was found not difficult to believe it.

These gifted Latin monks never do anything by halves. If they were to show you the Brazen Serpent that was elevated in the wilderness, you could depend upon it that they had on hand the pole it was elevated on also, and even the hole it stood in. They have got the "Grotto" of the Annunciation here; and just as convenient to it as one's throat is to his mouth, they have also the Virgin's Kitchen, and even her sitting-room, where she and Joseph watched the infant Saviour play with Hebrew toys eighteen hundred years ago. All under one roof, and all clean, spacious, comfortable "grottoes." It seems curious that personages intimately connected with the Holy Family always lived in grottoes—in Nazareth, in Bethlehem, in imperial Ephesus—and yet nobody else in their day and generation thought of doing anything of the kind. If they ever did, their grottoes are all gone, and I suppose we ought to wonder at the peculiar marvel of the preservation of these I speak of. When the Virgin fled from Herod's wrath, she hid in a grotto in Bethlehem, and the same is there to this day. The slaughter of the innocents in Bethlehem was done in a grotto; the Saviour was born in a grotto —both are shown to pilgrims yet. It is exceedingly strange that these tremendous events all happened in grottoes—and exceedingly fortunate, likewise, because the strongest houses must crumble to ruin in time, but a grotto in the living rock will last forever. It is an imposture—this grotto stuff—but it is one that all men ought to thank the Catholics for. Wherever they ferret out a lost locality made holy by some Scriptural event, they straightway build a massive—almost imperishable—church there, and preserve the memory of that locality for the gratification of future generations. If it had been left to Protestants to do this most worthy work, we would not even know where Jerusalem is to-day, and the man who could go and put his finger on Nazareth would be too wise for this world. The world owes the Catholics its good will even for the happy rascality of hewing out these bogus grottoes in the rock; for it is infinitely more satisfactory to look at a grotto, where people have faithfully believed for centuries that the Virgin once lived, than to have to imagine a dwelling-place for her somewhere, anywhere, nowhere, loose and at large all over this town of Nazareth. There is too large a scope of country. The imagination cannot work. There is no one particular spot to chain your eye, rivet your interest, and make you think. The memory of the Pilgrims cannot perish while Plymouth Rock remains to us. The old monks are wise. They know how to drive a stake through a pleasant tradition that will hold it to its place forever.

We visited the places where Jesus worked for fifteen years as a carpenter, and where he attempted to teach in the synagogue and was driven out by a mob. Catholic chapels stand upon these sites and protect the little fragments of the ancient walls which remain. Our pilgrims broke off specimens. We visited, also, a new chapel, in the midst of the town, which is built around a boulder some twelve feet long by four feet thick; the priests discovered, a few years ago, that the disciples had sat upon this rock to rest once, when they had walked up from Capernaum. They hastened to preserve the relic. Relics are very good property. Travelers are expected to pay for seeing them, and they do it cheerfully. We like the idea. One's conscience can never be the worse for the knowledge that he has paid his way like a man. Our pilgrims would have liked very well to get out their lampblack and stencil-plates and paint their names on that rock, together with the names of the villages they hail from in America, but the priests permit nothing of that kind. To speak the strict truth, however, our party seldom offend in that way, though we have men in the ship who never lose an opportunity to do it. Our pilgrims' chief sin is their lust for "specimens." I suppose that by this time they know the dimensions of that rock to an inch, and its weight to a ton; and I do not hesitate to charge that they will go back there to-night and try to carry it off.

This "Fountain of the Virgin" is the one which tradition says Mary used to get water from, twenty times a day, when she was a girl, and bear it away in a jar upon her head. The water streams through faucets in the face of a wall of ancient masonry which stands removed from the houses of the village. The young girls of Nazareth still collect about it by the dozen and keep up a riotous laughter and sky-larking. The Nazarene girls are homely. Some of them have large, lustrous eyes, but none of them have pretty faces. These girls wear a single garment, usually, and it is loose, shapeless, of undecided color; it is generally out of repair, too. They wear, from crown to jaw, curious strings of old coins, after the manner of the belles of Tiberias, and brass jewelry upon their wrists and in their ears. They wear no shoes and stockings. They are the most human girls we have found in the country yet, and the best natured. But there is no question that these picturesque maidens sadly lack comeliness.

A pilgrim—the "Enthusiast"—said: "See that tall, graceful girl! look at the Madonna-like beauty of her countenance!"

Another pilgrim came along presently and said: "Observe that tall, graceful girl; what queenly Madonna-like gracefulness of beauty is in her countenance."

I said: "She is not tall, she is short; she is not beautiful, she is homely; she is graceful enough, I grant, but she is rather boisterous."

The third and last pilgrim moved by, before long, and he said: "Ah, what a tall, graceful girl! what Madonna-like gracefulness of queenly beauty!"

The verdicts were all in. It was time, now, to look up the authorities for all these opinions. I found this paragraph, which follows. Written by whom? Wm. C. Grimes:

After we were in the saddle, we rode down to the spring to have a last look at the women of Nazareth, who were, as a class, much the prettiest that we had seen in the East. As we approached the crowd a tall girl of nineteen advanced toward

Miriam and offered her a cup of water. Her movement was graceful and queenly. We exclaimed on the spot at the Madonna-like beauty of her countenance. Whitely was suddenly thirsty, and begged for water, and drank it slowly, with his eyes over the top of the cup, fixed on her large black eyes, which gazed on him quite as curiously as he on her. Then Moreright wanted water. She gave it to him and he managed to spill it so as to ask for another cup, and by the time she came to me she saw through the operation; her eyes were full of fun as she looked at me. I laughed outright, and she joined me in as gay a shout as ever country maiden in old Orange County. I wished for a picture of her. A Madonna, whose face was a portrait of that beautiful Nazareth girl, would be a " thing of beauty " and " a joy forever."

That is the kind of gruel which has been served out from Palestine for ages. Commend me to Fenimore Cooper to find beauty in the Indians, and to Grimes to find it in the Arabs. Arab men are often fine-looking, but Arab women are not. We can all believe that the Virgin Mary was beautiful; it is not natural to think otherwise; but does it follow that it is our duty to find beauty in these present women of Nazareth?

I love to quote from Grimes, because he is so dramatic. And because he is so romantic. And because he seems to care but little whether he tells the truth or not, so he scares the reader or excites his envy or his admiration.

He went through this peaceful land with one hand forever on his revolver, and the other on his pocket-handkerchief. Always, when he was not on the point of crying over a holy place, he was on the point of killing an Arab. More surprising things happened to him in Palestine than ever happened to

any traveler here or elsewhere since Munchausen
died.

At Beit Jin, where nobody had interfered with
him, he crept out of his tent at dead of night and
shot at what he took to be an Arab lying on a
rock, some distance away, planning evil. The ball
killed a wolf. Just before he fired, he makes a
dramatic picture of himself—as usual, to scare the
reader:

Was it imagination, or did I see a moving object on the
surface of the rock? If it were a man, why did he not now drop
me? He had a beautiful shot as I stood out in my black burnoose against the white tent. I had the sensation of an entering bullet in my throat, breast, brain.

Reckless creature!

Riding toward Gennesaret, they saw two Bedouins,
and "we looked to our pistols and loosened them
quietly in our shawls," etc. Always cool.

In Samaria, he charged up a hill, in the face of a
volley of stones; he fired into the crowd of men
who threw them. He says:

*I never lost an opportunity* of impressing the Arabs with the
perfection of American and English weapons, and the danger
of attacking any one of the armed Franks. I think the lesson
of that ball not lost.

At Beitin he gave his whole band of Arab mule-
teers a piece of his mind, and then—

I contented myself with a solemn assurance that if there
occurred another instance of disobedience to orders, I would
thrash the responsible party as he never dreamed of being
thrashed, and if I could not find who was responsible, I would
whip them all, from first to last, whether there was a governor
at hand to do it or I had to do it myself.

Perfectly fearless, this man.

He rode down the perpendicular path in the rocks, from the Castle of Banias to the oak grove, at a flying gallop, his horse striding "thirty feet" at every bound. I stand prepared to bring thirty reliable witnesses to prove that Putnam's famous feat at Horseneck was insignificant compared to this.

Behold him—always theatrical—looking at Jerusalem—this time, by an oversight, with his hand off his pistol for once.

I stood in the road, my hand on my horse's neck, and with my dim eyes sought to trace the outlines of the holy places which I had long before fixed in my mind, but the fast-flowing tears forbade my succeeding. There were our Mohammedan servants, a Latin monk, two Armenians, and a Jew in our cortège, and all alike gazed with overflowing eyes.

If Latin monks and Arabs cried, I know to a moral certainty that the horses cried also, and so the picture is complete.

But when necessity demanded he could be firm as adamant. In the Lebanon Valley an Arab youth—a Christian; he is particular to explain that Mohammedans do not steal—robbed him of a paltry ten dollars' worth of powder and shot. He convicted him before a sheik and looked on while he was punished by the terrible bastinado. Hear him:

He (Mousa) was on his back in a twinkling, howling, shouting, screaming, but he was carried out to the piazza before the door, where we could see the operation, and laid face down. One man sat on his back and one on his legs, the latter holding up his feet, while a third laid on the bare soles a rhinoceros-hide

269

# MARK TWAIN

koorbash[1] that whizzed through the air at every stroke. Poor
Moreright was in agony, and Nama and Nama the Second
(mother and sister of Mousa) were on their faces begging and
wailing, now embracing my knees and now Whitely's, while
the brother, outside, made the air ring with cries louder than
Mousa's. Even Yusef came and asked me on his knees to
relent, and last of all Betuni—the rascal had lost a feed-bag in
their house and had been loudest in his denunciations that
morning—besought the Howajji to have mercy on the fellow.

But not he! The punishment was "suspended,"
at the *fifteenth blow*, to hear the confession. Then
Grimes and his party rode away, and left the entire
Christian family to be fined and as severely punished
as the *Mohammedan sheik* should deem proper.

As I mounted, Yusef once more begged me to interfere and
have mercy on them, but I looked around at the dark faces
of the crowd, and I couldn't find one drop of pity in my heart
for them.

He closes his picture with a rollicking burst of
humor which contrasts finely with the grief of the
mother and her children.

One more paragraph:

Then once more I bowed my head. It is no shame to have
wept in Palestine. I wept when I saw Jerusalem, I wept when
I lay in the starlight at Bethlehem, I wept on the blessed shores
of Galilee. My hand was no less firm on the rein, my finger did
not tremble on the trigger of my pistol when I rode with it in
my right hand along the shore of the blue sea [weeping]. My

[1] "A koorbash is Arabic for cowhide, the cow being a rhinoceros.
It is the most cruel whip known to fame. Heavy as lead and
flexible as India-rubber, usually about forty inches long and tapering gradually from an inch in diameter to a point, it administers a
blow which *leaves its mark for time*."—*Scow Life in Egypt*, by the
same author.

eye was not dimmed by those tears nor my heart in aught weakened. Let him who would sneer at my emotion close this volume here, for he will find little to his taste in my journeyings through Holy Land.

He never bored but he struck water.

I am aware that this is a pretty voluminous notice of Mr. Grimes's book. However, it is proper and legitimate to speak of it, for *Nomadic Life in Palestine* is a representative book—the representative of a *class* of Palestine books—and a criticism upon it will serve for a criticism upon them all. And since I am treating it in the comprehensive capacity of a representative book, I have taken the liberty of giving to both book and author fictitious names. Perhaps it is in better taste, anyhow, to do this.

## CHAPTER XXIV

NAZARETH is wonderfully interesting because the town has an air about it of being precisely as Jesus left it, and one finds himself saying, all the time, "The boy Jesus has stood in this doorway—has played in that street—has touched these stones with his hands—has rambled over these chalky hills." Whoever shall write the Boyhood of Jesus ingeniously, will make a book which will possess a vivid interest for young and old alike. I judge so from the greater interest we found in Nazareth than any of our speculations upon Capernaum and the Sea of Galilee gave rise to. It was not possible, standing by the Sea of Galilee, to frame more than a vague, far-away idea of the majestic Personage who walked upon the crested waves as if they had been solid earth, and who touched the dead and they rose up and spoke. I read among my notes, now with a new interest, some sentences from an edition of 1621 of the Apocryphal New Testament. [Extract.]

Christ, kissed by a bride made dumb by sorcerers, cures her. A leprous girl cured by the water in which the infant Christ was washed, and becomes the servant of Joseph and Mary. The leprous son of a Prince cured in like manner.

A young man who had been bewitched and turned into a

mule, miraculously cured by the infant Saviour being put on his back, and is married to the girl who had been cured of leprosy. Whereupon the bystanders praise God.

Chapter 16. Christ miraculously widens or contracts gates, milk pails, seives, or boxes not properly made by Joseph, he not being skilful at his carpenter's trade. The King of Jerusalem gives Joseph an order for a throne. Joseph works on it for two years and makes it two spans too short. The King being angry with him, Jesus comforts him—commands him to pull one side of the throne while he pulls the other, and brings it to its proper dimensions.

Chapter 19. Jesus, charged with throwing a boy from the roof of a house, miraculously causes the dead boy to speak and acquit him; fetches water for his mother, breaks the pitcher and miraculously gathers the water in his mantle and brings it home.

Sent to a schoolmaster, refuses to tell his letters, and the schoolmaster going to whip him, his hand withers.

Further on in this quaint volume of rejected gospels is an epistle of St. Clement to the Corinthians, which was used in the churches and considered genuine fourteen or fifteen hundred years ago. In it this account of the fabled phœnix occurs:

1. Let us consider that wonderful type of the resurrection, which is seen in the Eastern countries, that is to say, in Arabia.

2. There is a certain bird called a phœnix. Of this there is never but one at a time, and that lives five hundred years. And when the time of its dissolution draws near, that it must die, it makes itself a nest of frankincense, and myrrh, and other spices, into which, when its time is fulfilled, it enters and dies.

3. But its flesh, putrefying, breeds a certain worm, which being nourished by the juice of the dead bird, brings forth feathers; and when it is grown to a perfect state, it takes up the nest in which the bones of its parent lie, and carries it from Arabia into Egypt, to a city called Heliopolis:

4. And flying in open day in the sight of all men, lays it upon the altar of the sun, and so returns from whence it came.

5. The priests then search into the records of the time, and find that it returned precisely at the end of five hundred years.

Business is business, and there is nothing like punctuality, especially in a phœnix.

The few chapters relating to the infancy of the Saviour contain many things which seem frivolous and not worth preserving. A large part of the remaining portions of the book read like good Scripture, however. There is one verse that ought not to have been rejected, because it so evidently prophetically refers to the general run of Congresses of the United States:

199. They carry themselves high, and as prudent men; and though they are fools, yet would seem to be teachers.

I have set these extracts down, as I found them. Everywhere, among the cathedrals of France and Italy, one finds traditions of personages that do not figure in the Bible, and of miracles that are not mentioned in its pages. But they are all in this Apocryphal New Testament, and though they have been ruled out of our modern Bible, it is claimed that they were accepted gospel twelve or fifteen centuries ago, and ranked as high in credit as any. One needs to read this book before he visits those venerable cathedrals, with their treasures of tabooed and forgotten tradition.

They imposed another pirate upon us at Nazareth —another invincible Arab guard. We took our last look at the city, clinging like a whitewashed wasp's nest to the hillside, and at eight o'clock in the morning, departed. We dismounted and drove the horses down a bridle-path which I think was fully as crooked as a corkscrew; which I know to be as steep as the downward sweep of a rainbow, and which I believe to be the worst piece of road in the geography, except one in the Sandwich Islands, which I remember painfully, and possibly one or two mountain-trails in the Sierra Nevadas. Often, in this narrow path, the horse had to poise himself nicely on a rude stone step and then drop his forefeet over the edge and down something more than half his own height. This brought his nose near the ground, while his tail pointed up toward the sky somewhere, and gave him the appearance of preparing to stand on his head. A horse cannot look dignified in this position. We accomplished the long descent at last, and trotted across the great Plain of Esdraelon.

Some of us will be shot before we finish this pilgrimage. The pilgrims read *Nomadic Life* and keep themselves in a constant state of Quixotic heroism. They have their hands on their pistols all the time, and every now and then, when you least expect it, they snatch them out and take aim at Bedouins who are not visible, and draw their knives and make savage passes at other Bedouins who do not exist. I am in deadly peril always, for these spasms are sudden and irregular, and, of course, I cannot tell when to be getting out of the way. If I am accidentally murdered, some time, during one of these romantic frenzies of the pilgrims, Mr. Grimes must be rigidly held to answer as an accessory before the fact. If the pilgrims would take deliberate aim and shoot at a man, it would be all right and proper —because that man would not be in any danger;

but these random assaults are what I object to.
I do not wish to see any more places like Esdraelon,
where the ground is level and people can gallop.
It puts melodramatic nonsense into the pilgrims'
heads. All at once, when one is jogging along
stupidly in the sun, and thinking about something
ever so far away, here they come, at a stormy gallop, spurring and whooping at those ridgy old sore-
backed plugs till their heels fly higher than their
heads, and, as they whiz by, out comes a little potato-
gun of a revolver, there is a startling little pop, and
a small pellet goes singing through the air. Now
that I have begun this pilgrimage, I intend to go
through with it, though, sooth to say, nothing but
the most desperate valor has kept me to my purpose
up to the present time. I do not mind Bedouins,—
I am not afraid of them; because neither Bedouins
nor ordinary Arabs have shown any disposition to
harm us, but I *do* feel afraid of my own comrades.

Arriving at the furthest verge of the Plain, we
rode a little way up a hill and found ourselves at
Endor, famous for its witch. Her descendants are
there yet. They were the wildest horde of half-
naked savages we have found thus far. They
swarmed out of mud bee-hives; out of hovels of
the dry-goods-box pattern; out of gaping caves
under shelving rocks; out of crevices in the earth.
In five minutes the dead solitude and silence of the
place were no more, and a begging, screeching,
shouting mob were struggling about the horses' feet
and blocking the way. "Bucksheesh! buchsheesh!
bucksheesh! howajji, bucksheesh!" It was Magdala

over again, only here the glare from the infidel eyes was fierce and full of hate. The population numbers two hundred and fifty, and more than half the citizens live in caves in the rock. Dirt, degradation, and savagery are Endor's specialty. We say no more about Magdala and Deburieh now. Endor heads the list. It is worse than an Indian *campoodie*. The hill is barren, rocky, and forbidding. No sprig of grass is visible, and only one tree. This is a fig tree, which maintains a precarious footing among the rocks at the mouth of the dismal cavern once occupied by the veritable Witch of Endor. In this cavern, tradition says, Saul, the King, sat at midnight, and stared and trembled, while the earth shook, the thunders crashed among the hills, and out of the midst of fire and smoke the spirit of the dead prophet rose up and confronted him. Saul had crept to this place in the darkness, while his army slept, to learn what fate awaited him in the morrow's battle. He went away a sad man, to meet disgrace and death.

A spring trickles out of the rock in the gloomy recesses of the cavern, and we were thirsty. The citizens of Endor objected to our going in there. They do not mind dirt; they do not mind rags; they do not mind vermin; they do not mind barbarous ignorance and savagery; they do not mind a reasonable degree of starvation, but they *do* like to be pure and holy before their god, whoever he may be, and therefore they shudder and grow almost pale at the idea of Christian lips polluting a spring whose waters must descend into their sanctified gullets. We had no wanton desire to wound even *their* feelings or trample upon their prejudices, but we were out of water, thus early in the day, and were burning up with thirst. It was at this time and under these circumstances that I framed an aphorism which has already become celebrated. I said: "Necessity knows no law." We went in and drank.

We got away from the noisy wretches, finally, 'dropping them in squads and couples as we filed over the hills—the aged first, the infants next, the young girls further on; the strong men ran beside us a mile, and only left when they had secured the last possible piaster in the way of bucksheesh.

In an hour we reached Nain, where Christ raised the widow's son to life. Nain is Magdala on a small scale. It has no population of any consequence. Within a hundred yards of it is the original graveyard, for aught I know; the tombstones lie flat on the ground, which is Jewish fashion in Syria. I believe the Moslems do not allow them to have upright tombstones. A Moslem grave is usually roughly plastered over and whitewashed, and has at one end an upright projection which is shaped into exceedingly rude attempts at ornamentation. In the cities, there is often no appearance of a grave at all; a tall, slender marble tombstone, elaborately lettered, gilded and painted, marks the burial-place, and this is surmounted by a turban, so carved and shaped as to signify the dead man's rank in life.

They showed a fragment of ancient wall which they said was one side of the gate out of which the widow's dead son was being brought so many centuries ago when Jesus met the procession:

> Now when he came nigh to the gate of the city, behold there was a dead man carried out, the only son of his mother, and she was a widow; and much people of the city was with her.
>
> And when the Lord saw her, he had compassion on her, and said, Weep not.
>
> And he came and touched the bier: and they that bare him stood still. And he said, Young man, I say unto thee, arise.
>
> And he that was dead sat up, and began to speak. And he delivered him to his mother.
>
> And there came a fear on all. And they glorified God, saying, That a great prophet is risen up among us; and That God hath visited his people.

A little mosque stands upon the spot which tradition says was occupied by the widow's dwelling. Two or three aged Arabs sat about its door. We entered, and the pilgrims broke specimens from the foundation walls, though they had to touch, and even step, upon the "praying-carpets" to do it. It was almost the same as breaking pieces from the hearts of those old Arabs. To step rudely upon the sacred praying-mats, with booted feet—a thing not done by any Arab—was to inflict pain upon men who had not offended us in any way. Suppose a party of armed foreigners were to enter a village church in America and break ornaments from the altar railings for curiosities, and climb up and walk upon the Bible and the pulpit cushions? However, the cases are different. One is the profanation of a temple of our faith—the other only the profanation of a pagan one.

We descended to the Plain again, and halted a

# MARK TWAIN

moment at a well—of Abraham's time, no doubt.
It was in a desert place. It was walled three feet
above ground with squared and heavy blocks of
stone, after the manner of Bible pictures. Around
it some camels stood, and others knelt. There was a
group of sober little donkeys with naked, dusky
children clambering about them, or sitting astride
their rumps, or pulling their tails. Tawny, black-
eyed, barefooted maids, arrayed in rags and adorned
with brazen armlets and pinchbeck earrings, were
poising water jars upon their heads, or drawing water
from the well. A flock of sheep stood by, waiting
for the shepherds to fill the hollowed stones with
water, so that they might drink—stones which, like
those that walled the well, were worn smooth and
deeply creased by the chafing chins of a hundred
generations of thirsty animals. Picturesque Arabs
sat upon the ground, in groups, and solemnly
smoked their long-stemmed chibouks. Other Arabs
were filling black hogskins with water—skins which,
well filled, and distended with water till the short
legs projected painfully out of the proper line, looked
like the corpses of hogs bloated by drowning. Here
was a grand Oriental picture which I had worshiped
a thousand times in soft, rich steel engravings!
But in the engraving there was no desolation; no
dirt; no rags; no fleas; no ugly features; no sore
eyes; no feasting flies; no besotted ignorance in
the countenances; no raw places on the donkeys'
backs; no disagreeable jabbering in unknown tongues;
no stench of camels; no suggestion that a couple
of tons of powder placed under the party and touched

280

off would heighten the effect and give to the scene a genuine interest and a charm which it would always be pleasant to recall, even though a man lived a thousand years.

Oriental scenes look best in steel engravings. I cannot be imposed upon any more by that picture of the Queen of Sheba visiting Solomon. I shall say to myself, You look fine, madam, but your feet are not clean, and you smell like a camel.

Presently, a wild Arab in charge of a camel-train recognized an old friend in Ferguson, and they ran and fell upon each other's necks and kissed each other's grimy, bearded faces upon both cheeks. It explained instantly a something which had always seemed to me only a far-fetched Oriental figure of speech. I refer to the circumstance of Christ's rebuking a Pharisee, or some such character, and reminding him that from him he had received no "kiss of welcome." It did not seem reasonable to me that men should kiss each other, but I am aware, now, that they did. There was reason in it, too. The custom was natural and proper; because people must kiss, and a man would not be likely to kiss one of the women of this country of his own free will and accord. One must travel, to learn. Every day, now, old Scriptural phrases that never possessed any significance for me before take to themselves a meaning.

We journeyed around the base of the mountain—"Little Hermon,"—past the old Crusaders' castle of El Fuleh, and arrived at Shunem. This was another Magdala, to a fraction, frescoes and all.

Here, tradition says, the prophet Samuel was born, and here the Shunamite woman built a little house upon the city wall for the accommodation of the prophet Elisha. Elisha asked her what she expected in return. It was a perfectly natural question, for these people are and were in the habit of proffering favors and services and then expecting and begging for pay. Elisha knew them well. He could not comprehend that anybody should build for him that humble little chamber for the mere sake of old friendship, and with no selfish motive whatever. It used to seem a very impolite, not to say a rude question, for Elisha to ask the woman, but it does not seem so to me now. The woman said she expected nothing. Then, for her goodness and her unselfishness, he rejoiced her heart with the news that she should bear a son. It was a high reward— but she would not have thanked him for a daughter— daughters have always been unpopular here. The son was born, grew, waxed strong, died. Elisha restored him to life in Shunem.

We found here a grove of lemon trees—cool, shady, hung with fruit. One is apt to overestimate beauty when it is rare, but to me this grove seemed very beautiful. It *was* beautiful. I do not overestimate it. I must always remember Shunem gratefully, as a place which gave to us this leafy shelter after our long, hot ride. We lunched, rested, chatted, smoked our pipes an hour, and then mounted and moved on.

As we trotted across the Plain of Jezreel, we met half a dozen Digger Indians (Bedouins) with very long spears in their hands, cavorting around on old crow-bait horses, and spearing imaginary enemies; whooping, and fluttering their rags in the wind, and carrying on in every respect like a pack of hopeless lunatics. At last, here were the "wild, free sons of the desert, speeding over the plain like the wind, on their beautiful Arabian mares" we had read so much about and longed so much to see! Here were the "picturesque costumes"! This was the "gallant spectacle"! Tatterdemalion vagrants—cheap braggadocio—"Arabian mares" spined and necked like the ichthyosaurus in the museum, and humped and cornered like a dromedary! To glance at the genuine son of the desert is to take the romance out of him forever—to behold his steed is to long in charity to strip his harness off and let him fall to pieces.

Presently we came to a ruinous old town on a hill, the same being the ancient Jezreel.

Ahab, King of Samaria (this was a very vast kingdom, for those days, and was very nearly half as large as Rhode Island) dwelt in the city of Jezreel, which was his capital. Near him lived a man by the name of Naboth, who had a vineyard. The King asked him for it, and when he would not give it, offered to buy it. But Naboth refused to sell it. In those days it was considered a sort of crime to part with one's inheritance at any price—and even if a man did part with it, it reverted to himself or his heirs again at the next jubilee year. So this spoiled child of a King went and lay down on the bed with his face to the wall, and grieved sorely.

The Queen, a notorious character in those days, and whose name is a byword and a reproach even in these, came in and asked him wherefore he sorrowed, and he told her.  Jezebel said she could secure the vineyard; and she went forth and forged letters to the nobles and wise men, in the King's name, and ordered them to proclaim a fast and set Naboth on high before the people, and suborn two witnesses to swear that he had blasphemed.  They did it, and the people stoned the accused by the city wall, and he died.  Then Jezebel came and told the King, and said, Behold, Naboth is no more—rise up and seize the vineyard.  So Ahab seized the vineyard, and went into it to possess it.  But the Prophet Elijah came to him there and read his fate to him, and the fate of Jezebel; and said that in the place where dogs licked the blood of Naboth, dogs should also lick his blood—and he said, likewise, the dogs should eat Jezebel by the wall of Jezreel.  In the course of time, the King was killed in battle, and when his chariot wheels were washed in the pool of Samaria, the dogs licked the blood.  In after years, Jehu, who was King of Israel, marched down against Jezreel, by order of one of the Prophets, and administered one of those convincing rebukes so common among the people of those days: he killed many kings and their subjects, and as he came along he saw Jezebel, painted and finely dressed, looking out of a window, and ordered that she be thrown down to him.  A servant did it, and Jehu's horse trampled her underfoot.  Then Jehu went in and sat down to dinner; and presently he said, Go and bury this cursed woman, for she is a King's daughter. The spirit of charity came upon him too late, however, for the prophecy had already been fulfilled—the dogs had eaten her, and they "found no more of her than the skull and the feet, and the palms of her hands."

Ahab, the late King, had left a helpless family behind him, and Jehu killed seventy of the orphan sons. Then he killed all the relatives, and teachers, and servants and friends of the family, and rested from his labors, until he was come near to Samaria, where he met forty-two persons and asked them who they were; they said they were brothers of the King of Judah. He killed them. When he got to Samaria, he said he would show his zeal for the Lord; so he gathered all the priests and people together that worshiped Baal, pretending that he was going to adopt that worship and offer up a great sacrifice; and when they were all shut up where they could not defend themselves, he caused every person of them to be killed. Then Jehu, the good missionary, rested from his labors once more.

We went back to the valley, and rode to the Fountain of Ain Jelûd. They call it the Fountain of Jezreel, usually. It is a pond about one hundred feet square and four feet deep, with a stream of water trickling into it from under an overhanging ledge of rocks. It is in the midst of a great solitude. Here Gideon pitched his camp in the old times; behind Shunem lay the "Midianites, the Amalekites, and the Children of the East," who were "as grasshoppers for multitude; both they and their camels were without number, as the sand by the seaside for multitude." Which means that there were one hundred and thirty-five thousand men, and that they had transportation service accordingly.

Gideon, with only three hundred men, surprised them in the night, and stood by and looked on while they butchered each other until a hundred and twenty thousand lay dead on the field.

We camped at Jenin before night, and got up and started again at one o'clock in the morning. Somewhere toward daylight we passed the locality where the best authenticated tradition locates the pit into which Joseph's brethren threw him, and about noon, after passing over a succession of mountain-tops, clad with groves of fig and olive trees, with the Mediterranean in sight some forty miles away, and going by many ancient Biblical cities whose inhabitants glowered savagely upon our Christian procession, and were seemingly inclined to practise on it with stones, we came to the singularly terraced and unlovely hills that betrayed that we were out of Galilee and into Samaria at last.

We climbed a high hill to visit the city of Samaria, where the woman may have hailed from who conversed with Christ at Jacob's Well, and from whence, no doubt, came also the celebrated Good Samaritan. Herod the Great is said to have made a magnificent city of this place, and a great number of coarse limestone columns, twenty feet high and two feet through, that are almost guiltless of architectural grace of shape and ornament, are pointed out by many authors as evidence of the fact. They would

THE TOMB OF ADAM

not have been considered handsome in ancient Greece, however.

The inhabitants of this camp are particularly vicious, and stoned two parties of our pilgrims a day or two ago who brought about the difficulty by showing their revolvers when they did not intend to use them—a thing which is deemed bad judgment in the Far West, and ought certainly to be so considered anywhere. In the new Territories, when a man puts his hand on a weapon, he knows that he must use it; he must use it instantly or expect to be shot down where he stands. Those pilgrims had been reading Grimes.

There was nothing for us to do in Samaria but buy handfuls of old Roman coins at a franc a dozen, and look at a dilapidated church of the Crusaders and a vault in it which once contained the body of John the Baptist. The relic was long ago carried away to Genoa.

Samaria stood a disastrous siege, once, in the days of Elisha, at the hands of the King of Syria. Provisions reached such a figure that "an ass's head was sold for eighty pieces of silver and the fourth part of a cab of dove's dung for five pieces of silver."

An incident recorded of that heavy time will give one a very good idea of the distress that prevailed within these crumbling walls. As the King was walking upon the battlements one day, "a woman cried out, saying, Help, my lord, O King! And the King said, What aileth thee? and she answered, This woman said unto me, Give thy son, that we may eat him to-day, and we will eat my son to-morrow. So

we boiled my son, and did eat him; and I said unto
her on the next day, Give thy son that we may eat
him; and she hath hid her son."

The prophet Elisha declared that within four-and-
twenty hours the prices of food should go down to
nothing, almost, and it was so. The Syrian army
broke camp and fled, for some cause or other, the
famine was relieved from without, and many a
shoddy speculator in dove's dung and ass's meat was
ruined.

We were glad to leave this hot and dusty old
village and hurry on. At two o'clock we stopped
to lunch and rest at ancient Shechem, between the
historic Mounts of Gerizim and Ebal where in the
old times the books of the law, the curses and the
blessings, were read from the heights to the Jewish
multitudes below.

# CHAPTER XXV

THE narrow cañon in which Nablous, or Shechem, is situated, is under high cultivation, and the soil is exceedingly black and fertile. It is well watered, and its affluent vegetation gains effect by contrast with the barren hills that tower on either side. One of these hills is the ancient Mount of Blessings and the other the Mount of Curses; and wise men who seek for fulfilment of prophecy think they find here a wonder of this kind—to wit, that the Mount of Blessings is strangely fertile and its mate as strangely unproductive. We could not see that there was really much difference between them in this respect, however.

Shechem is distinguished as one of the residences of the patriarch Jacob, and as the seat of those tribes that cut themselves loose from their brethren of Israel and propagated doctrines not in conformity with those of the original Jewish creed. For thousands of years this clan have dwelt in Shechem under strict *tabu*, and having little commerce or fellowship with their fellow-men of any religion or nationality. For generations they have not numbered more than one or two hundred, but they still adhere to their ancient faith and maintain their ancient rites and ceremonies. Talk of family and old descent! Princes

and nobles pride themselves upon lineages they can
trace back some hundreds of years. What is this
trifle to this handful of old first families of Shechem,
who can name their fathers straight back without a
flaw for thousands—straight back to a period so
remote that men reared in a country where the days
of two hundred years ago are called "ancient" times
grow dazed and bewildered when they try to comprehend it! Here is respectability for you—here is
"family"—here is high descent worth talking about.
This sad, proud remnant of a once mighty community still hold themselves aloof from all the
world; they still live as their fathers lived, labor as
their fathers labored, think as they did, feel as they
did, worship in the same place, in sight of the same
landmarks, and in the same quaint, patriarchal way
their ancestors did more than thirty centuries ago.
I found myself gazing at any straggling scion of
this strange race with a riveted fascination, just as
one would stare at a living mastodon, or a megather-
ium that had moved in the gray dawn of creation and
seen the wonders of that mysterious world that was
before the flood.

Carefully preserved among the sacred archives of
this curious community is a MS. copy of the ancient
Jewish law, which is said to be the oldest document
on earth. It is written on vellum, and is some four
or five thousand years old. Nothing but bucksheesh
can purchase a sight. Its fame is somewhat dimmed
in these latter days, because of the doubts so many
authors of Palestine travels have felt themselves
privileged to cast upon it. Speaking of this MS.

reminds me that I procured from the high priest of this ancient Samaritan community, at great expense, a secret document of still higher antiquity and far more extraordinary interest, which I propose to publish as soon as I have finished translating it.

Joshua gave his dying injunction to the children of Israel at Shechem, and buried a valuable treasure secretly under an oak tree there about the same time. The superstitious Samaritans have always been afraid to hunt for it. They believe it is guarded by fierce spirits invisible to men.

About a mile and a half from Shechem we halted at the base of Mount Ebal, before a little square area, inclosed by a high stone wall, neatly whitewashed. Across one end of this inclosure is a tomb built after the manner of the Moslems. It is the tomb of Joseph. No truth is better authenticated than this.

When Joseph was dying he prophesied that exodus of the Israelites from Egypt which occurred four hundred years afterward. At the same time he exacted of his people an oath that when they journeyed to the land of Canaan, they would bear his bones with them and bury them in the ancient inheritance of his fathers. The oath was kept.

' And the bones of Joseph, which the children of Israel brought up out of Egypt, buried they in Shechem, in a parcel of ground which Jacob bought of the sons of Hamor the father of Shechem, for a hundred pieces of silver.

Few tombs on earth command the veneration of so many races and men of divers creeds as this of Joseph. "Samaritan and Jew, Moslem and Chris-

tian alike, revere it, and honor it with their visits.
The tomb of Joseph, the dutiful son, the affectionate, forgiving brother, the virtuous man, the wise
Prince and ruler. Egypt felt his influence—the
world knows his history."

In this same "parcel of ground" which Jacob
bought of the sons of Hamor for a hundred pieces
of silver, is Jacob's celebrated well. It is cut in the
solid rock, and is nine feet square and ninety feet
deep. The name of this unpretending hole in the
ground, which one might pass by and take no notice
of, is as familiar as household words to even the
children and the peasants of many a far-off country.

It is more famous than the Parthenon; it is older
than the Pyramids.

It was by this well that Jesus sat and talked with
a woman of that strange, antiquated Samaritan community I have been speaking of, and told her of the
mysterious water of life. As descendants of old
English nobles still cherish in the traditions of their
houses how that this king or that king tarried a day
with some favored ancestor three hundred years ago,
no doubt the descendants of the woman of Samaria,
living there in Shechem, still refer with pardonable
vanity to this conversation of their ancestor, held
some little time gone by, with the Messiah of the
Christians. It is not likely that they undervalue a
distinction such as this. Samaritan nature is human
nature, and human nature remembers contact with
the illustrious, always.

For an offense done to the family honor, the sons
of Jacob exterminated all Shechem once.

# THE INNOCENTS ABROAD

We left Jacob's Well and traveled till eight in the evening, but rather slowly, for we had been in the saddle nineteen hours, and the horses were cruelly tired. We got so far ahead of the tents that we had to camp in an Arab village, and sleep on the ground. We could have slept in the largest of the houses; but there were some little drawbacks; it was populous with vermin, it had a dirt floor, it was in no respect cleanly, and there was a family of goats in the only bedroom, and two donkeys in the parlor. Outside there were no inconveniences, except that the dusky, ragged, earnest-eyed villagers of both sexes and all ages grouped themselves on their haunches all around us, and discussed us and criticised us with noisy tongues till midnight. We did not mind the noise, being tired, but, doubtless, the reader is aware that it is almost an impossible thing to go to sleep when you know that people are looking at you. We went to bed at ten, and got up again at two and started once more. Thus are people persecuted by dragomans, whose sole ambition in life is to get ahead of each other.

About daylight we passed Shiloh, where the Ark of the Covenant rested three hundred years, and at whose gates good old Eli fell down and "brake his neck" when the messenger, riding hard from the battle, told him of the defeat of his people, the death of his sons, and, more than all, the capture of Israel's pride, her hope, her refuge, the ancient Ark her forefathers brought with them out of Egypt. It is little wonder that under circumstances like these he fell down and brake his neck. But Shiloh had no charms for us. We were so cold that there was no comfort but in motion, and so drowsy we could hardly sit upon the horses.

After a while we came to a shapeless mass of ruins, which still bears the name of Beth-el. It was here that Jacob lay down and had that superb vision of angels flitting up and down a ladder that reached from the clouds to earth, and caught glimpses of their blessed home through the open gates of Heaven.

The pilgrims took what was left of the hallowed ruin, and we pressed on toward the goal of our crusade, renowned Jerusalem.

The further we went the hotter the sun got and the more rocky and bare, repulsive and dreary the landscape became. There could not have been more fragments of stone strewn broadcast over this part of the world, if every ten square feet of the land had been occupied by a separate and distinct stone-cutter's establishment for an age. There was hardly a tree or a shrub anywhere. Even the olive and the cactus, those fast friends of a worthless soil, had almost deserted the country. No landscape exists that is more tiresome to the eye than that which bounds the approaches to Jerusalem. The only difference between the roads and the surrounding country, perhaps, is that there are rather more rocks in the roads than in the surrounding country.

We passed Ramah and Beroth, and on the right saw the tomb of the prophet Samuel, perched high upon a commanding eminence. Still no Jerusalem came in sight. We hurried on impatiently. We halted a moment at the ancient Fountain of Beira, but its stones, worn deeply by the chins of thirsty animals that are dead and gone centuries ago, had no interest for us—we longed to see Jerusalem. We spurred up hill after hill, and usually began to stretch our necks minutes before we got to the top —but disappointment always followed—more stupid hills beyond—more unsightly landscape—no Holy City.

At last, away in the middle of the day, ancient bits of wall and crumbling arches began to line the way—we toiled up one more hill, and every pilgrim and every sinner swung his hat on high! Jerusalem!

Perched on its eternal hills, white and domed and solid, massed together and hooped with high gray walls, the venerable city gleamed in the sun. So small! Why, it was no larger than an American village of four thousand inhabitants, and no larger than an ordinary Syrian city of thirty thousand. Jerusalem numbers only fourteen thousand people.

We dismounted and looked, without speaking a dozen sentences, across the wide intervening valley for an hour or more; and noted those prominent features of the city that pictures make familiar to all men from their school-days till their death. We could recognize the Tower of Hippicus, the Mosque of Omar, the Damascus Gate, the Mount of Olives, the Valley of Jehoshaphat, the Tower of David, and the Garden of Gethsemane—and dating from these landmarks could tell very nearly the localities of many others we were not able to distinguish.

I record it here as a notable but not discreditable fact that not even our pilgrims wept. I think there was no individual in the party whose brain was not teeming with thoughts and images and memories invoked by the grand history of the venerable city that lay before us, but still among them all was no "voice of them that wept."

There was no call for tears. Tears would have been out of place. The thoughts Jerusalem suggests are full of poetry, sublimity, and more than all, dignity. Such thoughts do not find their appropriate expression in the emotions of the nursery.

Just after noon we entered these narrow, crooked streets, by the ancient and the famed Damascus Gate, and now for several hours I have been trying to comprehend that I am actually in the illustrious old city where Solomon dwelt, where Abraham held converse with the Deity, and where walls still stand that witnessed the spectacle of the Crucifixion.

## CHAPTER XXVI

A FAST walker could go outside the walls of Jerusalem and walk entirely around the city in an hour. I do not know how else to make one understand how small it is. The appearance of the city is peculiar. It is as knobby with countless little domes as a prison door is with bolt-heads. Every house has from one to half a dozen of these white plastered domes of stone, broad and low, sitting in the center of, or in a cluster upon, the flat roof. Wherefore, when one looks down from an eminence, upon the compact mass of houses (so closely crowded together, in fact, that there is no appearance of streets at all, and so the city looks solid) he sees the knobbiest town in the world, except Constantinople. It looks as if it might be roofed, from center to circumference, with inverted saucers. The monotony of the view is interrupted only by the great Mosque of Omar, the Tower of Hippicus, and one or two other buildings that rise into commanding prominence.

The houses are generally two stories high, built strongly of masonry, whitewashed or plastered outside, and have a cage of wooden latticework projecting in front of every window. To reproduce a Jerusalem street, it would only be necessary to up-end a chicken-coop and hang it before each window in an alley of American houses.

The streets are roughly and badly paved with stone, and are tolerably crooked—enough so to make each street appear to close together constantly and come to an end about a hundred yards ahead of a pilgrim as long as he chooses to walk in it. Projecting from the top of the lower story of many of the houses is a very narrow porch-roof or shed, without supports from below; and I have several times seen cats jump across the street from one shed to the other when they were out calling. The cats could have jumped double the distance without extraordinary exertion. I mention these things to give an idea of how narrow the streets are. Since a cat can jump across them without the least inconvenience, it is hardly necessary to state that such streets are too narrow for carriages. These vehicles cannot navigate the Holy City.

The population of Jerusalem is composed of Moslems, Jews, Greeks, Latins, Armenians, Syrians, Copts, Abyssinians, Greek Catholics, and a handful of Protestants. One hundred of the latter sect are all that dwell now in this birthplace of Christianity. The nice shades of nationality comprised in the above list, and the languages spoken by them, are altogether too numerous to mention. It seems to me that all the races and colors and tongues of the earth must be represented among the fourteen thousand souls that dwell in Jerusalem. Rags, wretchedness, poverty, and dirt, those signs and symbols that indicate the presence of Moslem rule more surely than the crescent flag itself, abound. Lepers, cripples, the blind, and the idiotic, assail you on every hand, and they know but one word of but one language apparently—the eternal "bucksheesh." To see the numbers of maimed, malformed, and diseased humanity that throng the holy places and obstruct the gates, one might suppose that the ancient days had come again, and that the angel of the Lord was expected to descend at any moment to stir the waters of Bethesda. Jerusalem is mournful, and dreary, and lifeless. I would not desire to live here.

One naturally goes first to the Holy Sepulcher. It is right in the city, near the western gate; it and the place of the Crucifixion, and, in fact, every other place intimately connected with that tremendous event, are ingeniously massed together and covered by one roof—the dome of the Church of the Holy Sepulcher.

Entering the building, through the midst of the usual assemblage of beggars, one sees on his left a few Turkish guards—for Christians of different sects will not only quarrel, but fight, also, in this sacred place, if allowed to do it. Before you is a marble slab, which covers the Stone of Unction, whereon the Saviour's body was laid to prepare it for burial. It was found necessary to conceal the real stone in this way in order to save it from destruction. Pilgrims were too much given to chipping off pieces of it to carry home. Near by is a circular railing which marks the spot where the Virgin stood when the Lord's body was anointed.

# MARK TWAIN

Entering the great Rotunda, we stand before the most sacred locality in Christendom—the grave of Jesus. It is in the center of the church, and immediately under the great dome. It is inclosed in a sort of little temple of yellow and white stone, of fanciful design. Within the little temple is a portion of the very stone which was rolled away from the door of the Sepulcher, and on which the angel was sitting when Mary came thither "at early dawn." Stooping low, we enter the vault—the Sepulcher itself. It is only about six feet by seven, and the stone couch on which the dead Saviour lay extends from end to end of the apartment and occupies half its width. It is covered with a marble slab which had been much worn by the lips of pilgrims. This slab serves as an altar now. Over it hang some fifty gold and silver lamps, which are kept always burning, and the place is otherwise scandalized by trumpery gewgaws and tawdry ornamentation.

All sects of Christians (except Protestants) have chapels under the roof of the Church of the Holy Sepulcher, and each must keep to itself and not venture upon another's ground. It has been proven conclusively that they cannot worship together around the grave of the Saviour of the World in peace. The chapel of the Syrians is not handsome; that of the Copts is the humblest of them all. It is nothing but a dismal cavern, roughly hewn in the living rock of the Hill of Calvary. In one side of it two ancient tombs are hewn, which are claimed to be those in which Nicodemus and Joseph of Arimathea were buried.

3

# THE INNOCENTS ABROAD

As we moved among the great piers and pillars of another part of the church, we came upon a party of black-robed, animal-looking Italian monks, with candles in their hands, who were chanting something in Latin, and going through some kind of religious performance around a disk of white marble let into the floor. It was there that the risen Saviour appeared to Mary Magdalen in the likeness of a gardener. Near by was a similar stone, shaped like a star—here the Magdalen herself stood, at the same time. Monks were performing in this place, also. They perform everywhere—all over the vast building, and at all hours. Their candles are always flitting about in the gloom, and making the dim old church more dismal than there is any necessity that it should be, even though it is a tomb.

We were shown the place where our Lord appeared to His mother after the Resurrection. Here, also, a marble slab marks the place where St. Helena, the mother of the Emperor Constantine, found the crosses about three hundred years after the Crucifixion. According to the legend, this great discovery elicited extravagant demonstrations of joy. But they were of short duration. The question intruded itself: "Which bore the blessed Saviour, and which the thieves?" To be in doubt, in so mighty a matter as this—to be uncertain which one to adore—was a grievous misfortune. It turned the public joy to sorrow. But when lived there a holy priest who could not set so simple a trouble as this at rest? One of these soon hit upon a plan that would be a certain test. A noble lady lay very ill in Jerusalem. The wise priests ordered that the three crosses be taken to her bedside one at a time. It was done. When her eyes fell upon the first one, she uttered a scream that was heard beyond the Damascus Gate, and even upon the Mount of Olives, it was said, and then fell back in a deadly swoon. They recovered her and brought the second cross. Instantly she went into fearful convulsions, and it was with the greatest difficulty that six strong men could hold her. They were afraid, now, to bring in the third cross. They began to fear that possibly they had fallen upon the wrong crosses, and that the true cross was not with this number at all. However, as the woman seemed likely to die with the convulsions that were tearing her, they concluded that the third could do no more than put her out of her misery with a happy despatch. So they brought it, and behold, a miracle! The woman sprang from her bed, smiling and joyful, and perfectly restored to health. When we listen to evidence like this, we cannot but believe. We would be ashamed to doubt, and properly, too. Even the very part of Jerusalem where this all occurred is there yet. So there is really no room for doubt.

The priest tried to show us, through a small screen, a fragment of the genuine Pillar of Flagellation, to which Christ was bound when they scourged him. But we could not see it, because it was dark inside the screen. However, a baton is kept here, which the pilgrim thrusts through a hole in the screen, and then he no longer doubts that the true Pillar of Flagellation is in there. He cannot have any excuse to doubt it, for he can feel it with the stick. He can feel it as distinctly as he could feel anything.

Not far from here was a niche where they used to preserve a piece of the True Cross, but it is gone now. This piece of the cross was discovered in the sixteenth century. The Latin priests say it was stolen away, long ago, by priests of another sect. That seems like a hard statement to make, but we know very well that it *was* stolen, because we have seen it ourselves in several of the cathedrals of Italy and France.

But the relic that touched us most was the plain old sword of that stout Crusader, Godfrey of Bouillon —King Godfrey of Jerusalem. No blade in Christendom wields such enchantment as this—no blade of all that rust in the ancestral halls of Europe is able to invoke such visions of romance in the brain of him who looks upon it—none that can prate of such chivalric deeds or tell such brave tales of the warrior days of old. It stirs within a man every memory of the Holy Wars that has been sleeping in his brain for years, and peoples his thoughts with mail-clad images, with marching armies, with battles and with sieges. It speaks to him of Baldwin, and Tancred, the princely Saladin, and great Richard of the Lion Heart. It was with just such blades as these that these splendid heroes of romance used to segregate a man, so to speak, and leave the half of him to fall one way and the other half the other. This very sword has cloven hundreds of Saracen Knights from crown to chin in those old

times when Godfrey wielded it. It was enchanted,
then, by a genius that was under the command of
King Solomon. When danger approached its master's tent it always struck the shield and clanged
out a fierce alarm upon the startled ear of night. In
times of doubt, or in fog or darkness, if it were drawn
from its sheath it would point instantly toward
the foe, and thus reveal the way—and it would
also attempt to start after them of its own accord.
A Christian could not be so disguised that it would
not know him and refuse to hurt him—nor a Moslem so disguised that it would not leap from its
scabbard and take his life. These statements are all
well authenticated in many legends that are among
the most trustworthy legends the good old Catholic
monks preserve. I can never forget old Godfrey's
sword now. I tried it on a Moslem, and clove him
in twain like a doughnut. The spirit of Grimes was
upon me, and if I had had a graveyard I would have
destroyed all the infidels in Jerusalem. I wiped the
blood off the old sword and handed it back to the
priest—I did not want the fresh gore to obliterate
those sacred spots that crimsoned its brightness one
day six hundred years ago and thus gave Godfrey
warning that before the sun went down his journey
of life would end.

Still moving through the gloom of the Church of
the Holy Sepulcher we came to a small chapel,
hewn out of the rock—a place which has been
known as "The Prison of Our Lord" for many
centuries. Tradition says that here the Saviour was
confined just previously to the crucifixion. Under

an altar by the door was a pair of stone stocks for human legs. These things are called the "Bonds of Christ," and the use they were once put to has given them the name they now bear.

The Greek Chapel is the most roomy, the richest and the showiest chapel in the Church of the Holy Sepulcher. Its altar, like that of all the Greek churches, is a lofty screen that extends clear across the chapel, and is gorgeous with gilding and pictures. The numerous lamps that hang before it are of gold and silver, and cost great sums.

But the feature of the place is a short column that rises from the middle of the marble pavement of the chapel, and marks the exact *center of the earth*. The most reliable traditions tell us that this was known to be the earth's center, ages ago, and that when Christ was upon earth he set all doubts upon the subject at rest forever, by stating with his own lips that the tradition was correct. Remember He said that that particular column stood upon the center of the world. If the center of the world changes, the column changes its position accordingly. This column has moved three different times, of its own accord. This is because, in great convulsions of nature, at three different times, masses of the earth—whole ranges of mountains, probably—have flown off into space, thus lessening the diameter of the earth, and changing the exact locality of its center by a point or two. This is a very curious and interesting circumstance, and is a withering rebuke to those philosophers who would make us believe that it is not possible for any portion of the earth to fly off into space.

To satisfy himself that this spot was really the center of the earth, a skeptic once paid well for the privilege of ascending to the dome of the church to see if the sun gave him a shadow at noon. He came down perfectly convinced. The day was very cloudy and the sun threw no shadows at all; but the man was satisfied that if the sun had come out and made shadows it could not have made any for him. Proofs like these are not to be set aside by the idle tongues of cavilers. To such as are not bigoted, and are willing to be convinced, they carry a conviction that nothing can ever shake.

If even greater proofs than those I have mentioned are wanted, to satisfy the headstrong and the foolish that this is the genuine center of the earth, they are here. The greatest of them lies in the fact that from under this very column was taken the *dust from which Adam was made*. This can surely be regarded in the light of a settler. It is not likely that the original first man would have been made from an inferior quality of earth when it was entirely convenient to get first quality from the world's center. This will strike any reflecting mind forcibly. That Adam was formed of dirt procured in this very spot is amply proven by the fact that in six thousand years no man has ever been able to prove that the dirt was *not* procured here whereof he was made.

It is a singular circumstance that right under the roof of this same great church, and not far away from that illustrious column, Adam himself, the father of the human race, lies buried. There is no question that he is actually buried in the grave which is pointed out as his—there can be none—because it has never yet been proven that that grave is not the grave in which he is buried.

The tomb of Adam! How touching it was, here in a land of strangers, far away from home, and friends, and all who cared for me, thus to discover the grave of a blood relation. True, a distant one, but still a relation. The unerring instinct of nature thrilled its recognition. The fountain of my filial affection was stirred to its profoundest depths, and I gave way to tumultuous emotion. I leaned upon a pillar and burst into tears. I deem it no shame to have wept over the grave of my poor dead relative. Let him who would sneer at my emotion close this volume here, for he will find little to his taste in my journeyings through Holy Land. Noble old man— he did not live to see me—he did not live to see his child. And I—I—alas, I did not live to see *him*. Weighed down by sorrow and disappointment, he died before I was born—six thousand brief summers before I was born. But let us try to bear it with fortitude. Let us trust that he is better off where he is. Let us take comfort in the thought that his loss is our eternal gain.

The next place the guide took us to in the holy church was an altar dedicated to the Roman soldier who was of the military guard that attended at the Crucifixion to keep order, and who—when the veil of the Temple was rent in the awful darkness that followed; when the rock of Golgotha was split

asunder by an earthquake; when the artillery of
heaven thundered, and in the baleful glare of the
lightnings the shrouded dead flitted about the streets
of Jerusalem—shook with fear and said, "Surely
this was the Son of God!" Where this altar stands
now, that Roman soldier stood then, in full view of
the crucified Saviour—in full sight and hearing of
all the marvels that were transpiring far and wide
about the circumference of the Hill of Calvary.
And in this selfsame spot the priests of the Temple
beheaded him for those blasphemous words he had
spoken.

In this altar they used to keep one of the most
curious relics that human eyes ever looked upon—
a thing that had power to fascinate the beholder in
some mysterious way and keep him gazing for hours
together. It was nothing less than the copper plate
Pilate put upon the Saviour's cross, and upon which
he wrote, "THIS IS THE KING OF THE JEWS." I
think St. Helena, the mother of Constantine, found
this wonderful memento when she was here in the
third century. She traveled all over Palestine, and
was always fortunate. Whenever the good old enthusiast found a thing mentioned in her Bible, Old
or New, she would go and search for that thing, and
never stop until she found it. If it was Adam, she
would find Adam; if it was the Ark, she would find
the Ark; if it was Goliah, or Joshua, she would
find *them*. She found the inscription here that I
was speaking of, I think. She found it in this very
spot, close to where the martyred Roman soldier
stood. That copper plate is in one of the churches

in Rome now. Any one can see it there. The inscription is very distinct.

We passed along a few steps and saw the altar built over the very spot where the good Catholic priests say the soldiers divided the raiment of the Saviour.

Then we went down into a cavern which cavilers say was once a cistern. It is a chapel now, however—the Chapel of St. Helena. It is fifty-one feet long by forty-three wide. In it is a marble chair which Helena used to sit in while she superintended her workmen when they were digging and delving for the True Cross. In this place is an altar dedicated to St. Dimas, the penitent thief. A new bronze statue is here—a statue of St. Helena. It reminded us of poor Maximilian, so lately shot. He presented it to this chapel when he was about to leave for his throne in Mexico.

From the cistern we descended twelve steps into a large roughly shaped grotto, carved wholly out of the living rock. Helena blasted it out when she was searching for the true cross. She had a laborious piece of work here, but it was richly rewarded. Out of this place she got the crown of thorns, the nails of the cross, the true cross itself, and the cross of the penitent thief. When she thought she had found everything and was about to stop, she was told in a dream to continue a day longer. It was very fortunate. She did so, and found the cross of the other thief.

The walls and roof of this grotto still weep bitter tears in memory of the event that transpired on Calvary, and devout pilgrims groan and sob when these sad tears fall upon them from the dripping rock. The monks call this apartment the "Chapel of the Invention of the Cross"—a name which is unfortunate, because it leads the ignorant to imagine that a tacit acknowledgment is thus made that the tradition that Helena found the true cross here is a fiction—an invention. It is a happiness to know, however, that intelligent people do not doubt the story in any of its particulars.

Priests of any of the chapels and denominations in the Church of the Holy Sepulcher can visit this sacred grotto to weep and pray and worship the gentle Redeemer. Two different congregations are not allowed to enter at the same time, however, because they always fight.

Still marching through the venerable Church of the Holy Sepulcher, among chanting priests in coarse long robes and sandals; pilgrims of all colors and many nationalities, in all sorts of strange costumes; under dusky arches and by dingy piers and columns; through a somber cathedral gloom, freighted with smoke and incense, and faintly starred with scores of candles that appeared suddenly and as suddenly disappeared, or drifted mysteriously hither and thither about the distant aisles like ghostly jack-o'-lanterns—we came at last to a small chapel which is called the "Chapel of the Mocking." Under the altar was a fragment of a marble column; this was the seat Christ sat on when he was reviled, and mockingly made King, crowned with a crown of thorns and sceptered with a reed. It was here that they blindfolded him and struck him, and said in derision, "Prophesy who it is that smote thee." The tradition that this is the identical spot of the mocking is a very ancient one. The guide said that Saewulf was the first to mention it. I do not know Saewulf, but still, I cannot well refuse to receive his evidence—none of us can.

They showed us where the great Godfrey and his brother Baldwin, the first Christian Kings of Jerusalem, once lay buried by that sacred sepulcher they had fought so long and so valiantly to wrest from the hands of the infidel. But the niches that had contained the ashes of these renowned crusaders were empty. Even the coverings of their tombs were gone—destroyed by devout members of the Greek church, because Godfrey and Baldwin were Latin princes, and had been reared in a Christian faith whose creed differed in some unimportant respects from theirs.

We passed on, and halted before the tomb of Melchisedek! You will remember Melchisedek, no doubt; he was the King who came out and levied a tribute on Abraham the time that he pursued Lot's captors to Dan, and took all their property from them. That was about four thousand years ago, and Melchisedek died shortly afterward. However, his tomb is in a good state of preservation.

When one enters the Church of the Holy Sepulcher, the Sepulcher itself is the first thing he desires to see, and really is almost the first thing he does see. The next thing he has a strong yearning to see is the spot where the Saviour was crucified. But this they exhibit last. It is the crowning glory of the place. One is grave and thoughtful when he stands in the little Tomb of the Saviour—he could not well be otherwise in such a place—but he has not the slightest possible belief that ever the Lord lay there, and so the interest he feels in the spot is very, very greatly marred by that reflection. He looks at the place where Mary stood, in another part of the church, and where John stood, and Mary Magdalen; where the mob derided the Lord; where the angel sat; where the crown of thorns was found, and the true cross; where the risen Saviour appeared—he looks at all these places with interest, but with the same conviction he felt in the case of the Sepulcher, that there is nothing genuine about them, and that they are imaginary holy places created by the monks. But the place of the Crucifixion affects him differently. He fully believes that he is looking upon the very spot where the Saviour gave up his life. He remembers that Christ was very celebrated, long before he came to Jerusalem; he knows that his fame was so great that crowds followed him all the time; he is aware that his entry into the city produced a stirring sensation, and that his reception was a kind of ovation; he cannot overlook the fact that when he was crucified there were very many in Jerusalem who believed that he was the true Son of God. To publicly execute such a personage was sufficient in itself to make the locality of the execution a memorable place for ages; added to this, the storm, the darkness, the earthquake, the rending of the veil of the Temple, and the untimely waking of the dead, were events calculated to fix the execution

and the scene of it in the memory of even the most
thoughtless witness. Fathers would tell their sons
about the strange affair, and point out the spot; the
sons would transmit the story to their children, and
thus a period of three hundred years would easily
be spanned[1]—at which time Helena came and built
a church upon Calvary to commemorate the death
and burial of the Lord and preserve the sacred place
in the memories of men; since that time there has
always been a church there. It is not possible that
there can be any mistake about the locality of the
Crucifixion. Not half a dozen persons knew where
they buried the Saviour, perhaps, and a burial is not
a startling event, anyhow; therefore, we can be
pardoned for unbelief in the Sepulcher, but not
in the place of the Crucifixion. Five hundred
years hence there will be no vestige of Bunker Hill
Monument left, but America will still know where
the battle was fought and where Warren fell. The
crucifixion of Christ was too notable an event in
Jerusalem, and the Hill of Calvary made too celebrated by it, to be forgotten in the short space of
three hundred years. I climbed the stairway in the
church which brings one to the top of the small inclosed pinnacle of rock, and looked upon the place
where the true cross once stood, with a far more
absorbing interest than I had ever felt in anything
earthly before. I could not believe that the three
holes in the top of the rock were the actual ones the
crosses stood in, but I felt satisfied that those crosses

[1] The thought is Mr. Grime's, not mine, and is full of good sense.
I borrowed it from his *Tent Life.*—M. T.

313

had stood so near the place now occupied by them, that the few feet of possible difference were a matter of no consequence.

When one stands where the Saviour was crucified, he finds it all he can do to keep it strictly before his mind that Christ was not crucified in a Catholic church. He must remind himself every now and then that the great event transpired in the open air, and not in a gloomy, candle-lighted cell in a little corner of a vast church, up-stairs—a small cell all bejeweled and bespangled with flashy ornamentation, in execrable taste.

Under a marble altar like a table, is a circular hole in the marble floor, corresponding with the one just under it in which the true cross stood. The first thing every one does is to kneel down and take a candle and examine this hole. He does this strange prospecting with an amount of gravity that can never be estimated or appreciated by a man who has not seen the operation. Then he holds his candle before a richly engraved picture of the Saviour, done on a massy slab of gold, and wonderfully rayed and starred with diamonds, which hangs above the hole within the altar, and his solemnity changes to lively admiration. He rises and faces the finely wrought figures of the Saviour and the malefactors uplifted upon their crosses behind the altar, and bright with a metallic luster of many colors. He turns next to the figures close to them of the Virgin and Mary Magdalen; next to the rift in the living rock made by the earthquake at the time of the crucifixion, and an extension of which he had seen before in the wall of one of the grottoes below; he looks next at the showcase with a figure of the Virgin in it, and is amazed at the princely fortune in precious gems and jewelry that hangs so thickly about the form as to hide it like a garment almost. All about the apartment the gaudy trappings of the Greek church offend the eye and keep the mind on the rack to remember that this is the Place of the Crucifixion—Golgotha—the Mount of Calvary. And the last thing he looks at is that which was also the first—the place where the true cross stood. That will chain him to the spot and compel him to look once more, and once again, after he has satisfied all curiosity and lost all interest concerning the other matters pertaining to the locality.

And so I close my chapter on the Church of the Holy Sepulcher—the most sacred locality on earth to millions and millions of men, and women, and children, the noble and the humble, bond and free. In its history from the first, and in its tremendous associations, it is the most illustrious edifice in Christendom. With all its claptrap side-shows and unseemly impostures of every kind, it is still grand, reverend, venerable—for a god died there; for fifteen hundred years its shrines have been wet with the tears of pilgrims from the earth's remotest confines; for more than two hundred, the most gallant knights that ever wielded sword wasted their lives away in a struggle to seize it and hold it sacred from infidel pollution. Even in our own day a war, that cost millions of treasure and rivers of blood, was fought because two rival nations claimed the sole right to put a new dome upon it. History is full of this old Church of the Holy Sepulcher—full of blood that was shed because of the respect and the veneration in which men held the last resting-place of the meek and lowly, the mild and gentle Prince of Peace!

## CHAPTER XXVII

WE were standing in a narrow street, by the Tower of Antonio. "On these stones that are crumbling away," the guide said, "the Saviour sat and rested before taking up the cross. This is the beginning of the Sorrowful Way, or the Way of Grief." The party took note of the sacred spot, and moved on. We passed under the "Ecce Homo Arch," and saw the very window from which Pilate's wife warned her husband to have nothing to do with the persecution of the Just Man. The window is in an excellent state of preservation, considering its great age. They showed us where Jesus rested the second time, and where the mob refused to give him up, and said, "Let his blood be upon our heads, and upon our children's children forever." The French Catholics are building a church on this spot, and with their usual veneration for historical relics, are incorporating into the new such scraps of ancient walls as they have found there. Further on, we saw the spot where the fainting Saviour fell under the weight of his cross. A great granite column of some ancient temple lay there at the time, and the heavy cross struck it such a blow that it broke in two in the middle. Such was the guide's story when he halted us before the broken column.

We crossed a street, and came presently to the former residence of St. Veronica. When the Saviour passed there, she came out, full of womanly compassion, and spoke pitying words to him, undaunted by the hootings and the threatenings of the mob, and wiped the perspiration from his face with her handkerchief. We had heard so much of St. Veronica, and seen her picture by so many masters, that it was like meeting an old friend unexpectedly to come upon her ancient home in Jerusalem. The strangest thing about the incident that has made her name so famous, is, that when she wiped the perspiration away, the print of the Saviour's face remained upon the handkerchief, a perfect portrait, and so remains unto this day. We knew this, because we saw this handkerchief in a cathedral in Paris, in another in Spain, and in two others in Italy. In the Milan cathedral it costs five francs to see it, and at St. Peter's, at Rome, it is almost impossible to see it at any price. No tradition is so amply verified as this of St. Veronica and her handkerchief.

At the next corner we saw a deep indentation in the hard stone masonry of the corner of a house, but might have gone heedlessly by it but that the guide said it was made by the elbow of the Saviour, who stumbled here and fell. Presently we came to just such another indentation in a stone wall. The guide said the Saviour fell here, also, and made this depression with his elbow.

There were other places where the Lord fell, and others where he rested; but one of the most curious

landmarks of ancient history we found on this morning walk through the crooked lanes that lead toward
Calvary, was a certain stone built into a house—a
stone that was so seamed and scarred that it bore a
sort of grotesque resemblance to the human face.
The projections that answered for cheeks were worn
smooth by the passionate kisses of generations of
pilgrims from distant lands. We asked "Why?"
The guide said it was because this was one of "the
very stones of Jerusalem" that Christ mentioned
when he was reproved for permitting the people to
cry "Hosannah!" when he made his memorable
entry into the city upon an ass. One of the pilgrims said, "But there is no evidence that the stones
*did* cry out—Christ said that if the people stopped
from shouting Hosannah, the very stones *would* do
it." The guide was perfectly serene. He said,
calmly, "This is one of the stones that *would* have
cried out." It was of little use to try to shake this
fellow's simple faith—it was easy to see that.

And so we came at last to another wonder, of
deep and abiding interest—the veritable house where
the unhappy wretch once lived who has been celebrated in song and story for more than eighteen
hundred years as the Wandering Jew. On the
memorable day of the Crucifixion he stood in this
old doorway with his arms akimbo, looking out upon
the struggling mob that was approaching, and when
the weary Saviour would have sat down and rested
him a moment, pushed him rudely away and said,
"Move on!" The Lord said, "Move on, thou,
likewise," and the command has never been revoked

from that day to this. All men know how that the miscreant upon whose head that just curse fell has roamed up and down the wide world, for ages and ages, seeking rest and never finding it—courting death but always in vain—longing to stop, in city, in wilderness, in desert solitudes, yet hearing always that relentless warning to march—march on! They say—do these hoary traditions—that when Titus sacked Jerusalem and slaughtered eleven hundred thousand Jews in her streets and byways, the Wandering Jew was seen always in the thickest of the fight, and that when battle-axes gleamed in the air, he bowed his head beneath them; when swords flashed their deadly lightnings, he sprang in their way; he bared his breast to whizzing javelins, to hissing arrows, to any and to every weapon that promised death and forgetfulness, and rest. But it was useless—he walked forth out of the carnage without a wound. And it is said that five hundred years afterward he followed Mohammed when he carried destruction to the cities of Arabia, and then turned against him, hoping in this way to win the death of a traitor. His calculations were wrong again. No quarter was given to any living creature but one, and that was the only one of all the host that did not want it. He sought death five hundred years later, in the wars of the Crusades, and offered himself to famine and pestilence at Ascalon. He escaped again—he could not die. These repeated annoyances could have at last but one effect—they shook his confidence. Since then the Wandering Jew has carried on a kind of desultory toying with the most promising of the aids and implements of destruction, but with small hope, as a general thing. He has speculated some in cholera and railroads, and has taken almost a lively interest in infernal machines and patent medicines. He is old, now, and grave, as becomes an age like his; he indulges in no light amusements save that he goes sometimes to executions, and is fond of funerals.

There is one thing he cannot avoid; go where he will about the world, he must never fail to report in Jerusalem every fiftieth year. Only a year or two ago he was here for the thirty-seventh time since Jesus was crucified on Calvary. They say that many old people, who are here now, saw him then, and had seen him before. He looks always the same—old, and withered, and hollow-eyed, and listless, save that there is about him something which seems to suggest that he is looking for some one, expecting some one—the friends of his youth, perhaps. But the most of them are dead, now. He always pokes about the old streets looking lonesome, making his mark on a wall here and there, and eying the oldest buildings with a sort of friendly half-interest; and he sheds a few tears at the threshold of his ancient dwelling, and bitter, bitter tears they are. Then he collects his rent and leaves again. He has been seen standing near the Church of the Holy Sepulcher on many a starlight night, for he has cherished an idea for many centuries that if he could only enter there, he could rest. But when he approaches, the doors slam to with a crash, the earth trembles, and all the lights in Jerusalem burn a ghastly blue! He does this every fifty years, just the same. It is hopeless, but then it is hard to break habits one has been eighteen hundred years accustomed to. The old tourist is far away on his wanderings, now. How he must smile to see a pack of blockheads like us, galloping about the world, and looking wise, and imagining we are finding out a good deal about it! He must have a consuming contempt for the ignorant, complacent asses that go scurrying about the world in these railroading days and call it traveling.

When the guide pointed out where the Wandering Jew had left his familiar mark upon a wall, I was filled with astonishment. It read:

S. T.—1860—X.

All I have revealed about the Wandering Jew can be amply proven by reference to our guide.

The mighty Mosque of Omar, and the paved court around it, ⸤ ccupy *a fourth part* of Jerusalem. They are upon Mount Moriah, where King Solomon's Temple stood. This Mosque is the holiest place the Mohammedan knows, outside of Mecca. Up to within a year or two past, no Christian could gain admission to it or its court for love or money. But the prohibition has been removed, and we entered freely for bucksheesh.

I need not speak of the wonderful beauty and the exquisite grace and symmetry that have made this Mosque so celebrated—because I did not see them. One cannot see such things at an instant glance— one frequently only finds out how really beautiful a really beautiful woman is after considerable acquaintance with her; and the rule applies to Niagara Falls, to majestic mountains, and to mosques—especially to mosques.

The great feature of the Mosque of Omar is the prodigious rock in the center of its rotunda. It was upon this rock that Abraham came so near offering up his son Isaac—this, at least, is authentic—it is very much more to be relied on than most of the traditions, at any rate. On this rock, also, the angel stood and threatened Jerusalem, and David persuaded him to spare the city. Mohammed was well acquainted with this stone. From it he ascended to heaven. The stone tried to follow him, and if the angel Gabriel had not happened by the merest good luck to be there to seize it, it would have done it. Very few people have a grip like Gabriel—the prints of his monstrous fingers, two inches deep, are to be seen in that rock to-day.

This rock, large as it is, is suspended in the air. It does not touch anything at all. The guide said so. This is very wonderful. In the place on it where Mohammed stood, he left his footprints in the solid stone. I should judge that he wore about eighteens. But what I was going to say, when I spoke of the rock being suspended, was, that in the floor of the cavern under it they showed us a slab which they said covered a hole which was a thing of extraordinary interest to all Mohammedans, because that hole leads down to perdition, and every soul that is transferred from thence to Heaven must pass up through this orifice. Mohammed stands there and lifts them out by the hair. All Mohammedans shave their heads, but they are careful to leave a lock of hair for the Prophet to take hold of. Our guide observed that a good Mohammedan would consider himself doomed to stay with the damned forever if he were to lose his scalp-lock and die before it grew again. The most of them that I have seen ought to stay with the damned, anyhow, without reference to how they were barbered.

For several ages no woman has been allowed to enter the cavern where that important hole is. The reason is that one of the sex was once caught there blabbing everything she knew about what was going on above-ground, to the rapscallions in the infernal regions down below. She carried her gossiping to such an extreme that nothing could be kept private —nothing could be done or said on earth but everybody in perdition knew all about it before the sun went down. It was about time to suppress this woman's telegraph, and it was promptly done. Her breath subsided about the same time.

The inside of the great mosque is very showy with variegated marble walls and with windows and inscriptions of elaborate mosaic. The Turks have their sacred relics, like the Catholics. The guide showed us the veritable armor worn by the great son-in-law and successor of Mohammed, and also the buckler of Mohammed's uncle. The great iron railing which surrounds the rock was ornamented in one place with a thousand rags tied to its open work. These are to remind Mohammed not to forget the worshipers who placed them there. It is considered the next best thing to tying threads around his finger by way of reminders.

THE INNOCENTS ABROAD

Just outside the mosque is a miniature temple, which marks the spot where David and Goliah used to sit and judge the people.[1]

Everywhere about the Mosque of Omar are portions of pillars, curiously wrought altars, and fragments of elegantly carved marble—precious remains of Solomon's Temple. These have been dug from all depths in the soil and rubbish of Mount Moriah, and the Moslems have always shown a disposition to preserve them with the utmost care. At that portion of the ancient wall of Solomon's Temple which is called the Jew's Place of Wailing, and where the Hebrews assemble every Friday to kiss the venerated stones and weep over the fallen greatness of Zion, any one can see a part of the unquestioned and undisputed Temple of Solomon, the same consisting of three or four stones lying one upon the other, each of which is about twice as long as a seven-octave piano, and about as thick as such a piano is high. But, as I have remarked before, it is only a year or two ago that the ancient edict prohibiting Christian rubbish like ourselves to *enter* the Mosque of Omar and see the costly marbles that once adorned the inner Temple was annulled. The designs wrought upon these fragments are all quaint and peculiar, and so the charm of novelty is added to the deep interest they naturally inspire. One meets with these venerable scraps at every turn, especially in the neighboring Mosque el Aksa, into whose inner walls a very

[1] A pilgrim informs me that it was not David and Goliah, but David and Saul. I stick to my own statement—the guide told me, and he ought to know.

large number of them are carefully built for preservation. These pieces of stone, stained and dusty with age, dimly hint at a grandeur we have all been taught to regard as the princeliest ever seen on earth; and they call up pictures of a pageant that is familiar to all imaginations—camels laden with spices and treasure—beautiful slaves, presents for Solomon's harem—a long cavalcade of richly caparisoned beasts and warriors—and Sheba's Queen in the van of this vision of "Oriental magnificence." These elegant fragments bear a richer interest than the solemn vastness of the stones the Jews kiss in the Place of Wailing can ever have for the heedless sinner.

Down in the hollow ground, underneath the olives and the orange trees that flourish in the court of the great Mosque, is a wilderness of pillars—remains of the ancient Temple; they supported it. There are ponderous archways down there, also, over which the destroying "plow" of prophecy passed harmless. It is pleasant to know we are disappointed, in that we never dreamed we might see portions of the actual Temple of Solomon, and yet experience no shadow of suspicion that they were a monkish humbug and a fraud.

We are surfeited with sights. Nothing has any fascination for us, now, but the Church of the Holy Sepulcher. We have been there every day, and have not grown tired of it; but we are weary of everything else. The sights are too many. They swarm about you at every step; no single foot of ground in all Jerusalem or within its neighborhood

seems to be without a stirring and important history
of its own.   It is a very relief to steal a walk of a
hundred yards without a guide along to talk unceas-
ingly about every stone you step upon and drag you
back ages and ages to the day when it achieved
celebrity.

It seems hardly real when I find myself leaning
for a moment on a ruined wall and looking *listlessly*
down into the historic pool of Bethesda.   I did not
think such things *could* be so crowded together as to
diminish their interest.   But, in serious truth, we
have been drifting about, for several days, using our
eyes and our ears more from a sense of duty than any
higher and worthier reason.   And too often we have
been glad when it was time to go home and be distressed no more about illustrious localities.

Our pilgrims compress too much into one day.
One can gorge sights to repletion as well as sweet-
meats.   Since we breakfasted, this morning, we have
seen enough to have furnished us food for a year's
reflection if we could have seen the various objects
in comfort and looked upon them deliberately.   We
visited the Pool of Hezekiah, where David saw
Uriah's wife coming from the bath and fell in love
with her.

We went out of the city by the Jaffa gate, and of
course were told many things about its Tower of
Hippicus.

We rode across the Valley of Hinnom, between
two of the Pools of Gihon, and by an aqueduct
built by Solomon, which still conveys water to the
city.   We ascended the Hill of Evil Counsel, where

Judas received his thirty pieces of silver, and we also
lingered a moment under the tree a venerable tradition says he hanged himself on.

We descended to the cañon again, and then the
guide began to give name and history to every bank
and boulder we came to: "This was the Field of
Blood; these cuttings in the rocks were shrines and
temples of Moloch; here they sacrificed children;
yonder is the Zion Gate; the Tyropean Valley; the
Hill of Ophel; here is the junction of the Valley of
Jehoshaphat—on your right is the Well of Job."
We turned up Jehoshaphat. The recital went on.

"This is the Mount of Olives; this is the Hill of
Offense; the nest of huts is the Village of Siloam;
here, yonder, everywhere, is the King's Garden;
under this great tree Zacharias, the high priest, was
murdered; yonder is Mount Moriah and the Temple
wall; the tomb of Absalom; the tomb of St. James;
the tomb of Zacharias; beyond, are the Garden of
Gethsemane and the tomb of the Virgin Mary; here
is the Pool of Siloam, and—"

We said we would dismount, and quench our
thirst, and rest. We were burning up with the heat.
We were failing under the accumulated fatigue of
days and days of ceaseless marching. All were
willing.

The Pool is a deep, walled ditch, through which a
clear stream of water runs, that comes from under
Jerusalem somewhere, and passing through the
Fountain of the Virgin, or being supplied from it,
reaches this place by way of a tunnel of heavy
masonry. The famous pool looked exactly as it

looked in Solomon's time, no doubt, and the same
dusky, Oriental women came down in their old
Oriental way and carried off jars of the water on
their heads, just as they did three thousand years
ago, and just as they will do fifty thousand years
hence if any of them are still left on earth.

We went away from there and stopped at the
Fountain of the Virgin. But the water was not
good, and there was no comfort or peace anywhere,
on account of the regiment of boys and girls and beggars that persecuted us all the time for bucksheesh.
The guide wanted us to give them some money, and
we did it; but when he went on to say that they
were starving to death we could not but feel that we
had done a great sin in throwing obstacles in the way
of such a desirable consummation, and so we tried
to collect it back, but it could not be done.

We entered the Garden of Gethsemane, and we
visited the Tomb of the Virgin, both of which we
had seen before. It is not meet that I should speak
of them now. A more fitting time will come.

I cannot speak now of the Mount of Olives or its
view of Jerusalem, the Dead Sea, and the mountains
of Moab; nor of the Damascus Gate or the tree that
was planted by King Godfrey of Jerusalem. One
ought to feel pleasantly when he talks of these things.
I cannot say anything about the stone column that
projects over Jehoshaphat from the Temple wall
like a cannon, except that the Moslems believe Mohammed will sit astride of it when he comes to judge
the world. It is a pity he could not judge it from
some roost of his own in Mecca, without trespass-

ing on *our* holy ground. Close by is the Golden
Gate, in the Temple wall—a gate that was an
elegant piece of sculpture in the time of the Temple,
and is even so yet. From it, in ancient times, the
Jewish High Priest turned loose the scapegoat and
let him flee to the wilderness and bear away his
twelvemonth load of the sins of the people. If
they were to turn one loose now, he would not get
as far as the Garden of Gethsemane, till these miserable vagabonds here would gobble him up,[1] sins and
all. *They* wouldn't care. Mutton-chops and sin is
good enough living for them. The Moslems watch
the Golden Gate with a jealous eye, and an anxious
one, for they have an honored tradition that when
it falls, Islamism will fall, and with it the Ottoman
Empire. It did not grieve me any to notice that the
old gate was getting a little shaky.

We are at home again. We are exhausted. The
sun has roasted us, almost.

We have full comfort in one reflection, however.
Our experiences in Europe have taught us that in
time this fatigue will be forgotten; the heat will be
forgotten; the thirst, the tiresome volubility of the
guide, the persecutions of the beggars—and then,
all that will be left will be pleasant memories of
Jerusalem, memories we shall call up with always in-
creasing interest as the years go by, memories which
some day will become all beautiful when the last
annoyance that encumbers them shall have faded out
of our minds never again to return. School-boy days
are no happier than the days of after life, but we look

[1] Favorite pilgrim expression.

back upon them regretfully because we have forgotten our punishments at school, and how we
grieved when our marbles were lost and our kites
destroyed—because we have forgotten all the sorrows
and privations of that canonized epoch and remember only its orchard robberies, its wooden-sword
pageants, and its fishing holidays.  We are satisfied.
We can wait.  Our reward will come.  To us, Jerusalem and to-day's experiences will be an enchanted
memory a year hence—a memory which money
could not buy from us.

# CHAPTER XXVIII.

WE cast up the account. It footed up pretty fairly. There was nothing more at Jerusalem to be seen, except the traditional houses of Dives and Lazarus of the parable, the Tombs of the Kings, and those of the Judges; the spot where they stoned one of the disciples to death, and beheaded another; the room and the table made celebrated by the Last Supper; the fig tree that Jesus withered; a number of historical places about Gethsemane and the Mount of Olives, and fifteen or twenty others in different portions of the city itself.

We were approaching the end. Human nature asserted itself, now. Overwork and consequent exhaustion began to have their natural effect. They began to master the energies and dull the ardor of the party. Perfectly secure now against failing to accomplish any detail of the pilgrimage, they felt like drawing in advance upon the holiday soon to be placed to their credit. They grew a little lazy. They were late to breakfast and sat long at dinner. Thirty or forty pilgrims had arrived from the ship, by the short routes, and much swapping of gossip had to be indulged in. And in hot afternoons, they showed a strong disposition to lie on the cool divans in the hotel and smoke and talk about pleasant experiences of a month or so gone by—for even thus early do episodes of travel which were sometimes annoying, sometimes exasperating, and full as often of no consequence at all when they transpired, begin to rise above the dead level of monotonous reminiscences and become shapely landmarks in one's memory. The fog-whistle, smothered among a million of trifling sounds, is not noticed a block away, in the city, but the sailor hears it far at sea, whither none of those thousands of trifling sounds can reach. When one is in Rome, all the domes are alike; but when he has gone away twelve miles, the city fades utterly from sight and leaves St. Peter's swelling above the level plain like an anchored balloon. When one is traveling in Europe, the daily incidents seem all alike; but when he has placed them all two months and two thousand miles behind him, those that were worthy of being remembered are prominent, and those that were really insignificant have vanished. This disposition to smoke and idle and talk was not well. It was plain that it must not be allowed to gain ground. A diversion must be tried, or demoralization would ensue. The Jordan, Jericho, and the Dead Sea were suggested. The remainder of Jerusalem must be left unvisited, for a little while. The journey was approved at once. New life stirred in every pulse. In the saddle—abroad on the plains—sleeping in beds bounded only by the horizon: fancy was at work with these things in a moment. It was painful to note how readily these town-bred men had taken to the free life of the camp and the desert. The nomadic

instinct is a human instinct; it was born with Adam
and transmitted through the patriarchs, and after
thirty centuries of steady effort, civilization has not
educated it entirely out of us yet. It has a charm
which, once tasted, a man will yearn to taste again.
The nomadic instinct cannot be educated out of an
Indian at all.

The Jordan journey being approved, our dragoman
was notified.

At nine in the morning the caravan was before the
hotel door and we were at breakfast. There was
a commotion about the place. Rumors of war and
bloodshed were flying everywhere. The lawless
Bedouins in the Valley of the Jordan and the deserts
down by the Dead Sea were up in arms, and were
going to destroy all comers. They had had a battle
with a troop of Turkish cavalry and defeated them;
several men killed. They had shut up the inhabitants of a village and a Turkish garrison in an old
fort near Jericho, and were besieging them. They
had marched upon a camp of our excursionists by
the Jordan, and the pilgrims only saved their lives by
stealing away and flying to Jerusalem under whip
and spur in the darkness of the night. Another of
our parties had been fired on from an ambush and
then attacked in the open day. Shots were fired on
both sides. Fortunately, there was no bloodshed.
We spoke with the very pilgrim who had fired one of
the shots, and learned from his own lips how, in this
imminent deadly peril, only the cool courage of the
pilgrims, their strength of numbers and imposing
display of war material, had saved them from utter

destruction. It was reported that the Consul had requested that no more of our pilgrims should go to the Jordan while this state of things lasted; and further, that he was unwilling that any more should go, at least without an unusually strong military guard. Here was trouble. But with the horses at the door and everybody aware of what they were there for, what would *you* have done? Acknowledged that you were afraid, and backed shamefully out? Hardly. It would not be human nature, where there were so many women. You would have done as we did: said you were not afraid of a million Bedouins—and made your will and proposed quietly to yourself to take up an unostentatious position in the rear of the procession.

I think we must all have determined upon the same line of tactics, for it did seem as if we never would get to Jericho. I had a notoriously slow horse, but somehow I could not keep him in the rear, to save my neck. He was forever turning up in the lead. In such cases I trembled a little, and got down to fix my saddle. But it was not of any use. The others all got down to fix their saddles, too. I never saw such a time with saddles. It was the first time any of them had got out of order in three weeks, and now they had all broken down at once. I tried walking, for exercise—I had not had enough in Jerusalem searching for holy places. But it was a failure. The whole mob were suffering for exercise, and it was not fifteen minutes till they were all on foot and I had the lead again. It was very discouraging.

This was all after we got beyond Bethany. **We**
stopped at the village of Bethany, an hour out from
Jerusalem. They showed us the tomb of Lazarus.
I had rather live in it than in any house in the town.
And they showed us also a large "Fountain of
Lazarus," and in the center of the village the ancient
dwelling of Lazarus. Lazarus appears to have been
a man of property. The legends of the Sunday-
schools do him great injustice; they give one the
impression that he was poor. It is because they get
him confused with that Lazarus who had no merit
but his virtue, and virtue never has been as respectable as money. The house of Lazarus is a three-
story edifice, of stone masonry, but the accumulated
rubbish of ages has buried all of it but the upper
story. We took candles and descended to the
dismal cell-like chambers where Jesus sat at meat
with Martha and Mary, and conversed with them
about their brother. We could not but look upon
these old dingy apartments with a more than common interest.

We had had a glimpse, from a mountain-top, of
the Dead Sea, lying like a blue shield in the plain of
the Jordan, and now we were marching down a close,
flaming, rugged, desolate defile, where no living
creature could enjoy life, except, perhaps, a sal-
amander. It was such a dreary, repulsive, horrible
solitude! It was the "wilderness" where John
preached, with camel's hair about his loins—raiment enough—but he never could have got his
locusts and wild honey here. We were moping
along down through this dreadful place, every man

in the rear. Our guards—two gorgeous young Arab sheiks, with cargoes of swords, guns, pistols, and daggers on board—were loafing ahead.

"Bedouins!"

Every man shrunk up and disappeared in his clothes like a mud-turtle. My first impulse was to dash forward and destroy the Bedouins. My second was to dash to the rear to see if there were any coming in that direction. I acted on the latter impulse. So did all the others. If any Bedouins had approached us, then, from that point of the compass, they would have paid dearly for their rashness. We all remarked that afterward. There would have been scenes of riot and bloodshed there that no pen could describe. I know that, because each man told what he would have done, individually; and such a medley of strange and unheard-of inventions of cruelty you could not conceive of. One man said he had calmly made up his mind to perish where he stood, if need be, but never yield an inch; he was going to wait, with deadly patience, till he could count the stripes upon the first Bedouin's jacket, and then count them and let him have it. Another was going to sit still till the first lance reached within an inch of his breast, and then dodge it and seize it. I forbear to tell what he was going to do to that Bedouin that owned it. It makes my blood run cold to think of it. Another was going to scalp such Bedouins as fell to his share, and take his bald-headed sons of the desert home with him alive for trophies. But the wild-eyed pilgrim rhapsodist was silent. His orbs gleamed with a deadly light, but his lips moved not. Anxiety grew, and he was questioned. If he had got a Bedouin, what would he have done with him—shot him? He smiled a smile of grim contempt and shook his head. Would he have stabbed him? Another shake. Would he have quartered him—flayed him? More shakes. Oh! horror, what *would* he have done?

"Eat him!"

Such was the awful sentence that thundered from his lips. What was grammar to a desperado like that? I was glad in my heart that I had been spared these scenes of malignant carnage. No Bedouins attacked our terrible rear. And none attacked the front. The new-comers were only a reinforcement of cadaverous Arabs, in shirts and bare legs, sent far ahead of us to brandish rusty guns, and shout and brag, and carry on like lunatics, and thus scare away all bands of marauding Bedouins that might lurk about our path. What a shame it is that armed white Christians must travel under guard of vermin like this as a protection against the prowling vagabonds of the desert—those sanguinary outlaws who are always going to do something desperate, but never do it. I may as well mention here that on our whole trip we saw no Bedouins, and had no more use for an Arab guard than we could have had for patent-leather boots and white kid gloves. The Bedouins that attacked the other parties of pilgrims so fiercely were provided for the occasion by the Arab guides of those parties, and shipped from Jerusalem for temporary service as Bedouins. They met together in full view of the pilgrims, after the battle, and took lunch, divided the bucksheesh extorted in the season of danger, and then accompanied the cavalcade home to the city! The nuisance of an Arab guard is one which is created by the Sheiks and the Bedouins together, for mutual profit, it is said, and no doubt there is a good deal of truth in it.

We visited the fountain the prophet Elisha sweetened (it is sweet yet); where he remained some time and was fed by the ravens.

Ancient Jericho is not very picturesque as a ruin. When Joshua marched around it seven times, some three thousand years ago, and blew it down with his trumpet, he did the work so well and so completely that he hardly left enough of the city to cast a shadow. The curse pronounced against the rebuilding of it has never been removed. One king, holding the curse in light estimation, made the attempt, but was stricken sorely for his presumption. Its site will always remain unoccupied; and yet it is one of the very best locations for a town we have seen in all Palestine.

At two in the morning they routed us out of bed —another piece of unwarranted cruelty, another stupid effort of our dragoman to get ahead of a rival. It was not two hours to the Jordan. However, we were dressed and under way before any one thought of looking to see what time it was, and so we drowsed on through the chill night air and dreamed of camp-fires, warm beds, and other comfortable things.

There was no conversation. People do not talk when they are cold, and wretched, and sleepy. We nodded in the saddle, at times, and woke up with a start to find that the procession had disappeared in the gloom. Then there was energy and attention to business until its dusky outlines came in sight again. Occasionally the order was passed in a low voice down the line: "Close up—close up! Bedouins lurk here, everywhere!" What an exquisite shudder it sent shivering along one's spine!

We reached the famous river before four o'clock, and the night was so black that we could have ridden into it without seeing it. Some of us were in an unhappy frame of mind. We waited and waited for daylight, but it did not come. Finally we went away in the dark and slept an hour on the ground, in the bushes, and caught cold. It was a costly nap, on that account, but otherwise it was a paying investment because it brought unconsciousness of the dreary minutes and put us in a somewhat fitter mood for a first glimpse of the sacred river.

With the first suspicion of dawn, every pilgrim took off his clothes and waded into the dark torrent, singing:

> On Jordan's stormy banks I stand,
>   And cast a wistful eye
> To Canaan's fair and happy land,
>   Where my possessions lie.

But they did not sing long. The water was so fearfully cold that they were obliged to stop singing and scamper out again. Then they stood on the bank shivering, and so chagrined and so grieved, that they merited honest compassion. Because another dream, another cherished hope, had failed.

They had promised themselves all along that they would cross the Jordan where the Israelites crossed it when they entered Canaan from their long pilgrimage in the desert. They would cross where the twelve stones were placed in memory of that great event. While they did it they would picture to themselves that vast army of pilgrims marching through the cloven waters, bearing the hallowed ark of the covenant and shouting hosannahs, and singing songs of thanksgiving and praise. Each had promised himself that he would be the first to cross. They were at the goal of their hopes at last, but the current was too swift, the water was too cold!

It was then that Jack did them a service. With that engaging recklessness of consequences which is natural to youth, and so proper and so seemly, as well, he went and led the way across the Jordan, and all was happiness again. Every individual waded over, then, and stood upon the further bank. The water was not quite breast-deep, anywhere. If it had been more, we could hardly have accomplished the feat, for the strong current would have swept us down the stream, and we would have been exhausted and drowned before reaching a place where we could make a landing. The main object compassed, the drooping, miserable party sat down to wait for the sun again, for all wanted to see the water as well as feel it. But it was too cold a pastime. Some cans were filled from the holy river, some canes cut from its banks, and then we mounted and rode reluctantly away to keep from freezing to death. So we saw the Jordan very dimly. The thickets of bushes that bordered its banks threw their shadows across its shallow, turbulent waters ("stormy," the hymn makes them, which is rather a complimentary stretch of fancy), and we could not judge of the width of the stream by the eye. We knew by our wading experience, however, that many streets in America are double as wide as the Jordan.

Daylight came, soon after we got under way, and in the course of an hour or two we reached the Dead Sea. Nothing grows in the flat, burning desert around it but weeds and the Dead Sea apple the poets say is beautiful to the eye, but crumbles to ashes and dust when you break it. Such as we found were not handsome, but they were bitter to the taste. They yielded no dust. It was because they were not ripe, perhaps.

The desert and the barren hills gleam painfully in the sun, around the Dead Sea, and there is no pleasant thing or living creature upon it or about its borders to cheer the eye. It is a scorching, arid, repulsive solitude. A silence broods over the scene that is depressing to the spirits. It makes one think of funerals and death.

The Dead Sea is small. Its waters are very clear, and it has a pebbly bottom and is shallow for some distance out from the shores. It yields quantities of asphaltum; fragments of it lie all about its banks; this stuff gives the place something of an unpleasant smell.

All our reading had taught us to expect that the first plunge into the Dead Sea would be attended with distressing results—our bodies would feel as if they were suddenly pierced by millions of red-hot needles; the dreadful smarting would continue for hours; we might even look to be blistered from head to foot, and suffer miserably for many days. We were disappointed. Our eight sprang in at the same time that another party of pilgrims did, and nobody screamed once. None of them ever did complain of anything more than a slight pricking sensation in places where their skin was abraded, and then only for a short time. My face smarted for a couple of hours, but it was partly because I got it badly sunburned while I was bathing, and stayed in so long that it became plastered over with salt.

No, the water did not blister us; it did not cover us with a slimy ooze and confer upon us an atrocious fragrance; it was not very slimy; and I could not discover that we smelt really any worse than we have always smelt since we have been in Palestine. It was only a different kind of smell, but not conspicuous on that account, because we have a great deal of variety in that respect. We didn't smell, there on the Jordan, the same as we do in Jerusalem; and we don't smell in Jerusalem just as we did in Nazareth, or Tiberias, or Cesarea Philippi, or any of those other ruinous ancient towns in Galilee. No, we change all the time, and generally for the worse. We do our own washing.

It was a funny bath. We could not sink. One could stretch himself at full length on his back, with his arms on his breast, and all of his body above a line drawn from the corner of his jaw past the middle of his side, the middle of his leg and through his

ankle-bone, would remain out of water. He could
lift his head clear out if he chose. No position
can be retained long; you lose your balance and
whirl over, first on your back and then on your
face, and so on. You can lie comfortably, on your
back, with your head out, and your legs out from
your knees down, by steadying yourself with your
hands. You can sit, with your knees drawn up to
your chin and your arms clasped around them, but
you are bound to turn over presently, because you
are top-heavy in that position. You can stand up
straight in water that is over your head, and from
the middle of your breast upward you will not be
wet. But you cannot remain so. The water will
soon float your feet to the surface. You cannot
swim on your back and make any progress of any
consequence, because your feet stick away above
the surface, and there is nothing to propel yourself
with but your heels. If you swim on your face,
you kick up the water like a stern-wheel boat. You
make no headway. A horse is so top-heavy that he
can neither swim nor stand up in the Dead Sea. He
turns over on his side at once. Some of us bathed
for more than an hour, and then came out coated
with salt till we shone like icicles. We scrubbed it
off with a coarse towel and rode off with a splendid
brand-new smell, though it was one which was not
any more disagreeable than those we have been for
several weeks enjoying. It was the variegated villainy and novelty of it that charmed us. Salt crystals
glitter in the sun about the shores of the lake. In
places they coat the ground like a brilliant crust of ice.

# THE INNOCENTS ABROAD

When I was a boy I somehow got the impression that the river Jordan was four thousand miles long and thirty-five miles wide. It is only ninety miles long, and so crooked that a man does not know which side of it he is on half the time. In going ninety miles it does not get over more than fifty miles of ground. It is not any wider than Broadway in New York. There is the Sea of Galilee and this Dead Sea—neither of them twenty miles long or thirteen wide. And yet when I was in Sunday-school I thought they were sixty thousand miles in diameter.

Travel and experience mar the grandest pictures and rob us of the most cherished traditions of our boyhood. Well, let them go. I have already seen the Empire of King Solomon diminish to the size of the State of Pennsylvania; I suppose I can bear the reduction of the seas and the river.

We looked everywhere, as we passed along, but never saw grain or crystal of Lot's wife. It was a great disappointment. For many and many a year we had known her sad story, and taken that interest in her which misfortune always inspires. But she was gone. Her picturesque form no longer looms above the desert of the Dead Sea to remind the tourist of the doom that fell upon the lost cities.

I cannot describe the hideous afternoon's ride from the Dead Sea to Mars Saba. It oppresses me yet, to think of it. The sun so pelted us that the tears ran down our cheeks once or twice. The ghastly, treeless, grassless, breathless cañons smothered us as if we had been in an oven. The sun had

345

positive *weight* to it, I think. Not a man could sit erect under it. All drooped low in the saddles. John preached in this "Wilderness"! It must have been exhausting work. What a very heaven the massy towers and ramparts of vast Mars Saba looked to us when we caught a first glimpse of them!

We stayed at this great convent all night, guests of the hospitable priests. Mars Saba, perched upon a crag, a human nest stuck high up against a perpendicular mountain wall, is a world of grand masonry that rises, terrace upon terrace, away above your head, like the terraced and retreating colonnades one sees in fanciful pictures of Belshazzar's Feast and the palaces of the ancient Pharaohs. No other human dwelling is near. It was founded many ages ago by a holy recluse who lived at first in a cave in the rock—a cave which is inclosed in the convent walls now, and was reverently shown to us by the priests. This recluse, by his rigorous torturing of his flesh, his diet of bread and water, his utter withdrawal from all society and from the vanities of the world, and his constant prayer and saintly contemplation of a skull, inspired an emulation that brought about him many disciples. The precipice on the opposite side of the cañon is well perforated with the small holes they dug in the rock to live in. The present occupants of Mars Saba, about seventy in number, are all hermits. They wear a coarse robe, an ugly, brimless stove-pipe of a hat, and go without shoes. They eat nothing whatever but bread and salt; they drink nothing but water. As long as they live they can never go outside the walls, or look upon a woman—for no woman is permitted to enter Mars Saba, upon any pretext whatsoever.

Some of those men have been shut up there for thirty years. In all that dreary time they have not heard the laughter of a child or the blessed voice of a woman; they have seen no human tears, no human smiles; they have known no human joys, no wholesome human sorrows. In their hearts are no memories of the past, in their brains no dreams of the future. All that is lovable, beautiful, worthy, they have put far away from them; against all things that are pleasant to look upon, and all sounds that are music to the ear, they have barred their massive doors and reared their relentless walls of stone forever. They have banished the tender grace of life and left only the sapped and skinny mockery. Their lips are lips that never kiss and never sing; their hearts are hearts that never hate and never love; their breasts are breasts that never swell with the sentiment, "I have a country and a flag." They are dead men who walk.

I set down these first thoughts because they are natural—not because they are just or because it is right to set them down. It is easy for bookmakers to say "I thought so and so as I looked upon such and such a scene"—when the truth is, they thought all those fine things afterward. One's first thought is not likely to be strictly accurate, yet it is no crime to think it and none to write it down, subject to modification by later experience. These hermits *are* dead men, in several respects, but not in all; and it is not proper that, thinking ill of them at first, I should go on doing so, or, speaking ill of them, I should reiterate the words and stick to them. No, they treated us too kindly for that. There is something human about them somewhere. They knew we were foreigners and Protestants, and not likely to feel admiration or much friendliness toward them. But their large charity was above considering such things. They simply saw in us men who were hungry, and thirsty, and tired, and that was sufficient. They opened their doors and gave us welcome. They asked no questions, and they made no self-righteous display of their hospitality. They fished for no compliments. They moved quietly about, setting the table for us, making the beds, and bringing water to wash in, and paid no heed when we said it was wrong for them to do that when we had men whose business it was to perform such offices. We fared most comfortably, and sat late at dinner. We walked all over the building with the hermits afterward, and then sat on the lofty battlements and smoked while we enjoyed the cool air, the wild scenery, and the sunset. One or two chose cozy bedrooms to sleep in, but the nomadic instinct prompted the rest to sleep on the broad divan that extended around the great hall, because it seemed like sleeping out-of-doors, and so was more cheery and inviting. It was a royal rest we had.

When we got up to breakfast in the morning, we were new men. For all this hospitality no strict charge was made. We could give something if we chose; we need give nothing, if we were poor or if we were stingy. The pauper and the miser are as free as any in the Catholic convents of Palestine. I have been educated to enmity toward everything that is Catholic, and sometimes, in consequence of this, I find it much easier to discover Catholic faults than Catholic merits. But there is one thing I feel no disposition to overlook, and no disposition to forget; and that is, the honest gratitude I and all pilgrims owe to the Convent Fathers in Palestine. Their doors are always open, and there is always a welcome for any worthy man who comes, whether he comes in rags or clad in purple. The Catholic convents are a priceless blessing to the poor. A pilgrim without money, whether he be a Protestant or a Catholic, can travel the length and breadth of Palestine, and in the midst of her desert wastes find wholesome food and a clean bed every night, in these buildings. Pilgrims in better circumstances are often stricken down by the sun and the fevers of the country, and then their saving refuge is the convent. Without these hospitable retreats, travel in Palestine would be a pleasure which none but the strongest men could dare to undertake. Our party, pilgrims and all, will always be ready and always willing to touch glasses and drink health, prosperity, and long life to the Convent Fathers of Palestine.

So, rested and refreshed, we fell into line and filed away over the barren mountains of Judea, and along rocky ridges and through sterile gorges, where eternal silence and solitude reigned. Even the scattering groups of armed shepherds we met the afternoon before, tending their flocks of long-haired goats, were wanting here. We saw but two living

creatures. They were gazelles of "soft-eyed" notoriety. They looked like very young kids, but they
annihilated distance like an express-train. I have
not seen animals that moved faster, unless I might
say it of the antelopes of our own great plains.

At nine or ten in the morning we reached the
Plain of the Shepherds, and stood in a walled garden
of olives where the shepherds were watching their
flocks by night, eighteen centuries ago, when the
multitudes of angels brought them the tidings that
the Saviour was born. A quarter of a mile away
was Bethlehem of Judea, and the pilgrims took some
of the stone wall and hurried on.

The Plain of the Shepherds is a desert, paved
with loose stones, void of vegetation, glaring in the
fierce sun. Only the music of the angels it knew
once could charm its shrubs and flowers to life again
and restore its vanished beauty. No less potent
enchantment could avail to work this miracle.

In the huge Church of the Nativity, in Bethlehem,
built fifteen hundred years ago by the inveterate St.
Helena, they took us below-ground, and into a grotto cut in the living rock. This was the "manger"
where Christ was born. A silver star set in the
floor bears a Latin inscription to that effect. It
is polished with the kisses of many generations of
worshiping pilgrims. The grotto was tricked out
in the usual tasteless style observable in all the
holy places of Palestine. As in the Church of the
Holy Sepulcher, envy and uncharitableness were
apparent here. The priests and the members of the
Greek and Latin churches cannot come by the

same corridor to kneel in the sacred birthplace of the Redeemer, but are compelled to approach and retire by different avenues, lest they quarrel and fight on this holiest ground on earth.

I have no "meditations," suggested by this spot where the very first "Merry Christmas!" was uttered in all the world, and from whence the friend of my childhood, Santa Claus, departed on his first journey to gladden and continue to gladden roaring firesides on wintry mornings in many a distant land forever and forever. I touch, with reverent finger, the actual spot where the infant Jesus lay, but I think—nothing.

You *cannot* think in this place any more than you can in any other in Palestine that would be likely to inspire reflection. Beggars, cripples, and monks compass you about, and make you think only of bucksheesh when you would rather think of something more in keeping with the character of the spot.

I was glad to get away, and glad when we had walked through the grottoes where Eusebius wrote, and Jerome fasted, and Joseph prepared for the flight into Egypt, and the dozen other distinguished grottoes, and knew we were done. The Church of the Nativity is almost as well packed with exceeding holy places as the Church of the Holy Sepulcher itself. They even have in it a grotto wherein twenty thousand children were slaughtered by Herod when he was seeking the life of the infant Saviour.

We went to the Milk Grotto, of course—a cavern where Mary hid herself for a while before the flight into Egypt. Its walls were black before she entered, but in suckling the Child, a drop of her milk fell upon the floor and instantly changed the darkness of the walls to its own snowy hue. We took many little fragments of stone from here, because it is well known in all the East that a barren woman hath need only to touch her lips to one of these and her failing will depart from her. We took many specimens, to the end that we might confer happiness upon certain households that we wot of.

We got away from Bethlehem and its troops of beggars and relic-peddlers in the afternoon, and after spending some little time at Rachel's tomb, hurried to Jerusalem as fast as possible. I never was *so* glad to get home again before. I never have enjoyed rest as I have enjoyed it during these last few hours. The journey to the Dead Sea, the Jordan, and Bethlehem was short, but it was an exhausting one. Such roasting heat, such oppressive solitude, and such dismal desolation cannot surely exist elsewhere on earth. And *such* fatigue!

The commonest sagacity warns me that I ought to tell the customary pleasant lie, and say I tore myself reluctantly away from every noted place in Palestine. Everybody tells that, but with as little ostentation as I may, I doubt the word of every he who tells it. I could take a dreadful oath that I have never heard any one of our forty pilgrims say anything of the sort, and they are as worthy and as sincerely devout as any that come here. They will say it when they get home, fast enough, but why should they not? They do not wish to array themselves against all the Lamartines and Grimeses in the world. It does not stand to reason that men are reluctant to leave places where the very life is almost badgered out of them by importunate swarms of beggars and peddlers who hang in strings to one's sleeves and coat-tails and shriek and shout in his ears and horrify his vision with the ghastly sores and malformations they exhibit. One is *glad* to get away. I have heard shameless people say they were glad to get away from Ladies' Festivals where they were importuned to buy by bevies of lovely young ladies. Transform those houris into dusky hags and ragged savages, and replace their rounded forms with shrunken and knotted distortions, their soft hands with scarred and hideous deformities, and the persuasive music of their voices with the discordant din of a hated language, and *then* see how much lingering reluctance to leave could be mustered. No, it is the neat thing to say you were reluctant, and then append the profound thoughts that "struggled for utterance" in your brain; but it is the true thing to say you were not reluctant, and found it impossible to think at all—though in good sooth it is not respectable to say it, and not poetical, either.

We do not think, in the holy places; we think in bed, afterward, when the glare, and the noise, and the confusion are gone, and in fancy we revisit alone the solemn monuments of the past, and summon the phantom pageants of an age that has passed away.

## CHAPTER XXIX

WE visited all the holy places about Jerusalem which we had left unvisited when we journeyed to the Jordan, and then, about three o'clock one afternoon, we fell into procession and marched out at the stately Damascus gate, and the walls of Jerusalem shut us out forever. We paused on the summit of a distant hill and took a final look and made a final farewell to the venerable city which had been such a good home to us.

For about four hours we traveled down-hill constantly. We followed a narrow bridle-path which traversed the beds of the mountain gorges, and when we could we got out of the way of the long trains of laden camels and asses, and when we could not we suffered the misery of being mashed up against perpendicular walls of rock and having our legs bruised by the passing freight. Jack was caught two or three times, and Dan and Moult as often. One horse had a heavy fall on the slippery rocks, and the others had narrow escapes. However, this was as good a road as we had found in Palestine, and possibly even the best, and so there was not much grumbling.

Sometimes, in the glens, we came upon luxuriant orchards of figs, apricots, pomegranates, and such

354

things, but oftener the scenery was rugged, mountainous, verdureless, and forbidding. Here and there, towers were perched high up on acclivities which seemed almost inaccessible. This fashion is as old as Palestine itself, and was adopted in ancient times for security against enemies.

We crossed the brook which furnished David the stone that killed Goliah, and, no doubt, we looked upon the very ground whereon that noted battle was fought. We passed by a picturesque old gothic ruin whose stone pavements had rung to the armed heels of many a valorous Crusader, and we rode through a piece of country which we were told once knew Samson as a citizen.

We stayed all night with the good monks at the convent of Ramleh, and in the morning got up and galloped the horses a good part of the distance from there to Jaffa, or Joppa, for the plain was as level as a floor and free from stones, and besides this was our last march in Holy Land. These two or three hours finished, we and the tired horses could have rest and sleep as long as we wanted it. This was the plain of which Joshua spoke when he said, "Sun, stand thou still on Gibeon, and thou moon in the valley of Ajalon." As we drew near to Jaffa, the boys spurred up the horses and indulged in the excitement of an actual race—an experience we had hardly had since we raced on donkeys in the Azores islands.

We came finally to the noble grove of orange trees in which the Oriental city of Jaffa lies buried; we passed through the walls, and rode again down narrow streets and among swarms of animated rags, and saw other sights and had other experiences we had long been familiar with. We dismounted, for the last time, and out in the offing, riding at anchor, we saw the ship! I put an exclamation-point there because we felt one when we saw the vessel. The long pilgrimage was ended, and somehow we seemed to feel glad of it.

[For description of Jaffa, see Universal Gazetteer.] Simon the Tanner formerly lived here. We went to his house. All the pilgrims visit Simon the Tanner's house. Peter saw the vision of the beasts let down in a sheet when he lay upon the roof of Simon the Tanner's house. It was from Jaffa that Jonah sailed when he was told to go and prophesy against Nineveh, and, no doubt, it was not far from the town that the whale threw him up when he discovered that he had no ticket. Jonah was disobedient, and of a faultfinding, complaining disposition, and deserves to be lightly spoken of, almost. The timbers used in the construction of Solomon's temple were floated to Jaffa in rafts, and the narrow opening in the reef through which they passed to the shore is not an inch wider or a shade less dangerous to navigate than it was then. Such is the sleepy nature of the population Palestine's only good seaport has now and always had. Jaffa has a history and a stirring one. It will not be discovered anywhere in this book. If the reader will call at the circulating library and mention my name, he will be furnished with books which will afford him the fullest information concerning Jaffa.

So ends the pilgrimage. We ought to be glad

that we did not make it for the purpose of feasting
our eyes upon fascinating aspects of nature, for we
should have been disappointed—at least at this
season of the year. A writer in *Life in the Holy
Land* observes:

' Monotonous and uninviting as much of the Holy Land will
appear to persons accustomed to the almost constant verdure
of flowers, ample streams, and varied surface of our own country,
we must remember that its aspect to the Israelites after the
weary march of forty years through the desert must have been
very different.

Which all of us will freely grant. But it truly *is*
"monotonous and uninviting," and there is no sufficient reason for describing it as being otherwise.

Of all the lands there are for dismal scenery, I
think Palestine must be the prince. The hills are
barren, they are dull of color, they are unpicturesque
in shape. The valleys are unsightly deserts fringed
with a feeble vegetation that has an expression about
it of being sorrowful and despondent. The Dead
Sea and the Sea of Galilee sleep in the midst of a
vast stretch of hill and plain wherein the eye rests
upon no pleasant tint, no striking object, no soft
picture dreaming in a purple haze or mottled with
the shadows of the clouds. Every outline is harsh,
every feature is distinct, there is no perspective—
distance works no enchantment here. It is a hopeless, dreary, heartbroken land.

Small shreds and patches of it must be very beautiful in the full flush of spring, however, and all the
more beautiful by contrast with the far-reaching
desolation that surrounds them on every side. I

357

would like much to see the fringes of the Jordan in springtime, and Shechem, Esdraelon, Ajalon, and the borders of Galilee—but even then these spots would seem mere toy gardens set at wide intervals in the waste of a limitless desolation.

Palestine sits in sackcloth and ashes. Over it broods the spell of a curse that has withered its fields and fettered its energies. Where Sodom and Gomorrah reared their domes and towers, that solemn sea now floods the plain, in whose bitter waters no living thing exists—over whose waveless surface the blistering air hangs motionless and dead—about whose borders nothing grows but weeds, and scattering tufts of cane, and that treacherous fruit that promises refreshment to parching lips, but turns to ashes at the touch. Nazareth is forlorn; about that ford of Jordan where the hosts of Israel entered the Promised Land with songs of rejoicing, one finds only a squalid camp of fantastic Bedouins of the desert; Jericho the accursed lies a moldering ruin to-day, even as Joshua's miracle left it more than three thousand years ago; Bethlehem and Bethany, in their poverty and their humiliation, have nothing about them now to remind one that they once knew the high honor of the Saviour's presence; the hallowed spot where the shepherds watched their flocks by night, and where the angels sang Peace on earth, good will to men, is untenanted by any living creature, and unblessed by any feature that is pleasant to the eye. Renowned Jerusalem itself, the stateliest name in history, has lost all its ancient grandeur, and is become a pauper village; the riches of Solomon are no longer there to compel the admiration of visiting Oriental queens; the wonderful temple which was the pride and the glory of Israel is gone, and the Ottoman crescent is lifted above the spot where, on that most memorable day in the annals of the world, they reared the Holy Cross. The noted Sea of Galilee, where Roman fleets once rode at anchor and the disciples of the Saviour sailed in their ships, was long ago deserted by the devotees of war and commerce, and its borders are a silent wilderness; Capernaum is a shapeless ruin; Magdala is the home of beggared Arabs; Bethsaida and Chorazin have vanished from the earth, and the "desert places" round about them where thousands of men once listened to the Saviour's voice and ate the miraculous bread sleep in the hush of a solitude that is inhabited only by birds of prey and skulking foxes.

Palestine is desolate and unlovely. And why should it be otherwise? Can the *curse* of the Deity beautify a land?

Palestine is no more of this work-day world. It is sacred to poetry and tradition—it is dream-land.

## CHAPTER XXX

IT was worth a kingdom to be at sea again. It was a relief to drop all anxiety whatsoever—all questions as to where we should go; how long we should stay; whether it were worth while to go or not; all anxieties about the condition of the horses; all such questions as "Shall we *ever* get to water?" "Shall we *ever* lunch?" "Ferguson, how many *more* million miles have we got to creep under this awful sun before we camp?" It was a relief to cast all these torturing little anxieties far away—ropes of steel they were, and every one with a separate and distinct strain on it—and feel the temporary contentment that is born of the banishment of all care and responsibility. We did not look at the compass; we did not care, now, where the ship went to, so that she went out of sight of land as quickly as possible. When I travel again, I wish to go in a pleasure ship. No amount of money could have purchased for us, in a strange vessel and among unfamiliar faces, the perfect satisfaction and the sense of being *at home* again which we experienced when we stepped on board the *Quaker City,—our own ship*—after this wearisome pilgrimage. It is a something we have felt always when we returned to her, and a something we had no desire to sell.

360

# THE INNOCENTS ABROAD

We took off our blue woolen shirts, our spurs and heavy boots, our sanguinary revolvers and our buckskin-seated pantaloons, and got shaved, and came out in Christian costume once more. All but Jack, who changed all other articles of his dress, but clung to his traveling-pantaloons. They still preserved their ample buckskin seat intact; and so his short pea-jacket and his long, thin legs assisted to make him a picturesque object whenever he stood on the forecastle looking abroad upon the ocean over the bows. At such times his father's last injunction suggested itself to me. He said:

"Jack, my boy, you are about to go among a brilliant company of gentlemen and ladies, who are refined and cultivated, and thoroughly accomplished in the manners and customs of good society. Listen to their conversation, study their habits of life, and learn. Be polite and obliging to all, and considerate toward every one's opinions, failings, and prejudices. Command the just respect of all your fellow-voyagers, even though you fail to win their friendly regard. And Jack—don't you ever dare, while you live, appear in public on those decks in fair weather, in a costume unbecoming your mother's drawing-room!"

It would have been worth any price if the father of this hopeful youth could have stepped on board some time, and seen him standing high on the fore-castle, pea-jacket, tasseled red fez, buckskin patch and all,—placidly contemplating the ocean—a rare spectacle for anybody's drawing-room.

After a pleasant voyage and a good rest, we drew

# MARK TWAIN

near to Egypt, and out of the mellowest of sunsets
we saw the domes and minarets of Alexandria rise
into view. As soon as the anchor was down, Jack
and I got a boat and went ashore. It was night by
this time, and the other passengers were content to
remain at home and visit ancient Egypt after breakfast. It was the way they did at Constantinople.
They took a lively interest in new countries, but
their school-boy impatience had worn off, and they
had learned that it was wisdom to take things easy
and go along comfortably—these old countries do not
go away in the night; they stay till after breakfast.

When we reached the pier we found an army of
Egyptian boys with donkeys no larger than themselves, waiting for passengers—for donkeys are the
omnibuses of Egypt. We preferred to walk, but
we could not have our own way. The boys crowded
about us, clamored around us, and slewed their
donkeys exactly across our path, no matter which
way we turned. They were good-natured rascals,
and so were the donkeys. We mounted, and the
boys ran behind us and kept the donkeys in a
furious gallop, as is the fashion at Damascus. I
believe I would rather ride a donkey than any beast
in the world. He goes briskly, he puts on no airs,
he is docile, though opinionated. Satan himself
could not scare him, and he is convenient—very
convenient. When you are tired riding you can
rest your feet on the ground and let him gallop from
under you.

We found the hotel and secured rooms, and were
happy to know that the Prince of Wales had stopped

362

there once. They had it everywhere on signs. No
other princes had stopped there since, till Jack and
I came. We went abroad through the town, then,
and found it a city of huge commercial buildings,
of broad, handsome streets brilliant with gaslight.
By night it was a sort of reminiscence of Paris.
But finally Jack found an ice-cream saloon, and that
closed investigations for that evening. The weather
was very hot, it had been many a day since Jack
had seen ice-cream, and so it was useless to talk of
leaving the saloon till it shut up.

In the morning the lost tribes of America came
ashore and infested the hotels and took possession
of all the donkeys and other open barouches that
offered. They went in picturesque procession to
the American Consul's; to the great gardens; to
Cleopatra's Needles; to Pompey's Pillar; to the
palace of the Viceroy of Egypt; to the Nile; to the
superb groves of date-palms. One of our most
inveterate relic-hunters had his hammer with him,
and tried to break a fragment off the upright Needle
and could not do it; he tried the prostrate one
and failed; he borrowed a heavy sledge-hammer
from a mason and failed again. He tried Pompey's
Pillar, and this baffled him. Scattered all about the
mighty monolith were sphinxes of noble countenance, carved out of Egyptian granite as hard as
blue steel, and whose shapely features the wear of
five thousand years had failed to mark or mar. The
relic-hunter battered at these persistently, and
sweated profusely over his work. He might as well
have attempted to deface the moon. They regarded

him serenely with the stately smile they had worn
so long, and which seemed to say, "Peck away,
poor insect; we were not made to fear such as you;
in tenscore dragging ages we have seen more of
your kind than there are sands at your feet; have
they left a blemish upon us?"

But I am forgetting the Jaffa Colonists. At Jaffa
we had taken on board some forty members of a
very celebrated community. They were male and
female; babies, young boys and young girls; young
married people, and some who had passed a shade
beyond the prime of life. I refer to the "Adams
Jaffa Colony." Others had deserted before. We
left in Jaffa Mr. Adams, his wife, and fifteen unfor-
tunates who not only had no money but did not
know where to turn or whither to go. Such was
the statement made to us. Our forty were miserable
enough in the first place, and they lay about the
decks seasick all the voyage, which about completed
their misery, I take it. However, one or two young
men remained upright, and by constant persecution
we wormed out of them some little information.
They gave it reluctantly and in a very fragmentary
condition, for, having been shamefully humbugged
by their prophet, they felt humiliated and unhappy.
In such circumstances people do not like to talk.

The colony was a complete fiasco. I have already
said that such as could get away did so, from time
to time. The prophet Adams — once an actor,
then several other things, afterward a Mormon and
a missionary, always an adventurer—remains at
Jaffa with his handful of sorrowful subjects. The

forty we brought away with us were chiefly destitute, though not all of them. They wished to get to Egypt. What might become of them then they did not know and probably did not care—anything to get away from hated Jaffa. They had little to hope for; because after many appeals to the sympathies of New England, made by strangers of Boston, through the newspapers, and after the establishment of an office there for the reception of moneyed contributions for the Jaffa colonists, one dollar was subscribed. The consul-general for Egypt showed me the newspaper paragraph which mentioned the circumstance, and mentioned also the discontinuance of the effort and the closing of the office. It was evident that practical New England was not sorry to be rid of such visionaries and was not in the least inclined to hire anybody to bring them back to her. Still, to get to Egypt was something, in the eyes of the unfortunate colonists, hopeless as the prospect seemed of ever getting further.

Thus circumstanced, they landed at Alexandria from our ship. One of our passengers, Mr. Moses S. Beach, of the New York *Sun*, inquired of the consul-general what it would cost to send these people to their home in Maine by the way of Liverpool, and he said fifteen hundred dollars in gold would do it. Mr. Beach gave his check for the money, and so the troubles of the Jaffa colonists were at an end.[1]

[1] It was an unselfish act of benevolence; it was done without any ostentation, and has never been mentioned in any newspaper, I think. Therefore it is refreshing to learn now, several months after the above narrative was written, that another man received all the credit of this rescue of the colonists. Such is life.

# MARK TWAIN

Alexandria was too much like a European city to be novel, and we soon tired of it. We took the cars and came up here to ancient Cairo, which *is* an Oriental city and of the completest pattern. There is little about it to disabuse one's mind of the error if he should take it into his head that he was in the heart of Arabia. Stately camels and dromedaries, swarthy Egyptians, and likewise Turks and black Ethiopians, turbaned, sashed, and blazing in a rich variety of Oriental costumes of all shades of flashy colors, are what one sees on every hand crowding the narrow streets and the honeycombed bazars. We are stopping at Shepherd's Hotel, which is the worst on earth except the one I stopped at once in a small town in the United States. It is pleasant to read this sketch in my note-book, now, and know that I can stand Shepherd's Hotel, sure, because I have been in one just like it in America and survived:

I stopped at the Benton House. It used to be a good hotel, but that proves nothing—I used to be a good boy, for that matter. Both of us have lost character of late years. The Benton is not a good hotel.

The Benton lacks a very great deal of being a good hotel. Perdition is full of better hotels than the Benton.

It was late at night when I got there, and I told the clerk I would like plenty of lights, because I wanted to read an hour or two. When I reached No. 15 with the porter (we came along a dim hall that was clad in ancient carpeting, faded, worn out in many places, and patched with old scraps of oil-cloth—a hall that sank under one's feet, and creaked dismally to every footstep) he struck a light—two inches of sallow, sorrowful, consumptive tallow candle, that burned blue, and sputtered, and got discouraged and went out. The porter lit it again, and I asked if that was all the light the clerk sent.

366

He said, "Oh no, I've got another one here," and he produced another couple of inches of tallow candle. I said, "Light them both—I'll have to have one to see the other by." He did it, but the result was drearier than darkness itself. He was a cheery, accommodating rascal. He said he would go "somewheres" and steal a lamp. I abetted and encouraged him in his criminal design. I heard the landlord get after him in the hall ten minutes afterward.

"Where are you going with that lamp?"

"Fifteen wants it, sir."

"Fifteen! why he's got a double lot of candles—does the man want to illuminate the house?—does he want to get up a torchlight procession?—what *is* he up to, anyhow?"

"He don't like them candles—says he wants a lamp."

"Why, what in the nation does—why I never heard of such a thing. What on earth can he want with that lamp?"

"Well, he only wants to read—that's what he says."

"Wants to read, does he?—ain't satisfied with a thousand candles, but has to have a lamp!—I do wonder what the devil that fellow wants that lamp for? Take him another candle, and then if—"

"But he wants the lamp—says he'll burn the d—d old house down if he don't get a lamp!" [A remark which I never made.]

"I'd like to see him at it once. Well, you take it along—but I swear it beats *my* time, though—and see if you can't find out what in the very nation he *wants* with that lamp."

And he went off growling to himself and still wondering and wondering over the unaccountable conduct of No. 15. The lamp was a good one, but it revealed some disagreeable things—a bed in the suburbs of a desert of room—a bed that had hills and valleys in it, and you'd have to accommodate your body to the impression left in it by the man that slept there last, before you could lie comfortably; a carpet that had seen better days; a melancholy washstand in a remote corner, and a dejected pitcher on it sorrowing over a broken nose; a looking-glass split across the center, which chopped your head off at the chin and made you look like some dreadful unfinished monster or other; the paper peeling in shreds from the walls.

I sighed and said: "This is charming; and now don't you think you could get me something to read?"

The porter said, "Oh, certainly; the old man's got dead loads of books"; and he was gone before I could tell him what sort of literature I would rather have. And yet his countenance expressed the utmost confidence in his ability to execute the commission with credit to himself. The old man made a descent on him.

"What are you going to do with that pile of books?"

"Fifteen wants 'em, sir."

"Fifteen, is it? He'll want a warming-pan, next—he'll want a nurse! Take him everything there is in the house—take him the barkeeper—take him the baggage-wagon—take him the chambermaid! Confound me, I never saw anything like it. What did he say he wants with those books?"

"Wants to read 'em, like enough; it ain't likely he wants to eat 'em, I don't reckon."

"Wants to read 'em—wants to read 'em this time of night, the infernal lunatic! Well he can't have them."

"But he says he's mor'ly bound to have 'em: he says he'll just go a-rairin' and a-chargin' through this house and raise more—well, there's no tellin' what he won't do if he don't get 'em; because he's drunk and crazy and desperate, and nothing 'll soothe him down but them cussed books." [I had not made any threats and was not in the condition ascribed to me by the porter.]

"Well, go on; but I will be around when he goes to rairing and charging, and the first rair he makes I'll make him rair out of the window." And then the old gentleman went off growling as before.

The genius of that porter was something wonderful. He put an armful of books on the bed and said "Good night" as confidently as if he knew perfectly well that those books were exactly my style of reading-matter. And well he might. His selection covered the whole range of legitimate literature. It comprised *The Great Consummation*, by Rev. Dr. Cummings—theology; *Revised Statutes of the State of Missouri*—law; *The Complete Horse-Doctor*—medicine; *The Toilers of the Sea*, by Victor Hugo—romance; the works of William Shakespeare—poetry. I shall never cease to admire the tact and the intelligence of that gifted porter.

But all the donkeys in Christendom, and most of the Egyptian boys, I think, are at the door, and

there is some noise going on, not to put it in stronger
language. We are about starting to the illustrious
Pyramids of Egypt, and the donkeys for the voyage
are under inspection. I will go and select one before
the choice animals are all taken.

## CHAPTER XXXI

THE donkeys were all good, all handsome, all strong and in good condition, all fast and all willing to prove it. They were the best we had found anywhere, and the most *recherché*. I do not know what *recherché* is, but that is what these donkeys were, anyhow. Some were of a soft mouse-color, and the others were white, black, and vari-colored. Some were close-shaven, all over, except that a tuft like a paint-brush was left on the end of the tail. Others were so shaven in fanciful land-scape-garden patterns, as to mark their bodies with curving lines, which were bounded on one side by hair and on the other by the close plush left by the shears. They had all been newly barbered, and were exceedingly stylish. Several of the white ones were barred like zebras with rainbow stripes of blue and red and yellow paint. These were indescribably gorgeous. Dan and Jack selected from this lot be-cause they brought back Italian reminiscences of the "old masters." The saddles were the high, stuffy, frog-shaped things we had known in Ephesus and Smyrna. The donkey-boys were lively young Egyptian rascals who could follow a donkey and keep him in a canter half a day without tiring. We had plenty of spectators when we mounted, for the hotel was full of English people bound overland to India and officers getting ready for the African campaign against the Abyssinian King Theodorus. We were not a very large party, but as we charged through the streets of the great metropolis, we made noise for five hundred, and displayed activity and created excitement in proportion. Nobody can steer a donkey, and some collided with camels, dervishes, effendis, asses, beggars, and everything else that offered to the donkeys a reasonable chance for a collision. When we turned into the broad avenue that leads out of the city toward Old Cairo, there was plenty of room. The walls of stately date-palms that fenced the gardens and bordered the way, threw their shadows down and made the air cool and bracing. We rose to the spirit of the time and the race became a wild rout, a stampede, a terrific panic. I wish to live to enjoy it again.

Somewhere along this route we had a few startling exhibitions of Oriental simplicity. A girl apparently thirteen years of age came along the great thorough-fare dressed like Eve before the fall. We would have called her thirteen at home; but here girls who look thirteen are often not more than nine, in reality.

Occasionally we saw stark-naked men of superb build, bathing, and making no attempt at conceal-ment. However, an hour's acquaintance with this cheerful custom reconciled the pilgrims to it, and then it ceased to occasion remark. Thus easily do even the most startling novelties grow tame and spiritless to these sight-surfeited wanderers.

# MARK TWAIN

Arrived at Old Cairo, the camp-followers took up the donkeys and tumbled them bodily aboard a small boat with a lateen sail, and we followed and got under way. The deck was closely packed with donkeys and men; the two sailors had to climb over and under and through the wedged mass to work the sails, and the steersman had to crowd four or five donkeys out of the way when he wished to swing his tiller and put his helm hard down. But what were their troubles to us? We had nothing to do; nothing to do but enjoy the trip; nothing to do but shove the donkeys off our corns and look at the charming scenery of the Nile.

On the island at our right was the machine they call the Nilometer, a stone column whose business it is to mark the rise of the river and prophesy whether it will reach only thirty-two feet and produce a famine, or whether it will properly flood the land at forty and produce plenty, or whether it will rise to forty-three and bring death and destruction to flocks and crops—but how it does all this they could not explain to us so that we could understand. On the same island is still shown the spot where Pharaoh's daughter found Moses in the bulrushes. Near the spot we sailed from, the Holy Family dwelt when they sojourned in Egypt till Herod should complete his slaughter of the innocents. The same tree they rested under when they first arrived was there a short time ago, but the Viceroy of Egypt sent it to the Empress Eugénie lately. He was just in time, otherwise our pilgrims would have had it.

The Nile at this point is muddy, swift, and turbid,

and does not lack a great deal of being as wide as the Mississippi.

We scrambled up the steep bank at the shabby town of Ghizeh, mounted the donkeys again, and scampered away. For four or five miles the route lay along a high embankment which they say is to be the bed of a railway the Sultan means to build for no other reason than that when the Empress of the French comes to visit him she can go to the Pyramids in comfort. This is true Oriental hospitality. I am very glad it is our privilege to have donkeys instead of cars.

At the distance of a few miles the Pyramids, rising above the palms, looked very clean-cut, very grand and imposing, and very soft and filmy, as well. They swam in a rich haze that took from them all suggestions of unfeeling stone, and made them seem only the airy nothings of a dream—structures which might blossom into tiers of vague arches, or ornate colonnades, maybe, and change and change again into all graceful forms of architecture while we looked, and then melt deliciously away and blend with the tremulous atmosphere.

At the end of the levee we left the mules and went in a sailboat across an arm of the Nile or an overflow, and landed where the sands of the Great Sahara left their embankment, as straight as a wall, along the verge of the alluvial plain of the river. A laborious walk in the flaming sun brought us to the foot of the great Pyramid of Cheops. It was a fairy vision no longer. It was a corrugated, unsightly mountain of stone. Each of its monstrous sides

was a wide stairway which rose upward, step above
step, narrowing as it went, till it tapered to a point
far aloft in the air. Insect men and women—pilgrims from the *Quaker City*—were creeping about
its dizzy perches, and one little black swarm were
waving postage-stamps from the airy summit—handkerchiefs will be understood.

Of course we were besieged by a rabble of muscular Egyptians and Arabs who wanted the contract
of dragging us to the top—all tourists are. Of course
you could not hear your own voice for the din that
was around you. Of course the Sheiks said *they* were
the only responsible parties; that all contracts must
be made with them, all moneys paid over to them,
and none exacted from us by any but themselves
alone. Of course they contracted that the varlets
who dragged us up should not mention bucksheesh
once. For such is the usual routine. Of course
we contracted with them, paid them, were delivered
into the hands of the draggers, dragged up the
Pyramids, and harried and bedeviled for bucksheesh from the foundation clear to the summit.
We paid it, too, for we were purposely spread very
far apart over the vast side of the Pyramid. There
was no help near if we called, and the Herculeses
who dragged us had a way of asking sweetly and
flatteringly for bucksheesh, which was seductive, and
of looking fierce and threatening to throw us down
the precipice, which was persuasive and convincing.

Each step being full as high as a dinner-table;
there being very, very many of the steps; an Arab
having hold of each of our arms and springing up-

ward from step to step and snatching us with them, forcing us to lift our feet as high as our breasts every time, and do it rapidly and keep it up till we were ready to faint,—who shall say it is not lively, exhilarating, lacerating, muscle-straining, bone-wrenching, and perfectly excruciating and exhausting pastime, climbing the Pyramids? I beseeched the varlets not to twist *all* my joints asunder; I iterated, reiterated, even *swore* to them that I did not wish to beat anybody to the top; did all I could to convince them that if I got there the last of all I would feel blessed above men and grateful to them forever; I begged them, prayed them, pleaded with them to let me stop and rest a moment—only one little moment: and they only answered with some more frightful springs, and an unenlisted volunteer behind opened a bombardment of determined boosts with his head which threatened to batter my whole political economy to wreck and ruin.

Twice, for one minute, they let me rest while they extorted bucksheesh, and then continued their maniac flight up the Pyramid. They wished to beat the other parties. It was nothing to them that I, a stranger, must be sacrificed upon the altar of their unholy ambition. But in the midst of sorrow joy blooms. Even in this dark hour I had a sweet consolation. For I knew that except these Mohammedans repented they would go straight to perdition some day. And *they* never repent—they never forsake their paganism. This thought calmed me, cheered me, and I sank down, limp and exhausted, upon the summit, but happy, *so* happy and serene within.

# MARK TWAIN

On the one hand, a mighty sea of yellow sand stretched away toward the ends of the earth, solemn, silent, shorn of vegetation, its solitude uncheered by any forms of creature life; on the other, the Eden of Egypt was spread below us—a broad green floor, cloven by the sinuous river, dotted with villages, its vast distances measured and marked by the diminishing stature of receding clusters of palms. It lay asleep in an enchanted atmosphere. There was no sound, no motion. Above the date-plumes in the middle distance, swelled a domed and pinnacled mass, glimmering through a tinted, exquisite mist; away toward the horizon a dozen shapely pyramids watched over ruined Memphis; and at our feet the bland impassible Sphinx looked out upon the picture from her throne in the sands as placidly and pensively as she had looked upon its like full fifty lagging centuries ago.

We suffered torture no pen can describe from the hungry appeals for bucksheesh that gleamed from Arab eyes and poured incessantly from Arab lips. Why try to call up the traditions of vanished Egyptian grandeur; why try to fancy Egypt following dead Rameses to his tomb in the Pyramid, or the long multitude of Israel departing over the desert yonder? Why try to think at all? The thing was impossible. One must bring his meditations cut and dried, or else cut and dry them afterward.

The traditional Arab proposed, in the traditional way, to run down Cheops, cross the eighth of a mile of sand intervening between it and the tall pyramid of Cephren, ascend to Cephren's summit and return to us on the top of Cheops—all in nine minutes by the watch, and the whole service to be rendered for a single dollar. In the first flush of irritation, I said let the Arab and his exploits go to the mischief. But stay. The upper third of Cephren was coated with dressed marble, smooth as glass. A blessed thought entered my brain. He must infallibly break his neck. Close the contract with despatch, I said, and let him go. He started. We watched. He went bounding down the vast broadside, spring after spring, like an ibex. He grew small and smaller till he became a bobbing pygmy, away down toward the bottom—then disappeared. We turned and peered over the other side—forty seconds—eighty seconds—a hundred—happiness, he is dead already?—two minutes—and a quarter—"There he goes!" Too true—it was too true. He was very small, now. Gradually, but surely, he overcame the level ground. He began to spring and climb again. Up, up, up —at last he reached the smooth coating—now for it. But he clung to it with toes and fingers, like a fly. He crawled this way and that—away to the right, slanting upward—away to the left, still slanting upward—and stood at last, a black peg on the summit, and waved his pygmy scarf! Then he crept downward to the raw steps again, then picked up his agile heels and flew. We lost him presently. But presently again we saw him under us, mounting with undiminished energy. Shortly he bounded into our midst with a gallant war-whoop. Time, eight minutes, forty-one seconds. He had won. His bones were intact. It was a failure. I reflected. I said to myself, he is tired, and must grow dizzy. I will risk another dollar on him.

He started again. Made the trip again. Slipped on the smooth coating—I almost had him. But an infamous crevice saved him. He was with us once more—perfectly sound. Time, eight minutes, forty-six seconds.

I said to Dan, "Lend me a dollar—I can beat this game, yet."

Worse and worse. He won again. Time, eight minutes, forty-eight seconds. I was out of all patience, now. I was desperate. Money was no longer of any consequence. I said, "Sirrah, I will give you a hundred dollars to jump off this pyramid head first. If you do not like the terms, name your bet. I scorn to stand on expenses now. I will stay right here and risk money on you as long as Dan has got a cent."

I was in a fair way to win, now, for it was a dazzling opportunity for an Arab. He pondered a moment, and would have done it, I think, but his mother arrived, then, and interfered. Her tears moved me —I never can look upon the tears of woman with indifference—and I said I would give her a hundred to jump off, too.

But it was a failure. The Arabs are too high-priced in Egypt. They put on airs unbecoming to such savages.

We descended, hot and out of humor. The dragoman lit candles, and we all entered a hole near the base of the pyramid, attended by a crazy rabble of Arabs who thrust their services upon us uninvited. They dragged us up a long inclined chute, and dripped candle-grease all over us. This chute was not more than twice as wide and high as a Saratoga trunk, and was walled, roofed, and floored with solid blocks of Egyptian granite as wide as a wardrobe, twice as thick, and three times as long. We kept on climbing, through the oppressive gloom, till I thought we ought to be nearing the top of the pyramid again, and then came to the "Queen's Chamber," and shortly to the Chamber of the King. These large apartments were tombs. The walls were built of monstrous masses of smoothed granite, neatly joined together. Some of them were nearly as large square as an ordinary parlor. A great stone sarcophagus like a bathtub stood in the center of the King's Chamber. Around it were gathered a picturesque group of Arab savages and soiled and tattered pilgrims, who held their candles aloft in the gloom while they chattered, and the winking blurs of light shed a dim glory down upon one of the irrepressible memento-seekers who was pecking at the venerable sarcophagus with his sacrilegious hammer. We struggled out to the open air and the bright sunshine, and for the space of thirty minutes received ragged Arabs by couples, dozens, and platoons, and paid them bucksheesh for services they swore and proved by each other that they had rendered, but which we had not been aware of before—and as each party was paid, they dropped into the rear of the procession and in due time arrived again with a newly invented delinquent list for liquidation.

We lunched in the shade of the pyramid, and in

the midst of this encroaching and unwelcome company, and then Dan and Jack and I started away for a walk. A howling swarm of beggars followed us—surrounded us—almost headed us off. A sheik, in flowing white burnoose and gaudy headgear, was with them. He wanted more bucksheesh. But we had adopted a new code—it was millions for defense, but not a cent for bucksheesh. I asked him if he could persuade the others to depart if we paid him. He said yes—for ten francs. We accepted the contract, and said—

"Now persuade your vassals to fall back."

He swung his long staff round his head and three Arabs bit the dust. He capered among the mob like a very maniac. His blows fell like hail, and wherever one fell a subject went down. We had to hurry to the rescue and tell him it was only necessary to damage them a little, he need not kill them. In two minutes we were alone with the sheik, and remained so. The persuasive powers of this illiterate savage were remarkable.

Each side of the Pyramid of Cheops is about as long as the Capitol at Washington, or the Sultan's new palace on the Bosporus, and is longer than the greatest depth of St. Peter's at Rome—which is to say that each side of Cheops extends seven hundred and some odd feet. It is about seventy-five feet higher than the cross on St. Peter's. The first time I ever went down the Mississippi, I thought the highest bluff on the river between St. Louis and New Orleans—it was near Selma, Missouri—was probably the highest mountain in the world. It is four

hundred and thirteen feet high. It still looms in
my memory with undiminished grandeur. I can
still see the trees and bushes growing smaller and
smaller as I followed them up its huge slant with my
eye, till they became a feathery fringe on the distant
summit. This symmetrical Pyramid of Cheops—
this solid mountain of stone reared by the patient
hands of men—this mighty tomb of a forgotten
monarch—dwarfs my cherished mountain. For it
is four hundred and eighty feet high. In still earlier
years than those I have been recalling, Holliday's
Hill, in our town, was to me the noblest work of
God. It appeared to pierce the skies. It was
nearly three hundred feet high. In those days I
pondered the subject much, but I never could understand why it did not swathe its summit with
never-failing clouds, and crown its majestic brow with
everlasting snows. I had heard that such was the
custom of great mountains in other parts of the world.
I remembered how I worked with another boy, at
odd afternoons stolen from study and paid for with
stripes, to undermine and start from its bed an immense boulder that rested upon the edge of that hilltop; I remembered how, one Saturday afternoon, we
gave three hours of honest effort to the task, and saw
at last that our reward was at hand; I remembered
how we sat down, then, and wiped the perspiration
away, and waited to let a picnic party get out of the
way in the road below—and then we started the
boulder. It was splendid. It went crashing down
the hillside, tearing up saplings, mowing bushes
down like grass, ripping and crushing and smashing

everything in its path—eternally splintered and scattered a woodpile at the foot of the hill, and then sprang from the high bank clear over a dray in the road—the negro glanced up once and dodged—and the next second it made infinitesimal mincemeat of a frame cooper shop, and the coopers swarmed out like bees. Then we said it was perfectly magnificent, and left. Because the coopers were starting up the hill to inquire.

Still, that mountain, prodigious as it was, was nothing to the Pyramid of Cheops. I could conjure up no comparison that would convey to my mind a satisfactory comprehension of the magnitude of a pile of monstrous stones that covered thirteen acres of ground and stretched upward four hundred and eighty tiresome feet, and so I gave it up and walked down to the Sphinx.

After years of waiting, it was before me at last. The great face was so sad, so earnest, so longing, so patient. There was a dignity not of earth in its mien, and in its countenance a benignity such as never anything human wore. It was stone, but it seemed sentient. If ever image of stone thought, it was thinking. It was looking toward the verge of the landscape, yet looking *at* nothing—nothing but distance and vacancy. It was looking over and beyond everything of the present, and far into the past. It was gazing out over the ocean of Time—over lines of century-waves which, further and further receding, closed nearer and nearer together, and blended at last into one unbroken tide, away toward the horizon of remote antiquity. It was thinking of

the wars of departed ages; of the empires it had
seen created and destroyed; of the nations whose
birth it had witnessed, whose progress it had watched,
whose annihilation it had noted; of the joy and
sorrow, the life and death, the grandeur and decay,
of five thousand slow revolving years. It was the
type of an attribute of man—of a faculty of his
heart and brain. It was MEMORY—RETROSPEC-
TION—wrought into visible, tangible form. All
who know what pathos there is in memories of days
that are accomplished and faces that have vanished
—albeit only a trifling score of years gone by—will
have some appreciation of the pathos that dwells in
these grave eyes that look so steadfastly back upon
the things they knew before History was born—before Tradition had being—things that were, and
forms that moved, in a vague era which even Poetry
and Romance scarce know of—and passed one by
one away and left the stony dreamer solitary in the
midst of a strange new age, and uncomprehended
scenes.

The Sphinx is grand in its loneliness; it is impossible in its magnitude; it is impressive in the mystery
that hangs over its story. And there is that in the
overshadowing majesty of this eternal figure of stone,
with its accusing memory of the deeds of all ages,
which reveals to one something of what he shall feel
when he shall stand at last in the awful presence of
God.

There are some things which, for the credit of
America, should be left unsaid, perhaps; but these
very things happen sometimes to be the very things

which, for the real benefit of Americans, ought to have prominent notice. While we stood looking, a wart, or an excrescence of some kind, appeared on the jaw of the Sphinx. We heard the familiar clink of a hammer, and understood the case at once. One of our well-meaning reptiles—I mean relic-hunters—had crawled up there and was trying to break a "specimen" from the face of this the most majestic creation the hand of man has wrought. But the great image contemplated the dead ages as calmly as ever, unconscious of the small insect that was fretting at its jaw. Egyptian granite that has defied the storms and earthquakes of all time has nothing to fear from the tack-hammers of ignorant excursionists—highwaymen like this specimen. He failed in his enterprise. We sent a sheik to arrest him if he had the authority, or to warn him, if he had not, that by the laws of Egypt the crime he was attempting to commit was punishable with imprisonment or the bastinado. Then he desisted and went away.

The Sphinx: a hundred and twenty-five feet long, sixty feet high, and a hundred and two feet around the head, if I remember rightly—carved out of one solid block of stone harder than any iron. The block must have been as large as the Fifth Avenue Hotel before the usual waste (by the necessities of sculpture) of a fourth or a half of the original mass was begun. I only set down these figures and these remarks to suggest the prodigious labor the carving of it so elegantly, so symmetrically, so faultlessly, must have cost. This species of stone is so hard that figures cut in it remain sharp and unmarred after exposure to the weather for two or three thousand years. Now did it take a hundred years of patient toil to carve the Sphinx? It seems probable.

Something interfered, and we did not visit the Red Sea and walk upon the sands of Arabia. I shall not describe the great mosque of Mehemet Ali, whose entire inner walls are built of polished and glistening alabaster; I shall not tell how the little birds have built their nests in the globes of the great chandeliers that hang in the mosque, and how they fill the whole place with their music and are not afraid of anybody because their audacity is pardoned, their rights are respected, and nobody is allowed to interfere with them, even though the mosque be thus doomed to go unlighted; I certainly shall not tell the hackneyed story of the massacre of the Mamelukes, because I am glad the lawless rascals were massacred, and I do not wish to get up any sympathy in their behalf; I shall not tell how that one solitary Mameluke jumped his horse a hundred feet down from the battlements of the citadel and escaped, because I do not think much of that—I could have done it myself; I shall not tell of Joseph's well which he dug in the solid rock of the citadel hill and which is still as good as new, nor how the same mules he bought to draw up the water (with an endless chain) are still at it yet and are getting tired of it, too; I shall not tell about Joseph's granaries which he built to store the grain in, what time the Egyptian brokers were "selling short," unwitting that there would be no corn in all the land when it should be time for them to deliver;

# MARK TWAIN

I shall not tell anything about the strange, strange city of Cairo, because it is only a repetition, a good deal intensified and exaggerated, of the Oriental cities I have already spoken of; I shall not tell of the Great Caravan which leaves for Mecca every year, for I did not see it; nor of the fashion the people have of prostrating themselves and so forming a long human pavement to be ridden over by the chief of the expedition on its return, to the end that their salvation may be thus secured, for I did not see that either; I shall not speak of the railway, for it is like any other railway!—I shall only say that the fuel they use for the locomotive is composed of mummies three thousand years old, purchased by the ton or by the graveyard for that purpose, and that sometimes one hears the profane engineer call out pettishly, "D—n these plebeians, they don't burn worth a cent—pass out a King";[1] I shall not tell of the groups of mud cones stuck like wasps' nests upon a thousand mounds above high-water mark the length and breadth of Egypt— villages of the lower classes; I shall not speak of the boundless sweep of level plain, green with luxuriant grain, that gladdens the eye as far as it can pierce through the soft, rich atmosphere of Egypt; I shall not speak of the vision of the Pyramids seen at a distance of five and twenty miles, for the picture is too ethereal to be limned by an uninspired pen; I shall not tell of the crowds of dusky women who flocked to the cars when they stopped a moment at

[1] Stated to me for a fact. I only tell it as I got it. I am willing to believe it. I can believe anything.

a station, to sell us a drink of water or a ruddy, juicy pomegranate; I shall not tell of the motley multitudes and wild costumes that graced a fair we found in full blast at another barbarous station; I shall not tell how we feasted on fresh dates and enjoyed the pleasant landscape all through the flying journey; nor how we thundered into Alexandria, at last, swarmed out of the cars, rowed aboard the ship, left a comrade behind (who was to return to Europe, thence home), raised the anchor, and turned our bows homeward finally and forever from the long voyage; nor how, as the mellow sun went down upon the oldest land on earth, Jack and Moult assembled in solemn state in the smoking-room and mourned over the lost comrade the whole night long, and would not be comforted. I shall not speak a word of any of these things, or write a line. They shall be as a sealed book. I do not know what a sealed book is, because I never saw one, but a sealed book is the expression to use in this connection, because it is popular.

We were glad to have seen the land which was the mother of civilization—which taught Greece her letters, and through Greece Rome, and through Rome the world; the land which could have humanized and civilized the hapless children of Israel, but allowed them to depart out of her borders little better than savages. We were glad to have seen that land which had an enlightened religion with future eternal rewards and punishment in it, while even Israel's religion contained no promise of a hereafter. We were glad to have seen that land which had glass three thousand years before England had it, and could paint upon it as none of us can paint now; that land which knew, three thousand years ago, well-nigh all of medicine and surgery which science has *discovered* lately; which had all those curious surgical instruments which science has *invented* recently; which had in high excellence a thousand luxuries and necessities of an advanced civilization which we have gradually contrived and accumulated in modern times and claimed as things that were new under the sun; that had paper untold centuries before we dreamt of it—and waterfalls before our women thought of them; that had a perfect system of common schools so long before we boasted of our achievements in that direction that it seems forever and forever ago; that so embalmed the dead that flesh was made almost immortal—which we cannot do; that built temples which mock at destroying time and smile grimly upon our lauded little prodigies of architecture; that old land that knew all which we know now, perchance, and more; that walked in the broad highway of civilization in the gray dawn of creation, ages and ages before we were born; that left the impress of exalted, cultivated Mind upon the eternal front of the Sphinx to confound all scoffers who, when all the other proofs had passed away, might seek to persuade the world that imperial Egypt, in the days of her high renown, had groped in darkness.

# CHAPTER XXXII

WE were at sea now, for a very long voyage—we were to pass through the entire length of the Levant; through the entire length of the Mediterranean proper, also, and then cross the full width of the Atlantic—a voyage of several weeks. We naturally settled down into a very slow, stay-at-home manner of life, and resolved to be quiet, exemplary people, and roam no more for twenty or thirty days. No more, at least, than from stem to stern of the ship. It was a very comfortable prospect, though, for we were tired and needed a long rest.

We were all lazy and satisfied, now, as the meager entries in my note-book (that sure index, to me, of my condition) prove. What a stupid thing a note-book gets to be at sea, anyway. Please observe the style:

*Sunday*—Services, as usual, at four bells. Services at night, also. No cards.

*Monday*—Beautiful day, but rained hard. The cattle purchased at Alexandria for beef ought to be shingled. Or else fattened. The water stands in deep puddles in the depressions forward of their after shoulders. Also here and there all over their backs. It is well they are not cows—it would soak in and ruin the milk. The poor devil eagle[1] from Syria looks miserable and droopy in the rain perched on the forward capstan. He

[1] Afterward presented to the Central Park.

# MARK TWAIN

appears to have his own opinion of a sea voyage, and if it were put into language and the language solidified, it would probably effectually dam the widest river in the world.

*Tuesday*—Somewhere in the neighborhood of the island of Malta. Cannot stop there. Cholera. Weather very stormy. Many passengers seasick and invisible.

*Wednesday*—Weather still very savage. Storm blew two land-birds to sea, and they came on board. A hawk was blown off, also. He circled round and round the ship, wanting to light, but afraid of the people. He was so tired, though, that he had to light, at last, or perish. He stopped in the foretop, repeatedly, and was as often blown away by the wind. At last Harry caught him. Sea full of flying-fish. They rise in flocks of three hundred and flash along above the tops of the waves a distance of two or three hundred feet, then fall and disappear.

*Thursday*—Anchored off Algiers, Africa. Beautiful city, beautiful green hilly landscape behind it. Stayed half a day and left. Not permitted to land, though we showed a clean bill of health. They were afraid of Egyptian plague and cholera.

*Friday*—Morning, dominoes. Afternoon, dominoes. Evening, promenading the deck. Afterward, charades.

*Saturday*—Morning, dominoes. Afternoon, dominoes. Evening, promenading the decks. Afterward, dominoes.

*Sunday*—Morning service, four bells. Evening service, eight bells. Monotony till midnight.—Whereupon, dominoes.

*Monday*—Morning, dominoes. Afternoon, dominoes. Evening, promenading the decks. Afterward, charades and a lecture from Dr. C. Dominoes.

*No date*—Anchored off the picturesque city of Cagliari, Sardinia. Stayed till midnight, but not permitted to land by these infamous foreigners. They smell inodorously—they do not wash—they dare not risk cholera.

*Thursday*—Anchored off the beautiful cathedral city of Malaga, Spain.—Went ashore in the captain's boat—not ashore, either, for they would not let us land. Quarantine. Shipped my newspaper correspondence, which they took with tongs, dipped it in sea-water, clipped it full of holes, and then fumigated it with villainous vapors till it smelt like a Spaniard. Inquired about chances to run the blockade and visit the Alham-

# THE INNOCENTS ABROAD

bra at Granada. Too risky—they might hang a body. Set sail—middle of afternoon.

And so on, and so on, and so forth, for several days. Finally, anchored off Gibraltar, which looks familiar and homelike.

It reminds me of the journal I opened with the New Year, once, when I was a boy and a confiding and a willing prey to those impossible schemes of reform which well-meaning old maids and grandmothers set for the feet of unwary youths at that season of the year—setting oversized tasks for them, which, necessarily failing, as infallibly weaken the boy's strength of will, diminish his confidence in himself, and injure his chances of success in life. Please accept of an extract:

*Monday*—Got up, washed, went to bed.
*Tuesday*—Got up, washed, went to bed.
*Wednesday*—Got up, washed, went to bed.
*Thursday*—Got up, washed, went to bed.
*Friday*—Got up, washed, went to bed.
*Next Friday*—Got up, washed, went to bed.
*Friday fortnight*—Got up, washed, went to bed.
*Following month*—Got up, washed, went to bed.

I stopped, then, discouraged. Startling events appeared to be too rare, in my career, to render a diary necessary. I still reflect with pride, however, that even at that early age I washed when I got up. That journal finished me. I never have had the nerve to keep one since. My loss of confidence in myself in that line was permanent.

The ship had to stay a week or more at Gibraltar to take in coal for the home voyage.

It would be very tiresome staying here, and so

391

four of us ran the quarantine blockade and spent
seven delightful days in Seville, Cordova, Cadiz, and
wandering through the pleasant rural scenery of
Andalusia, the garden of Old Spain. The experiences of that cheery week were too varied and
numerous for a short chapter, and I have not room
for a long one. Therefore I shall leave them all
out.

# CHAPTER XXXIII

TEN or eleven o'clock found us coming down to breakfast one morning in Cadiz. They told us the ship had been lying at anchor in the harbor two or three hours. It was time for us to bestir ourselves. The ship could wait only a little while because of the quarantine. We were soon on board, and within the hour the white city and the pleasant shores of Spain sank down behind the waves and passed out of sight. We had seen no land fade from view so regretfully.

It had long ago been decided in a noisy public meeting in the main cabin that we could not go to Lisbon, because we must surely be quarantined there. We did everything by mass-meeting, in the good old national way, from swapping off one empire for another on the program of the voyage down to complaining of the cookery and the scarcity of napkins. I am reminded, now, of one of these complaints of the cookery made by a passenger. The coffee had been steadily growing more and more execrable for the space of three weeks, till at last it had ceased to be coffee altogether and had assumed the nature of mere discolored water—so this person said. He said it was so weak that it was transparent an inch in depth around the edge of the cup. As

he approached the table one morning he saw the
transparent edge—by means of his extraordinary
vision—long before he got to his seat. He went
back and complained in a high-handed way to Captain Duncan. He said the coffee was disgraceful.
The captain showed his. It seemed tolerably good.
The incipient mutineer was more outraged than
ever, then, at what he denounced as the partiality
shown the captain's table over the other tables in
the ship. He flourished back and got his cup and
set it down triumphantly, and said:

"Just try that mixture once, Captain Duncan."

He smelt it—tasted it—smiled benignantly—then
said:

"It *is* inferior—for *coffee*—but it is pretty fair
*tea.*"

The humbled mutineer smelt it, tasted it, and
returned to his seat. He had made an egregious ass
of himself before the whole ship. He did it no
more. After that he took things as they came.
That was me.

The old-fashioned ship-life had returned, now that
we were no longer in sight of land. For days and
days it continued just the same, one day being exactly
like another, and, to me, every one of them pleasant.
At last we anchored in the open roadstead of Fun-
chal, in the beautiful islands we call the Madeiras.

The mountains looked surpassingly lovely, clad as
they were in living green; ribbed with lava ridges;
flecked with white cottages; riven by deep chasms
purple with shade; the great slopes dashed with
sunshine and mottled with shadows flung from the

drifting squadrons of the sky, and the superb picture fitly crowned by towering peaks whose fronts were swept by the trailing fringes of the clouds.

But we could not land. We stayed all day and looked, we abused the man who invented quarantine, we held half a dozen mass-meetings and crammed them full of interrupted speeches, motions that fell still-born, amendments that came to naught, and resolutions that died from sheer exhaustion in trying to get before the house. At night we set sail.

We averaged four mass-meetings a week for the voyage—we seemed always in labor in this way, and yet so often fallaciously that whenever at long intervals we were safely delivered of a resolution, it was cause for public rejoicing, and we hoisted the flag and fired a salute.

Days passed—and nights; and then the beautiful Bermudas rose out of the sea, we entered the tortuous channel, steamed hither and thither among the bright summer islands, and rested at last under the flag of England and were welcome. We were not a nightmare here, where were civilization and intelligence in place of Spanish and Italian superstition, dirt and dread of cholera. A few days among the breezy groves, the flower-gardens, the coral caves, and the lovely vistas of blue water that went curving in and out, disappearing and anon again appearing through jungle walls of brilliant foliage, restored the energies dulled by long drowsing on the ocean, and fitted us for our final cruise—our little run of a thousand miles to New York—America—HOME.

We bade good-by to "our friends the Bermudians," as our program hath it — the majority of those we were most intimate with were negroes— and courted the great deep again. I said the majority. We knew more negroes than white people, because we had a deal of washing to be done, but we made some most excellent friends among the whites, whom it will be a pleasant duty to hold long in grateful remembrance.

We sailed, and from that hour all idling ceased. Such another system of overhauling, general littering of cabins and packing of trunks we had not seen since we let go the anchor in the harbor of Beirout. Everybody was busy. Lists of all purchases had to be made out, and values attached, to facilitate matters at the custom-house. Purchases bought by bulk in partnership had to be equitably divided, outstanding debts canceled, accounts compared, and trunks, boxes, and packages labeled. All day long the bustle and confusion continued.

And now came our first accident. A passenger was running through a gangway, betweendecks, one stormy night, when he caught his foot in the iron staple of a door that had been heedlessly left off a hatchway and the bones of his leg broke at the ankle. It was our first serious misfortune. We had traveled much more than twenty thousand miles, by land and sea, in many trying climates, without a single hurt, without a serious case of sickness, and without a death among five-and-sixty passengers. Our good fortune had been wonderful. A sailor had jumped overboard at Constantinople one night, and was seen no more, but it was suspected that his object was to desert, and there was a slim chance, at least, that he reached the shore. But the passenger-list was complete. There was no name missing from the register.

At last, one pleasant morning, we steamed up the harbor of New York, all on deck, all dressed in Christian garb—by special order, for there was a latent disposition in some quarters to come out as Turks—and, amid a waving of handkerchiefs from welcoming friends, the glad pilgrims noted the shiver of the decks that told that ship and pier had joined hands again, and the long, strange cruise was over. Amen.

# A NEWSPAPER VALEDICTORY

IN this place I will print an article which I wrote
for the New York *Herald* the night we arrived.
I do it partly because my contract with my publisher
makes it compulsory; partly because it is a proper,
tolerably accurate, and exhaustive summing-up of
the cruise of the ship and the performances of the
pilgrims in foreign lands; and partly because some
of the passengers have abused me for writing it,
and I wish the public to see how thankless a task
it is to put one's self to trouble to glorify unappre-
ciative people. I was charged with "rushing into
print" with these compliments. I did not rush. I
had written news letters to the *Herald* sometimes,
but yet when I visited the office that day I did not
say anything about writing a valedictory. I did go
to the *Tribune* office to see if such an article was
wanted, because I belonged on the regular staff of
that paper and it was simply a duty to do it. The
managing editor was absent, and so I thought no
more about it. At night when the *Herald's* request
came for an article, I did not "rush." In fact, I
demurred for a while, because I did not feel like
writing compliments, then, and therefore was afraid
to speak of the cruise lest I might be betrayed into
using other than complimentary language. How-

ever, I reflected that it would be a just and righteous thing to go down and write a kind word for the Hadjis—Hadjis are people who have made the pilgrimage—because parties not interested could not do it so feelingly as I, a fellow-Hadji, and so I penned the valedictory. I have read it, and read it again; and if there is a sentence in it that is not fulsomely complimentary to captain, ship, and passengers, *I* cannot find it. If it is not a chapter that any company might be proud to have a body write about them, my judgment is fit for nothing. With these remarks I confidently submit it to the unprejudiced judgment of the reader:

### RETURN OF THE HOLY LAND EXCURSIONISTS—THE STORY OF THE CRUISE

To the Editor of the Herald:

The steamer *Quaker City* has accomplished at last her extraordinary voyage and returned to her old pier at the foot of Wall Street. The expedition was a success in some respects, in some it was not. Originally it was advertised as a "pleasure excursion." Well, perhaps it was a pleasure excursion, but certainly it did not look like one; certainly it did not act like one. Anybody's and everybody's notion of a pleasure excursion is that the parties to it will of a necessity be young and giddy and somewhat boisterous. They will dance a good deal, sing a good deal, make love, but sermonize very little. Anybody's and everybody's notion of a well-conducted funeral is that there must be a hearse and a corpse, and chief mourners and mourners by courtesy, many old people, much solemnity, no levity, and a prayer and a sermon withal. Three-fourths of the *Quaker City's* passengers were between forty and seventy years of age! There was a picnic crowd for you! It may be supposed that the other fourth was composed of young girls. But it was not. It was chiefly composed of rusty old bachelors and a child of six years. Let us average the ages of the *Quaker City's* pilgrims and set the figure down as fifty years. Is any man insane enough to imagine that this picnic of patriarchs sang, made love, danced, laughed, told anecdotes, dealt in ungodly levity? In my experience they sinned little in these matters. No doubt it was presumed here at home that these frolicsome veterans laughed and sang and romped all day, and day after day, and kept up a noisy excitement from one end of the ship to the other; and that they played blindman's buff or danced quadrilles and waltzes on moonlight evenings on the quarter-deck; and that at odd moments of unoccupied time they jotted a laconic item or two in the journals they opened on such an elaborate plan when they left home, and then scurried off to their whist and euchre labors under the cabin lamps. If these things were presumed, the presumption was at fault. The venerable excursionists were not gay and frisky. They played no blindman's buff; they dealt not in whist; they shirked not the irksome journal, for alas! most of them were even writing books. They never romped, they talked but little, they never sang, save in the nightly prayer-meeting. The pleasure ship was a synagogue, and the pleasure trip was a funeral excursion without a corpse. (There is nothing exhilarating about a funeral excursion without a corpse.) A free, hearty laugh was a sound that was not heard oftener than once in seven days about those decks or in those cabins, and when it was heard it met with precious little sympathy. The excursionists danced, on three separate evenings, long, long ago (it seems an age) quadrilles, of a single set, made up of three ladies and five gentlemen (the latter with handkerchiefs around their arms to signify their sex), who timed their feet to the solemn wheezing of a melodeon; but even this melancholy orgie was voted to be sinful, and dancing was discontinued.

The pilgrims played dominoes when too much Josephus or Robinson's Holy Land Researches, or book-writing, made recreation necessary—for dominoes is about as mild and sinless a game as any in the world, perhaps, excepting always the ineffably insipid diversion they call croquet, which is a game where you don't pocket any balls and don't carom on any thing of any consequence, and when you are done nobody has to pay, and there are no refreshments to saw off, and, consequently, there isn't any satisfaction whatever about it—they played dominoes till they were rested, and then they black-guarded each other privately till prayer-time. When they were not seasick they were uncommonly prompt when the dinner-gong sounded. Such was our daily life on board the ship—solemnity, decorum, dinner, dominoes, devotions, slander. It was not lively enough for a pleasure trip; but if we had only had a corpse it would have made a noble funeral excursion. It is all over now; but when I look back, the idea of these venerable fossils skipping forth on a six-months picnic seems exquisitely refreshing. The advertised title of the expedition—"The Grand Holy Land Pleasure Excursion"—was a misnomer. "The Grand Holy Land Funeral Procession" would have been better—much better.

Wherever we went, in Europe, Asia, or Africa, we made a sensation, and, I suppose I may add, created a famine. None of us had ever been anywhere before; we all hailed from the interior; travel was a wild novelty to us, and we conducted ourselves in accordance with the natural instincts that were in us, and trammeled ourselves with no ceremonies, no conventionalities. We always took care to make it understood that we were Americans—Americans! When we found that a good many foreigners had hardly ever heard of America, and that a good many more knew it only as a barbarous province away off ·somewhere, that had lately been at war with somebody, we pitied the ignorance of the Old World, but abated no jot of our importance. Many and many a simple community in the Eastern hemisphere will remember for years the incursion of the strange horde in the year of our Lord 1867, that called themselves Americans, and seemed to imagine in some unaccountable way that they had a right to be proud of it. We generally created a famine, partly because the coffee on the *Quaker City* was unendurable, and sometimes the more substantial fare was not strictly first class; and partly because one naturally tires of sitting long at the same board and eating from the same dishes.

The people of those foreign countries are very, very ignorant. They looked curiously at the costumes we had brought from the wilds of America. They observed that we talked loudly at table sometimes. They noticed that we looked out for expenses, and got what we conveniently could out of a franc, and wondered where in the mischief we came from. In Paris they just simply opened their eyes and stared when we spoke to them in French! We never did succeed in making those idiots understand their own language. One of our passengers said to a shopkeeper, in reference to a proposed return to buy a pair of gloves, *"Allong restay trankeel—maybe ve coom Moonday";* and would you believe it, that shopkeeper, a born Frenchman, had to ask what it was that had been said. Sometimes it seems to me, somehow, that there must be a difference between Parisian French and *Quaker City* French.

The people stared at us everywhere, and we stared at them. We generally made them feel rather small, too, before we got done with them, because we bore down on them with America's greatness until we crushed them. And yet we took kindly to the manners and customs, and especially to the fashions of the various people we visited. When we left the Azores, we wore awful capotes and used fine-tooth combs—successfully. When we came back from Tangier, in Africa, we were topped with fezzes of the bloodiest hue, hung with tassels like an Indian's scalp-lock. In France and Spain we attracted some attention in these costumes. In Italy they naturally took us for distempered Garibaldians, and set a gunboat to look for anything significant in our changes of uniform. We made Rome howl. We could have made any place howl when we had all our clothes on. We got no fresh raiment in Greece—they had but little there of any kind. But at Constantinople, how we turned out! Turbans, simitars, fezzes, horse-pistols, tunics, sashes, baggy trousers, yellow slippers—Oh, we were gorgeous! The illustrious dogs of Constantinople barked their under-jaws off, and even then failed to do us justice. They are all dead by this time. They could not go through such a run of business as we gave them and survive.

And then we went to see the Emperor of Russia. We just called on him as comfortably as if we had known him a century or so, and when we had finished our visit we variegated ourselves with selections from Russian costumes and sailed away again more picturesque than ever. In Smyrna we picked up camel's-hair shawls and other dressy things from Persia; but in Palestine—ah, in Palestine—our splendid career ended. They didn't wear any clothes there to speak of. We were satisfied, and stopped. We made no experiments. We did not try their costume. But we astonished the natives of that country. We astonished them with such eccentricities of dress as we could muster. We prowled through the Holy Land, from Cesarea Philippi to Jerusalem and the Dead Sea, a weird procession of pilgrims, gotten up regardless of expense, solemn, gorgeous, green-spectacled, drowsing under blue umbrellas, and astride of a sorrier lot of horses, camels, and asses than those that came out of Noah's ark, after eleven months of seasickness and short rations. If ever those children of Israel in Palestine forget when Gideon's Band went through there from America, they ought to be cursed once more and finished. It was the rarest spectacle that ever astounded mortal eyes, perhaps.

Well, we were at home in Palestine. It was easy to see that that was the grand feature of the expedition. We had cared nothing much about Europe. We galloped through the Louvre, the Pitti, the Uffizzi, the Vatican—all the galleries—and through the pictured and frescoed churches of Venice, Naples, and the cathedrals of Spain; some of us said that certain of the great works of the old masters were glorious creations of genius (we found it out in the guide-book, though we got hold of the wrong picture sometimes), and the others said they were disgraceful old daubs. We examined modern and ancient statuary with a critical eye in Florence, Rome, or anywhere we found it, and praised it if we saw fit, and if we didn't we said we preferred the wooden Indians in front of the cigar stores of America. But the Holy Land brought out all our enthusiasm. We fell into raptures by the barren shores of Galilee; we pondered at Tabor and at Nazareth; we exploded into poetry over the questionable loveliness of Esdraelon; we meditated at Jezreel and Samaria over the missionary zeal of Jehu; we rioted—fairly rioted among the holy places of Jerusalem; we bathed in Jordan and the Dead Sea, reckless whether our accident-insurance policies were extra-hazardous or not, and brought away so many jugs of precious water from both places that all the country from Jericho to the mountains of Moab will suffer from drought this year, I think. Yet, the pilgrimage part of the excursion was its pet feature—there is no question about that. After dismal, smileless Palestine, beautiful Egypt had few charms for us. We merely glanced at it and were ready for home.

# MARK TWAIN

They wouldn't let us land at Malta—quarantine; they would not let us land in Sardinia; nor at Algiers, Africa; nor at Malaga, Spain, nor Cadiz, nor at the Madeira Islands. So we got offended at all foreigners and turned our backs upon them and came home. I suppose we only stopped at the Bermudas because they were in the program. We did not care anything about any place at all. We wanted to go home. Homesickness was abroad in the ship—it was epidemic. If the authorities of New York had known how badly we had it, they would have quarantined us here.

The grand pilgrimage is over. Good-by to it, and a pleasant memory to it, I am able to say in all kindness. I bear no malice, no ill will toward any individual that was connected with it, either as passenger or officer. Things I did not like at all yesterday I like very well to-day, now that I am home, and always hereafter I shall be able to poke fun at the whole gang if the spirit so moves me to do, without ever saying a malicious word. The expedition accomplished all that its program promised that it should accomplish, and we ought all to be satisfied with the management of the matter, certainly. By-by!

MARK TWAIN.

I call that complimentary. It *is* complimentary; and yet I never have received a word of thanks for it from the Hadjis; on the contrary, I speak nothing but the serious truth when I say that many of them even took exceptions to the article. In endeavoring to please them I slaved over that sketch for two hours, and had my labor for my pains. I never will do a generous deed again.

# CONCLUSION

NEARLY one year has flown since this notable pilgrimage was ended; and as I sit here at home in San Francisco thinking, I am moved to confess that day by day the mass of my memories of the excursion have grown more and more pleasant as the disagreeable incidents of travel which encumbered them flitted one by one out of my mind—and now, if the *Quaker City* were weighing her anchor to sail away on the very same cruise again, nothing could gratify me more than to be a passenger. With the same captain and even the same pilgrims, the same sinners. I was on excellent terms with eight or nine of the excursionists (they are my stanch friends yet), and was even on speaking terms with the rest of the sixty-five. I have been at sea quite enough to know that that was a very good average. Because a long sea-voyage not only brings out all the mean traits one has, and exaggerates them, but raises up others which he never suspected he possessed, and even creates new ones. A twelve months' voyage at sea would make an ordinary man a very miracle of meanness. On the other hand, if a man has good qualities, the spirit seldom moves him to exhibit them on shipboard, at least with any sort of emphasis. Now I am satisfied that our pilgrims are pleasant old people on shore; I am also satisfied that at sea on a second voyage they would be pleasanter, somewhat, than they were on our grand excursion, and so I say without hesitation that I would be glad enough to sail with them again. I could at least enjoy life with my handful of old friends. They could enjoy life with *their* cliques as well—passengers invariably divide up into cliques, on *all* ships.

And I will say, here, that I would rather travel with an excursion party of Methuselahs than have to be changing ships and comrades constantly, as people do who travel in the ordinary way. Those latter are always grieving over some *other* ship they have known and lost, and over *other* comrades whom diverging routes have separated from them. They learn to love a ship just in time to change it for another, and they become attached to a pleasant traveling-companion only to lose him. They have that most dismal experience of being in a strange vessel, among strange people who care nothing about them, and of undergoing the customary bully-ing by strange officers and the insolence of strange servants, repeated over and over again within the compass of every month. They have also that other misery of packing and unpacking trunks—of running the distressing gantlet of custom-houses—of the anxieties attendant upon getting a mass of baggage from point to point on land in safety. I had rather sail with a whole brigade of patriarchs than suffer so. We never packed our trunks but twice—when we sailed from New York, and when

THE INNOCENTS ABROAD

we returned to it.  Whenever we made a land journey, we estimated how many days we should be gone and what amount of clothing we should need, figured it down to a mathematical nicety, packed a valise or two accordingly, and left the trunks on board.  We chose our comrades from among our old, tried friends, and started.  We were never dependent upon strangers for companionship.  We often had occasion to pity Americans whom we found traveling drearily among strangers with no friends to exchange pains and pleasures with.  Whenever we were coming back from a land journey, our eyes sought one thing in the distance first —the ship—and when we saw it riding at anchor with the flag apeak, we felt as a returning wanderer feels when he sees his home.  When we stepped on board, our cares vanished, our troubles were at an end—for the ship was home to us.  We always had the same familiar old stateroom to go to, and feel safe and at peace and comfortable again.

I have no fault to find with the manner in which our excursion was conducted.  Its program was faithfully carried out—a thing which surprised me, for great enterprises usually promise vastly more than they perform.  It would be well if such an excursion could be gotten up every year and the system regularly inaugurated.  Travel is fatal to prejudice, bigotry, and narrow - mindedness, and many of our people need it sorely on these accounts.  Broad, wholesome, charitable views of men and things cannot be acquired by vegetating in one little corner of the earth all one's lifetime.

# MARK TWAIN

The excursion is ended, and has passed to its place among the things that were. But its varied scenes and its manifold incidents will linger pleasantly in our memories for many a year to come. Always on the wing, as we were, and merely pausing a moment to catch fitful glimpses of the wonders of half a world, we could not hope to receive or retain vivid impressions of all it was our fortune to see. Yet our holiday flight has not been in vain— for above the confusion of vague recollections, certain of its best prized pictures lift themselves and will still continue perfect in tint and outline after their surroundings shall have faded away.

We shall remember something of pleasant France; and something also of Paris, though it flashed upon us a splendid meteor, and was gone again, we hardly knew how or where. We shall remember, always, how we saw majestic Gibraltar glorified with the rich coloring of a Spanish sunset and swimming in a sea of rainbows. In fancy we shall see Milan again, and her stately cathedral with its marble wilderness of graceful spires. And Padua—Verona— Como, jeweled with stars; and patrician Venice, afloat on her stagnant flood — silent, desolate, haughty—scornful of her humbled state—wrapping herself in memories of her lost fleets, of battle and triumph, and all the pageantry of a glory that is departed.

We cannot forget Florence—Naples—nor the foretaste of heaven that is in the delicious atmosphere of Greece—and surely not Athens and the broken temples of the Acropolis. Surely not venerable

Rome—nor the green plain that compasses her round about, contrasting its brightness with her gray decay—nor the ruined arches that stand apart in the plain and clothe their looped and windowed raggedness with vines. We shall remember St. Peter's; not as one sees it when he walks the streets of Rome and fancies all her domes are just alike, but as he sees it leagues away, when every meaner edifice has faded out of sight and that one dome looms superbly up in the flush of sunset, full of dignity and grace, strongly outlined as a mountain.

We shall remember Constantinople and the Bosporus—the colossal magnificence of Baalbec—the Pyramids of Egypt—the prodigious form, the benignant countenance of the Sphinx—Oriental Smyrna —sacred Jerusalem—Damascus, the "Pearl of the East," the pride of Syria, the fabled Garden of Eden, the home of princes and genii of the Arabian Nights, the oldest metropolis on earth, the one city in all the world that has kept its name and held its place and looked serenely on while the Kingdoms and Empires of four thousand years have risen to life, enjoyed their little season of pride and pomp, and then vanished and been forgotten!

**THE END**

Printed in the United States
75247LV00001BA/1

9 780809 531646